The Tannhäuser

A Swan Knights Story

STEFAN SCHEUERMANN

"The Tannhäuser," by Stefan Scheuermann. ISBN 978-1-951985-51-6 (softcover); 978-1-951985-52-3 (hardcover); 978-1-949756-53-0 (eBook).

Published 2020 by Virtualbookworm.com Publishing Inc., P.O. Box 9949, College Station, TX 77842, US. ©2020, Stefan Scheuermann.

II

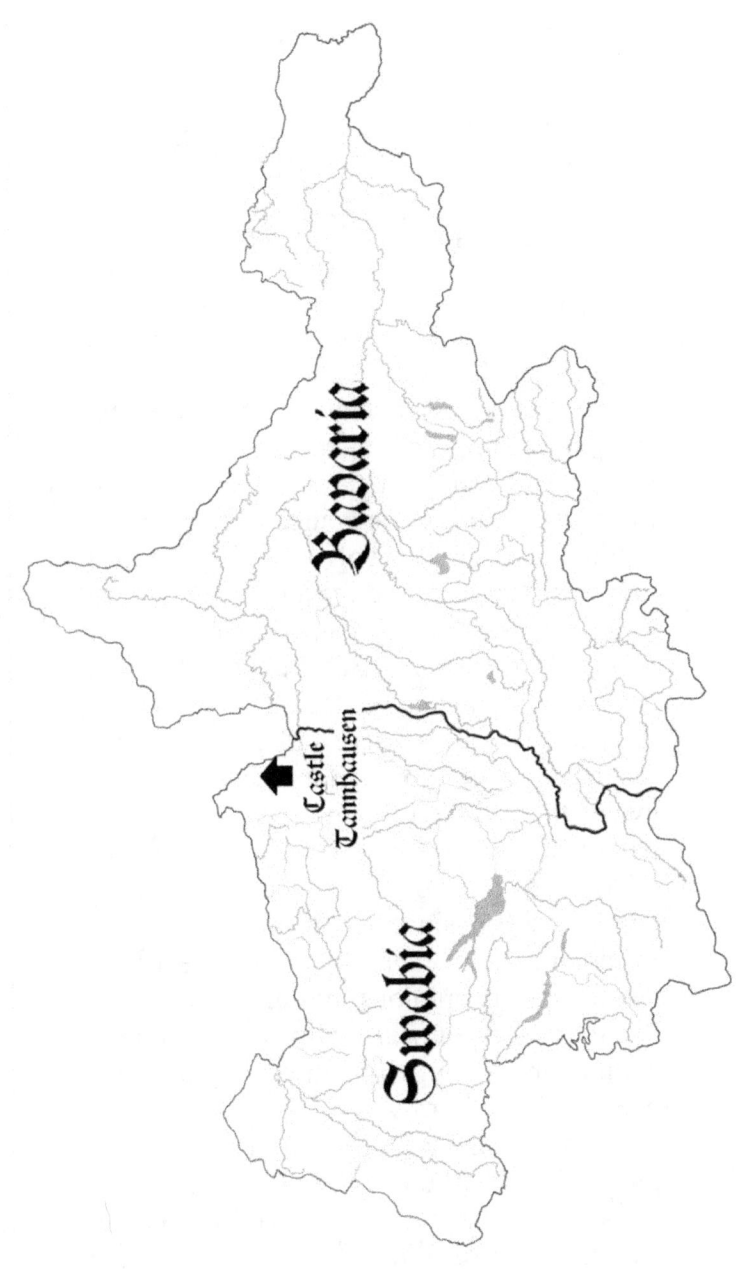

Bavaria

Swabia

Castle Tannhausen

NOTE FROM THE NARRATOR

Dear Reader,

Allow me to introduce myself. I am your narrator for this story — not to be mistaken for the author. Mr. Scheuermann is a decent enough fellow, and although I am but a product of his imagination, a creation of his, if you will, during the course of this book's production, I have evolved and developed into something beyond the author.

I hope Mr. Scheuermann appreciates my telling of this story. But frankly, it is not necessary to me that he does. This is now *my* story to tell, and I sit here with my own voice and my own opinions on the characters and events that fill the following pages. He and I have had some rather heated disagreements of late, as to how this story should be presented. But since technically I still live inside of Mr. Scheuermann's head, rent-free, I will bear his opinions in mind. His skull is a cluttered apartment, with strange guests coming and going, night and day, but he has been a fair landlord.

I don't believe it necessary to give you a physical description of myself, since I don't physically exist. Sufficed to say, I have my reading glasses on, clothes that are comfortable enough for a long read, but not distracting, a fire or candles, or whatever suits your tastes, and a passion for the figures in this story, who developed alongside me while Mr. Scheuermann worked on this book.

I hope you do not gather around me with no intention of being altered by the experience. Whether the author meant it or not, there are moral lessons to be gained here, and I, your fictional narrator, will hold you to them. So place on my head whatever face suits you — your grandfather's, an uncle's, or even your mother's, it is all the same to me, so long as you listen intently and open your hearts to the story of *The Tannhäuser*.

With Sincere Well-Wishes,
The Narrator

TABLE OF CONTENTS

CHAPTER 1
The Rustic Defender

11 NOVEMBER, 1197

The clop of horse hooves harmonized exquisitely with the roll of wagon wheels and the late-morning song of the birds to serenade a dulcet and hypnotic lullaby to the Baroness. It was also heard, no doubt, by the unborn child within her. The sixth baby of Baron Luitpold von Tannhausen and his wife Methildis was usually quite active, tossing, turning, and kicking through day and night. But the sounds and the motions that conspired to weight the Baroness' eyelids also lulled the baby to rest. Although it was cold on the open cart, the sun was direct, and aside from a little nip on her shaded ear, Methildis was warm and comfortable.

They were both well-at-ease. Methildis was secure under the guard of her husband's men. One drove the cart and two rode beside her. She was returning from a visit to her father and mother, Count Egon von Urach and Elizabeth von Zähringen. Methildis' mind drifted in that strange place between dreaming and conscious thought. For her, there was little difference between the two. Her life had been privileged, and there was nothing her dreams could offer that the circumstances of her life could not match. Her dreamy thoughts that morning were ended abruptly by the holler of men in anguish, the rearing of the horses, and the splatter of blood across her face. They were under attack.

By the time her eyes were wide and her wits fully about her, her husband's men were dead. In her swollen state, nearly full term in her pregnancy, she faced the attackers alone. They were two, dirty, crude men, who barked vulgarities so crass, so savage that they were hardly intelligible to the Baroness, while they waved rusty, bloody tools in the air above their heads. They did not seem to notice the blood of the Baron's men drop into their hair and fling from their flailing hands like the rusty-red rays of a sunset. Nor did they seem to notice the sixth child of Luitpold von Tannhausen, who kicked against Methildis' belly in violent competition with the terrified heart that pounded against her chest.

The attackers stood side by side and yelled at Methildis. She could make no sense of their shrill howling. Were they going to rob her, capture her, or kill her? Perhaps *they* did not know. It was hard for Methildis to imagine *any* sort of plan behind those wild eyes. She mustered the courage to speak to them, but when she opened her mouth, the only new sound added to the scene was a low and dull —thud—. It accompanied the immediate silence of one of the wild men. He fell to his face, revealing behind him a simple farmer, humbly but neatly dressed, holding a long staff in his hands.

The other attacker turned on him, raising his voice as if to compensate for his cohort's sudden silence. The farmer struck the wild man in the belly with the point of the staff, doubling him over. With the attacker face down, the farmer held the staff horizontally with two hands and raised it across the foul face of his enemy, who rebounded off of the staff to stand tall with his eyes closed and blood streaming from his nose. He rocked back on his heels, and teetered slightly for a moment before falling flat on his back.

The farmer mounted the cart, introduced himself to the Baroness as Her Loyal Servant, Wikerus, took the reins, hollered at the horses, and drove them both away, toward her home and destination, Castle Tannhausen. Wikerus carried none of the airs of Methildis' usual company. He was rustic. He was raw. Yet there was an undeniable nobility in the calm decisiveness of his actions and in the genuine reverence he paid to the lady beside him.

They rolled along, neither fast nor slow, conversing only with polite pleasantries, through the afternoon and into the evening, stopping twice to eat beneath the local linden trees. As the sun set, Methildis fell asleep. She awoke hysterical from a vicious dream, with the clear image of her attackers' wild eyes embroidered to her inner-eye. The thrill brought Methildis into labor. Wikerus revealed his unpolished coarseness when he stood, yelled at the horses, and shook the reins wildly. But even this provincial display appeared heroic to Methildis. She fell to her back and rolled to her side, growling in pain. From that angle, Wikerus appeared twice his size, like a giant from the ancient legends, belting commands to the horses in what seemed a lost and forgotten language. These were the sights and sounds that accompanied Methildis' pain until the cart rolled to the front doors of Castle Tannhausen.

One, maybe two minutes earlier would have placed the Baroness on a soft bed when the child was born. But she did not have that minute. Wikerus delivered a small but healthy boy in the back of the cart, under the Swabian star-lit sky of a clear night. It was not the screams of his wife that woke Baron Tannhausen, but the first cry of his son.

Half-asleep, the Baron charged through the doors of the castle and witnessed Wikerus placing the baby to Methildis' breast. His foggy mind struggled to make sense of the scene before his eyes. He yelled at the farmer and charged toward his wife. Wikerus leaped from the wagon and ran in fear, disappearing quickly into the dark of the surrounding woods. Methildis tried to defend her rescuer. But servants, guards, and family erupted from the castle and rushed her and her baby behind the thick wooden doors of the family home.

The hours between the birth and the dawn seemed eternal to all within the walls of Castle Tannhausen. During that time, Methildis regaled them all with a vivid recitation of the previous day's events, including a spirited depiction of the heroics of Farmer Wikerus.

Luitpold was a fair man, an honest man. But under the shock of the evening, he had little compassion or gratitude to grant the poor hero he frightened away. Methildis on the other hand, aside from her comfort and relief, thought of little else.

The Baron gave the boy his own name, Luitpold. It was an old family name, decided well before the events that initiated this story. But Methildis insisted upon the right to grant the second name. She named her son Wikerus, after a figure whose heroics, like the tales of old, grew larger and more legendary with every retelling, and with every silent, solitary remembrance of the Baroness.

Castle Tannhausen

CHAPTER 2
His Mother's Child

ONE STAR — ONE TWINKLING STAR, seeming to sit alone in the deep blackness of an endless night sky. It was the earliest memory of Luitpold Wikerus von Tannhausen. Perhaps it was his imagination, or the first thing his infant eyes ever focused upon. In any case, it remained with him, in him. The only remaining light in his eyes when his eyelids closed off the rest of the world each night, it was his constant companion, through a privileged childhood, a tumultuous adolescence, and a violent adulthood, until it leaped from his eyes to sparkle from the face of his only lover.

Beneath that deep black, Swabian sky stood the bulky grey castle, the home of the Lords of Tannhausen. The stone of the castle interior served as the blank canvas that beckoned young Wikerus' imagination to create a much more colorful world.

His father's name was Luitpold, as was his great-grandfather's. His uncle on his mother's side and four cousins were also called Luitpold. They all had much more in common than the name. Those traits that bound them were distasteful – abominably repugnant to the subject of this story. And the name of Luitpold held the same odious repulsion. For this reason, our young Tannhäuser did not go by the ancient family name given to him at his birth. Instead, he used his second, Wikerus, given to him by his mother in honor of the humble farmer who secured his entrance into this world.

Young Wikerus heard the heroic tale of the simple farmer, told with passion from his mother's lips, while chills ran across her skin, since the boy was old enough to sit up straight. Wikerus' father and brothers, while eternally grateful to the farmer, believed that the naming of the child was reward enough. They saw no reason to mention the dirty little man and no reason to think of him at all.

The farmer, whose heroic actions earned as its prize young Wikerus' healthy delivery, and saved the life of a most cherished mother, was gilded and deified in the bright and searing young heart of this story's hero. The tale of the rescue lifted dusty old farmers to the level of Wikerus' noble relatives, and higher. Bravery and romanticism carried more prestige in his wandering little mind than birthrights and banners, castles and crests.

The woods that surrounded the castle, the castle walls, the stables, and even the young noble's own bedroom served as the backdrop of many an exotic and imaginative fantasy — each featuring the courage and grace of a commoner. From his earliest musings, the culture and stories of the simple folk of the region fascinated Wikerus much more than did the knightly exploits of his own kin. And such a romantic beginning to his life put him in constant and perpetual expectation that the rest of his life would be equally mythological.

As the fifth son of a prominent regional baron, Wikerus was quite at liberty to pursue his rustic fantasies. His four older brothers held the family banner high enough. His sister had been sent to the convent when Wikerus was very young, and none in the family had seen her since. Wikerus, dearest of all to his mother, could have disappeared for months at a time without catching the notice of the men of the manor. And disappear he did, perhaps not for months, but for many drifty, wandering, imaginative hours.

The regimental restraints that bound his brothers tightly had no grip on Wikerus. By the age of twelve, by which point his brothers had mastered the sword, the horse, and the tools of oratory, when their minds and bodies had been focused toward a future that was scripted generations before their births, Wikerus was as free as the poor but valiant farmer who saved his mother.

In the mornings, Wikerus' eyes did not open in automatic, subconscious obedience to long established habits. He opened his eyes with excitement and intention, drawing his eyelids like curtains, opening that window to his heart and inhaling into those same organs, with freshness and delight, the old, mundane sights that adorned the castle for generations. Wikerus greeted those sights very differently than the many ancestors who awakened to the same walls. He expected something, something his life in the castle did not have to offer him. He expected magic to charm him and love to sweep him away to exotic lands, with sights, sounds, and tastes to tantalize his eagerly receptive soul.

Wikerus did not roll out of bed, place his feet on the floor, stand and walk in a mindless recitation of any other day's beginning. No — each gesture, each step, each twitch of his brow was performed with purpose and motive, in agitated searching for some unknown delight that he believed hid around every corner and in every shadow, waiting for its moment to pounce on him and permanently transform the nature of his existence.

This is how he began each morning, how he faced each second of his day. And when the shadows of the courtyard made their full journey from west to east, and dissolved into the darkness of night, Wikerus expected the twinkle of each star to shake free a piece of heavenly wonder that would fall to his feet and declare him to be, as he believed himself to be, special among all that he knew. Of course, nothing pounced from the shadows and nothing fell from the stars. Wikerus went to bed each night wondering what he had done wrong, who he offended, and why, against all he hoped and believed, he ended the day in the same circumstances that saw him to bed the night before. But each night, his dreams refreshed his passions, and he began the next morning with the same fiery fervor and the same expectations.

Methildis was intelligent and wise. She had vision, both practical and fantastical, well beyond her husband's. No doubt, the Tannhausen estate would have fared better with her influence spread in healthy proportion across all family matters. But that was not the sort of man she married. The Baron kept a tyrannically jealous grip on the affairs of the household, the estate, and the community. This liberated Methildis' mind to canvas a broad range of topics, academic, artistic, and spiritual. She wrote poetry and music. She drew and she painted. She studied every subject represented in the family's substantial library. Manuscripts as elegantly illustrated as they were informative patiently took their turns under her richly capable eyes.

Wikerus' older siblings were plenty to occupy the attentions of the tutors and trainers engaged for their education, leaving Wikerus almost entirely to his mother's attention. He was educated by his mother's voice reading poetry, her fingers plucking the lute, and her devout hymns sung in intimate adoration to God. With her many talents and accomplishments, Methildis was, above all else, a pious woman. This too was transferred directly to Wikerus' sensibilities, with little in the way to filter it.

Both of Wikerus' parents kept close eyes on the Church and were obedient to the Pope, but for different reasons. Methildis' allegiance was spiritual. Luitpold's was political. The Baron closely monitored the movements of the Papacy and the ripples that the various hands sent across the political waters of Europe. In 1208, Pope Innocent III sent missionaries to convert the heretical Cathars in Southern France. The Cathars, while not officially breaking from the Church, spread beliefs so distant from the Church's fundamental precepts. They believed in two gods — Satan, creator of the physical world and god of the Old Testament, and the good God, creator of the spiritual world and God of the New Testament. This stood firmly against the Church's teaching of one God, Creator of all things visible and invisible.

Pope Innocent believed that missionary teachers could be dispatched to educate the Cathars and bring them in-line with Church teachings. He sent his papal legate Pierre de Castelnau to excommunicate Count Raymond VI of Toulouse, whose sympathy for Catharism jeopardized the missionaries. But de Castelnau was murdered while returning to Rome. Innocent had no choice but to admit the facts before him, that teachers and missionaries could not educate the Cathars into compliance, and their growing movement threatened Christianity in Europe. For these reasons, Innocent announced the Cathar Crusade, or Albigensian Crusade as it was also called, to wipe the heretical beliefs from Europe with the sharpened edges of Crusader swords.

Baron Luitpold's ever-keen political senses saw before him an opportunity to place his sons in the path of heroism and raise the prestige of the Lords of Tannhausen. In May of 1210, Wikerus' three oldest brothers joined the crusading army of Adolf VI, Count of Berg. The move could purchase favor with the Pope and with the rising influence of Düsseldorf. The Pope promised crusading families that their lands would come under the protection of the Church, making them immune from the secular claims of other nobles.

Well-trained and suited for battle, the three eldest sons of Baron Luitpold von Tannhausen rode north to the ruins of Castle Saarbrücken, where the Berg army camped. A new castle was being built, and the surrounding grounds were set with tents and a kitchen, and everything needed to sustain a substantial construction force. It was the ideal location to stage the army before entering France. The workers cleared out and the tools of construction were replaced with the accoutrements of war.

Castle Tannhausen was left with only two sons, a fact that should have secured Wikerus a greater portion of his father's attention. But the Baron was blind to the one who trained and entirely unaware of the one who spent his days in prayer with his mother. All talk in the castle was of the crusade and the glories that would be brought upon their household by the holy heroics of the eldest sons. This was fine with Wikerus. His obscurity within the walls of his own home was his most cherished possession. It allowed him liberties never known by his brothers. With all attention and hopes bent upon the crusade, Wikerus became even less his father's, and in so, even more his mother's.

In his earliest years, Wikerus' head pushed forth, in wild waves, light-brown hair that matched his mother's identically. It had colorful depth, seeming to possess simultaneously every shade on a broad spectrum of amber, that is, until his eleventh year. In the spring of 1208, as circumstances pushed Wikerus further from his father, the Baron's thinner, straight, black hair evicted his glorious locks in a transition that took only weeks to complete. Wikerus mourned the transformation, particularly as it accompanied other alterations in his maturing body that brought him nearer the image of his father. To his disgust and frustration, his reflection appeared as a shorter, soft-featured version of the Baron, and of every other Tannhäuser whose likenesses lined the hallways, locked in hardened oils and framed within grand and gilded woodwork. But Wikerus' straight, long, black hair framed a pair of eyes that were, in both color and fire, distinctly from Methildis.

Aside from the physical changes, Wikerus became a magnified replica of everything that was quintessentially Methildis. He had an unyielding sense of justice, a zealous desire to serve the needs of the less fortunate, a passionate devotion to beauty, and an amorous reverence to God and the Church. In other words, Wikerus' childhood prepared him to be too pure for the world around him, and entirely ill-equipped to face the realities that the wider world held in store for him. The household talk of battlefield heroism for the Glory of God infused into him, with his mother's strong spiritual influence, to spawn in the young boy visions and imaginings unlike anything seen on Earth. He had never left the immediate surroundings of the castle. So his imagination filled in what his experience could not, painting a surreal portrait of the lives of his oldest brothers and of the other knights who joined Innocent's crusade.

Each passing day of Wikerus' youth pushed him one step closer to the edge of a cliff, where he would fall from his mother's bosom and plunge headlong into an ocean of humanity, as enigmatic to him as the mysteries beyond that one twinkling star, held in the very first chamber of his memory. He was not kin with mankind, a fact, above all else in his life, that would steer his destiny.

CHAPTER 3
Into the Wider World

"THUD — THUMP — WHACK," the fourteen year-old Wikerus shouted, as he swooshed a stick from the courtyard recklessly through the air of the castle dining room, in imitation of well-notorious and often-fantasized events from the day of his birth.

But unlike his farmer-namesake, young Wikerus did not abandon the wild men on the road and drive off in a cart with the rescued lady. He knelt beside the imaginary bodies of his beastly attackers.

"In the name of the Father, and the Son, and the Holy Spirit," he spoke slowly and precisely while making the Sign of the Cross. "Lord Christ, save these men from the violence of my staff, and from their own natures. Redeem them, that they may serve you as I do."

He followed this prayer with a hymn of thanksgiving — a slightly higher pitched but uncannily similar rendition of his mother's nightly lullaby. As I mentioned earlier, his mother's goodness and her naivety magnified inside of him. It is sort of pathetically adorable how much authentic compassion he felt for these smelly, hairy phantoms that lay invisibly vanquished on the dining room floor. He wept for them, but smiled through his tears in full faith that his prayers for their redemption would be heard and answered by a nurturing and omnipresent God. This faith freed him to rise to his feet, raise his stick, and face the next horde of enemies swinging from the chandelier and climbing over the chairs and tables to attack his dear mother.

These fanciful, gallant, and splendidly benevolent imaginings occupied the largest portion of Wikerus' days until September, 1211, two months before his fifteenth birthday. His nearest brother had left the castle to join the forces in defense of the Holy Roman Emperor, Otto IV of Brunswick. It was only when Wikerus remained alone in the halls of the castle that the Baron realized how unprepared his son was for life. At nearly fifteen years-old, he had no employable skills and no realistic understanding of the world beyond the castle courtyard. This was a predicament that needed desperate and immediate attention. And the full force of every teacher and tutor at the Baron's disposal crashed against Wikerus' daily habits with destructive violence.

It mattered little to the boy that he spent his days with strangers, learning and training in subjects not particularly dear to his heart. His savage imagination could make fanciful the most humdrum situation. What bothered Wikerus was his separation from his mother. Her sounds, her touch, and her smell had been as regular to his days as the vibrations of his own footsteps. But once his father seized his life and crammed him forcefully into the centuries-old Tannhäuser mold, his mother was virtually gone from his waking hours, as if abducted by wild, smelly men.

For the first few weeks of his training, Wikerus was lethargic, and little from his books and from the lips of his tutors saturated deeply into his contemplations. He missed his mother terribly, and he cried during every solitary moment of his day. But in time, he adjusted admirably. The chivalric codes of Tannhäuser behavior that lined each lesson easily donned the cloak of Wikerus' fantasies. Although faith and religion were all but entirely absent from his training, his mother's spiritual influence slid stealthily between the cracks of the subjects taught in the classroom, and of the practical lessons with the sword and horse. It was Methildis' faith and sense of divine purpose, instilled in Wikerus from his earliest lullabies, which powered his enthusiasm for training. He quickly became a much more dedicated and diligent student than any of his brothers had been.

His father was blind to the maternal influence that drove his son's ambitions. But that mattered little. He watched his youngest child grow as quick and accurate with the sword as with the pen, strong of shoulder and sharp of wit. The image of Wikerus in the Baron's eyes created an ambitious itch that could only be scratched by more and harder training. Not only did Wikerus have the advantage of solitary attention from his tutors, he showed promise that enflamed his father. Luitpold added little to his son's education, but was almost always present, watching and plotting how his youngest pawn could be played to political advantage.

At the end of his long days, Wikerus belonged to his mother. He skipped no detail, however minute, in relaying to her the events of his day. The religious sensibilities that had hidden successfully in the cracks of his training poured forth in the evenings as he reenacted with dramatic fervor every flick of his wrist from the day's activities. Methildis laughed until her belly ached, and cried until she laughed her tears away again.

In these evening dramatics, Wikerus described in detail every fantastical adventure that played out silently in his head while he trained. Methildis thanked God with more beholden gratitude than any mother had ever prayed. Every evening, she saw what her husband and the boy's teachers did not see — a beautifully balanced and divine blend of extraordinary abilities and a faithful, righteous sense of divine purpose. A dynamic fire shone from his eyes that, as familiar as she was with it, still struck Methildis and felt as if it heated her from skin to marrow. In short, she watched her son become all that she hoped, prayed, and believed he would be, since that thrilling day when he came into her life.

Until discovering Wikerus' talents, the Baron had little interest in dining with his youngest child and hearing reports of his day. But after such demonstrative excellence in the classroom, and promise beyond his illustrious brothers, Luitpold insisted upon it. Mother, father, and son sat together late each evening, dining and conversing until the dining room fires dwindled.

After dinner, Wikerus and his mother retreated to the chapel, where the most recent addition to the castle poked awkwardly from the whole, like a mole on the skin. It was commissioned by the Baroness, and was where she spent most of her day, particularly after the initiation of Wikerus' studies. They prayed and sang and read scripture to each other. It was in these prayerful sessions that the lessons of the day were solidified into Wikerus' heart, and gilded with his mother's uniquely devout spirituality. It was on the wings of those shared prayers that Wikerus flew into his nightly dreams, allowing him to awaken each day even more driven with divine purpose than the morning before.

The following May saw Wikerus' training take a practical turn.

"You have learned much, my treasure," his mother whispered dotingly. But adding gravity to her tone, she continued, "That knowledge is not meant to reside in your head, a reclusive hermit, sharing nothing and receiving nothing from others. I have liberated you from your lessons today. Go…, go from the castle. Roam for one day and see men, women, and nature through the filter of your new understanding. Then return home and tell me what the world looks like through your eyes."

As Methildis spoke, the hairs across Wikerus' body rose to attention in repeating waves across him, dragging chills in their wake. He was excited *and* nervous. He wanting everything to happen to him, and he wanted nothing to happen. His mind was new and his heart was ancient. Despite their differences, those dueling organs collaborated to jolt Wikerus to his feet. One demanded a quick kiss from his mother before a single step would be taken. The other yanked him from the castle and onto the surrounding paths the very next second. Wikerus was outside, exposed for the first time to a world, the size and diversity of which he could not begin to fathom.

Clouds, breezes, leaves dancing on trees, birds singing or flying overhead — none of these things were new to Wikerus. He experienced all of these from the castle courtyard. But those identical occurrences were peculiar to him as he walked the road away from his home. They were sharper, and seemed to sting his senses, almost uncomfortably, with freshness that took him by surprise. He was alert in the extreme, as his eyes, ears, nose, and skin grasped covetously at everything within their reach. It was too much to bear. Not one hundred paces from the large wooden doors, he dropped to his knees, opened his eyes wider, and through a laughing cry he swung open a submissive invitation for the world to take him and do with him as it pleased.

From her opened window, Methildis could hear her darling son's eccentric wailings. A subdued version of the same sounds came through her nose, denied their preferred escape by her tightly sealed lips. The sounds were not in imitation of Wikerus, rather in an authentic expression of similar feelings. It was not the stinging freshness of nature, but an equally acute and equally shocking sensation in her heart, hearing Wikerus' reaction to his first steps into the world and knowing that much newer and much more stinging experiences awaited her son.

Wikerus knelt and wailed and absorbed the freedom of nature until the severity of the sensations subsided. They were replaced by a rush of ambitions into his head. Standing paramount above them all was his lifelong desire to meet the man whose heroics with a staff animated a lifetime of romantic dining room adventures. The farmer Wikerus — how honored he would be to learn that the unborn child he saved fifteen years earlier bore his name and the noble woman he met on the path that day featured him prominently in her daily prayers of thanksgiving to God.

Wikerus had little go on to begin his search for the farmer. Although his mother's stories of the event were vivid, the matters of the heart, her feelings, her fears and gratitude, were more finely detailed than were the geographical particulars. So he followed his *own* heart, resulting in a whimsical meandering from path to road to path again. He was too faithful to be frightened. But the truth is, he was quite lost.

He wandered until the sun was directly above, when he came across a tilled field where dozens of farmers had been sowing seeds. They were at rest then, and a dull murmur betrayed the calm nature of conversational topics without Wikerus discerning a single word. Richly dressed and demonstratively conspicuous among the soiled earth tones of the resting farmers, he walked among them and drew their attention.

"Wikerus?" he shouted.

His voice seemed to echo back to him, not into his ears, but as an instant memory of how awkwardly his own name rang out across the silent field. His throat seized to proclaim the name more loudly, but froze before a sound escaped. The crowd did not know him to be the son of their landlord. But they assumed him to be connected to the family in some way. They waited attentively for him to make his intentions clearer.

He volleyed his eyes from left to right and back again, across the curious faces that sat amid the tilled soil and took their midday break. He settled his sights on one woman. Of the lot of strange faces, hers looked most familiar, and therefore most welcoming. She was like his mother in some features — the point of the nose and slightness of the chin. But mostly it was the hair, that light wavy hair that had once been his, before it yielded to his father's influence.

Aside from the minutely similar facial features and the hair, the woman bore no resemblance to anyone in the line of Tannhäusers or Zähringens. But it was enough for Wikerus to single her out and approach her comfortably. When he was within a few feet of her, she rose from the dirt, followed clumsily by an older man, grey at the temples and leathery of face, who looked too old to be her husband and too young to be her father.

"What may I do for you, young sir?" she spoke to break the silent air.

The anticipation of the following exchange was so intense among the farmers in the field that the very breeze seemed to pause for his answer.

Wikerus bumbled, "I am looking for a hero…, well, *my* hero, my mother's hero… I am looking… Do you know a man named Wikerus?"

The woman spent little time pondering, answering quickly, "I know of the Baron's son, who goes by that name. Are you looking for him? I would not know him from any other young man. I am afraid we will be of little help. Are you a friend of his?"

Wikerus began to answer, "I am…," followed by a few grunts and an irritated roll of his neck. He scratched his head above both ears for a few seconds, threw his hands to his side, stood taller, and raised his voice to all in the field, "Does anyone know a farmer named Wikerus?"

The woman and the older man who stood beside her turned to the workers behind them, many of whom had risen to their feet and inched closer to the richly dressed, neatly groomed, but peculiarly behaved young visitor to their field. Wikerus' jigging extremities, his jerking shoulders, and the desperation in his voice combined to draw from the simple farmers that pure and powerful brand of compassion that one only sees in that sort of folk. They had a desire to ease and comfort him that slowly grew frenzied.

They continued to inch toward him while scanning their eyes across the others, hoping that someone would stand forth and offer the poor boy what he so frantically desired.

Time distorted in this awkward, pastoral scene, stretching the seconds to seven times their natural length, until a withered old voice pushed through the thick tension of the air, shouting, "I know Wikerus."

Gasps, sighs, and oohs shot forth from every face in the field, followed by, "Who is that?" and "Bring him forward," and many sympathetic, vocalized hums.

The crowd of farmers, who had crept into a rather tight cluster after having been spread throughout the field, parted in half to create a corridor for a single, withered old man to pass directly to the young Tannhäuser. Wikerus stood and stared motionless, with held breath, as the man approached him. When they stood face to face, they examined each other closely. The old man looked puzzled at Wikerus, unsure how this young man could possibly know the name he shouted. Wikerus studied the face in front of him, trying, hoping to recognize any part of the hero described by his mother in the face of the stranger before him.

Wikerus' eyes crept from contour to contour, around and across the man's face, until settling upon the eyes. Every tense muscle and skin that writhed until hard, across Wikerus' entire body, suddenly softened. Every harsh and jagged, angular feature melted and rounded.

The eyes — he found the familiarity he sought, barely exposing themselves from behind a pair of wrinkled eyelids. They were exactly as his mother had described — amber in the middle, crusted along the outside with deep, dark brown, but exploding from the center and pouring in streaks through the amber, as if erupting from the pupils and flowing downward, was a glorious and sparkling gold.

The farmer saw clearly that profound thoughts worked rigorously through Wikerus' head. How could he not? Everything inside of the boy had been on bold display his entire life, as if he was born inside out.

"How do you know that name?" the raspy old voice asked him.

"It is the name of my rescuer," Wikerus answered tenderly, assuming he addressed his hero.

"I think not," the man pushed forward, tilting his head and folding his arms, "You are too young, and Wikerus has been gone for… at least fifteen years."

Wikerus' cheeks sank as he drew them into his mouth to chew on them from the inside.

"So, you are not he?" he struggled to whisper.

"No, I am not. And you could not have known him."

Wikerus dropped his eyes to the toes of the man in front of him, and spoke more to himself than to any audience, but just loud enough for those nearest him to hear, "I did *not* know him…, and I have *always* known him."

After allowing himself a few moments to recover from his disappointment, Wikerus raised his head to see the confounded expression on the farmers surrounding him. The old man did not look puzzled. His penetrating glare demanded an explanation for the contradiction of the last statement to break the otherwise silent air of the field.

Wikerus cleared his throat and explained, "He saved my mother's life on the night that I was born. He delivered me from my mother's womb. His were the first hands to touch me. But he fled from the scene and never received the gratitude owed to him."

"Your story does not surprise me. He was drawn to trouble, for better and worse, like flies to refuse. He never sought adventure. But adventure was certainly drawn to him."

"Who is he?"

"He is my brother, or was my brother."

"Was?"

"I have not seen him in almost fifteen years."

Without warning, the man plopped onto the ground and crossed his legs in front of him. He made himself comfortable, adjusting for what he intended to be a long sit in the field. He gestured for Wikerus to sit beside him. Wikerus quickly obeyed, lifting his feet from the dirt before his weight was supported by another limb. He plopped hard and awkwardly to the ground, but he did not care. The book of his childhood hero was about to receive more pages and his spirit bloated within him, exposing itself to the farmers of the field through the raised hairs on his arms, the shiver of his skin, and the bursts of air that popped from his nose in infantile giggles.

The other farmers gathered tightly for the story. Some sat and some stood, but all gave their ears to the old man. He told this story.

Wikerus is my younger half-brother. We were raised far to the north of here. Both of our fathers died, leaving us with a tender, doting, but sickly mother. My brother fell in love and married. But he remained committed to our mother, and committed to me. Wikerus' wife was a lively and radiant woman. She tended to our mother and to us, running our household effectively and affectionately. She was father, mother, and sister to me.

But not one full year into their marriage, she grew ill. We both watched the poor woman transition from the vibrancy of the angels, from a ripe fruit at its peak of brightness and sweetness to a grey and withered casing that held to life by the thinnest of threads. The decline took mere hours. Together, my brother and I nursed this woman who had taken custody of our affairs like we were children. Two days later, she died. That very evening we lost our mother. Our home was bitter with despair.

Wikerus' love for his wife was of the rarest and purest sort. He was stricken so violently by the loss that I thought I would lose him too. And three weeks later, Wikerus showed no signs of recovery. He withdrew. He spoke little and ate even less. I had to do something for my brother. So I took him away. We had little to lose. Without the matriarch of the house, all fell quickly to pieces. So we took little more than could be stored in our pockets and we sought people, places, and work with as few reminders of our broken lives as could be found in a month of travel by foot.

I took him here. We found work, with these fine folks, here in the Baron's fields. The toil of manual labor and the support of this community worked an unexpected magic on our spirits. Wikerus showed immediate signs of revival. But he often went for long walks alone and came back crying. One night, he did not come back. It was, I assume, the night you were born. It was in November, about fifteen years ago. There was always some distraught maiden or helpless child being thrown in his path by fate. I am not surprised to encounter one of them today.

While telling the story, the old man's eyes remained stuck on a single thread of his pants. He looked up to catch the sun's sparkle from the glossy, tear-drenched cheeks of young Wikerus. The other farmers had tightened in formation around them, many clinging to each other or holding hands.

After a long pause, while hardly an exhale entered the air of the field from the captivated audience, Wikerus dared to ask, "Have you no idea where he has gone, what has happened to him?"

After a slow shake of his head, performed in a thoughtful trance, the old man shifted his eyes to Wikerus' and remarked, "I rather hoped you might tell me."

"He delivered me from my mother's womb, handed me to her, and disappeared into the surrounding woods. That is the last any Tannhäuser ever saw of him."

At the mention of his family name, the farmers stood and shuffled. The field belonged to the Baron. The farmers were his workers. The old man simply smiled, able to his own delight to put a face to the woman rescued by his brother — the face of the notoriously beautiful Baroness.

Wikerus eyed the old man up and down. Aroused out of the fog that had swallowed his brain since his hero's brother stepped forward, he finally saw clearly the condition of the man who still sat cross-legged in front of him. Wikerus stood quickly and offered the man his hand. The man gave it and Wikerus helped him to his feet. He looked worn and dirty, conditions not noticed by Wikerus while his curiosity still held its despotic grip on his attention. Pity for the man blended with a tremendous sense of debt.

"What is your name?" he asked the man.

"I am Alawich, young lord. And you must be young Luitpold von Tannhausen."

Wikerus placed his hand gently on the man's shoulder and answered, "I am Luitpold Wikerus von Tannhausen, named after my father and after your brother."

All dirtiness, all tiredness and squalor evaporated from Alawich, heated to oblivion by the warmth that radiated from within him as his smile broadened and his eyes, which were locked on Wikerus', dewed with emotion.

The farmers stood torn between absorbing the tender moment and showing their young lord how industriously they work, resulting in awkward steps and double-steps, turns and shifting, which Wikerus found hilarious.

He slid his hand from Alawich's shoulder to his palm and pulled the man forward, back toward the castle, saying, "Come. You are like family to me, and a grateful household will want to thank you for your brother's heroics."

"Thank me?" Alawich asked.

"Of course. You brought your brother here, and he saved my mother. If not for you, I would not have been born alive."

As they walked through the crowd of farmers, he and Alawich smiled at the comments, "That's right," and "Young lord is correct," and "Alawich saved the Baron's son," spouting gracefully from the smiling faces of the farmers like the springtime blossoms on the trees that surrounded the field.

CHAPTER 4
The Poet Awakens

Alawich returned to Castle Tannhausen with Wikerus. The boy had no notion of direction and could have found London as easily as his own home. Fortunately, the old man knew the way. The journey should have been short. A tall man in his prime, with the breeze at his back and a warm sun ahead to beckon him forward could make the walk from the field to the castle in less than an hour. Alawich was not a tall man in his prime. But that was not what drew the journey out the length of the day.

Wikerus had two reasons to meander an indirect route and keep his walking companion to himself as long as possible. Firstly, he wanted to know as much about Alawich's brother as could be pried from his memory. Secondly, he wanted Alawich to be comfortable and accepted in the castle. He rather hoped that the old man would be able to remain there, living with Wikerus and collecting the rewards of gratitude and goodwill that should have been paid to the Baroness' rescuer. To ensure this, Wikerus wanted to prepare Alawich for his family, to teach the rustic farmer what should be said and done to make his presence in the castle less irksome to the Baron, the tutors, and all others who might have a harsh judgment too sly to keep caged behind noble etiquette and decorum.

It is unlikely Wikerus would have admitted this to himself, but his greater fear was that his family would somehow offend Alawich. Noble and pastoral sensibilities were very different in rural Swabia. Alawich and his kind had their own set of social expectations, as beyond the comprehension of the nobility as a Baron's expectation were from the farmers of the field, making Alawich as much above them as beneath them. Wikerus was terrified that his father, or tutors, or even the castle servants would offend Alawich and drive him away as his father drove away the brother fifteen years earlier.

Behavior was not the only concern. The Lords of Tannhausen bore magnificent physical beauty. They were tall. Most had the Baron's black hair, framing pale faces with distinguished jaw lines. They were naturally muscular with deep, dark eyes. Alawich, on the other hand, was quite cut up by his years under the sun. His face was tanned and wrinkled well beyond the natural effect of his years. He was only eight years older than the Baroness, but he looked as ancient as the linden trees that surrounded the castle, an apt comparison considered by Wikerus as they walked among them, for Alawich's face bore the same color and texture as the bark.

Everything about the castle was beautiful. Antique wood, leather, and spectacular gilding greeted every turn of the head. Nothing was accidental or haphazard in the castle. Each piece of furniture, each work of art, each trinket was placed painstakingly by the castle curator. Wikerus also feared that Alawich would betray his simplicity by uncouth gawking at the splendor of his surroundings.

The two of them walked to the front doors, which were opened in perfect timing by the attendants, so that neither Wikerus nor Alawich had to retard their pace or shorten a single stride to part the swinging doors. The squeak of the hinges, which Wikerus' ears had long gone deaf to, spoke loudly to Alawich. Whether it was a greeting or a warning, he could not tell. But he entered the castle nevertheless, side by side with the young lord, as equals, as comrades, as old friends might enter a home together.

None of Wikerus' fears materialized immediately. Alawich was not overcome by the splendor of the castle. He spoke cordially and returned greetings with an appropriate amount of formality, albeit without the elegance of the castle's frequent visitors. The servants were kind and attentive. Once it was determined that Alawich would be remaining through the night, a bath was drawn, a room made ready, and a place was set for him at the table, not at all unlike the efforts put forth for any honored member of the aristocracy paying a visit to the Lords of Tannhausen. Wikerus held his breath through each introduction, through each opportunity for awkwardness or embarrassment to leap from a word or gesture to mortify him. Each instance of such an opportunity that passed without incident relieved Wikerus in increasing degrees, like a hiker removing one pebble at a time from his shoes.

At dinner, Wikerus removed the final pebble, leaving nothing in his shoes but relieved feet. Alawich adhered surprisingly to the pageantry and refinement of a Baron's dinner table. He did not spin delicious phrases from a silver tongue, as Wikerus did. But once bathed and dressed for the occasion, his mannerisms and speech did nothing to sink him beneath his appearance. Methildis would not have noticed either way. Being a woman of more spiritual than physical sensibilities, she recognized traits of her hero inside of his surviving brother. She looked through those familiar eyes to those reticent qualities that do not readily declare themselves, those virtues ablaze behind the eyes, which can only be seen by others with the same sort of fire burning in them.

The Baron was a moral landlord. More than that, he was a good businessman. He saw clearly the connection between a worker's happiness and productivity. He was more than fair, giving his farmers and tenants a much higher standard of living than could generally be expected by their level of society. At dinner, he did not see Alawich as a hero's brother. This was an employee. But that alone was enough to push his best foot forward.

"He will not stay here forever," the Baron thought to himself, "He must go back. And when he does, he will speak to the others of his experience under my roof."

Baron Luitpold foresaw a short stay. Methildis gave no thought at all to the subject. But Wikerus' musings were in stark contradiction to his father's. He imagined Alawich residing indefinitely in the castle, calling it home and calling its residents family. The matter was never allowed to bubble to the surface in the form of an argument. After dinner, Alawich drew from Methildis everything she could remember about the day of her rescue. Each tiny, fragmented memory provided a shard to a mosaic, which Alawich glued to his mind while he rolled his eyes around and chewed on his thumbnails. Once Methildis' memories were fully exhausted, Alawich thanked his hosts and announced his intention to depart in the morning, early enough to join the other workers for the full length of their long day's work.

Wikerus tried to argue, imploring Alawich to remain longer, speaking of obligations and debt.

"There is no debt to be paid to me," he answered, "Your father gives me a respectable living. I do not expect more from him than that."

Wikerus spoke of the heroics of the brother. Like all fifteen-year-old stories, it came from Wikerus' mouth more splendid and polished than the events it was meant to reflect.

Alawich responded, "If my brother were here, it would be right for him to accept whatever reward your hearts needed to give. But I am here, having rescued nobody. I will leave early tomorrow morning, grateful for the meal and the company, and for a few shared memories of my lost brother."

When the dining room emptied, Alawich went directly to bed. He had begun his day as he always did, before dawn. He was in the field by the dimmest light of the infant day. Dinner was late and Alawich went to bed having eye-witnessed virtually every second of the entire day. When his body hit a bed much softer than his own, with a belly full of delicious foods and his mind full of forgotten images, he fell quickly to sleep.

Wikerus could not sleep. Although Alawich was not the discovery he had hoped to make, he was thrilled by the connection to his childhood hero, and he paced the hallways of the castle through the wee hours, in severe agitation. After a day of liberty and discovery, he dreaded his return to the classroom and the castle's return to normalcy. He fell asleep in a hallway, sitting against the wall, beneath the portrait of some ancestor or another. He was awakened by the resounding boom of the front doors, closing behind Alawich. Wikerus followed the sound, pushed the heavy doors open with his own desperate strength, and ran several steps past the threshold of the castle entrance. But the sky was still dim, the surrounding woods still shrouded by darkness, and his honored visitor had disappeared into it as quickly and completely as his brother had fifteen years earlier.

Wikerus crawled to his bed determined to sleep for a few hours before returning to the field and fetching his new friend for a day of idle storytelling. He awoke several hours into his schedule of training, and not a minute was wasted by the tutors, who rushed to make up the lost time. So quickly and challenging did the lessons come at him, that Wikerus could think of little else. Alawich did exactly as the Baron hoped. He returned to his comrades with stories of the hospitality he received at the hands of their lord. He put in another hard day of work, but with one eye on the path that leads from the castle to the farm, half-expecting Wikerus to come bounding across the freshly sowed field, as he did the day before.

The Baron feared the intimacy his son wished to develop with their farmer-guest. He kept Wikerus busy and forbade him to venture beyond the immediate circle of trees around their home. Although Alawich had no expectation of a deepening intimacy with the Lords of Tannhausen, and Wikerus knew it, Wikerus still feared how his silence and absence would be interpreted by the farmer. After several days of panic on this subject, he contented himself to write a letter.

He drew his pen from the well and hovered it over the paper with no notion of what to write. He drifted into a million haphazard thoughts, and only realized he was writing when his ears discerned the scratch of the pen. He looked down to his fingers and saw that his heart had spoken directly to them, bypassing his head and expressing itself in verse.

Der winter ist zergangen,
daz prüeve ich ûf der heide.
aldar kam ich gegangen;
guot wart mîn ougenweide
Von den bluomen wolgetân.
wer sach ie sô schoenen plân?

(The winter has gone away
So the pasture has told me
As I traveled there
Many sights pleased me
Of the blossoms fairly made.

Who has seen so lovely a glade?)

His head bumbled clumsily onto the scene, frightening his heart back into hiding, like a rabbit that sat peacefully eating until spooked and sent in a flash into the safety of the underbrush. The feelings were incompletely expressed. The story was yet untold. But his mind could not coax his heart to return to its delicate dance with his fingers. His pen stood frozen above the parchment, with one bulbous drop of ink clinging to the tip, refusing to release itself to the other scribblings, as if its life depended on it. He tried to continue the stanza, but his consciousness provided implacable impediments. As long as his head stood present, his eloquent heart hid away. The moment was over and the verses ended as they stood.

The poetry remained as an introduction to an exquisitely praiseful letter to a man he obviously admired. He finished the letter in prose, stating no expectations, no desires beyond the expression of his affection. He concluded the letter, signed it, sealed it with wax and his *mother's* seal, and tucked it into his tunic. There it rested against his heart until the end of the day. Late in the evening, after his nightly prayers, he kissed the letter, whispered his well-wishes to the old man, set the letter on the small, round table beside his bed, and he went to sleep.

Vivid were his dreams that night, and clear his later recollection of them. But he could not have known how prophetic they were, how prescriptive of a life he would not step into for many years to come. He dreamed that he rode his horse down a narrow path in the woods. His heart leaped from his chest and flew like a bird ahead of the horse. The path opened into a wide road, which led him through towns and over mountains, through fields of violent battle and peaceful gardens. His heart led the way, weaving into song and verse descriptions and interpretations of everything it encountered. Wikerus rode directly behind, experiencing the sights along with the songs of his heart.

As hard as he rode, he could not catch his singing heart, until it crossed into a forbidden land. He was imprisoned in that empty, forsaken realm. But it did not matter to Wikerus. He reunited with his heart, welcomed it back into his chest, and begged it to continue its songs. It obeyed him. He yielded control of his right hand to his heart and watched and wept as the loveliest verses came into being before his eyes, scratched onto expensive imported paper. The words were as lovely as they were strange to him, for they did not pass through his mind until perceived by his eyes. His right hand was not controlled by his head, but by his heart, and it wrote things that Wikerus felt but did not think.

When he awoke, he tried to broker a similar arrangement with his heart. He sat at his writing table and offered himself as servant to that passionate organ, that anxious muscle. But his right hand stared motionless up to him, barely engaged enough to grip the pen. And all conscious attempts to recreate his heart's songs failed colossally. Frustrated, but not disheartened, he hid his letter to Alawich among his sacred items, rather than sending it, so that the verses within might serve as inspiration once his heart is not so easily spooked out of expression. He gave his daily routine every bit of attention it deserved, but with memories of his dream haunting him like a phantom that can be heard but not seen.

CHAPTER 5
The Forbidding Priest

AFTER MEETING ALAWICH, Wikerus trained more industriously, partially from a sense of obligation, as if the debt he believed himself to owe to his mother's rescuer, one he did not know how to pay, could be relieved by the sweat, tears, and blood he shed during his long days. But this was not the only agitator spurring his heart into perpetual motion. He had intense feelings and opinions on *every* matter he encountered. He remembered every face he saw in the field when he met Alawich, and believed himself responsible for their fortunes.

His tutors spoke of the responsibilities that came with his education and training. They were training a noble knight whose behavior, at least among company, would have to adhere to the Chivalric Code. His father fastened him tightly to the expectations of nobility and of carrying the Tannhausen name. And his mother spoke to him of God. Her devotion to Christ and the Church had a sincerity and purity beyond anything he saw in his father or tutors. Baron Luitpold's words to his son were heavy with obligation, but smacked distinctly of ambition, which bore a repugnant odor to Wikerus.

When the boy was only ten, Philip Duke of Swabia and King of the Germans was assassinated. The dukedom remained vacant for four years while the Welf and Hohenstaufen dynasties fought for control of Germany. During that time, the power void swelled the ambitions of

35

every Swabian noble, from the most notorious counts to the most obscure barons. Luitpold was not immune to the siren call of power, and he believed that the military prowess and political exploits of his sons were his greatest tools for advancement.

When Duke Ludwig of Bavaria threw his support behind Friedrich of Hohenstaufen, and the winds seemed to blow in that direction, Baron Luitpold von Tannhausen offered all that he could to gain favor with Friedrich, including the lives and services of his sons. But his fourth son was already sworn into the service of the Welf enemy. Just one month after Wikerus' fifteenth birthday, Friedrich celebrated his coronation as King of Germany, and his assumption of the Duchy of Swabia. Wikerus' three oldest brothers, able soldiers in their own right, were not remarkable among the many sons of nobles who served Friedrich's cause. But Wikerus was proving himself well beyond the abilities of his brothers, and the Baron bent all of his hopes around his youngest son's skills.

Friedrich lost his parents at a young age, and Pope Innocent III assumed guardianship. His childhood tutor was Cencio Savelli, who became Pope Honorius III, after the death of Innocent III. Friedrich's affections were tightly stitched to the affairs of the Church. When Innocent announced his desire to launch a Fifth Crusade to recapture Jerusalem, Friedrich's support was guaranteed. At his coronation, he announced his support of the Crusade and his intention to personally oversee their victory. In April of 1213, Pope Innocent released the *Quia Maior*, a public decree in support of a crusade. Baron Luitpold's ambitious eyes saw his son Wikerus as just the hero to catch Friedrich's eye and raise the fortunes of the Lords of Tannhausen. He placed that weight on young Wikerus' shoulders, telling his son, "I have taught you, now you will make me a duke."

As self-motivated as Luitpold's pride was, it was still pride — pride in Wikerus. And Wikerus' chest puffed with every exaggerated compliment and every dreamy fantasy of his future heroics that rolled so freely from his father's tongue. When Holy Roman Emperor Otto of Brunswick suffered his defeat in the Battle of Bouvines, in July of 1214, all of Europe knew that Friedrich would someday be emperor, and Luitpold's dreams of becoming the Duke of Swabia had a shimmering glint of possibility. Wikerus was sixteen. He handled the sword like a seasoned knight. He was as prepared for battle as any sixteen-year-old could be. And Luitpold was ready to hand his son's life over to Friedrich.

Wikerus' mother did not subscribe to the life her husband had meticulously scripted for her favorite son. She saw much deeper into Wikerus' soul than any of his other relations. She prayed with him every night and witnessed first-hand her son's devotion to God. She intended for him a life in the Church. Methildis had a copy of the *Quia Maior*. Wikerus read it and dreamed of glory. As he approached his seventeenth birthday, discussions of a contentious and fiery nature filled the air of the castle — air that had known generations of placidity, and was angry to have to carry the yelling voices of the Baron and Baroness through its hallowed halls.

The Baron had much to gain through his ambitions for Wikerus, but much to lose in the tenderness of an affectionate wife. His fantasized dukedom drifted from him as his wife asserted her authority — until a compromise came to mind. Luitpold presumed upon an old family debt, a service long forgotten by most. The Lords of Tannhausen were instrumental in the elevation of many ministeriales — families who were raised from serfdom. They became knights and unfree nobles. But through deeds and connections, they rose through the ranks of the German nobility.

One of these ministeriales was the grandfather of Hermann von Salza. In 1189, Hermann fought as a knight in the Siege of Acre, in the Third Crusade, securing Christendom's most valuable stronghold in the Holy Land. He was among those first forty German knights initiated into the Order of Teutonic Knights, a religious order of warrior monks under the command of the Pope. In 1209, Hermann became Grand Master of the Teutonic Knights, a prestigious position in both religious and secular circles. The fame and appeal of the order grew throughout Germany since its founding in 1190.

The debt the von Salza owed to the Lords of Tannhausen grew in value with Hermann's successes. He was a friend and counselor to Friedrich. And when the Pope raised the Teutonic Knights to the level of the Templars, his position as Grand Master placed him among the most powerful and notorious names in Europe.

It was Methildis, not Luitpold, who first recalled the connection. She reminded her husband of what was owed to them by the head of the Teutonic Order. It was a compromise that pleased them both. Methildis' treasured son would join a holy order sanctioned by the Pope, where he would take vows of poverty, chastity, and service to the Church. Luitpold would see his warrior son under the eye of Hermann von Salza and in the service of King Friedrich. On 20 October, 1214, twenty-two days before his seventeenth birthday, the old debt was collected and Wikerus was accepted into the Order of Teutonic Knights under the particularly watchful eye of its Grand Master.

Wikerus was excited to embark on his new life. The compromise between his parents also reconciled two opposing facets of his character — his devotion to God and the Church and his thirst for gallant heroics. His vows would demand a pious existence, which pleased his mother. It would also place Wikerus into battle, where his uncommon abilities would raise the prestige of the family. For Wikerus, the dining room battles of his imagination would soon become quite tangible. The sticks from the courtyard, which his imagination had worked into the finest steel, would be replaced with a Teutonic Knight's sword.

These things were exciting to all within Castle Tannhausen, until 9 November, 1214, two days before Wikerus' seventeenth birthday, when he stood beside a wagon in front of the large wooden doors of the castle. He had grown tall and beautiful. In his mother's farewell embrace, the crown of her head fit snugly into the left side of his neck. He leaned his jaw against her and squeezed tightly. It must have hurt, or at least restricted her breath. He was strong and had been flicking his father's heavy sword with ease, and leaping obstacles, and throwing weighted barrels during his training.

He squeezed his mother with all that he had, as if trying to press her through his skin and between his ribs. Regardless of the discomfort, Methildis savored every moment of it, and she whispered a prayer to Christ that only Wikerus could hear. At the end of her prayer, mother and son sighed a simultaneous "Amen". He kissed the top of her head and mounted the wagon. He waved to his father and the servants and tutors. The entire household poured through the large doorway to see their young master off. When the wagon was out of sight, the household returned indoors, all except Methildis, who remained frozen in place, staring into the surrounding woods, straining to hear the horses or the wagon, or any sound of her departing son. When her ears finally had to admit that Wikerus was entirely gone, the Baroness went straight to the chapel and sequestered herself in prayer and fasting for days, begging the Lord to protect her son, but asking much more fervently that he find his purpose in the hands of God.

Wikerus was so unaccustomed to the world that he quickly lost his bearings on the winding paths and roads that took him from his home and mother. Two knights and a priest rode with him on the cart. The knights wore white cloaks with a black cross over the left shoulder. One wore a blue tunic with a black cross over the chest. The other's tunic was grey with an identical cross. Wikerus burned with questions for them. But their mouths transitioned seamlessly from conversations with each other to intensely focused prayers and chants, leaving Wikerus' curiosity no window to interject.

The priest spoke little to the knights and did not appear to engage in particularly fervent prayers. It was his scowl that warded off Wikerus' questions. Several times within the first few hours of travel, Wikerus' lips parted. His lungs pushed forward the air that was intended to carry language from his mouth. But the words did not mount his breath, scared of the scowling priest. They hid inside of him, and the air flew quietly from the boy, sounding only like a sigh that was incongruent with the inquisitive expression that held relentlessly to his face.

Once beyond the fields of his family, once beyond all that bore any semblance of familiarity to Wikerus, the meandering roads turned south. Of course Wikerus did not know this. They could have turned upward to the sky, or downward into the earth and he would not have known better. The commonest things, Swabian wildlife that played in the woods and fields of the area since before time, were strange and mystical to Wikerus' virgin eyes and ears.

Birds that did not make homes near Castle Tannhausen may as well have been God's heavenly Angels. They were as strange as magical, and they sang to him like the Angels sang of the birth of Christ to the shepherds of the pastures near Bethlehem. The hills were higher than he had imagined them, the fields more expansive. And the wonders that befell his senses were as responsible for his muted voice as the forbidding scowl of the priest who piloted the cart.

The day grew old and the cart did not stop rolling forward. They did not break for rest or refreshments, though they had passed many homes, villages, and quiet fields that begged for their attention. Wikerus was hungry and his legs protested against their long hours of idleness. The knights beside him did not appear at all as uncomfortable as he was. They told stories to each other of distant lands and bloody battles against exotic enemies. They spoke to one another, not to Wikerus. But they must have known how they captivated their stowaway. They could not have missed the sighs and the startled jumps from the young recruit beside them.

Not the excitement of the stories, nor the freshness of the scenery, nor the flight of his imagination could take Wikerus' mind off of his grumbling stomach and aching legs. The knights continued to laugh and carry on as if they were machines that required none of the things that Wikerus craved. The priest's scowl was so miserably fierce, no degree of discomfort could make it fowler. Wikerus was convinced that his lips puckered just as tightly, and his eyes squinted just as angrily while the priest slept and ate and during the pleasantest moments of his life.

The sun set and the road in front of them disappeared.

"This is intolerable," Wikerus thought loudly to himself. His lips moved with his thoughts and he was thankful for the darkness for hiding the subtle outward expression of his thoughts.

Finally, a dim light appeared in front of them. As they approached, it grew into a cluster, lighting the houses and structures of a town. Wikerus wished desperately to stop, eat, and sleep in a bed. But he did not expect it. They did stop. To Wikerus' relief, they dismounted the cart and were greeted by two friars. The friars spoke to the priest, welcoming him to Ulm. Wikerus knew well of Ulm. It was a Free Imperial City and housed in its outskirts one of the Emperor's palaces. He knew that dining halls with grand tables and expansive stores of wine, large bedrooms with plush beds awaited them. But they did not go to the palace. The friars led them to a humble building on the far southern edge of town, one which, in the darkness, appeared in much worse condition than the light of day would have revealed.

The friars led them to a small dining room with just enough chairs for the four travelers and hardly enough table for the four chairs. Wikerus was given no more than the others — two small pieces of flatbread and a few dried apple slices. As he ate, he tried to revive his imagination to its former liveliness, in order that it might transform his food and surroundings into something pleasanter, something more like home. His imagination went to bed before him. It slept soundly and left Wikerus with the realities of his circumstances. He ate his food and went to a small bedroom, with two small beds, where he shared with the scowling priest a bed not quite made for *one* normal sized man, while the knights shared the other without any sign of protest.

Half of Wikerus' long body hung precariously from his side of the bed, while his other half pressed against the old priest. The priest said nothing. He made no noise or gesture of rejection. But his coldness chilled Wikerus to the bone. He wanted nothing more than to roll out of the bed and sleep on the cold, hard floor, disconnected from contact with the priest. But he feared to do so, to offend a man he could hardly image being less congenial. So he remained pressed against his bunkmate, straining to focus

42

his thoughts on anything but those parts of him that were touching the old man.

Wikerus must have sleepwalked in the morning. By the time his wits were gathered, he was again in the cart, his stomach full of God-knows-what breakfast, and his eyes were being poked by the first rays of the rising sun to his left. He did not resent the early start, but he mourned the loss of the morning's memories, wishing to have had the chance to savor every second outside of the rumbling cart.

The second day of travel was worse than the first. By mid-morning, Wikerus' bones could not sit still and be rattled by the violent love affair between the rough road and the hard wheels of the cart. He reminded himself that he is Luitpold Wikerus von Tannhausen, son of the Baron von Tannhausen. His ancient lineage should purchase him a demand or two from the scowling priest and the two knights beside him. The reminder bolstered his courage enough to ask for a brief stop, which was reluctantly granted by the priest, whose level of disappointment was entirely undiscernible behind his perpetual grimace. The knights, having never considered stopping to rest, discussed the matter for a moment then concurred with Wikerus.

They stopped the cart and Wikerus jumped off first. He walked three or four quick laps around the cart, unsettling the horses.

In a disagreeable, repellent, almost sinister voice that did not invite an honest answer, the priest asked, "Good God, boy, are you quite all right?"

Wikerus ceased his paces and stared at the man, trying to allow the angry wrinkles to tell him what sort of answer they expected. They gave him no such hints and he simply answered, "Yes."

He turned his attention to the knights, who had not moved from their seats on the cart. They stared at him puzzled, as if he had grown a set of horns from his head, each with bright flowers blooming on the tips. He was not about to allow them to pressure him back onto the cart so quickly. He scanned the full circle around him and chose the direction where the surrounding woods were thickest, and he marched quickly out of their sight.

He listened for them to call to him and demand his return. But no noise came from behind him. He worked his way between trees and around bushes, allowing his mind to wander between tender thoughts of home and clanging, hollering, violent heroics in the throes of holy battle. He meandered quite mindlessly until he had circled around and noticed that the road and cart were in front of him. The sound of low chanting entered his ears simultaneously as the sight of the cart met his eyes. He followed the sound around to the other side of the cart, where all three of his fellow travelers were on their knees in prayer. There was a one-man space between the knights and the priest, as if it had been left there specifically for Wikerus to fill. He took it as an invitation and he knelt among them.

Wikerus joined in the prayers, knowing them well by-heart. The voices of the knights were coarse and raspy. The priest's was no pleasanter than his face. Wikerus' voice carried the others, lifting them to well beyond their natural abilities. With the strong efforts of Wikerus' contribution, the four of them sounded almost angelic. Wikerus' eyes were closed in focused communication with God. The others, while still singing their prayer, stared at Wikerus in mesmerized bewilderment. Theirs was a devoted life, a pious life, a righteous life, but not one filled with beauty. Wikerus' voice swept them away and laid them gently into the arms of their earliest memories. They felt comfort and soothing in ways they had long forgotten. They also felt closer to God, like Wikerus' voice was a brightly paved road on which their own prayers rode smoothly and quickly to heaven.

The prayer ended. The song ended. And Wikerus' throat settled to stillness as he felt the hands of the knights on his shoulders. They looked directly into him with eyes that smiled as widely as their lips. The priest also looked Wikerus in the face, still scowling, but his deep wrinkles seemed a bit shallower and the harsh lines that framed his mouth seemed softer, as if they were almost willing to uncage the man's lips and allow a smile to subtly lift on their far edges. No smile came, not remotely, but the fact that Wikerus expected it was improvement enough for him and he returned the smile that the priest's harshness could not offer.

The travelers mounted the cart, led eagerly by Wikerus. The knights jumped beside him and sat on either side of him, not clustered together on the opposite end, as they had been before. The priest took his place at the seat in the front of the cart, took the reins, shook them, hollered at the horses, and set the cart back into motion. The knights resumed the same sort of conversations they had been volleying between them since they left Castle Tannhausen, but this time with eyes and ears to Wikerus, inviting the boy's contribution. Wikerus' sheltered life gave him little to subsidize the knight's tales. But he relished his inclusion and sprinkled his mother's signature morality in appropriate moments during conversation.

That day would have passed much like the last. The surroundings were similar. The company was the same. The road was no smoother, and the opportunities to rest and eat were just as scarce. But the day *was* different. Wikerus was not cargo on the cart, but another passenger, a person to be spoken to and listened to. They asked him to sing the songs of his childhood, which he sang with tender, reminiscent pride. The day passed much more quickly than the last, and the low sun was striking the right side of the cart with the last few rays of its elderly, out-stretched fingertips.

The dark played games with them all, and silenced the jovial songs and discussions that had carried them through the day. In the absence of distractions, the hunger and the achiness took center stage of Wikerus' contemplations.

They rolled into another town, much smaller than Ulm. Again, two men met them in the road. They walked the cart between the sparsely scattered houses, into the largest building in the town. The darkness forbade vivid study of his surroundings. But Wikerus did not care. His physical needs greatly outweighed his curiosity. The monks welcomed them to the Salem Monastery in the town of Ostrach. The structures of the monastery were beautiful, even in the dim light. The monks led the travelers into a dining hall, where Wikerus devoured stew, bread, and beer. After the meal, his head grew light and his eyelids heavy. In the morning, he hardly remembered having been shown his lodgings, or changing into the robe provided by his hosts, or sliding into a bed that, while much rougher and harder than his bed at home, was as welcoming to him as his mother's arms. His feet hung from the edge of the small bed. But while he lie awake, before rising, he savored the fact that he occupied the bed alone, and did not press the full length of one side of his body against the callused old priest, as he had done the night before.

They did not return to the dining hall for breakfast, nor did they trade stories with their hosts. Before the eastern sky blushed with the slightest hint of rose, Wikerus and his companions were on the road again.

CHAPTER 6
Count Konradin von Buchhorn

THE TRAVELERS RODE SOUTH OUT OF OSTRACH. This morning was different than the one before. The slaps on the back and shoulders that the knight had been giving each other during the voyage were passed along to Wikerus' back and shoulders. There was an obvious air of mutual respect about them all, not due to Wikerus' ancient lineage, not from anything inherited from his father, but from his voice, something that was his alone to offer to any ear in need of it, any spirit able to be satiated by its soothing waters. His curt and timid contributions to the conversations of the previous afternoon were much more earnestly appreciated than Wikerus knew. He wasted no time on the third day of travel. He sang the sun out of hiding and into the sky. The first beams of soft morning light hit Wikerus directly on his singing tongue, appearing to him and to the knights as if the sun itself sought healing from his prayerful songs.

The day passed in conversation and song, excluding from this, of course, the priest, whose thoughts were impossible for Wikerus to guess. Surprisingly, before Wikerus had given the first thought to a walk and a stretch, the priest stopped the cart and invited the others to dismount for a rest. He was the first off of the cart and he knelt for prayer exactly as Wikerus had found him the day before. The knights smiled at each other, then to Wikerus,

47

and followed in kind, again leaving a space for the boy. Wikerus took the hint. He knew what the priest wanted, what he needed. Wikerus knelt in his designated place and led the chant. Again the others placed their voices on Wikerus' to be taken on that divine chariot to their destination among the clouds.

During the song, Wikerus opened his eyes and watched the others as they sang together. The knights held expressions of calmness on the faces, as if sleeping with their mouths in motion. The priest looked like a different human being entirely. A softness settled over his harsh face. His wrinkles no longer spoke of repudiation and dismissal, but of understanding, of countless years filled with endless experiences, all in service to something larger than what saw the light of the sun at that moment. Wikerus was enchanted by this new vision of the priest, and he wondered why he was unable to see the man in that light before. Such rich and pure devotion, such zealous commitment swam through the trenches of those deep facial wrinkles. From that point, Wikerus had no fear of the priest, only admiration. The scowl was a battle scar of life, of a life that did more and witnessed more than even Wikerus' wild imagination could frame.

After the prayerful pause, they set back to motion. But this time, Wikerus sat beside the priest. Nothing was said between them. There were no words of welcome or encouragement inviting Wikerus to remain hip to hip. But there was not the slightest hint of rejection either. The two of them looked straight ahead while the knights took advantage of the extra room in the back to stretch themselves out and fall asleep. Wikerus was not pressed against the priest as tightly as he had been in the tiny bed at Ulm. But what contact they had was of a very different nature. There was something alluring in Wikerus' connection to the priest, something to be gained by the alliance that might rub from one shoulder to another.

The previous days' travel was brisk and with purpose. Wikerus did not understand the necessity of expedience, but imagined that the constant flick of the whip, squeezed tightly in the priest's hand, that prodded the horses into their pace must have had its reasons. But the third day was different. An altered air surrounding the cart lulled the travelers and the horses into greater leisure. Wikerus could not imagine what might have transpired to so drastically reduce their need for fleetness. He relished an atmosphere much nearer that of his home, and allowed himself to drift in and out of nostalgic trances, featuring the smells, tastes, sounds, and warm embraces he had known in the castle.

The voyage from Ostrach to the shore of Lake Constance would have taken half a day at their previous pace. The cart carrying Wikerus and his fellow travelers exhausted the length of the day before the battlements of Meersburg Castle dominated the southern horizon in front of them. Once the lakeside castle was in sight, the road seemed to straighten, as if its attention to its destiny had been focused by the revelation of the grey stone walls and pointed peaks of Meersburg's most prominent feature.

Regardless of what communication passed between the castle and the road, Meersburg spoke clearly to Wikerus. This was no paltry country monastery. The grandeur of the dwelling revealed itself more resplendently with every clip-clop of the hooves in front of him. Wikerus stared as the spires reached higher into the southern sky. His eyes and heart cooperated to lead the way, beckoned by what familiar comforts surely awaited him there.

The wheels of the wagon tripled in loudness as the rural road gave way to the cobblestone of Meersburg. The hearts of Wikerus and the knights rose to meet that sound, thumping against their ribs with an excitement that Wikerus could not precisely explain.

The cart rolled to a stop while sunset colors decorated every wall, wagon, tree, and face willing to reflect its beauty. Wikerus was the first to leap from the cart. He ran a few paces to a rickety old wooden bridge that crossed a stone ravine, the far side of which was made of the neatly laid rows of grey bricks that rose to support the walls of the castle façade. To his right were more rows of brick, extending outward and upward, the extremities of which slyly ducked behind the growing darkness. To his left was a sight both foreign and magnificent.

Framed on the right by the edge of the castle, and on the left by a cluster of tall pines, was a swath of shimmering Lake Constance, reflecting the orange of the sunset back to the sky with gleeful gratitude. Wikerus had never imagined such an expanse of water. He squinted his eyes to make out, in the deep distance, the faded outline of the opposite shore. One thousand nautical fantasies spurred into action in his head as the brilliant orange struck the back of his eyes.

The lake, the sunset, and the fantasies all lost Wikerus' attention to a booming voice on the other side of the rickety bridge. A large, broad figure stood under the arched entrance to the castle, too shrouded by the castle's shadow to reveal any details. But the voice was rich and oily, diverse and apparently on good terms with the air that divided them, for the air carried the voice to Wikerus' ears with pride and alacrity. Above the man, mounted on the wall atop the archway, was a large Crucifix. The figure of Christ on the Cross stood only barely shorter than Wikerus' mother and lent a divine credibility to the savory voice that welcomed them to Meersburg.

The grand silhouette from which the jovial greeting came was more enticing than the dining room of Castle Tannhausen on Christmas Eve. The figure rolled back and forth from right leg to left, pleasantly lumbering across the bridge. Wikerus moved forward at the same pace, but gracefully, with silent boots that barely touched the old wood beneath them, relieved of half their weight by a light and eager heart. The large man was not like Baron Luitpold or Wikerus' brothers, or even like the honored Alawich. He was unlike any man Wikerus had ever encountered.

They met in the center of the bridge, where proximity revealed a round face, incongruently youthful, almost boyish, beneath the rolling grey locks of hair that capped it. A thin grey beard hung from the man's bubble of a chin, with a narrow string of its previous black just to the left of center, seeming to dangle freely from the grey hairs around it as he spoke, like the tail of a jubilant dog seeing its good master.

"Luitpold Wikerus von Tannhausen," the man belted from his abundant, richly red lips, "you honor these old eyes with beauty that could only have come from your mother's womb."

With the mention of Methildis, a sparkle in the man's happy eyes and a tilt of his stately head betrayed an intimate tenderness and undeniable adoration held in those twinkling eyes for Wikerus' beloved mother. If the expansive orange water and the life-sized crucifix, the splendid old castle and the rich voice of its proprietor were not enough to cradle and suckle our young hero's heart, this obvious connection to his mother would alone have seduced him to throw himself at the large, round feet of the man before him. Wikerus had no time to do so. No sooner had his heart been pulled into the man's embrace than a pair of remarkably powerful arms enveloped his stout frame and submerged him into the breast of his host.

The man shook Wikerus, hummed a tune unrecognized by his young guest, and kissed the boy repeatedly on the crown of his head. This should have seemed odd, even unsettling to a stranger in these unfamiliar surroundings. But familial warmth and paternal care shone from the deepest parts of that thick chest, and heated Wikerus inside and out.

The man released Wikerus and gestured toward the others. Wikerus turned to follow the man's hands, where the old priest stood with open jaw at the unexpected familiarity and warmth on display in the center of the rickety bridge. The knights squeezed around the lord of the castle, passing him on either side with a smile and a hearty pat on the man's shoulders. They disappeared behind the girthy obstruction, who still stood gesturing to the priest.

"Stefan!" the rich, oily voice boomed forward, "come introduce this poor boy to his oldest family friend."

The priest responded to the command. He walked to the center of the bridge, placed one hand on Wikerus' shoulder with shocking tenderness, and spoke, "Luitpold, this is Count Konradin von Buchhorn. We are to be his guests tonight."

He turned to the Count and continued, "It appears, old friend, that I need not tell you of young Luitpold von Tannhausen."

"No father, I know well of young Luitpold."

Wikerus hesitatingly interrupted, "I prefer to be called..."

"Yes, yes, WIKERUS!" the Count laughed. "Of course you choose the name your lovely mother gave you."

As he stared into Wikerus' eyes, the Count's face turned grave. His gaze seemed to penetrate far beyond what his eyes could naturally see. The silent pause that followed seemed an eternity to Wikerus.

Finally a chuckle shattered the frozen moment and pulled from deep in the Count's throat, "You have your mother's eyes in that skull of yours. I felt for a moment that I stood in front of her, years ago, in her father's fields, instead of here and now, at my own home. My boy, you are welcome here. While you are within my walls, this castle and all within it are to be considered yours."

With those words, Wikerus' image in the eyes of the priest completed its drastic transition from the spoiled, useless adolescent that broke his mother's embrace to mount the cart in front of Castle Tannhausen, to a figure of almost mystical intrigue just a few days later.

The Count took Wikerus by the hand, swallowing him from fingertip to wrist in a tight grip. He pulled the boy through the archway that led into the castle, as if stout young Wikerus was but a scarf in his hand. The priest followed behind with a curious but delighted grin that Wikerus was unable to look back and witness. It would not be the last such expression the wrinkled priest would pass to the youngest Tannhäuser.

What happened to his traveling companions Wikerus could not say. The Count whisked him away with much more agility than a man of his age and girth should have been able. Beyond the castle door was a foyer, lit just dimly by the lights from the hallway ahead and by the weak dusk-light from a courtyard to his right. Fully lit, there would have been little more to see. The foyer was grey and dingy. The floors were dirty cobblestone. It seemed to Wikerus that his boots scraped more dirt and sand than stone. The courtyard was framed by a tremendous, thick, bold proscenium arch that stood as a mystical barrier between the archaic foyer and the heavenly garden beyond.

In the foyer, directly across from the castle entrance was another over-sized Crucifix, with statues of feminine figures on either side, like prayerful bookends. The Christ-figure on the cross towered over the castle's guest. But this is not what froze the young Tannhäuser in a fixed gaze. Unlike the crucifix outside of the castle, weather-worn and undistinguished beyond its size, this Crucifix captivated with extraordinary realism. The flesh of Christ was painted so vividly that it looked as if it could have been pinched and lifted from the body, rather than hardened oils on hardened wood. The bruises on the knees, the droplets of blood from the thorny crown, which ran down the cheeks and gathered in droplets at the ridge of the jaw, the wincing expression, conveying great anguish and understanding, mourning and hope, all worked in unison to give the viewer the distinct sensation that time held still while a precise moment of the crucifixion of Christ stood on display in the dark, dirty foyer of Meersburg Castle. Wikerus resisted the pull of the Count, as he continued to stare at the Crucifix, expecting the release of its held breath and the flow of blood to resume. Of course it did not, and Wikerus yielded to the insistent tug of the Count's meaty hand.

Jutting out from the wall, to the left of the Crucifix, was a small, mounted fountain. The Count indicated its purpose when he dipped his right hand into its shallow supply and made the Sign of the Cross. Wikerus, whose right hand was not under his own control, twisted behind himself as they passed the fountain, trying to reach his left hand for the water, but he was pulled too quickly through the stone arches that ribbed the hallway ceiling like vertebrae.

Wikerus could make no sense of the sudden expedience, particularly after a much more leisurely day of travel and the casual, familial greeting he received on the bridge. While he tried to compose an appropriately phrased question on that point, his curiosity was satiated.

"How fortunate that you arrive this evening, my boy," the Count belted with an increased pace and a tighter squeeze of the much smaller hand within his, "for of every night in the long year, this one is most celebrated in this castle."

The mad rush of input into his senses and his sensibilities had not pushed from young Tannhäuser's mind that this was his birthday — his seventeenth birthday. For a moment, he allowed his vanity to presume the purpose of the excitement and the need for haste. The thought was amended by the Count's following statement.

"It is Martinstag, the feast of our beloved Saint Martin, and Meersburg's oldest and most cherished tradition will welcome its newest practitioner."

With that, the Count released Wikerus' hand and gave him a firm slap on the back, sending him three or four rapid steps forward to avoid finding himself belly-down at the base of a rising stairwell. The stairs were welcoming. In stark contrast against the dirty floors, each step was polished wood — deep brown brought to a reflective gleam. The walls were not old grey stone, but brilliant white, made brighter by copious mirrored sconces. A dozen candles lit the stairwell. At last, Wikerus thought, the castle matches its proprietor in richness and taste.

The Count led Wikerus up the stairs to a corridor from which many rooms branched. Most were occupied. The castle was filled with honored guests for the celebration of Saint Martin's Day. But one room was kept empty, kept for the son of Baroness Tannhausen, Methildis von Urach, the best room in the castle, except for the Master's Chamber. It was a southern room with a large southern-facing window. The lateness of the day forbade Wikerus' eyes from witnessing what he knew would be a breath-taking view of the lake beyond. But his imagination paused to see what his senses could not.

"So much your mother's son," the Count roared, shaking Wikerus quite violently from his musings, "No time for that, son. The wardrobe is full. Choose whatever you like. But wear a cloak atop. You must wear a cloak. The evening depends upon it."

He spoke the last word with a dynamic but playful growl in his voice before disappearing quickly from the doorway. His hearty footsteps echoed through the entire castle, masking from Wikerus their position and direction of travel.

Strange it seemed to Wikerus, this insistence upon a cloak. He traveled for three days and had rather hoped to remain indoors at least through the night. But the necessity of a cloak suggested outdoor activities. The thought exhausted him and he plopped upon the supple reception of the bed, with its ample folds of luxurious bedding. He allowed himself a few slow breaths, followed by a curt, forced sigh, before rising with determination to his feet. Wikerus wanted badly to maintain this intimacy with his host and would not jeopardize it by being late for the Martinstag festivities. He chose clothing most closely resembling those of the Count and topped it with the richest, fur-lined cloak in the wardrobe.

In the few minutes of his dressing, the most fantastically diverse wreath of aromas found its way through the arched hallways and across cobblestone floor and polished step, into Wikerus' room and to his eagerly accommodating nose. The humble meals of his last few days were but whiffs of air beside the feast that must have sent forth its cordial invitation in the form of that magnificent smell. There were meats — quite obviously a variety of meats, cooked in various methods. And the far subtler aroma of breads and beers rode stealthily upon the more dominant smells, only to pounce from their carriage in a brave attack on Wikerus' senses. His eagerness to please the Count may have fueled his heart. But the smells that had so gloriously ransacked his nostrils took possession of his extremities, and his feet were clumsily, greedily, and ambitiously shuffling Wikerus out of his bedroom.

He had no idea in which direction the Count had gone, no concept of the layout of the castle, and no indication as to where and when he should join the Martinstag festivities. He did not wonder for long. Doors on both sides of his flung open, one, two, three at a time, from which other richly clothed guests, each pulling a lush cloak in their wake, poured out in jovial spirits. They seemed to know the way, like water knows the way from spring to sea, subconsciously, amid their conversations, but equally determined to reach their destination. Oh, what a happy, babbling little stream they were! Wikerus' eyes stayed fixed on the backs of the heads in front of him, simply following and marking nothing in his mind for future reference, an oversight he would later regret. Up, down, left, and right — Wikerus would have sworn that the herd of revelers traveled seven times the length of all of the castle's corridors and hallways combined. But finally, their crammed passage opened to a grand dining hall. The water had reached the sea and dispersed into the new expanse, dispensing into small groups of two, three, or four, except for a lone group of one — Wikerus — who once again felt like an observer of life much more than a participant.

CHAPTER 7
Martinslag

THE COUNT TOOK HIS SEAT at the head of a long, low table. The table was plain, dark, heavy, bulky wood. But the chairs around it shone like a halo over a poor, dirty saint. They were ornately carved with high backs, of a variety of styles from a variety of cultures. Diverse figures from myths and legends, from as near as the Black Forest and as far as the Orient, from all corners of the Mediterranean to the southern tip of Africa, were worked masterfully into the arms and the crests of the high backs of the chairs. Gilded snakes and birds and beasts that Wikerus could not identify seemed animated as they wrapped around the chairs. Gods and goddesses and bejeweled dancers, siren busts and exotic foliage all gathered around the plain old table, carved into the magnificent collection of chairs, and seducing the eye into a closer look until Wikerus and all other guests were seated upon them.

The glorious collection of chairs seemed to embrace the company, encircling them in a crown of warmth and imagination, and shielding them from whatever anxious or mundane thoughts had been clinging to them all day. Wikerus and the guests became overwhelmed with an inexplicable affection for all who gathered around that table. A very familiar sparkle gleamed in the eyes of complete strangers. To Wikerus, the voices, laughs, and smiles of the room were as warm and familial as his own mother's scent. Faces that just minutes earlier were entirely unrecognizable and could not have been distinguished from any random face from the farthest stretches of his father's maps spoke to Wikerus, and their warm voices were received with adoring, gracious, congenial ears.

Without a drop of the beer yet to blame, or a pinch of the meats, a shared intoxication gripped the entire room. Nothing of the physical world had infiltrated his mind, no narcotic that can be eaten, drunk, or injected into the body. But Wikerus was giddy to the point of delirium. They all were. They were drunk with some spiritual toxin that the day or the ancient castle, the boisterous host or the rich clothing, the mystic chairs or the tantalizing aromas had worked into them with cunning stealth.

The Count pounded his substantial fist twice on the table, shaking the floor beneath their feet. In response, servants poured into the room with the feast. Roast beef, boiled beef, ham shanks on the bone, pork roasts, whole geese roasted and piled atop each other, looking like a poultry shrub, all billowing with steam and dripping with juices, were loaded onto the table. Steaming beans and tender vegetables filled in the spaces between the meats, leaving little more space on the table than what was necessary for the beers and wines that followed.

Wikerus used to boast of the extravagance of his father's Christmas night table. The Martinstag feast of Count Konradin von Buchhorn was something Olympic in comparison. Baron Luitpold's entire Christmas feast could have been used to stuff the poultry on the Meersburg table. The wine came from the vines that could be seen from the castle windows. The beer was under the supervision of the Count's personal brew master. Large, bulbous, mugs of polished pottery wore the caps of foam with pride. The Martinstag brew was served only once a year and the entire year was spent on its perfection. It was indeed perfect. The most discerning palate would struggle to decipher and categorize the multitude of splendid flavors in this rich and complex brew.

The entire scene was dreamy and Wikerus' head swam before his lips touched the mug. No king, no emperor in all of recorded history could have boasted of such a scene. But of all of it, the most peculiar thing to Wikerus was the behavior of the servants. They served as expected. But they reached between the noble guests to pull from the table portions for their own consumption. With one hand, they served a fresh beer. With the other, they pulled a leg from a goose and ate it on the spot. Nobody, none of the other guests, nor Count Konradin himself seemed to find anything unusual in the behavior. On occasion, when a fist-full of meat was just out of reach from a servant, a guest would break off a piece and hand it over. Such would have never been acceptable at the Tannhäuser table. Any servant to reach between the Baron and Baroness for a piece of goose from the table would surely have been sent away for lunacy.

Wikerus startled and shook the first several times his shoulder was nudged by a servant reaching across the table for something to eat. But he quickly realized that the behavior was expected, and the service was not in the least diminished by the practice. Once his father's rigid dining room decorum was fully shattered, Wikerus delighted in passing meats and breads to the many servants who buzzed around the table like bees. In each of their faces, he saw the rugged smiles of the farmers in his father's fields. He saw his honored Alawich, and he was pleased to serve them.

When the devouring slowed, and more burps than swallows were heard, the Count stood, still holding the oversized ham on the bone. What a monstrous beast of a pig in must have been. Although it appeared in standard proportion in the grip of Konradin's substantial hand,

Wikerus stared at it in doubt that he could have held it out in front of him with one hand for more than a few seconds without lowering it in exhaustion.

For those whose attention was not already drawn to him, the Count cleared his thick throat — just a little rumble at the front of his neck that seemed to reverberate throughout his entire body like the toll of a colossal bell through an empty cathedral, as though the Count had hollowed himself for the occasion. That short, low, echoing growl pierced every conversation in the chaotic room and spun every chin in attendance to point at the Count and his fist-full of ham.

Shaking the well-cooked ham so that pieces of it flew from the whole like droplets of water from a dog shaking itself dry, Count Konradin announced, "Two days we mark with this feast. It is the birthday of my dear friend and most honored guest, Luitpold Wikerus von Tannhausen, the son of Swabia's noblest woman. And of course, it is the feast of our beloved Saint Martin. So, in keeping with tradition…"

The Count took one more bite of his ham, washed it down with a single gulp of beer that could have drowned four men of average size, and clapped his mighty hands loudly together. The castle servants rushed to attention and cleared away every remnant of the feast. The slow creak of an opening door came into the room from some side hallway. In single-file, poor men, women, and children walked into the dining hall, gasping at the rich clothing of the guests and relishing the general splendor. The children carried lanterns, clearly made by their own humble hands. They held them above the levels of their own eyes, wishing to spread the light to the full expanse of the room. They were proud of the lanterns, these glowing displays that shone just a little less brightly than the luminous young faces that processed into the room. The line of dirty, leathery people wrapped around the table until they circled the guests entirely. They stopped, with the end of the line still trailing down the hallway beyond sight, and posted themselves near the seated guests.

The children placed their lanterns on the floor against the walls. The room doubled in warm brightness. They returned to their parents with the gasps and compliments of the nobles. Each was praised thoroughly for the lovely artistry of their lanterns, each child being told that their particular lantern is the prettiest ever brought into Meersburg Castle.

The purpose of the cloaks became clear. The Count, still standing with the attention of all upon him, recounted a story from the life of Saint Martin, when the Saint tore his own cloak in half to share with a cold peasant. At the completion of the story, Count Konradin removed his cloak, gripped it at the neck with both hands, and tore the sturdy fabric in half like it was a dried old leaf. He threw one half over his shoulder. The other half he draped across the poor, dirty old woman who stood beside him.

Half of Konradin's cloak was more than enough for the old woman. It enshrouded her completely and folded several times upon itself at her feet. The room went silent. The old woman closed her eyes and tilted her head hard to one side to rub her cheek against the fur on the cloak's collar. She smiled widely, pushing wrinkles to crash against her ears like waves. She whispered "Thank you". The Count bent low to her and turned his head, offering his cheek to her grateful lips. She kissed him, and in the silent room, the smack from those tiny lips echoed. When the echo died, the nobles of the room erupted in cheers.

They cheered and embraced those around them, nobles and peasants alike. Wikerus' generous heart required no instructions. In unison with the other nobles, he removed his cloak and draped it across the poor young man who had posted himself near Wikerus' chair. Once all of the poor who stood around the table were clad in fine cloaks, the nobles offered their chairs. The peasants sat and the castle servants entered from the kitchen with a feast as large as the last. The Count led the way, serving to the poor as much food as he could hold, placing it in front of them, patting them on the backs, calling them brothers, sisters, and friends. All of the nobles served, and when one of Meersburg's poor was too full for another bite, the chair was surrendered and filled by another.

The line of poor continued to file into the dining hall as others departed with new cloaks and full bellies. It was clear that this year's attendance was higher than expected. Amid all of his laughter and handshakes, the Count kept an accurate tally of the heads entering his home. When the last poor visitor crossed the bridge and passed under the large Crucifix, and the castle was sealed shut, the Count left the dining hall and returned within a few minutes, his massive arms piled high with cloaks and coats, scarves and hats, and anything else he could plunder from the wardrobes and storage closets of the castle. They were stacked so high upon his outstretched arms that the highest robe appeared to be growing from his upper lip. He was not three steps returned to the dining hall when the other nobles lightened him of his load and gleefully passed the garments among the newcomers. There was food and clothes for all.

Each of Meersburg's poor left with something — a cloak, a hat, a scarf, a robe, a pair of boots, a ring or bracelet, and each ate well by the humble hands of their noble servants. It was a scene that reached directly to Wikerus' Urach sensibilities. He was in ecstasy serving the heroic poor. This was keenly noticed by Count Konradin, who often throughout the evening went deaf and blind to the activities around him, adoringly captivated by the familiar tender nobility of Methildis' heart beating passionately inside the chest of her youngest son.

Wikerus had always seen his mother as a solitary star in an expanse of blackness, as the only heavenly sparkle of light above a dark world. But there, in Meersburg Castle, on Saint Martin's Day, there were stars aplenty, filling Wikerus' eyes with light, reflecting with gratitude from the bright eyes on the worn faces of Meersburg's destitute. The spectacle could not help but bring to Wikerus' mind the tenderest thoughts of his mother. This Martinstag tradition is precisely the sort of thing that would have enflamed her righteous sensibilities.

For the briefest of moments, Wikerus wondered why such a tradition never took root in Castle Tannhausen. But the fleeting thought of Alawich's people receiving cloaks and eating at his mother's table was replaced by the clear image of his father. Baron Luitpold was capable of performing immense acts of goodness, but never altruistically. There was always as his ultimate aim something personal to be gained by his acts of kindness, some profit either monetary or otherwise, either immediate or eventual, that fueled his efforts. Such was not the case in Meersburg Castle that night. The nobles served the poor and gave to them, weighing no gain for themselves beyond the lightening of their hearts and the eternal memories of the delighted faces of people whose lives were infinitely less fortunate than their own. Saint Martin himself smiled with honored eyes over what was done in his name that evening, and every Martinstag since before anyone could remember. Let there be no doubt at all about that.

The last of the poor stood from the table together and exchanged well-wishes with the nobles who served them. They made their own way through and out of the castle, without supervision and without suspicion. Father Stefan entered the dining hall as most of the nobles returned to their quarters. He had not been at the feast. In fact, Wikerus had not seen the old priest since being pulled into the castle by the Count's tugging hand.

Father Stefan informed the Count that Wikerus was expected at Mainau Island, the Teutonic Knight stronghold across Lake Constance from Meersburg, early the following morning.

"Oh no!" the Count boomed in response, "I just got him. You cannot take him from me so soon. Three days, Stefan, I insist upon that. *I* will answer to Hermann von Salza."

The priest shook his head and hummed a low note.

"Relax, my friend," Konradin insisted, "and stay here with us. Say our mass tomorrow and share my home with your old friend."

The priest slowly softened, realizing that he had no chance of conquering the Count's stated desires.

"Your rooms are all full, Konradin," the priest noted.

Before another breath could escape any of them, Wikerus interjected, "Please, Father, please share my room. It is much more than I need. And besides, we shared a cart of much smaller proportions for three days. I suspect we will be quite comfortable in that room."

Over his many decades, the priest had developed a mastery at shielding his brighter emotions behind a well-rehearsed and almost constantly worn scowl. Those forbidding wrinkles proved a feeble resistance against the swell of emotion that rose from Wikerus' invitation. The very air around him seemed to grow sweeter and easier to draw as his smile and blush grew beyond what even the Count had ever witnessed. Count Konradin escorted Wikerus and Father Stefan to their room personally. He kissed and patted his old friend, but held his new friend in an embrace of the truest affection before closing the door behind them and retiring to the master's chambers.

Before sleep, Wikerus asked the priest for a blessing. What he got was a pouring forth of all of Father Stefan's deepest fears and most wretched prognostications. Stefan pleaded the Lord to hold the young Tannhäuser's hand through the horrors that await him. With a hand on Wikerus' head, gently caressing his hair, the priest spoke of torment and loss, of pain and regrets, and he did so with a wincing face that seemed to be experiencing the predicted miseries first-hand. He prayed that the strength of the Holy Spirit inhabit the boy and hold him erect through what would most assuredly be a tumultuous life.

"Keep him in your light," the priest begged, "so that the miseries that await him will not purge from within him the pious generosity and holy innocence that inspires all who encounter him. And if there is a pain you may spare him and pass to me, I beg for it, my Lord. Do not give this faithful servant of yours any more than can be borne by the stoutest Christian."

With his right thumb, Father Stefan marked the Sign of the Cross on Wikerus' forehead, as he whispered, "I ask this in the Name of the Father, the Son, and the Holy Spirit, Amen."

Wikerus echoed in a voice broken by surprise and fear, "Amen."

Father Stefan took him firmly by the back of the neck and pulled him to his face. He pressed his tightly puckered lips against Wikerus forehead and held him in that manner while silent prayers, those too wretched to speak aloud, were relayed directly to God. He ended his silent prayer with a tender kiss and a softly spoken, "Goodnight Wikerus." Wikerus returned the pleasantry, changed into his robe, curled himself into such minute dimensions that his long body took less than a third of the bed, and he fell quickly into an uneasy sleep.

The blessing from the priest had primed Wikerus' dreams to be haunted by the foulest of demons, both earthly and hellish. Horrors beyond the reach of the wildest imaginations played themselves out in seamless sequence on the stage of his unconscious mind. Beings and events far more terrible than anything his waking thoughts could conjure on command were born and lived out their wretchedness in his night of endless dreaming. Flesh being slashed, bones shattering, death and guilt, demons and creatures even older and fouler cycled through his unconscious mind. To the conscious world, to Father Stefan, Wikerus lay as still and peaceful and a stone cherub. But he was a hollow statue that held within its core a blistering storm of evils.

Wikerus awoke before the sun. He sat and held his pale face in his trembling hands. His breaths were shallow and were forced from his gaping mouth by tragic whimpers. He had suffered ten lifetimes of evils in one short night of vivid dreaming. When he calmed and convinced himself that his senses took in the physical world, free from the spiritual demons that lacerated him from within, he shook off the sensation of the dreams. He remembered the priest's blessing from the night before and embraced the notion that his nightmares were some sort of spiritual training, placed in his sleeping head by God, in response to the prayers of the priest.

Wikerus stood at the chamber window and stared into the blackness of pre-dawn. He remained in this manner until the pink sky lit Lake Constance from above. He left the room before Father Stefan awoke and wandered aimlessly through what he believed was a sleeping household. He was wrong. The servants were up and long about the business of recovery from the evening's activities. The Count was in his study, industriously shuffling through ledgers and accounts. This was the perfect time for a lonely and solemn exploration of Meersburg Castle.

CHAPTER 8
The Pit of Starvation

THE CASTLE WAS NOT SILENT. It did not slumber early in the morning as Wikerus began his self-guided tour. But it took its rise slowly. The dinner guests were still locked away in their chambers. Count Konradin was already working at his desk, with papers and ledgers piled about him, as Wikerus discovered when he stumbled across the castle's study. Servants were lighting fires and setting about the home all the things that the household required.

Martinstag was over, and the Count bore a different air during the infant hours of a humdrum day. Oh, he was still kind to Wikerus, still delighted to host him. But the face of a businessman, with worldly concerns of every sort, wished the young Tannhäuser a good morning that day — the same rich, oily voice that greeted him on the bridge, but with a tone entirely bereft of the celebratory jubilance of Saint Martin's Day. Wikerus did not know what to expect as he roamed the castle that day, but it was certainly not this bold alteration in the Count's general air.

An understated, "Good morning, my boy," was followed by an even subtler, "The castle is to be considered yours while you are here. Help yourself around. I will speak with you this afternoon."

Wikerus responded with a shallow bow and a whispered "Thank you". He backed out of the study, rather than turning around and walking forward. He did so slowly, inviting the boisterous and exuberant Count he had met on the bridge to immerge through the stoic expression of the man in front of him. It did not come. The Count looked down at the figures on his ledger and scratched his head, comprehensively engrossed, as if Wikerus vanished from the earth the moment they broke eye contact.

Wikerus backed around the corner until the study and the Count were out of his vision. The awkwardness and disappointment evaporated by the fires of his curiosity. He was very interested in seeing the kitchen — the origin of the previous night's feast that fed so many and bound in kinship and pleasure such a diverse company of rich and poor, of educated and ignorant, of nobles and commoners. He expected a grand and magical chamber, with unearthly spirits under the disguise of men and women, flying like the wind from counter to oven and back again. What he found was altogether different, but just as intriguing.

The kitchen was not easy to find, and he refused to ask the many servants he encountered on his search. The aimless wandering brought him multiple times through the same corridors and into the same rooms. He learned much about the castle and about those who called it home during the turn of five centuries. The walls of every room were adorned with relics of the castle's history. One room was filled with trophies from hunting expeditions. The heads of huge beasts were mounted on the walls, with bows and spears beside them, and plaques with the names of the hunters involved. Each plaque was marked with a date, from as early as June, 828.

Another room was devoted to the military history of the region. Suits of armor were mounted on the walls, in styles from the late Roman Empire to the most current technology and designs. Some were dented and rusty, and still wore the stains of battle. Some were clearly ceremonial and had never met an enemy's sword. In the military room was a scale model of the castle. It had soldier figurines and knights on horseback, sculpted and painted to realistic accuracy. This commandeered Wikerus' imagination and took it down several fantastic and adventurous roads, while his eyes anatomized every precise detail of the model.

Nagging him from just beneath the surface, and keeping him pressing forward, was his relentless desire to see the kitchen. He eventually made his way down to a long hallway. The first evidence of his destination came at his face in the form of wafting heat. This was among the oldest parts of the castle. The large, grey stones were ancient and well-worn. Wikerus followed the heat. No rooms opened in the corridor. There were no doors. The hallway bulbed out on the sides, where things were stored. Nestled snuggly inside the second of these bulbs was the castle forge.

The blacksmith was already at work. A tall, thin man pulled on a bellows cramp that was so large it could have swallowed him like Jonah. But this "Jonah" had a friendly, playful relationship with *his* whale. He spoke with it, and giggled as he stretched his long body with the bellows' inhale and curled into a tiny ball as he forced the exhale. The kiln responded, surging with glowing orange and a rush of warm air blown down the long hallway with each contraction of the blacksmith's long body.

Wikerus' imagination stayed with the biblical metaphor, for the blacksmith appeared to be underwater. His long, wavy, chestnut hair floated about his head, dancing in the hot vapors of the kiln. He was youthful in his gleeful expression, like a child at play with his friends. But a few wrinkles around his eyes and mouth, happy wrinkles, the sort one develops after decades of excessive laughter, along with a scar that ran from his temple to his jaw on the right side of his face, hinted at a history that toyed with Wikerus' imagination.

There was something about this man, toiling away, glistening so early in the day with sweat, smiling and playing with his work like they were old friends, that held Wikerus' attention with a covetous grasp. He was jolted free when that youthful face broke from his watery dance with his whale and turned to lock eyes with Wikerus. The blacksmith broadened his smile as he nodded to his curious visitor, who responded with alternating steps sideward and backward, never breaking his stare until the bellows-whale swam between them.

At the very moment Wikerus lost eye contact with the blacksmith, his senses were seized by another seductive magician. Wafting from the kitchen just a few steps behind him came the elevating, cradling, nurturing aroma of freshly baked bread. Wikerus turned on his heels and united his eyes with his nose. The kitchen bulbed out from the hallway much like the forge, but on both sides. It capped the hallway like a sphere at the end of a scepter. It was not large, not grand in any way except for the mood of its employees.

The kitchen was small, but bustled with activity. This would seem to be the literal manifestation of the old, hackneyed cliché "too many cooks in the kitchen". But as Wikerus watched them buzz about their work, he realized that the old saying had no place in this crowded place. There are many organs in the body. Thank God for them all. Each plays its own part while working in unison with the whole. Such was the case in the "body" of the castle kitchen. No stumbling, no bumps or collisions, but a tight flow of concerted chaos that volleyed our hero's eyes back and forth at a frenzied rate across the busy scene.

Wikerus thought of the Martinstag feast and struggled to imagine it all coming from such a tiny kitchen. His mind tried to cram every ham, every goose, every fruit and vegetable that flowed into the dining hall into the nooks and crannies of the small kitchen, but he could not make it fit.

"What miracle workers," he thought to himself, "Where did it all come from?"

Far more intriguing than that were the attitudes and airs of the kitchen staff. Like the blacksmith, they seemed to take earnest joy in the duties assigned to them. They joked and laughed and cooperated as if their work was some beloved hobby they performed excitedly during their moments of leisure.

One of the cooks took notice of Wikerus and greeted him, "You must be our noble guest, the Tannhäuser."

Wikerus acknowledged the truth of the assumption and was immediately seized by the arms from many directions and rushed to a tall stool beside the counter.

A voice came from behind him, "Thank you for visiting us in the kitchen. Here, eat."

A callused old hand, scarred from burns, reached around him with a plate full of warm bread, a thick slice of ham, and a wedge of cheese. Before he could begin to thank them, a mug appeared on the table as if delivered by a ghost. It was filled with some bubbling, light-green tonic. It had a distinctly herbal flavor and sparkled in his nose. Wikerus ate and exchanged every polite pleasantry with his servant-hosts, while they continued about their work, not skipping a beat.

Precisely as Wikerus lifted the last nibble of cheese from his plate, it was lifted away and whisked out of sight. He poured the last of the green tonic down his throat and stood from the stool, offering his gratitude and compliments randomly in all directions, for no matter where he looked there was a cook moving at an inhuman pace. The woman who greeted him handed him two small rolls of bread and invited him to visit them whenever he desires, assuring him that a succulent meal would great him, any time, day or night. With a few firm pats on his back, which would have been grossly inappropriate from a servant in Castle Tannhausen, the woman sent him back where he came, past the blacksmith and through the passages that had led him to the kitchen.

With a warm roll in each hand, Wikerus continued his tour of the castle. He rambled up and down, inside and out, until he came across a curious room. At its center was a hole — a well of sorts, with a dark wood, circular banister surrounding it. This curiosity became, in an instant, a mortification. A weak and pathetically mournful moan came from the hole. Wikerus stood against the rail and looked downward. It opened into a pit, only the center of which could be seen from Wikerus' vantage point. A man walked from the hidden extremities of the pit to stand directly under Wikerus' glance. He wore only a short pair of pants, covering him just beneath the knees. He had no shirt, making his emaciated state all too visible. The bones of his shoulders seemed to poke out of him, like he was smuggling thin, poky tools under his skin. The spaces between his ribs were so sunken that their depths were difficult to determine.

The man looked up at Wikerus. He was no savage, no wild man to be isolated from peaceful people. A keen and undeniable intelligence shone from his eyes. A face of peace and understanding looked up from the pit to the confounded young guest. Wikerus' mind scurried in a thousand directions, trying to make some sense of what he was witnessing. What was this pit? For what crime was this man being starved inside of it? How could good Count Konradin condone such torture? Perhaps a full minute of frenzied contemplation occurred in poor Wikerus' head before he recollected the bread in his hands. With no thought of consequences, in mindless obedience to his compassion, he tossed a roll into the pit.

74

The man lifted his hand to catch the roll, but he was too weak, too slow. The roll bounced twice at his feet before his hand reached the height of his head. He bent down and picked up the bread, and stared at it as if entirely unsure what was to be done with it.

"Eat it," Wikerus growled down to him in a half-cry.

The man squatted down and placed the roll ceremoniously in the center of the floor, directly under the opening. He looked up to Wikerus with a face that expressed nothing — no gratitude, no pain, no confusion. He looked upward in this manner for a few seconds, then walked out of Wikerus' sight, away from the offering. Wikerus threw the other roll into the pit. It bounced out of his sight, in the direction the man had walked. He waited to hear the sounds of bread being devoured by a ravenous beast. What he heard instead were slow and intentional footsteps.

The man came back into view, this time not looking upward. He placed the second roll beside the first, while reciting in a parched, rusty, barely functional voice, "Not by bread alone shall I live."

The man turned away from the bread, took one step, and collapsed. He surely heard Wikerus' sorrowful gasp. But he made no acknowledgement of it. He simply regathered himself and walked out of sight. Wikerus' anger surpassed his decorum. He squeezed and wrenched the wooden railing until his hands blistered. He pictured the good Count in his head, which ignited a fierce battle within him. He had a violent internal reaction to the conflicting thoughts. The man who knew and loved his mother, who greeted him so warmly on the bridge, who fed the poor of his city from his own kitchen and clothed them from his own wardrobes kept this dying man inside of a pit — a pit of starvation. Whatever the man's crimes, surely a just lord, a man of Christ could find a gentler means of punishment. Such was the battle raging within him.

These swirling thoughts and the man's refusal to eat the bread, plus the very existence of such a pit, so clearly designed to torture, under the roof of a man whom Wikerus had so quickly come to love and respect, set his head to swoon. His knees buckled. If not for the height of the banister around the pit, Wikerus surely would have joined the starving man. But he caught the rail with his armpit and struggled to return to his weakened legs. He returned to his room to find Father Stefan gone. He fell face-first onto his bed and was unconscious before his body stopped moving.

There would be no peaceful rest, no graceful repose after what he had experienced at the pit. With rigid muscles and tormented spirits, his dream that morning was truly wretched. In his dream, a large man who walked and breathed and appeared from behind much like the Count, dragged Wikerus by the wrist. Wikerus could not see the man's face, nor could he get to his feet. He was being dragged too quickly to get his boots beneath him. –Stomp- and –pound- and –thud- went the massive boots in front of him, with determination that seemed distinctly malignant. The massive figure dragged Wikerus through forests and old stone hallways, through deserts and over hills, until finally stopping on a white dune.

In the middle of the dune was the hauntingly familiar wooden banister rail of the Pit of Starvation. Wikerus knew his punishment, but not his crime. The man flung Wikerus into the pit like he was discarding a chicken bone. With his face to the hole above him, he watched the banister rapidly reduce in dimension as he fell downward. He awaited the ground's painful strike on his backside. But it did not come. He continued to fall until there was nothing at all to be seen above him, or in any other direction. There was nothing for his eyes or hands to grab, just nothingness in all directions. He closed his eyes and prayed.

Suddenly, he became aware of the sensation of water pouring onto his head. He opened his eyes to see and feel a narrow fall of crystal-clear water, an infinite line of falling fluid, no wider than his shoulders, falling at his rate beside him. But he could not see the beginning or end of it. It came from some source far beyond his vision above, and fell to some depth his worldly eyes could not reach. He grabbed at the column of water, squeezing at it with his hands and wrapping his arms around it. It responded as water does. It gave him nothing of substance to slow his descent. His arms and hands passed through it but returned to him dry.

Feeling no impact, he became aware of solid ground beneath him, precisely as he noticed an end to the sensation of falling. He sat in a grassy field. The column of water continued to fall beside him, and pool around him. He was struck hard in the center of his chest by an inner sensation that was foreign to him. He loved the water. He could not explain how or why, not while he dreamed or in his attempts to understand it after he awoke. But he loved the water. He wanted to be in it, surrounded and embraced by it. The column of falling water ceased and the sound of it crashing into the rising pool around him suddenly silenced. Wikerus stood as the water level rose to his hips.

After the scene had gone still and silent, and he stood in an endless, glistening pool, he had an insatiable desire to taste the water. He cupped his right hand and drew a sip to his mouth. It was warm but refreshing. It soothed him and healed him, relieving every pain and sorrow, washing away bruises as if they were light smudges of dirt, and patching the holes in his troubled soul. He was complete and pristine. He was reborn.

As comprehensively satisfying as the sip was, he craved more. The desire to drink was desperate, not because he was thirsty, but that he wanted the water inside of him, as a part of him. He bent low to touch his eager lips to the surface of the pool, but as he lowered his head, the level of the water lowered in equal measure. His mouth could draw no nearer the surface. He dropped to his knees and continued to lower his head until every remnant of the magical water sank into the low grass and disappeared beneath him.

He mourned the loss of the water like it had washed away with it everything beautiful, everything worth celebrating, everything capable of being enjoyed in the world. The grass was dry, the ground beneath it also dry. He dug his finger beneath the blades and into the dirt. Nothing of the water remained. It was gone from his life forever. He buried his face in the grass and begged it to come back to him. But the only fluid to be found was Wikerus' own tears, which also disappeared into the soil between his knees.

Wikerus awoke in his bed, precisely as he knelt in his dream, with his cheeks soaked in tears and the same ache in his chest. As he elevated through those layers of consciousness between his dream and the tangible world, the ache in his chest subsided. But the memory of it remained with him for weeks.

Wikerus stood from the bed in time to hear a knock at his door. Two quick taps were all that preceded the opening of the door just wide enough for the Count to squeeze his abundant cheeks into the room.

"The cooks told me you have already eaten well. Unlikely you'll need lunch. Do as you wish, my boy. I must eat lunch and I will come for you after."

He smiled so widely at Wikerus that his broadening face pushed the door open further. Wikerus returned the warm expression with one of embittered confusion.

Ignorant of Wikerus' encounter with the Pit of Starvation, and misunderstanding the boy's grimace, he amended, "Unless of course you are hungry, or would like simply to sit with me while I eat."

"No!" Wikerus retorted sharply, before containing himself and adding more genteelly and with an undeniably forced deference, "No thank you, my lord."

The Count raised an eyebrow and forced out a quick sigh, and reminded Wikerus, "Whatever you like. The castle is yours while you are here."

Wikerus thought loudly inside his own head, "If it is mine, I wish to free that man from the pit and to fill it in so that it is never used again."

By the time this thought finished, he was thinking it to the inside of his closed door. The Count was off to lunch. Still disturbed by the lingering sensation of his dream, but focusing more clearly by the second on the more disdainful, Wikerus paced his chamber, alternating rubbing his temples and his eyes, with more force than could do him any good. His paces quickened until the room could no longer hold him. He burst from the room and marched with determined and unchecked zeal for the Pit of Starvation.

With his senses and wits heightened, he found the room directly. He ran to the pit and placed his hands on the rail, but leaning backward so that he could not look inside. Something inside of him forbade another look at the starving man. But his thoughts were intensely on the poor soul, so intensely that his heart flew into his throat when a firm hand took his shoulder. He spun around and stumbled backward, almost falling into the pit. The Count caught him by the wrist and pulled him squarely to his feet.

With a laugh in his voice that Wikerus found disturbingly irreverent in such proximity to the pit's pathetic captive, the Count said, "Whoa now. If you decide that you wish to go into my pit, I'll gladly lower you myself. But best not to go in headfirst."

Wikerus took this as a threat, and shivered in a moment of intense fear. He only relaxed in remembering the Count's affections for his mother and the fact that Father Stefan was charged with bringing him to the Teutonic Knights. He could not just disappear into the castle's cruel pit.

The realization emboldened him enough to confront his host, "How could you do this? I have seen the man in there. If he deserves death, kill him. But what crime can deliver a sentence of starvation?"

The Count's jovial face turned intensely grave.

"You misunderstand, young man. He is not a criminal. He is a friend."

The fear returned to Wikerus' skin, where it waved inward until it shook his bones. He scooted quickly to the opposite side of the pit, placing the circular banister between them.

The Count's face softened with compassion as he asked, "You fear me, young Tannhäuser. Why? What do you think is happening here?"

The Count was so genuinely sympathetic, so authentically concerned for Wikerus' state of mind, that fear evaporated in an instant and was replaced by curiosity.

"I don't know... That is to say... I can't imagine why... I ..."

It was clear to the Count that Wikerus was shaken out of his wits and was no more capable of constructing a coherent sentence than of eating the entire Martinstag feast by himself. So he decided to go directly to the point.

"The man in the pit is Andreas. He is the son of a nearby baron and friend. Andreas wishes to join my knights."

Wikerus slowly shook his head back and forth, still unable to make sense of it all.

Konradin continued, "I tried to deny his entrance into the pit. But he insisted upon it."

"I saw him," Wikerus stuttered. "He asked for this?"

"It is the only passageway into my army, the only passageway to heaven… if not this pit, then some other."

"Some other?"

"Mark these words, my boy. Mark this moment, for you will never hear more profound advice from these lips."

The Count's solemnity of tone and severity of expression sent another wave of chills through Wikerus.

He continued, "There are many varieties of beasts in this world. Some run around the wilderness on four legs, scavenging for survival. Others walk on two legs through the streets of civilization. Of those, some reek of the gutters and wear ragged, dirty clothes. Others are adorned in the finest garments. Some wear the robes of clergy. Others ride on horseback in polished armor. But do not mistake them for humans. They are beasts, only thinly removed from the wolves that run through these forests.

Wikerus, paying close attention and taking quickly to the lesson, began an internal inventory of everyone he had ever known in order to place them in the category of either beast or human. He struggled to tell them apart and asked the count how to know one from the other.

"Beasts are driven by the desires of the wild and the satisfaction of physical pleasures. Fear puts them in a mindless frenzy and to survive they will commit unspeakable horrors. Humans are spiritual… children of God and well beyond that which mandates the behavior of the beasts. Our spirituality lifts us beyond the physical. This pit does not make you human. Rather it reveals the beast, if a beast lies within you, that you may battle it. What is pulled from the pit will either be fully beast or an angelic

81

creature who requires only that divine nourishment of God, entirely free from the shackles of the physical world. They will be at peace and have, through their inner eye, the vision of God."

The Count assumed an ominous, frighteningly foreboding tone, and with a drastic deepening of his voice, he walked around the banister, took Wikerus by both shoulders and spoke, "You must face the pit, if not this one then some other. Your humanity will be tested by this world. I can assure you of that, and your spirit must raise you above the animals."

Wikerus looked into the pit, and back again to the Count, and asked, "Have you been in there?"

"My father put me in when I was twelve."

With mortified compassion, Wikerus commented more to himself than to the Count, "That is terrible."

"No!" the Count quickly retorted, "It was painful..., not terrible. It was glorious. The beast in me was weak and it yielded readily to the spirit, which raised me above the hunger, to the Saints. I took my place among God's cherished children. When I was lifted from the pit, no pleasure or pain, fear or desire in this world could hold me tightly. I can enjoy the pleasurable. But it will never grip me tightly enough to force me into evil. That, my son, is what the pit does for us."

Wikerus looked into the pit. The man inside revealed himself and looked upward. The Count allowed a moment of contemplation in his young friend's head before adding, "Would you deny this man his divinity?"

Wikerus was about to answer when the Count continued, "And will you deny yourself when your time comes?"

Wikerus continued to stare at Andreas, who stared back with deeply darkened and sunken eyes. But the horrors of his physical form no longer spoke of injustice or cruelty. Oh no. Someone quite heroic stood shakily beneath him. Health looked upward at him, spiritual health, liberated from the ravages of desire and fear. It was a look familiar to Wikerus. He saw that bliss in the blacksmith and in the cooks.

He asked, "Is it only your knights who face the pit, or do others who work for you?"

With his penetrating vision, the Count asked, "You recognize it, do you? The tests of God are not mine to allow or deny. Anyone who desires it may have it. But I require it of some."

Wikerus blurted, "The blacksmith!"

"Ah, you've met Rikard. Nobody has ever stayed down so long. Now he is the happiest man I have ever heard of."

"And the cooks?"

"Many of them... most of us. Yes, most of us have faced that trial."

This thing that Wikerus thought to be such an evil was the explanation for the true majesty of Meersburg Castle, for the servants who reach over nobles to share in their feast, for the playful joy with which the blacksmith and cooks perform their duties, for the delight taken in serving the poor. Andreas was the latest to join them.

The Count lowered a rope with a knotted loop at the end. Andreas sat in the loop and was pulled from the pit by Konradin's powerful arms. Andreas did not go directly to the dining hall, as Wikerus expected. He stopped at the chapel to thank God for his transcendence and for the good count who facilitated it.

CHAPTER 9
Mainau Island

THE LESSON AT THE PIT saturated to the deepest parts of Wikerus' inner-most self. From the moment he followed Andreas to the chapel, and later to the kitchen, he no longer had to ask who had faced the trials of the pit. Nothing he had ever seen, with either his physical or his internal eyes, had been clearer, plainer, or more boldly demonstrated. Those who had purged the beast and immerged truly human glowed with a golden halo, or so it seemed to him.

The glow was simply a manifestation of a complicated spiritual transcendence that Wikerus coveted. He did not rise to the level of those who had suffered the pit, yet he was above those who had not. He was caught between a world into which he never really fit and one he could not yet reach, making him even lonelier than he had been. Still, he delighted in his new spiritual vision. He roamed the castle and beyond in an intense study of the Meersburg inhabitants. He was fascinated with the lessons of the pit — with men and women, their relationship with God, their divinity, their subservient relationship with the physical world, and their ability and willingness to elevate themselves above it.

By that same evening, he had staunchly and resolutely determined to walk with his spiritual friends. To do so, he thought, he must go into the pit. And if he were to go into the pit, he saw no reason to delay its effects with meals in the meantime. He resigned to go early to bed, without dinner, wait until after the household had eaten breakfast the following morning, and ask the Count to lower him down himself. He followed his plan and was sound asleep, with a stomach slightly rumbling, while the rest of the castle and town were still aglow with fires, candles, and activity.

Father Stefan awoke the next morning with Wikerus. They rose and dressed simultaneously. He intended to keep an eye on his young charge. The spirit of Meersburg Castle had a seductive draw for its visitors, even those who could not know why. Stefan would have had him already to Mainau Island, stronghold of the Teutonic Order, if not for the Count's irrefusable insistence. And he knew the young Tannhäuser well enough to fear for the particularly beguiling effects it would most certainly have on a young man of his peculiar sensibilities.

Father Stefan took Wikerus by the hand and said, "Come with me, son. I want to speak with our host."

"Yes yes," Wikerus stuttered in return, "there is something I... I want to tell him, to ask him, to...to... to tell him."

Father Stefan had no reason to suspect Wikerus' intention to enter the pit, but every reason to fear for their timely departure from Meersburg. He subconsciously assumed a tighter grip on Wikerus' hand. But Wikerus did not notice the difference and he felt none of the discomfort that such a clenching grasp should have caused. You see, he had already begun the transformation. He already pushed his beast farther from the conscious portions of his mind than an average person might during the course of a long and fruitful lifetime. So they walked hand-in-hand to the Count's study, neither aware of the compressed bones of Wikerus' left hand.

They entered the study and stood before the Count's stately desk.

Father Stefan wasted no time, "Your lordship, old friend, I know that you would like to keep our noble young friend for a lengthy visit. But there are schedules to keep, and I fear for—"

Wikerus interrupted, as if he had been deaf to any other voice in the room, and blind to any other intentions, "I want to go into the pit!"

He subdued his voice and unclenched his body, took one deep, slow inhale, then continued, "That is, I am ready to accept its benefits."

Silence followed, with a solemn gaze from the Count. Father Stefan's gaze was much fiercer, and it spoke clearly of his disapproval. But Wikerus did not see Stefan's face. He did not break his attention on the Count, as he fearfully but eagerly anticipated his response.

With no immediate reply, Wikerus tried to beg his case, "I know I judged the pit harshly, before I knew what it did..., what it does, the service it provides. But I see it clearly now and I am ready to—"

His words were stopped in their tracks, not by a verbal interruption, but by the sudden broadening of the Count's smile, the beam of his glowing face, and one substantial step to the side. The Count lumbered around the side of the desk, reaching his hand to shake Wikerus'.

Father Stefan held his left arm out, signaling the Count to stop where he stood, while his other hand swatted at Wikerus, who was reaching to join the Count in a handshake.

"No, absolutely not!" he barked at them both, "There is no time for that."

Wikerus stepped backward, out of Stefan's reach, and addressed Konradin, as if he were the one who needed convincing, and argued, "You said Andreas comes from a baron's household, and he is the son of a friend. I come from a baron's household, and is my mother not your friend?"

"Dear boy," the Count responded with a parent's tenderness and pride, "Methildis' son graces any part of this castle he wishes to enter, even the hallowed depth of the pit. I am delighted to facilitate your journey."

Stefan took two steps forward and slapped his palm on the desk. It certainly drew their attention, and shook them both from the intimate little moment they were enjoying.

"No!" he shouted with deep clarity in his otherwise raspy old voice, "He is not going into your pit!"

The Count protested, "But Stefan, the boy is ready to join the—"

"Of course he is ready," Stefan snapped, "but his pit is not in this castle."

He turned his body to squarely face Wikerus, grabbed him by the fine hairs on the back of his neck, and added in a barely vocalized whisper, "His pit is elsewhere, and infinitely more terrible."

Father Stefan squeezed harder, nearly tearing the hairs from Wikerus' neck. Unlike the clenching of his hand, Wikerus felt this brutal embrace, but he demonstrated no sign of it in his face. He simply stared at the priest, awaiting another wicked prognostication.

In the same grave tone, he continued, "This man will face more horror and grief than any one person was design to withstand. Let us not add to it and bring his breaking point nearer."

The Count disagreed. He believed that the trial of the pit could only serve to galvanize Wikerus against the priest's foreseen horrors. But he dared not contradict his old friend. He parted his lips a few times, as if words of dispute knocked against the inside of his cheeks. But no words escaped, nor would they dare. The gravity of Father Stefan's address was not to be tested by debate.

"Well," the Count proclaimed with a sudden eruption of his lighter self, "he *is* your charge. Who am I to protest?"

Father Stefan released Wikerus and turned gently and calmly to the Count, "Thank you for yielding to me on this. For what it is worth, I agree with you. This boy is ready for such a trial. And I assure you, my friend, he will get it soon enough."

This satisfied the Count, whose limited vision forbade the sort of pity that came clearly through the priest's voice. Wikerus did not know how to feel. His disappointment in the sudden dashing of his plan was fully buried beneath a swell of emotions. Fear, yes of course fear, but the promise of a remarkable life, the anticipation of joining the Teutonic Order, missing his mother, and wanting to see more of God's world, were all ingredients poured into his head and stirred vigorously by Father Stefan's words. He stood silently dumbfounded as his heart and head fumbled equally for a grip on his thoughts.

Stefan took him by the hand and said with finality, "Good. There is nothing more to say on that and little more to do. We will leave for Mainau Island after lunch."

"So be it. As you see fit, Father," the Count readily yielded.

The three of them walked together from the study and through the gardens of the internal courtyards. Talk was light but moods were heavy. Any looker-on would have seen three jovial spirits, with a spring in their steps like giddy schoolboys. But a dark and heavy pall lay over them as they took in the morning sun, one that was unspoken, undemonstrated, but intimately shared between them.

It was Wikerus' demand to enter the pit that forced Stefan's hand and mandated their immediate departure. The two knights who traveled with them to Meersburg could not have known of those events. Yet they arrived in the dining hall for lunch, to share in Wikerus' final meal in Meersburg Castle. From that lunch until Wikerus was safely deposited into the hands of Hermann von Salza, Grand Master of the Teutonic Order, the two knights would not leave his company. After lunch, they accompanied Wikerus and Father Stefan to their room. They carried the priest's books to the cart that awaited them, exactly where it had dropped them off.

The four travelers rode by cart for only a few minutes, to a dock on the shore of Lake Constance. They boarded a small boat together, where two other knights, in matching white tunics with a large black cross upon the breast, and matching white mantles, also adorned with a black cross, rowed the party from the Meersburg dock to the Island of Mainau. The white with a black cross denoted their affiliation with the Grand Master. It would much later become the mantle of the entire Order. But in 1214, it was worn only by those immediately surrounding the Grand Master. Everyone in the boat knew this, everyone but Wikerus. They knew their youngest passenger was special, bound not for the outer tents of the compound, but for the headquarters of the Order, the office of the Grand Master himself.

The knights rowed tirelessly, not altering their rhythmic strokes in the slightest. Wikerus was amazed at their endurance. The year was late, the days short, so the boat arrived on the island with little of the day's light still revealing the island's details. Wikerus would have to content himself until morning with the minimal details provided to his hungry, darting eyes. The main building of the compound was already well lit. A large lodge with a bright-white façade and enormous twin doors blinded Wikerus from the many details of the island that hid in the dim dusk. Above the double doors was a bold wooden plaque, upon which was inscribed "Helfen - Wehren – Heilen" (Help – Defend – Heal). The slogan of the Order spoke directly to Wikerus' soul, as if whispered into his childhood ears by his own mother.

As he walked through the doors with the others, it felt right. It felt Providential. If misery did await Wikerus, as predicted by Father Stefan, it sure did not seem that it would come to him within these walls. When the heavy doors closed loudly behind him, they did not trap him or hold him against his will. That is not the feeling that struck Wikerus' heart. He felt cradled. He felt squarely and safely on his correct path. That path led him down a corridor that opened into a humble room. The majority of its floor was covered by a long table. It must have sat thirty. But only a small handful of knights sat around it, each with the Grand Master's signature white. One among them sat taller, broader, and more lavishly adorned with patches and medals. It was Hermann von Salza.

The knights from the boat and the two who traveled from Castle Tannhausen greeted the others, shook hands, and dispersed to God-knows-where, leaving Father Stefan and Wikerus alone with Hermann. Now, Count Konradin had been intimate with Wikerus before they met, a connection through Wikerus' mother. As is natural, the relationship bore his mother's spirit. Hermann von Salza also had an intimacy with Wikerus before they met, one through Wikerus' father. And the spirit of *that* intimacy bore the spirit of his father. The greeting was familiar, as if they had already met, but with the coldness of Baron Luitpold's address, not the warmth of Methildis'.

With only Father Stefan as witness, Wikerus knelt and swore his oath to the Order, with vows of poverty, chastity, and obedience. He rose and received an embrace from Hermann, then signed his name confirming his commitment. His life belonged to the Pope, the Grand

Master, and the Order, until released from his obligation. The ceremony was understated. It followed rigid formalities, painstakingly adhered to. Hermann draped a grey tunic with the Cross of the Order, signifying his having entered his training. A matching mantle of identical grey was folded and handed to Wikerus by the Grand Master. Two other knights, ones yet unknown to our hero, escorted Wikerus from the lodge to a tent on the far shore of the island. The tent was small, but slept four. There were no amenities beside a single wool blanket.

There was nothing between him and the frozen ground but the canvas bottom of the tent. Whatever was owed to Wikerus by Hermann's debt to Baron Luitpold, was paid in full by his admittance into the Order. No comfort was his that did not belong to any other recruit. But that was fine with Wikerus. He was denied his chance to enter the Meersburg pit. He was not only prepared for discomfort and trial. He desired it and celebrated it. He sought that glow of transcendence that enveloped Andreas and Rikard. And he would have welcomed any laceration of flesh or spirit to acquire it.

CHAPTER 10
Holy Orders

THE COLD AND HARD GROUND was hardly conducive to sleeping into a late and leisure morning. Wikerus awoke early, along with most other recruits. He was expecting action, immediate, thrilling, and life altering. He was ready to embrace his new life and eager to live up to the oath he had sworn the evening before.

He received no guidance upon awaking, no instructions from anyone. The other recruits passed pleasantries and little more. Most were as confused as Wikerus. A servant of the Order came along the tents passing out bread and water. One loaf and one cup per tent.

As the morning grew old, Wikerus grew antsy. He meandered through the tents and buildings, having not gained his bearings during his late arrival the night before. He found his way to the main building, but could not bring himself to enter. He could have presumed on his father's acquaintance with Hermann von Salza, or with his blossoming friendship with Father Stefan. But such was not in Wikerus' nature, nor was it in line with his desire to find and suffer within his own "pit". So he walked several laps around the building, expanding his radius with each turn, until he had canvased every part of the island, speaking to few and stopping only briefly, a few times throughout the long day, to rest his legs and contemplate. If another meal was served before dinner, he did not know of it and did not partake. He returned to his tent in the hour before sunset and followed a flow of recruits to the main hall, where a hearty meal of bread and stew was served to all.

With a satisfied belly, the ground did not seem so cold and not half as hard as it did on his first night. He could have slept into the day, were it allowed. The recruits were aroused by a banging pot and a town crier whose qualifications for the job were beyond reproach. Wikerus could not help but wonder if Count Konradin von Buchhorn, from his soft bed in Meersburg Castle, across Lake Constance, startled at the announcement. The recruits were ordered to gather in an opening near the center of the island.

An older knight, with a long grey and black beard, wearing the white tunic and mantle of the Grand Master's sect, stood upon a high table and gathered the attention of the recruits. A dense circle of full-member knights, in tunics and cloaks of various colors, wrapped around the gathered recruits. The older knight introduce himself as the Master-at-Arms. He commanded attention like only a Master-at-Arms can. This was *his* island, *his* stronghold. It was easy to imagine, for any soul gathered at that clearing, that even the Grand Master would yield to the opinions of the Master-at-Arms whenever they stood together on Mainau Island.

He grabbed his thick beard, as if shaking hands with it, squeezed it while he surveyed the pool of recruits in front of him, cleared his throat loudly, and asked, "Why are you here?"

Many answers were shouted, some fairly close to the mark and clearly pleasing to the Master-at-Arms. Many answers were in stark contradiction to all that the Order stood for. Some were against all that the Church and the Gospels teach. The further from the truth, the more loudly and boldly the answers were stated. Most spoke of war, of bloody battles and vanquishing enemies of the Church.

Wikerus remained quiet while Father Stefan and a few of the seasoned knights evaluated his reactions to the answers given by the other recruits. His opinions did not hide deeply in his face and were easily interpreted by anyone who looked closely enough.

One of the knights who had traveled with Wikerus, and knew by his subtle reactions to the answers, that Wikerus understood the mission and the spirit of the Order, yelled out, "What does the Tannhäuser think?"

He had every reason to expect a pleasing answer. During three days of travel, he and his comrade observed Wikerus closely. The devotion with which he led their prayerful chants, the deference with which he observed and learned from Father Stefan, and the humility with which he accepted humble lodgings and simple paltry meals left little doubt that Wikerus' answer would please the Master-at-Arms. All eyes that knew him turned to Wikerus in anticipation of his answer. All other eyes followed quickly behind.

With little pause to compose a proper answer, he spoke, "To leave behind my life and self, to take Holy Orders, adhere to my vows, and to give all that I am to God, the Church, and the Order."

The knight who prompted Wikerus' response smiled with satisfaction. Father Stefan nodded his head twice, then turned his eyes to the ground. The Master-at-Arms was harder to decipher.

He shook hands with his beard again, this time with two hands, stared hard at Wikerus, like there was nobody on the island but the two of them, and asked, "And after that, once you are a full member of the Order?"

Wikerus' tense shoulders relaxed and he spoke in a soft voice, "To help, to defend, and to heal."

With that, the circle of knights surrounding the recruits shouted in unison, "Helfen - Wehren – Heilen!"

Only the most stubborn and spoiled of the recruits could not see the effect that Wikerus' answers had on the knights and the Master-at-Arms. In imitation, they began amending their answers, shouting forth new ones, much more aligned with the Tannhäuser. Wikerus was entirely too humble to connect their new answers with his. But the knights knew. The Master-at-Arms knew. And most poignantly, Father Stefan knew. He tried to fight back the broad smile that shoved with giddiness from the inside of his skull. But it was useless. He swelled with pride in his former traveling companion and roommate. He allowed Wikerus one glance at the smile his answers had earned, and he turned away and walked from the congregation.

Holy Orders, with all of the study and sacrifices that accompany it, was the minutest of considerations driving most of the recruits to the Teutonic Order. Steeped much more deeply in his mother's sensibilities than his father's, Wikerus thought of that, of prayer, vows, and sacrifice, well above any thoughts of swords and shields and battle. He joined to become a monk and serve the Church, and often forgot completely that he was joining a military order. He still remembered his gallant childhood battles in the dining room of his father's home. He still dreamed of being a knight. But in his mind, the only road to that destination was through his monastic training.

To his delight, and the frustration of most others, his monastic training came first. Scriptures were placed in their hands well before swords. They began that very day. As in any monastic order, the recruits lived humbly. They were forbidden to leave the compound or receive correspondence from their homes. Each day, they were isolated for six hours of silent prayer. For most, that was the deepest cut of all. So, naturally, it was Wikerus' favorite part of his day.

During his isolated prayer, he spoke little to God. He asked for nothing but guidance. Mostly, he listened. He began with a prayer of gratitude for all that he had as a child, for placing him on his path, and for everyone he met since leaving his home. Then he cleared his mind and waited for God to speak to him.

In the morning, after gathering for breakfast but before eating, everyone on the island joined in singing the anthem of the Order — Christ Ist Erstanden.

Christ ist erstanden von den Toten
Im Tode bezwang er den Tod
Und schenkte den Entschlafenden das Leben

(Christ had risen from the dead
In death he conquered death
And gave life to those who slept)

The anthem was belted with fervor, not exactly the platform from which a voice like Wikerus' could make itself known. But in the evenings, before dinner, they sang The Lord's Prayer. Between dinner and retirement, they sang the Vespers Hymn. It was in these venues that Wikerus' soulful devotion united with his angelic voice to provide the same service to all that he had for Father Stefan and the two knights as they knelt beside their cart. Again, the sweet boy of the Baroness von Tannhausen paved a gilded road directly to God's ear on which the voices of others jubilantly traveled.

Wikerus quickly became favored, among his peers and superiors alike. He did not notice. He was focused. His kindness and selflessness made him fine company for anyone. The other recruits were guided by his behavior,

96

which made him an unwitting leader. But he did not seize the reins of leadership. His eye was inward and upward, not outward. He sought the effects of Konradin's pit. He fasted beyond the required hours and often flagellated himself with sticks, not in atonement for his sins, but to elevate his spirit above the physical world and receive from his lacerations what Andreas had received from hunger.

The harder Wikerus was on himself, the harder the others were in imitation. The Master-at-Arms had never been so impressed with a group of recruits to the Order. Even the boys who had given the most atrocious answers to the question "Why are you here?" redeemed themselves. And after just three months of witnessing the tightening of their brotherhood and the deepening of their faith, the Master-at-Arms accelerated their training. In late February 1215, the military trainers arrived on the island. The mornings and evenings remained the same. But the six hours of silent prayer was replaced by knight's training. They each received a set of leather armor to protect them, albeit minimally, from the perils of combat practice. They learned the sword, rode courses on horseback, and learned the strategic secrets of the Order.

They ran, and jumped, and crawled, returning to their meager tents bruised and bloody. The Order only accepted the sons of nobles. These young men had lived lives of comfort and indulgence. Had they begun immediately with battle training, as most of them had wished, without the three months of spiritual preparations, most would have fled the island after a few days. But while their bodies bore the brutality of their training, their spirits bonded more tightly.

Some of them came to the island with magnificent skills. Most were older than Wikerus, some quite a bit older. Still, Wikerus was far from the worst of them. The tutors that his father employed had laid a firm foundation.

He held his own against the most skilled, and was given a corps of weaker recruits to tutor.

After his years of loneliness, Wikerus was an honored student, a respected leader, and a cherished friend to many. As he wiped his own blood from his scraped knees, bruised legs, and lacerated forearms, he was keenly aware that he had never been happier. His gratitude numbed him from all pains and discomfort.

In July of 1215, a familiar visitor came to the island. From his tent, Wikerus heard and immediately recognized the rich voice and hearty laugh of Count Konradin von Buchhorn. He came with political news — Holy Roman Emperor Otto von Brunswick invaded Italy and lost the favor of the Pope. Innocent excommunicated him and all who fought for him. This included Wikerus' brother. The Count came also with a letter from Wikerus' parents. In it, Baron Luitpold poured forth, in desperate but tender terms, that the honor and fortunes of the family rested squarely on Wikerus' young shoulders.

Wikerus' distinguished service in the Teutonic Order, the Pope's army, was all that could recover the name of Tannhausen in the eyes of the Church. His training and studies had taken him far from such concerns. But included with his father's letter was a note from his mother. Methildis wrote nothing of family status, but only of her confidence that her son was on God's path, and her warnings of the Devil's attempts to pull him off. It came with one token — a ring. Wikerus knew it well. It was on his mother's hand since his earliest memories. On countless quiet evenings in Castle Tannhausen, it had run with Methildis' fingers through her son's hair until he slept.

The news enflamed the stronghold. Pope Innocent backed Friedrich II as the new King of Germany and Holy Roman Emperor, and the Teutonic Knights prepared to support the Pope's choice with the force of the Order. On

23 July 1215, Friedrich II was crowned King of Germany in the city of Aachen. In attendance at the coronation was Duke Ludwig I of Bavaria, a man who would soon be placed on Wikerus' path and forever alter the course of his life.

After the coronation of Friedrich, tensions subsided and life on Mainau Island settled into some semblance of normalcy. But for various reasons, many of those who trained with Wikerus left the island. Many returned home or died when sickness swept the compound. Some were pulled for reasons that Wikerus and the others could only speculate. As Wikerus' first year on Mainau Island approached its conclusion, less than two-thirds of the tents were full. But events would soon fill them.

The Christian world received the news, Hermann von Salza first among them, that Pope Innocent III was convening the Fourth Lateran Council. A growing desire throughout Christendom for another crusade to the Holy Land, to secure Jerusalem for Christian pilgrims and regain the True Cross, had swelled to envelope Rome. The Council, held in the Lateran Palace in Rome, was to set the canons of Innocent's pontificate. But chief among the orders of business was the satisfaction of Europe's appetite for a fifth crusade.

The True Cross was a golden Cross. Inside of it was embedded a plank of wood from the cross upon which Jesus was crucified. It is said that the blood stains of Christ were still in the grains. The True Cross was kept in the Church of the Holy Sepulcher, in Old Jerusalem, and marched ahead of Christian armies going to battle. In 1187, it was captured by the Egyptian Sultan, Saladin, at the Battle of Hattin.

Except for the Holy Grail, which had not been accounted for since the earliest days of Christianity, and had long slipped into legend, the True Cross was the most sacred relic in the faith, particularly for bearing the Blood of Christ. Demand for its return was ever-fervent. The Fourth Lateran Council convened on November 11, 1215, Saint Martin's Day and Wikerus' eighteenth birthday. The day already conjured a squall of lush and fresh memories, of a magical evening in Meersburg castle, and the christening of a spiritual voyage that defined his every breath. Wikerus did not allow for a moment that the timing of the Counsel was coincidental. This little sign was all that our hero needed to embrace a destiny he whole-heartedly believed to be ordained by God. After a night of prayerful listening, he determined — he would rescue the True Cross and return it to the Pope.

The Fourth Lateran Council was like nothing in the history of the Church. In attendance were 71 Patriarchs (the highest-ranking bishops in the Church), 412 bishops, and more than 900 Abbots and Abbesses. The proclamations of the Fourth Lateran Council carried greater weight than any decree to come out of Rome since Constantine.

The proclamation of the Council detailed many directives from the Pope, from heretical discipline to the Church's relationship with secular powers. But among it all, in accordance with expectations, Pope Innocent III called for the Fifth Crusade. The Council wrote its declarations and sent copies across Europe, beginning with those for whom the decision was most relevant, the Knights Templar, the Knights Hospitaller, and the Teutonic Knights, who, along with various secular armies, would be carrying out the directives of the crusade. Hermann posted across the island part of the *Quia Maior,* Innocent's first proclamation in support of a new crusade.

GOD, WHO DISPOSES ALL THINGS
WITH MARVELOUS PROVIDENCE,
WE HUMBLY BESEECH THEE TO
SNATCH FROM THE HANDS OF THE
ENEMIES OF THE CROSS THE
LAND WHICH THINE ONLY-
BEGOTTEN SON CONSECRATED
WITH HIS OWN BLOOD AND TO
RESTORE IT TO CHRISTIAN
WORSHIP BY MERCIFULLY
DIRECTING IN THE WAY OF
ETERNAL SALVATION THE VOWS
OF THE FAITHFUL HERE PRESENT,
MADE FOR ITS LIBERATION,
THROUGH THE SAME OUR LORD.

In response to the expectations of Innocent III, Hermann von Salza doubled recruitment, but fell short of the numbers expected by Rome. Recruitment into the Teutonic Order was reserved for the sons of German nobles, a pool with limited depth. Priests throughout Europe were instructed by Rome to deliver sermons designed to rally the people to pick up the Crusader's Cross. Father Stefan was one of these priests. Upon receiving the directive, he spent one long, sleepless night gathering his thoughts and writing sermons, and left the island in the hour before the following dawn.

Despite the efforts of the clergy and those of the secular rulers who supported the crusade, recruitment still fell well short. Frustrated and ambitious, the Pope opened the Order to working-class families and tradesmen. In addition to the indulgences offered by the Church, lifting the restrictions offered an avenue of social advancement for families who had been wedged tightly and fixedly into their socio-economic stratum. Training strongholds like Mainau Island were opened throughout Germany to accommodate the flood of lower-class recruits.

For the most part, Mainau Island received the crème of the crop. But the recruits that hailed from noble family were greatly outnumbered, and Mainau Island found itself soiled with characters whom, if not for the desperate need, would have never been fitted for a knight's armor. But there they were, mingling among the most renowned surnames in German nobility. The island was filled to double its previous capacity.

It was not their names that distinguished them. All recruits came to the island to lose their former selves, to live humbly and take monastic vows. It was the manners of the newest recruits that betrayed their upbringing. Some were as pure of heart and capable of mind as any knight. Those blended well with Tannhäuser and his fellows, and all social distinction was obliterated the moment they changed into the tunics of the Order. Others, however, were of the lowest possible standards of decorum and decency. Most of *them* were weeded out and sent away quickly and discretely.

Some came humbly to the island, but their pride in being with the Teutonic Order swelled beyond their ability to contain it. The noble recruits called them "Muschelschale" (sea shells), for the ugly crabs that resided beneath their newly polished exteriors. There was one in particular, named Meinrad, the son of an urban tradesman from Hamburg, a Free Imperial City with a growing middle-class. Meinrad was crass but charismatic, and he quickly developed a following of naïve recruits with pliable morality. He did not seek the spiritual advantages of monastic life, nor did he care much for the social advancement of his family. He was there to get a sword and armor, to go to war, and to kill. It was battle that he craved.

Meinrad fantasized loudly and boldly of battles in the Holy Land. He did not wish to regain the True Cross or liberate Jerusalem for Christian pilgrims. With his weak-minded young devotees gathered around him, he did not speak of helping, defending, and healing. He spoke only of killing, in glorious words from a fiery tongue. Wide-eyed, his friends listened to him describe how he would plunge his sword into his enemies, how he planned to spit on them and laugh at them as they died, so that those would be the images they would take into Hell.

Wikerus and his circle did not care to associate with the Muschelschale. They made a particular point of avoiding Meinrad. But they were often thrown together, and Wikerus, wishing to teach not embarrass, could not help but challenge Meinrad in front of his friends. This was not to be borne by the urban upstart. Meinrad retorted in such ferocious, insulting, and unreasonable ways, in no way resembling courteous debate, that Wikerus did not know how to engage the confrontation. He usually walked away and prayed, for Meinrad, for those young recruits influenced by him, and for the poor souls who would someday find themselves at the end of Meinrad's blood-thirsty sword.

Meinrad, being of infinitely inferior morality, saw Wikerus' disengagement as retreat, which only puffed him further and adhered his followers to him more securely. But one evening, in the brief moments between the Vespers

Hymn and retiring to the tents, Meinrad convened a symposium of his eager disciples.

With fire in his hungry eyes, he spoke, "I probably won't kill very many. I wouldn't enjoy that. I will kill them slowly. I want to push my sword into them bit by bit, so I can savor their pain. I want to see that they know it was I who took their lives. And I want to watch that moment when life leaves them."

Wikerus was nearby and overheard. These sorts of fantasies were not uncommonly sprayed from Meinrad's mouth, along with the saliva ejected in equal proportion. Wikerus was not extraordinarily disturbed by the spectacle. But he was sickened to the bone when the surrounding recruits applauded him, and when he scanned their ranks to see the same mindless, Godless fury in their eyes that had been so recognizable in Meinrad. Wikerus walked amid them and shouted for their attention.

Standing less than a sword's length from Meinrad and staring through him as if examining the interior of his skull, he declared, "The Pope has called us to crusade, not to kill our enemies, but to protect our Christian pilgrims, and to bring the True Cross home. If we can accomplish those things without drawing our swords, then we truly have God on our side."

Silence encircled them for a moment, until Meinrad sighed and followed it with rolling laughter, which in turn spawned the laughter of his friends.

The son of a Hamburg tradesman walked directly to Wikerus' face, but spoke loudly enough for all gathered around to hear, "Are you saying you would waste your journey and return home without drawing a drop of enemy blood? It is you who misunderstand the Crusade. The Pope has called us to slaughter the enemies of Christ. God wants them dead, and we have been ordained to execute them as viciously as possible."

The faces surrounding them grew red with bloodlust. Wikerus wanted to respond, to somehow pass his calm wisdom to Meinrad, who in turn could spread it to those he influenced. But he knew the futility of any such effort. He just stared at Meinrad while he prayed to God for the means to sway him, or eject him from his position of persuasion. He prayed so intensely that he did not feel the hand of Father Stefan resting on his shoulder, until that familiar grasp patted him a few times and stepped to stand beside him.

Wikerus had not seen Father Stefan in many months, while the old priest was traveling the towns of Swabia and Bavaria, preaching the virtues of the crusade and drumming support and recruitment. He wanted to embrace his old friend. But Stefan's face was as uninviting as ever, as he locked his blazing eyes on Meinrad.

With the fiercest version yet of his wrinkled old scowl, he silenced Meinrad's laugh, then broke the quiet air with the growl of his voice, "You have no idea what a fool you make of yourself each time you part your lips. I pray for your pain."

A little frightened by Stefan's sudden appearance among the tents of the recruits, Meinrad listened, but not with a heart opened to redemption, and he asked with half-hearted curiosity, "My pain, Father?"

Father Stefan grabbed the side of Meinrad's head with his right hand, and leaned toward him to say, in the utmost gravity of tone, "I pray that you suffer enough to grow wise. If you live long enough to have spent some time in this world, perhaps you will view this moment with as much disgust I do."

The young recruit twisted his face into the most contorted grimace, and he shifted and twitched his posture. He seemed like he was trying to pull his face from Stefan's palm, but was unable to, as a battle raged within him. On one side was his youthful pride, with a half-circle of his friends waiting for a witty comeback to the old man's chastisement. On the other was the full weight of the priest's influence — countless experiences, horrific and sublime, swimming through the deep trenches of each forbidding wrinkle on his face.

"Take our noble Tannhäuser as an example," the priest continued, "Seldom does he open his mouth. When he does, it is in praise to our Lord Jesus Christ, or in some endeavor to better himself. He is younger than you, but his spirit is infinitely your senior. The cross on his chest reflects what is inward. Yours hides it."

Meinrad stumbled through some clumsy clusters of consonants and vowels, not forming a single coherent word, before gathering his wits, such as they were, and replying in a much higher, childlike, whining voice than anyone had heard from him to that point, "Well, it is a good thing you are not in charge. Go do whatever it is that you do here, priest. I take my orders from the Master-at-Arms."

With that, the priest turned his hard features to Wikerus. Had a realist painted his portrait at that very glance, a viewer of the painting would have seen the same unpleasant, repellant face that stared Wikerus down on the day they met. But had his image been captured by an impressionist, with eyes that pierced into the spiritual, it would have borne a soft glow, and each wrinkle would have had a proud and approving smile of its own. Wikerus blushed deeply at receipt of the glance. It said much more to him than any words the priest had spoken.

Father Stefan again took Wikerus by the shoulder. He led him from the circle, to the same cold, little tent Wikerus had called home for more than a year. Stefan gave him a kiss, wished him goodnight, blessed him, and walked away. In the morning, Wikerus immerged from his tent to find Father Stefan waiting for him. They walked hand-in-hand to the main building and ate breakfast together.

Stefan smiled. And with that smile, Wikerus knew that Meinrad would no longer prejudice the young minds of Mainau Island. Wikerus had long been able to decipher those thoughts and feelings that hid behind Father Stefan's wrinkles, far better than the priest's oldest and closest friends. He read that weathered old face like reading a manuscript in a language that nobody else around him knew. That morning, Stefan's wrinkles spoke of satisfaction — the sort a wise old priest might have if he just accomplished something that he knows will save lives. In the short hours between his encounter with Meinrad and the following sunrise, Stefan exercised his significant influence to expel the pompous knight from the Order.

Stefan's smile that morning clung to his face and brightened with every glance across the table to his young friend. It was rooted deeply into his head by something infinitely more profound than the self-congratulations for ridding the Order of an arrogant and dangerous new knight. Wikerus saw this clearly, but could not read specifics in his friend's deep wrinkles. He did not need to.

Father Stefan spoke, "I have prayed for you, Tannhäuser, that God will lead your receptive heart down his path for you. Last night, he spoke back to me."

Wikerus froze in mid-chew, dropping what food remained in his hand. To say that he was captivated by Stefan's introduction would be to say that his own bones were *captivated* by the flesh around them. His attention had no ability and no desire to escape. He did not inhale in the swollen pause that followed, as if the only thing that could satiate his ravenous lungs was the next word from the priest's mouth. His spirit grew insanely desperate, like it was drowning in the silence. Although his body was comprehensively without motion, his soul thrashed for that breath of information so reluctant to leave Stefan's mouth.

At last, the old man spoke, "You are to retrieve the Blood of our Lord and deliver it to His faithful. That is what God has told me."

Wikerus had been leaning as far forward as the table between them allowed. But at those cryptic words, he drew back against his chair. His mind sprinted in one direction, only to stop in place and dart in another direction. It flew without his control in search of an understanding of this Providential directive.

"That is all," Stefan added in sympathy for Wikerus' disoriented turmoil, "But I have pondered its meaning, and I believe you are destined to retrieve the True Cross from the Holy Land. It is stained with the Blood that spilled from our Lord on the day of his crucifixion."

Every mystery, every unanswered question, and every conundrum that ever haunted Wikerus' brain since his supple mind gained self-awareness, in that instant gained lucid clarity. It was a moment of sublime certainty. He felt like Saul, knocked from his identity by the light of Christ. Wikerus lost all connection to the physical world around him, and he swam in the infinite. Father Stefan reached his hand across the table and grabbed Wikerus by the wrist, reconnecting him to his surroundings. Wikerus pulled away enough to take the priest's hand and return his squeeze. They held hands in this manner, silently, through the conclusion of their meal.

After breakfast with Father Stefan, Wikerus walked the compound as he usually did, but this time, his mind was on the True Cross. Wikerus had many opinions, on a broad array of topics. His views were rooted well, but not firmly cemented in place. The revelation of Stefan's vision, aligning with Wikerus' own prayerful musings, locked a firm destiny in his mind. Everything about the island and his life there felt perfectly right during that walk.

Wikerus also walked with an open eye for signs of Meinrad. There were none to be seen. He was gone from Mainau Island, presumably on his way back to Hamburg. Wikerus did not know and did not care. He was grateful for the wisdom and influence of his oldest friend. Meinrad had been expelled in the middle of the night, before his foul lips could spray another ungodly falsehood or seductively violent fantasy.

His leaderless disciples floated aimlessly through their next few days, waiting to be taken in by the next charismatic character to seize their loyalty. It would not be Wikerus. They sought a bold leader, loud, fast, and obvious. Wikerus' inward spirituality and subtle goodness only grabbed those with similar inclinations. Such is the way of things. Goodness is quieter than evil. Its calmness saturates over time, only after soaking in it. It does not grasp at its prey with quick, sharp, powerful arms. Many who had befriended Meinrad soaked in the slow influence of Wikerus and his friends long enough to become one with them. Many did not. The crusade could not afford to be selective. Those young knights who had been irreversibly tainted by Meinrad would see full membership in the Order, right alongside Wikerus. And their contribution to the coming events would be as impactful.

CHAPTER 11
To the Holy Land

POPE INNOCENT TRAVELED AROUND EUROPE that spring and early summer of 1216, brokering peace between feuding local powers, joining them together in a united cause. Soldiers and knights that were embroiled in petty local wars and land disputes collaborated in the Crusader cause. In July, while traveling north to arrange a peace between Genoa and Pisa, Pope Innocent III died, casting uncertainty across Christendom as to the fate of the planned crusade. His successor, Honorius III immediately dispelled the doubt and declared his intention to resume Innocent's efforts in the Holy Land. But it took several weeks for the declarations of Honorius to travel the roads of Europe. Mainau Island, along with the other Teutonic strongholds, froze in anticipation.

Wikerus and his colleagues received something of a holiday. They were not allowed to leave their cloisters. But rigorous training was on hold and the recruits had many daylight hours at their leisurely disposal. Wikerus spent much of it alone in prayer. Although he readily placed his fate in God's hands, with his mind always on the True Cross and Father Stefan's vision, he grew impatient and even on occasion, doubtful. Stefan remained on the island during this time and easily perceived his friend's faltering faith.

Late one August evening, Stefan consulted with the Master-at-Arms, and it was agreed — Wikerus had proven himself ready for his final oath and full initiation into the Order. The next morning, when the recruits gathered in their crowded cluster, and the knights of the Order encircled them, Wikerus was called forth. He and he alone, in front of every inhabitant of Mainau Island, received his final blessing and became a Teutonic Knight. After being handed his sword and shield, and his white mantle was ceremoniously draped upon his shoulders by the Master-at-Arms, he did not return to the crowd of recruits, but took his place among the circle of knights.

The event did much to galvanize Wikerus' spirits, but did much more for those recruits whom he had not been able to influence. As a Teutonic Knight, he carried respect and admiration. His signature goodness became a thing to imitate. He also gained a knight's share of dominion over the affairs of the island. He moved out of his tent, into the sturdier huts of the knights — still humble, but with a bed of his own and warm blankets.

He was immediately assigned to assist with training. He would have preferred spiritual training. But that was not where his character was most needed. He was placed with the knights who trained close battlefield combat. Father Stefan and the Master-at-Arms hoped that Wikerus might temper the fury and bloodlust growing rampant in the compound, while moderating his own compassion.

When word of Pope Honorius III's commitment to the crusade hit Mainau Island, the training regimen hit a new pitch. With his new position, Wikerus felt a much stronger obligation than before. He returned to his knight's hut every evening, and awoke every morning, sorer and more exhausted than he ever did as a recruit. Along with Honorius' commitment came his directives to the clergy. Father Stefan was ordered to resume his tour of sermons, with a new list of Papal indulgences offered by the new Pope.

Honorius wanted every Christian involved, regardless of age, sex, or physical capabilities. Nobles who were unable to crusade were offered the same indulgences if they would outfit a crusader with sword and armor. Poor Christians who could neither crusade nor pay the expenses of a crusader received indulgences for committing to a strict regimen of prayer for the crusade. This was the task of Father Stefan and the other priests — to stitch all of Europe to the effort as tightly as they could be stitched, and in whichever manner was possible. Months passed without Stefan seeing a single hour of leisure. But he did not mind. No, there was a fire beneath him. His faith that Wikerus would secure and return the True Cross, and prove himself to be the holy hero Stefan knew him to be, was the fuel that kept that fire burning.

On Mainau Island, and in each Teutonic stronghold, recruits gained full knighthood in groups of five to ten at a time, for another year, until the Order was ready to unite as the most massive army of holy knights ever to gather for a cause. The secular armies were slower to gather, as Honorius tried to continue Innocent's efforts to settle local disputes and liberate soldiers and knights from the petty conflicts that kept them from the Holy Land.

In August of 1217, after a year as a knight and teacher, Wikerus left Mainau Island. He rode in caravan with his former teachers and former students, to the Croatian city of Split, where they were to meet the other knights of their Order and sail to Egypt. Hermann von Salza, Grand Master of the Teutonic Order, was already in Split, awaiting his new knights, and he assumed command over each contingent as it arrived.

There was only one place to acquire the ships needed to transport so many knights, soldiers, and servants. The

Venetian Merchant Fleet could have hauled twice the numbers gathered. Venice gladly committed to the effort. The fleet sailed to Split, where it took on the massive invading army and sailed to Cyprus. With only a few days of solid ground beneath their feet, the crusaders boarded the Venetian fleet again and embarked for Acre, the only secure Christian stronghold in the Holy Land.

The voyage from Split to Cyprus was smooth, with a steady wind at their backs and a soft sea surface that seemed to be on their side. But as they sailed from Cyprus to Acre, the Mediterranean turned against them. The ships were tossed and rocked. At one moment, the bow of Tannhäuser's ship pointed directly to the stars above. A moment later, it aimed perilously to the abyss beneath them. The Venetian crew swarmed above boards, in frantic action. The knights were all hunkered below decks — all but our hero.

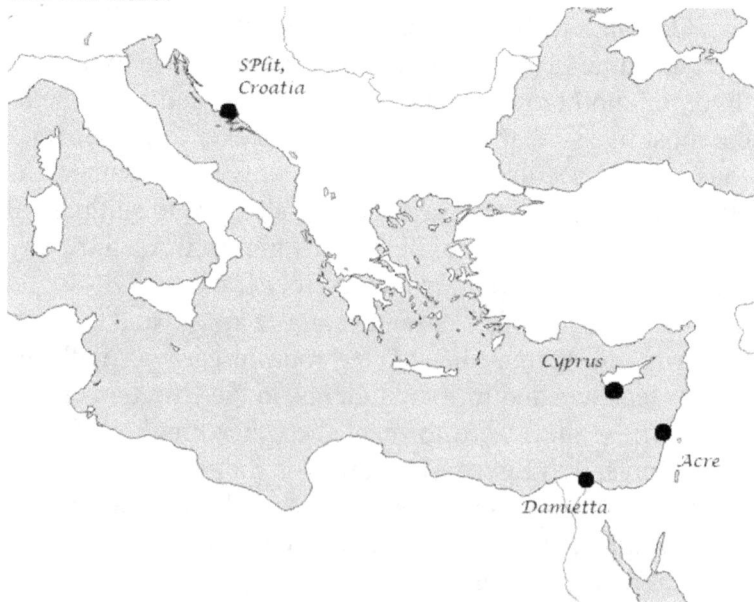

Wikerus tried to help, but until that week, he had never seen a body of water larger than Lake Constance. He had no nautical skills to offer, so he prayed. He prayed with a relentless eye upon the subject of his prayers, upon the Venetians who would save them or drown with them. The violence of the open sea was too much for the world's most notoriously skilled sailors. The Venetian captains turned the ships toward the shore and rode as near to the coast as possible without shredding their hulls on the rocks or running aground.

They moved at such a slow pace that they remained for hours within sight of the same costal landmarks. Sometimes they did not move at all. Such a tumult came upon them that each ship dropped three anchors to avoid being swept away. Yet the storm still had its way with them, taking them west, away from shore, into the old but powerful hands of the Mediterranean Sea.

The Venetian masters tirelessly worked their craft. Nevertheless, by the time the blue sky looked down on them again, returning to the daytime the light that is rightfully hers, two ships were lost, and crew members from each ship were unaccounted for. One of the lost ships disappeared entirely with no sign of board or passenger. The other remained capsized but afloat long enough for many to be rescued. Wikerus' ship fared well, and he put himself at the disposal of the Venetians, who directed the rescue. Wikerus was so eager to help, that he nearly leaped into the sea with full armor and sword. A Venetian grabbed him by the tails of his tunic, just as he was mounting the rails. He stripped from his armor, as if flinging off a loose shirt, and was in mid-air falling headlong into the water before his military accoutrements settled quietly on the deck above him. He saved many, and the journey to Acre continued.

Acre was a crusader city, won, maintained, and occupied by the holy orders of warrior monks. Being in Acre was not entirely unlike being in the training grounds of the Orders, like Mainau Island and its equivalents. Lay pilgrims also gathered there, and the city hosted hospitals and libraries. But it did not have the common markets and local festivals that were seen in Acre's neighboring cities, and almost everyone Wikerus saw wore the Crusader Cross on his tunic.

At a glance, one would never have known all of the planning and preparations that had gone into the crusade. Honorius wanted to keep the campaign in the hands of the Church and out of secular control. But disorder and confusion buzzed though Acre and nobody knew who to follow. Wikerus spent his first day searching for news or direction from everyone he passed. Nobody seemed to know what was going on or what was to be done next.

On his third day in Acre, three weathered old crusaders came to Wikerus, a Templar, a Hospitaller, and a Teutonic Knight. They ordered him to attend a special council that evening. Wikerus thought it rather preposterous that the elders of the Orders would seek his opinion on any matter. Of course he obeyed and attended the council. It was a dark room in an obscure house, in a hidden corner of the city — not at all the grandeur he expected. There were three members of each of the three military orders, including Wikerus. Also in attendance was John Brienne, King of Jerusalem. Brienne was a Frenchman and he wore a Templar tunic over a full set of armor. Wikerus felt underdressed, or unprepared. He wore his Teutonic tunic over the same understated clothes he wore during his training.

Duke Leopold VI of Austria and Andrew II, King of Hungary and Croatia, had already been in Acre for several weeks. They were in the council chamber, and they were the first to greet Wikerus. They gave hardy handshakes and affectionate kisses to our surprised hero. It was not so strange to be greeted and kissed. What struck Wikerus was the realization that a duke and a king, these illustrious figures whose ranks and titles were so far beyond the humble Lords of Tannhausen, seemed to know of him before he entered the room, and not because of his father's political connections. Wikerus' own reputation preceded him into the council chamber that evening. These great men had hand-picked Wikerus, desirous of his counsel. And they embraced him like he had gone most of his life by their side.

Three more joined the council, entering the room in mid-conversation among themselves. They were King Hugh I of Cyprus, who Wikerus had heard was on the Venetian fleet that departed with him from Cyprus, Prince Bohemund IV of Antioch, and renowned friar, Francis of Assisi, founder of the Friars Minor and the Order of Saint Claire. There were few names of greater notoriety in the Church than Francis. Yet there he stopped and there he stood, face to face with our young Tannhäuser. Francis stared at Wikerus with a delightfully puzzled look on his face, as if trying to reconcile some previous assumption with the figure that stood before him.

"You are the Tannhäuser, the young knight we have heard so much about," Francis spoke in a teasing tone.

"I am… I am Luitpold Wik-"

"Yes, yes," Francis interrupted, "Wikerus, the Tannhäuser of Swabia."

"You know of me? What have I done that could have reached your ears, or the ears of these noble men who seem to know me?"

Francis chuckled and answered, "Pope Honorius himself knows of you, as did Pope Innocent."

"Was it Father Stefan who told you of me?"

"Ah, Father Stefan. He *is* a trusted friend, and he *did* speak to me of you. But no. Word of your leadership on Mainau Island has reached the ear of every noble and every cleric committed to this campaign, by the eminent and almost incredible ramblings of your order's Grand Master, and by the crowing of your very proud Master-at-Arms. Father Stefan did not brag of you, as they did. No king or duke knows of you through him. But he spoke to me. He spoke of you with tenderness that is uncommon with him. He said nothing of your deeds. But he clearly loves you, and that told me more about your character than any report from Mainau Island."

Wikerus' first ten minutes in that chamber showered upon him many surprising honors, but none that touched him as deeply as the last. Father Stefan's love meant more to him than any notoriety, and hearing of that love from the lips of Francis warmed and energized him. He kissed Francis as he would have kissed Father Stefan. Francis received the kiss in his old friend's place.

After opening introductions and salutations, the purpose of the gathered council received its due attention. They were not there to strategize military actions. They were there to define the crusade, to discuss how peaceful or how bloody they wished it to be, to agree on the ultimate goals and debate what expense of time, blood, and political suffering they were willing to pay. They discussed what peace terms would be accepted if offered. Francis came to Acre with one goal — to avoid bloodshed by converting the enemy to Christianity. He had no childish assumption that it could be done in earnest. But he hoped to convince the enemy, in the face of the tremendous crusading army, that a declaration of conversion would appease the Pope and save the lives of their countrymen.

Wikerus clapped for Francis. But he clapped alone. None of the others believed that the Ayyubid Sultanate would agree to conversion, nor did they think that any such declaration would satiate the Pope's thirst for a military crusade. Still, the forum was open and all opinions invited.

The council debated each idea put forth. Wikerus was intimidated by the prominence of his fellow members, and he spoke little, even when his opinion was begged for. The reputation that preceded him to Acre was that of a young holy warrior who took his vows to heart, who sought the glory of God over his own or that of his family name. He was known to be free of the bloodlust that engulfed Europe as the zeal for crusading reached its fever-pitch.

It was for that reputation that Wikerus was invited to the council. It was from his lips that the others expected a moderating tone. They knew enough of their own natures to request the opinions of a young man who would choose peace if it were given as an option. So it came as a surprise to all when Wikerus finally spoke.

In a rare moment of silence among them, he ran his finger over a notch in the table, made nervously by some blade of some unknown person many years ago. He lifted his eyes from the notch, stood, and said plainly and calmly, "The Sultan will give us nothing that we do not take by force or terrify him into giving. He will not return the True Cross, the Blood stains of our Lord, nor will he guarantee the safety of our Christian pilgrims."

All heads in the dark and humble room dropped in contemplation. Nobody responded and Wikerus continued, "It is also not enough for us to secure Jerusalem. We must claim the path to the Holy Land. Egypt must be taken if any gains from this crusade are to last. Gentlemen, I pray. I pray with every beat of my heart that God will deliver that victory without battle. But I fear he will not."

Wikerus placed his palms over his face and drew a deep inhale. This drew the faces of the others in his direction. He held that breath well beyond its natural life before letting it go reluctantly and with difficulty.

He dropped his hands to his side and spoke in language cryptic to the others, but infinitely familiar to you, my audience, "This desert is our Pit of Starvation. God will not pull us out too soon, not before our transformation, not until we have forsaken everything but him."

All breath in the room was held during the silence that followed, while Wikerus' mystical prognostication was pondered by the great minds in attendance. They waited for more, for some key to the mystery laid before them.

He did not provide a key, but another ominous prediction, "We may all expect a great expense of blood before the objectives of this crusade are accomplished."

King Andrew replied, "Well, this is war. So long as it is their blood and not ours."

Wikerus slapped his hand down firmly and loudly on the table in front of him, standing briskly and responding not in the calm voice he had demonstrated to that point, but with a scolding tone that even his colleagues on Mainau Island had never heard from him, "Is one drop of blood more valuable than another? Do our wives mourn more deeply than theirs? Are their children better suited to grow up without fathers? We will kill in this crusade, and we will suffer our losses. But if we claim to fight for Christ, let us do so with Christian hearts. Please let us remember the value of our enemy's life. Otherwise, we fight for land. We fight for prize. We do not fight for God, and we cannot expect God to be beside us in battle."

King Andrew stood sharply. His face turned red, first in anger at this new knight, the last son of some obscure Swabian baron. But as the other heads at the table began to nod in agreement and understanding, Andrew's anger turned to embarrassment, and the redness of his face turned deeper. His harsh features softened. His shoulders relaxed and his huffing slowed to a normal rate of breath.

Francis stood and passed his glance along every face at the table before commenting to Wikerus for all to hear, "And that is why you were invited to this council. Not one knight in ten thousand would have shared that sentiment. Not one in a million would have addressed it to a king."

Francis sat down and King Andrew humbly thanked Wikerus for his opinion. Wikerus' heart pounded in his chest. He feared that the others would hear it as loudly as it thumped in his own ears. Of course they could not hear his heart beat. But even if they did, they understood the courage required to speak as he did. And that sort of courage was exactly what they wanted riding beside them in battle.

For the rest of the evening, all considerations, all plans and suggestions were made through the filter of Wikerus' morality. He left the council with the same pounding chest and weathered nerves. But as he walked back to his lodgings, he became prayerful, and with that, calmer and more confident in his actions that night. As he reclined into bed, he had just one thought left in his head. He thought of his mother, and hoped that all of the things he had done and said since he rode away from Castle Tannhausen would bring pride to her dear heart.

CHAPTER 12
God on Their Side

WEEKS WENT BY AFTER THE COUNCIL CONVENED. Wikerus had no way of knowing which of his words had taken root. None of the kings or dukes, nor the leaders of the military orders had reached out to him. He wandered the streets of Acre much like he did when he first arrived — ignorant of the future and feeling rather like he was drowning in the disordered chaos of the city. Nobody that he spoke to knew what was to happen next and very few seemed to care.

Several nationalities and languages were represented in Acre. Many of them had been recently at war with each other. The multinational armadas that sailed from European ports, carrying crusading knights to the Holy Land, were virtual floating cities. For example, more than three hundred ships embarked from the Netherlands on 29 May 1217. To govern them during the long voyage, leaders were elected among them. Laws were passed, to which each passenger signed a contract. They lived by these laws for the months it took to sail. Each convoy of ships developed something of a new nationality among them. When they arrived in Acre, and blended with other crusaders, from other regions, they still held to their nautical laws and leaders. There was a painful lack of central leadership tying the many contingents together, and it resulted in a wild and chaotic Acre.

Wikerus began to inquire widely and impatiently. He asked for his fellow council members by name. But none who mingled in his company had access to kings. As surprised as Wikerus was to have been included in the private council, he was equally astonished to be abandoned in the dark afterward. Eleven days after the council meeting, he made his way to the building that hosted it. It was dark and abandoned, like many rooms around it, as if nothing extraordinary ever occurred there. A dusty table sat in a dingy room. Wikerus sat at the place he held when he stood among royalty and spoke his mind.

The dreary aesthetics of the meeting hall made him question himself repeatedly, "Is this the same building, the same room? No doubt it must be," he assured himself as he fingered the same notch in the wood.

The room was evidence to the power of dynamic leaders. Graced by the men of the council, the walls gleamed like a royal palace. In their absence, it was just a room, a dirty room in an old, dirty city. Wikerus found it difficult to plunge from that brilliant company to the unfocused mindlessness of the streets. He slapped his hand on the table and stood, just as he had during the meeting, but gave no moral sermon to the empty room. He only asked the phantom leadership that haunted his mind, "Why?"

He did not govern his thoughts well, but allowed them to roam at will. A clear vision of the True Cross appeared in his head, though he had never seen an image of it and would not have known it from any gilded cross. The image scraped against the inside of his skull, begging to escape his thoughts and appear real and tangible in his hands. He felt the True Cross calling to him. A sense of urgency to recover it grabbed at his throat and squeezed. His confusion turned to panic, which coursed through his veins and set every muscle and organ to flutter. To cope, he turned to prayer. He buried himself so deeply in his correspondence with God that he did not notice himself standing from the table, leaving the building, and embarking on another aimless stroll through the streets.

Wikerus had few possessions in Acre, and even less money. The Order provided all that they thought he would need. But not surprisingly, their needs and his needs were not identical. Late one evening, while roaming Acre, he took the few coins in his possession and purchased a head wrap from a man on the street. He took it back to his chamber, tore it into strips, and tied and knotted it into a poor man's Rosary. It could have been made of horse manure. It would not have mattered to him. Simply holding it in his hands would have brought him peace. But he did not simply hold it. He prayed it — repetitively, day and night. And with his Rosary in hand, the leaderless chaos and frantic nothingness of Acre swirled outside of his perception.

Martinstag came and went without his notice, without him paying his ceremonial tribute to his experiences in Meersburg. Christmas passed, and the New Year. Outside of Wikerus' head, moods rose and fell among the other knights, ambitions and motivations came and went and came again. Cheers and song turned to disgruntled protestations, and cycled back into cheers. Wikerus took no notice, until one day in March of 1218. The streets were buzzing with a new energy. Still, Wikerus did not notice until, while walking a street, eyes to the ground, mumbling his prayers to himself and God, he bumped into a man.

He looked up to see a Teutonic tunic in front of him. Perched upon it was a head that he knew, with a glow of excitement unhidden by the long grey beard. It was one of the knights from the council.

"Tannhäuser?" the knight belted out in surprise, "Yes, it is you. Propitious timing, brother. Come with me to the docks. Leaders from Europe have arrived in Acre and things will finally begin to happen."

Wikerus had been in such a long and ceaseless habit of repeating his prayers, that he continued them internally as the old knight spoke. Having only half-listened, it took him a moment to piece the words together into their intended meaning. When the words "things will finally begin to happen" congealed inside of his head into an intelligible thought, Wikerus broke from the implacable rails of his Rosary prayers. He tucked the Rosary into his belt and begged the old knight to lead the way.

A tremendous crowd of eager crusaders were gathered at the docks. It was impossible to approach the ships or to see anything but the backs of the heads in front of him. But word made it through the crowd that Oliver of Paderborn, a teacher from Cologne who had been preaching the Crusade since the Fourth Lateran Council, had arrived, along with an army of Saxons. It was not the Saxon army that excited the crusaders. It was the news that Paderborn had struck a deal with the Sultan of Rum to attack the Ayyubid Sultanate in Syria, diverting the attentions of the enemy. This was the surest sign since the earliest proclamations of Innocent III that things would indeed finally begin to happen.

With Wikerus in tow, the old knight made directly for the building that had hosted the secret council. The two of them waited there for about twenty minutes before others began to arrive. Wikerus was seated at the same table around which he had chastised a king months earlier. The seats around him filled quickly with faces familiar and strange. One face in particular was sought by our hero, and he stared at the entrance waiting to see him. Finally, Francis of Assisi entered the room. With a gesture, he dismissed the knight who sat beside Wikerus so that he could take the spot.

Above the clamor of armor and voices, Wikerus heard only one. Francis could have whispered and Wikerus still would have heard only him.

Francis put his lips to Wikerus' ear and said, "Your words at the council were priceless to me. But I will need you much more now. We are at a crossroads. How Godly or how devilish this war will become shall be determined in this room today."

Francis propped his elbows on the table and buried his face in his palms.

"Have you so little faith in our leaders?" Wikerus asked.

"I do not doubt their hearts, nor their faith in God. It is their minds that frighten me. I pray for Ludwig to arrive."

Wikerus tilted his head like a dog that hears a strange sound. "Who is Ludwig? How will he help us?"

"Ludwig von Wittelsbach, Duke of Bavaria, he has been appointed by Emperor Friedrich to command the forces of the Holy Roman Empire. Were he standing here now, I would fear nothing from the mindless zeal of this crusading army. But he is delayed."

"If he is so important, what could be keeping him?"

"His own morality. He is war-weary and reluctant to take another life. He is a man of peace, of family, and of God. If he believes that nothing will happen without him, you may expect him to hold his arrival as long as possible, and delay the bloodshed."

"Do you think they will do nothing without him… until he arrives?"

"The fever of war is beginning to boil. Perhaps it will simmer until Ludwig arrives. Or maybe it will bubble over. The hearts of men are as mysterious as the Heavens themselves. That is why you are here. Your words have calmed and moderated before. I pray they will do so again."

At that final word, the room was brought to order by the banging of a thick, meaty fist on the table. It was attached to the massive arm of Peire de Montagut, Grand Master of the Templars. Montagut had only recently ascended to the lofty post and had already established a new, fiercer, more ruthlessly zealous Templar Order.

When Francis saw who had commanded the room, he leaned again into Wikerus and whispered with despair, "Ahh, here we go."

Montagut began a speech. With fiery words and with glowing eyes he spoke of his love of God, of his determination to free the holy sites of his faith, and his determination to free the True Cross from its infidel captors. Anyone listening to him, had they never read the Gospels and knew the words of Christ, would have believed Montagut to be the incarnation of Saint Michael the Archangel, raising and rallying an army to dispatch Satan into the underworld. But Wikerus *had* read the Gospels. He knew the words of Christ. But he was also not immune to the charisma of the Grand Master. Great duality tugged from opposite ends of his heart. One sentence from Montagut's lips would raise a fire in Wikerus' chest. The next would deflate him.

Wikerus watched Francis flinch and jig whenever Montagut spoke of the enemy. There was no doubt that Montagut was sincerely loyal to his faith. And he was ready and desirous to destroy anything that he deemed opposed to the Church and the Pope. Francis was equally desirous to see the return of the True Cross, and the peaceful pilgrimage of Christians to the Holy Land. But he weighed the value of enemy lives very differently than Montagut, and he was not equipped to stand against the flaming seduction of such charismatic speeches. He grabbed Wikerus by the wrist and held tightly while Montagut concluded his preamble.

When Montagut finished rallying religious bloodlust, he opened the floor for debate. The fire from his eyes had passed, without dampening, into the eyes of the others — all but Wikerus and Francis. It was clear that Egypt must be taken to secure any gains in the Holy Land, and the gateway to Egypt was Damietta. The Damietta Branch of the Nile River runs directly into Cairo. With control of Damietta, that crucial supply line to the crusading army would be open. Control of the port city would prevent counter attacks from the Ayyubid Sultanate navy, while providing a port for reinforcements and supplies from Europe. All were in agreement. Damietta had to fall to the crusaders before any other facet of the campaign could proceed. But Damietta was no easy target, even for such a large army.

Damietta was fortified, protected by high walls, a deep moat, and dozens of towers. The bay that accessed the city was guarded by a tall tower. A chain ran across the harbor from the tower, preventing ships from entering. There was no holding Jerusalem without Egypt, no taking Egypt without Damietta, and no capturing Damietta without the harbor tower. These assertions were indisputable. But how to take the tower and how to take the city afterward was a point of great contention.

Montagut weighed nothing more heavily than victory. He was ready to throw whatever volume of Christian lives were necessary to take Damietta. There was no chance at a direct assault from sea, and an assault by land on the city walls would come at a tremendous expense of crusader blood. Montagut was determined and zealous beyond reason. He proposed an assault on the city walls, despite many dissenting voices. To each protestation, each concern about the loss of life, he argued that each crusader had already purchased his place in God's Kingdom. He reminded them of the indulgences granted to them by the Pope.

"Death in this effort," he rumbled, "is no sacrifice, but a gift. It is an invitation to take a well-earned seat at God's table."

King Andrew argued that taking Damietta was only the beginning of the campaign to take the Holy Land, and that heavy losses in the siege of Damietta would leave them outnumbered in the battles to follow. Montagut insisted that God was on their side and the walls of Damietta would fall before the crusaders. They would be torn down by the hands of Heaven.

"I have no doubt of that," Andrew added, "but the hands of God are now in Acre. They are my knights and soldiers. And how many will still breathe air when the walls come down?"

"Does it matter?" Montagut proposed, "We leave it to God to secure our victory."

Francis argued, "Do we put this war in God's hands? It seems that God has put it in ours. There are things we control and things that only God controls. Be certain to know which is which, before you throw men at that wall."

Montagut slammed his fist on the table again, and insisted, "Their lives mean little. There is nothing more important to God than retaking the Holy Lands and the True Cross."

Wikerus, who had remained still and silent, stood sharply and looked at Montagut with disgust in his face, "How can you believe that? Is any possession of more value to a father than his children? How much more valuable are our lives to God?"

Montagut stared so harshly at Wikerus that the young knight's knees buckled and he returned to his seat.

"Who is this child, this Teutonic coward?" the Grand Master shouted, "And why does he have a seat among these men?"

Duke Leopold of Austria answered, "That is the Tannhäuser."

With no attempt to veil his distain, Montagut asked, "And why does this Swabian baron's son have a voice in this room?"

Everyone who had attended the secret council stood in defense of Wikerus. But their voices bounced off the side of Montagut's head, finding no port to enter his thoughts.

Francis, whose soft but rich voice had rarely risen above another's, silenced the room, yelling, "Enough!"

He gestured around the table for the participants to take a seat. All but Montagut obeyed. The two men stood opposite of each other while all others sat in expectation of the showdown.

Francis simply placed a hand on Wikerus' shoulder and spoke barely above a whisper, so that Montagut was forced to lean forward and strain his ears to hear, "There is no man in this room more ready to put down his life for God. And it means more from him, for *he* values life more than any of you... his own and that of others. Pope Honorius wants his opinions heard. Will you be the first to reject them, Grand Master?"

All eyes went to Montagut. No thundering response came, no response at all except for a drop of his head and rub of his chin through his thick beard. The only sound in the room was Montagut's subtle scratch at his bushy chin, which echoed in the otherwise silent room.

After an awkward pause, he spoke, "I have considered the words of the Tannhäuser, and I agree. The blood of our Christian knights is too valuable to throw recklessly on Egyptian soil. We must attack Damietta by sea."

The turnaround in Montagut's head was drastic. Francis patted Wikerus, believing that the Holy Spirit worked in the Grand Master's thoughts, after riding the chariot of righteous words from Wikerus' lips to Montagut's ears.

The details of the naval attack were left for another meeting. Official business broke at Montagut's surprising proclamation. Servants brought food and drink into the room and conversations turned away from war, to the mundane affairs of their lives and families. Montagut did not make eye contact with Wikerus for the rest of the day. It mattered little to Wikerus. He was surrounded by kings and dukes who honored him for his honesty and righteousness. And the hand of Francis remained on his shoulder or around his waist until he left the building and returned alone to the streets of Acre, thumbing his makeshift Rosary and lulling himself into a mindless trance with his repetitive prayers.

CHAPTER 13
Familiar Embraces

THE LEADERS OF THE CRUSADE did not again seek the
counsel of the Tannhäuser, nor did they seek his company,
not while they remained in Acre. Not even the affectionate
and supportive Francis of Assisi sought Wikerus' lodgings.
Wikerus knew that Damietta would be attacked by sea, but
he could not imagine how the harbor tower could be taken.
When he was invited to the secret council, he did not know
why, nor could he comprehend what he could have offered.
But having been in two such gatherings, he craved to be
informed and involved. He knew little more than the
wandering hordes of knights and soldiers flowing through
the streets of Acre by day and filling the city's dining halls
by night.

Although he had daily contact with several of his
Teutonic brothers from Mainau Island, Wikerus felt quite
alone. And each day seemed to peel them further away
from each other, in understanding, ambition, and vision of
their role in the crusade. Wikerus hungered for a close
personal connection, like that which he enjoyed with
Father Stefan, or Count Konradin, or even the mysterious
Francis. Over the next few weeks, that hunger turned to
starvation, and he cried openly in the streets, feeling more
lost than he did when he first roamed from his family home.
He was wedged tightly somewhere between the highest

leadership of the crusade and those people with whom he brushed shoulders every day. He was kin to none of them.

Five weeks after he ventured his opinions to the Grand Master of the Templars, satiation came in the most unexpected encounter. He wandered one afternoon into a chapel, one he had never noticed, but which called to him in some indescribably arcane way. The chapel was empty except for a solitary man, kneeling before the altar and staring awkwardly upward to the face on the Crucifix. At the quickest of glances, Wikerus knew who he beheld. The hair still seemed to float as if in water, though there was no bellows cramp pushing hot air toward him. His general air glowed as before, though he did not sweat. There, not twenty paces from our hero, knelt Rikard, the blacksmith of Meersburg.

The instant and delightful realization drew from Wikerus' lungs a sharp gasp. In response, Rikard's head snapped to the side, but not nearly so contorted as to be able to see Wikerus standing directly behind him. So please, my audience, explain to me how the blacksmith spoke as he did.

"Wikerus von Tannhausen, friend of my regal count, please come pray with me."

Wikerus was as perplexed as I am, as to how Rikard could have identified him by a curt gasp. But he gave it no more than a few seconds of consideration before abandoning the mystery and obeying the request. He knelt at the altar rail, to the right of Rikard. No sooner had he shifted his knees to tolerable comfort than a hand pressed gently on his right shoulder. The hand patted twice and disengaged, then its owner knelt beside Wikerus, opposite of Rikard. Wikerus turned to stare at the man, who looked directly into our hero's eyes. The face was fuller, entirely recovered from its ordeal in the Pit of Starvation. But Wikerus would have recognized those burning eyes behind the most concealing of masks. They belonged to Andreas, the knight he had thrown the bread to, the very man he saw elevated and removed from the pit by the powerful hands of Count Konradin.

There Wikerus knelt, before an elegant image of his Lord, pressed between Rikard and Andreas. He had not felt so warmly situated, so very at-home, since he was last held by his mother's arms. Simultaneously, without consultation or warning, Rikard and Andreas took Wikerus by the hand nearest them. The three of them dropped their heads together and sang in unison The Lord's Prayer, concluding in sustained harmony —

Denn Dein ist das Reich
und die Kraft
und die Herrlichkeit in
Ewigkeit.
Amen.

Rikard and Andreas rose at the conclusion of the prayer. They turned without a word to Wikerus and walked side by side from the chapel. Andreas was in full armor and wearing the tunic of the Buchhorn Army. Rikard appeared ready to work, in similar neat but understated earth-tones like he wore when Wikerus first beheld him in Meersburg Castle. At his hip was a small forging hammer, not half the size of what he wielded at his home kiln. Wikerus followed in confusion, not remotely ready to part from his newly reunited friends. From the chapel, the men turned left, away from Wikerus' lodgings. Several steps from the chapel, Rikard turned back to see if Wikerus followed. He smiled at his young friend and shrugged a shoulder forward to invite Wikerus nearer. Wikerus picked up his pace until he was toe-to-heel behind them. He put one hand on each of his friends and followed them through the streets.

They entered a small building not far from the docks. It was very small indeed, and appeared even smaller on the inside, a single-roomed building, with three beds, one large chest of drawers and a few lamps atop a three-shelf bookcase with about forty books, a fortune in hand-scribed and woodblock-printed works, with pages of cloth and parchment, for this was well before the invention of the printing press. There was a single cabinet, without doors, mounted on the wall. It held various ceramic dishes and a few bottles of wine. One dish stood out from the others. It was a shallow cup of brown marble.

As Wikerus scanned his eyes around the humble home, Rikard settled his curiosity, saying, "The Count purchased this home for us."

Wikerus pointed to the third bed, the one that was pristinely made and clearly unused, and asked, "Who else is with you?"

Andreas answered, "The third bed is for you."

Wikerus stuttered on his way to a response, "Bu... but... but I am not allowed to stay with you. The lodgings of the Order, I must stay there."

"We know that," Rikard said with a widening smile, "and so does the Count. Nevertheless, he wanted a place with us for you. He purchased lodgings for three and begged us to find you and give you his love."

Andreas interrupted, "It does not matter to him *or* us that you cannot use that bed, only that you know it is yours, as is our friendship and the Count's familial loyalty."

Wikerus' shoulders shook as he released an endearing and comical blend of laughter and sobs. His friends embraced him and laughed, washing the sobs from Wikerus' laughter until the voices of all three rolled in full-throated mirth.

Once the laugher subsided and the embraces released, Wikerus returned his attention to the marble bowl. He raised his hand to the shelf and ran a finger along the smooth brim.

"I suspected you might be drawn by that treasure, "Andreas interjected.

"What is it?" Wikerus asked, "I mean, I see it is a cup, but it is, what I mean to ask is… is it?"

Andreas put an end to Wikerus' clumsy interrogation, answering, "Yes, it is special. It is a replica of the Holy Grail."

"*THE* Holy Grail!" Wikerus shouted incredulously, "The cup of Christ?"

"Yes, it was a gift to the Count's father from Duke Otto von Wittelsbach of Bavaria. Their friendship began—"

Wikerus interrupted, "Otto von Wittelsbach? Otto the Red-Head? Hero of Verona?"

"The very same. He was friends with the Counts of Buchhorn since before he was given the Duchy of Bavaria by Emperor Friedrich Barbarossa."

"But this cannot be a replica of the Grail, this simple stone bowl. Surely the Cup of Christ is—"

"The Cup of Christ is, or at least was, exactly as you see it there," Andreas assured him, "The Count insists upon it, because his father told him and the Red-Head told his father."

"Well how would Otto have known?"

"There is something special about the Dukes of Bavaria, those Wittelsbachs. That I can tell you from my own encounters."

"It is interesting we should be having this conversation," Wikerus spoke with thoughtful quiet, "I was speaking recently of Otto's son, Duke Ludwig. Francis spoke of him similarly. He prays that Ludwig will soon join the crusade and guide it onto God's path."

"Francis?" Rikard leaned forward to ask, "You cannot mean the monk, Francis of Assisi?"

"Yes, of course. Technically, he is a friar."

Andreas mimicked his blacksmith's pose as he probed his young friend, "Are saying you have already met Francis of Assisi?"

"I have met with him twice. He is my friend."

Andreas turned to Rikard and placed a hand on his shoulder, saying, "The Count was right about our friend here. This should not surprise us, nor should any wonder we may witness from him."

Wikerus wanted to beg for elaboration. His vanity craved it, but his humility slammed that door shut and turned the conversation to other topics. He thumbed through the books on the shelves, inquiring about each, in what the other two could plainly see was an awkward diversion from the previous subject. They allowed Wikerus to navigate talk until they all sat, poured wine, and settled into comfortable and natural speech on the topics dearest to their hearts.

At the end of the evening, Wikerus rushed from the house of his friends to the lodgings of his Order, where he was required to attend the Verpers Hymn. The evening streets were still crowded. But he did not feel alone as before. He did not hunger for companionship. He walked with purpose, but feeling cradled by familial affection, with images of Meersburg Castle, Count Konradin, Father Stefan, and the Holy Grail running spritely through his head.

In the morning, the distance between Wikerus and his Mainau brothers grew at the proportionate rate as before. They hardly spoke, even those dearest to him during their training. He noticed the change as he had every morning since arriving in Acre. But it did not bother him. He was not alone. In that same city, laughing and praying together

136

in their humble house, or in the small abandoned chapel, were his friends, Rikard and Andreas, who served as both an anchor and a rudder, holding Wikerus to who he had been, while pointing him to who he must become.

CHAPTER 14
The Fleet in Motion

IN THE WEEKS THAT FOLLOWED Wikerus' reunion with his
Meersburg friends, the chaos of Acre began to be reined in
by a steady flow of leadership into the city. Hermann von
Salza appeared sporadically, tightening the daily schedule
of his Teutonic Knights and disposing almost entirely of
Wikerus' leisure time. A few weeks earlier, Wikerus would
have celebrated the change. But it separated him from
Rikard and Andreas, and that he mourned terribly. He
wished his father had not promised him to the Teutonic
Order — that he could have instead entered the Pit of
Starvation and earned himself a place in Count Konradin's
army. He could have filled that third bed in that humble
house with his friends. These thoughts soured what would
have otherwise been a refreshingly welcomed sense of
direction that the campaign in the Holy Land seemed to be
assuming.

Knights of different orders and different armies no
longer mingled in the streets of Acre. The regimen of the
Teutonic Order resembled that of the various training
encampments throughout Germany. The hours of mindless
meandering were replaced by grueling training sessions.
Clothing and armor that had begun to turn snug above
widening girths again fit as they were designed. It was
these changes, not intelligence gained in some secret

council, which told Wikerus that the siege on Damietta was near.

On 19 May 1218, the crusaders in Acre were drawn to order. The Siege of Damietta was soon to commence. Knights, soldiers, servants, blacksmiths, cooks, and squires all boarded ships. The docks of Acre could not accommodate the entire fleet at once. Those ships that were boarded early sailed out and linked together, waiting for the others. On the 24th of May, the ships were full and ready to embark. Wikerus was on one of the ships designated for the Teutonic Knights. On his ship, he was just one passenger, one knight out of hundreds. But he did not remain with his Teutonic brothers for long.

Once the fleet united offshore, a dingy bumped against Wikerus' ship.

"We seek the Tannhäuser," a smooth and melodic voice sang from below, in choppy German and a strong foreign accent.

The crew lifted the man aboard. He was a Hospitaller Knight, an English gentleman of polished and refined manner. He bowed low to the Venetian Captain and again requested possession of Wikerus. The Grand Marshal of the Order appeared above boards and reminded his English brother that the Tannhäuser was a Teutonic Knight and was not subordinate to the designs of any other Holy Order. The Hospitaller pulled from his cloak a note, hastily and sloppily scribbled upon.

The Grand Marshal's eyes widened at his first glance at the note. The signature at the bottom was unmistakable. It belonged to the hand of his master, Hermann von Salza. The note read as follows.

Grand Marshal,

Hand Luitpold von Tannhausen to this Hospitaller. He is to be delivered to the flagship, where his counsel is requested by the Grand Masters of all three of His Holiness' military orders. Do nothing to delay his delivery and by no means accept his refusal.

Hermann von Salza
Grand Master
Order of Brothers of the German House
of Saint Mary in Jerusalem

The Grand Marshal fetched Wikerus himself and rushed him above deck. The Hospitaller explained to Wikerus the reason and urgency of his compliance.

"I cannot go alone with him," Wikerus insisted to his Grand Marshal.

More defensive than insulted, the Marshal refuted, "You have no choice. I am forbidden by our Master to accept your refusal."

"You mistake me, Grand Marshal. I am not refusing to go. I am honored to go, delighted to go. But I will not go alone."

Every face in attendance displayed its owner's confusion. The Grand Marshal looked around him, trying to determine whom Wikerus wished to take.

Wikerus dispelled his curiosity, demanding, "There is a knight and a blacksmith. They travel together with the army of Buchhorn. I will not board the flagship without them."

"Absolutely not!" the Hospitaller rebutted, "I am to fetch you without delay."

Wikerus smiled and spoke softly, "Then I recommend we do not delay. Let us get my friends from their ship immediately."

The English gentleman's impatience and anger rose above his refinement's ability to mask it. He grimaced and growled. Wikerus turned to his Grand Marshal, and whether from the determination in his eyes or the calm righteousness in his voice, the Marshal submitted.

The Grand Marshal stepped away without a word, returned quickly with a note of his own, handed it to the Hospitaller, and said, "Take this to the Buchhorn ship. Ask for—"

He turned to Wikerus, who replied quickly, "Andreas, a knight, and Rikard, the army's blacksmith."

The Grand Marshal forced the note into the Hospitaller's hand and nodded in firm acquiescence to Wikerus' request.

The Hospitaller took the note, but added, "And will the army of Buchhorn hand over its blacksmith so easily?"

Wikerus put a hand firmly on the Hospitaller's shoulder and assured him, "They will return to their army as I will return to mine. But my counsel is demanded, and I have no counsel without theirs."

On that assurance, there was nothing left to be said. Wikerus boarded the dingy and left the Teutonic ship. They rowed toward the flagship, not toward Andreas and Rikard.

Wikerus looked sternly at the Hospitaller, who blurted in a defensive tone, "I will get your knight and blacksmith. But I was ordered to bring you without delay, and I will obey my orders. As soon as you are aboard the flagship, I will fetch your friends."

The very instant the last word left his lips, the Hospitaller's collected refinement returned to him. He gave Wikerus a long, subservient nod, keeping his eyes down until he heard Wikerus say "Very well."

Wikerus was helped aboard by the ship's crew. Hermann von Salza himself greeted his first step on deck. Wikerus had seen Hermann in Acre, as the Grand Master made sporadic appearances. It was the first time Hermann had seen Wikerus since leaving Mainau Island, and the first he had ever seen him in full armor and regalia.

In a gravelly voice, one clearly fending off sickness, von Salza spoke with a firm grasp of Wikerus' upper arm, "Luitpold! You have your father's hair." He released Wikerus' arm, took a step back, cocked his head in a tilt, and added with great thought, "but everything else is your mother."

Wikerus' preference for his mother leaped forth as he shouted at an uncomfortable volume considering the proximity of his audience, "You know my mother?"

"I stayed at your home for two weeks, when you were only a baby. I saw little of your mother during those days. But we dined together every evening. She is an angelic woman." Changing the subject toward the less pleasant, he added, "Your father is a loyal friend. He did much to help me, at a time when I needed him most. I can do little for him here, but I can do much for you."

Wikerus' face turned sour as he considered those words. Any favor shown to him on his father's behalf piled on his conscience as a debt to his father, which he did not want to owe. He would gladly have accepted whatever assistance was given in the name of his mother, as he did in Meersburg — but not his father. The thought disgusted him, and he shivered as if a thousand crawling insects waved across his skin.

In that shiver, words that would normally have remained caged by Wikerus' propriety sprang free, and he blurted, "Whatever you feel that you owe my father, repay to my father. I am a Teutonic Knight. You are my Grand Master. And I will serve my vows."

142

The two men stared at each other, one in impressed pride in his subordinate and the other in morbid regret.

Slowly, a grin surfaced on von Salza's face, and he spoke as gently as his gruff voice could manage, "Dear man, I did not pull you from your ship because of your father. It is your own merits that have purchased this honor. You will rejoin your brothers and fight in fulfillment of your vows. But not before your treasured counsel is given. Some of the most venerable voices in Christendom have requested you. Testimony of your moral wisdom has hit me in large, crashing waves, from many directions, and from those whose opinions carry the most weight with me."

Wikerus' grin grew to match his Grand Master's. He dropped to a knee and begged von Salza to forgive his impertinence.

The Grand Master stepped forward, closing the gap between them, so that he looked almost directly downward to Wikerus, and he said, "You swore yourself to the Order. In doing so, you owe not only your sword, but your judgment…, and your faith…, and your treasured counsel. You are admirably reluctant to give your opinion, but you are bound by your oath to speak what is in that heart of yours. Now, join me and the others. We will eat and drink, then talk."

Over refreshments, Wikerus told the Grand Masters that he had sent for Andreas and Rikard to join them. Nobody outside of the Buchhorn army had heard of them — certainly nobody aboard the flagship. Some in the crusade's leadership thought it irregular and unnecessary to seek the opinions of an unseasoned Teutonic Knight from northeast Swabia. Yet there our hero was. It was not so very much more peculiar to invite a knight and a blacksmith from the small military contribution of Count Konradin von Buchhorn. So they allowed it. If there was dissension on the matter, and I am sure there was, it went unspoken. By the time they broke from refreshments, Andreas and Rikard were boarding the flagship.

There was little time for introductions. The leaders of the Fifth Crusade gathered in the officers' mess, along with Wikerus, Andreas, and Rikard, the latter two of which had no idea why they were summoned or what they could possibly offer the venerable and notorious figures seated around them. Unfortunately, the leaders felt similarly.

It had been decided that an open attack on the walls of Damietta would be disastrous, and fruitless, as long as the harbor that feeds the city was still under control of the enemy. The tower that protected the harbor and controlled the chain that restricted entrance had to fall. The Grand Master of the Knights Hospitaller, Guérin de Montaigu, spoke with confidence about how the tower should be taken, how easily it would fall, and the speed at which Damietta would be under their control. The speech made the others uneasy, but none would speak up, until Rikard.

"Respectfully sir," the blacksmith budged in, "have you seen the tower?"

"Have you?" Montaigu returned.

"No sir, but I know of it, of its dimensions and capabilities. It will not fall so easily, nor will the city, once the tower is taken."

Hermann von Salza asked Rikard, "What are you saying… that our sea assault will not work?"

"It is the only way, and it will work, just not easily and not quickly. The tower will be unaffected by our ships. The harbor will not allow our armada. Only a few of our ships can assault the tower at once. But it would not matter if a hundred ships reached that tower."

Wikerus, with a blend of despair and pride, asked, "What do you suggest?"

"There must be some other way…, some attack that Damietta has not planned for, some new warfare that can give us the advantage."

Peire de Montagut of the Templars scolded him, "Do you expect us to discover this new warfare in the days it takes us to sail from Acre to Damietta, with only the people and supplies aboard our ships?"

Everyone saw the ridiculousness of Montagut's response, and none, including Montagut, expected Rikard to answer. The blacksmith only sighed quietly and dropped his head.

After the awkward silence that followed, Montagut continued, "Then we will attack the tower as planned. With luck they will surrender at the sight of our forces."

Rikard leaned to Andreas and spoke loudly enough for Wikerus to hear, "They have no reason to surrender the tower. We cannot take it."

Nobody else heard the comment. It would not have mattered if they had. It spoke of a truth that everyone already knew. They could have brought twice the knights, twice the ships, and it wouldn't matter. The tower was too tall to be taken by any naval force. And the city would not fall from a naval attack while the tower protected it.

One piece of good news was brought to the meeting. Paderborn had done as he promised, and the Sultan of Rum was good at his word. He attacked the Ayyubid forces from the south, turning the sultan's eyes and his swords away from Damietta. Whatever the crusaders did about Damietta, they would not be fighting on two fronts. The city was their only concern, and it was plenty. Nobody in the entire armada knew how to attack the city. The ships still sailed and Damietta approached. One way or another, they would be engaging in battle and the first blood of the crusade would spill.

The council broke and the various minds involved, like their bodies, went in different directions. Rikard sat a few minutes longer and rubbed his eyes, hoping that some flash of genius might place into his head the new form of warfare that could take the harbor tower of Damietta without hundreds of crusader bodies being thrown upon it. He and Andreas were taken back to their ship and Wikerus rejoined his Grand Marshal and the brothers of his order.

CHAPTER 15
The Siege of Damietta

ON 29 MAY 1218, the flagship made land outside of Damietta. They established a base without resistance. Count Simon III of Saarbrücken was given command of the camp. Later that same day, the other ships arrived and filled the camp with a force of knights like the world had never seen. There they were — a massive camp of European crusaders and a walled city protected by an unapproachable defense tower.

Early the next morning, with no other plan, no other options, five ships with skeleton crews and a hand-full of knights attacked the harbor tower. They were easily repelled. The ships took damage on their approach, and every knight who attempted to mount the tower was killed. The ships limped back to their landing camp and another five took their place. This continued for weeks without any hint of success, without any reason to believe that the tower would eventually fall.

The Teutonic Knights were not on any of the attacks. But that was a blessing that did not look to last. Eventually it would be Wikerus' turn, or maybe Andreas', to board one of the five ships and throw his life fruitlessly at the tower. As a blacksmith, one of the few in camp, Rikard's life was more precious than any knight's. But one day, he stopped mending swords and shoeing horses. He disappeared into

147

his tent, desperate to find a solution before one of his friends went on the pointless attack.

Nobody was allowed to interrupt him, and his services as a blacksmith were demanded. He did not care. Under intense pressure, and even violent threats, he remained at work in his tent. Four days after he sequestered himself, he appeared. His glowing spirits shone beyond his sleep-deprived complexion. He made directly for Wikerus and handed him a plan. Wikerus did not even glance at it. His faith in Rikard was absolute and unreserved. With no fear for his own reputation, he brought the plans to his Grand Master.

Hermann von Salza unrolled the plans and studied them. He hummed under his breath as he turned the parchment to gain different angles. In an instant, he rolled the plans and replaced the academic gaze that had been locked to his face with a wide and bright smile.

"Brilliant!" he exclaimed too loudly for the proximity of Wikerus' ears, "You are brilliant my boy."

"This is not mine," Wikerus tried to rebut.

But the Grand Master was too single-minded to care what came from Wikerus' lips. He grabbed the young knight by the hand and yanked him to Simon of Saarbrücken. The two of them thrusted themselves into Simon's tent.

Hermann slapped the plans on a table and declared, "The tower will fall before we lose another Christian knight! Let it be known that the Teutonic Order designed the fall of the tower!"

Wikerus was afraid to mention Rikard until Simon accepted the plan with the same enthusiastic vigor as von Salza.

Once he did, and Simon began to ask our hero questions about the plans, Wikerus drew the nerve to speak, "Do you remember the blacksmith I brought to the flagship? Rikard… Rikard is his name. These are his plans, from his mind. He is not of our Order. He is from Meersburg, part of the small army sent by Count Konradin of Buchhorn."

The Grand Master's pride fell very little, and he puffed his chest further and said, "And you, my brother, had the wisdom to bring it to me. The Teutonic Order delivers these plans."

It was not until those words, "these plans", that Wikerus looked down to see Rikard's sketches. The picture was unlike anything he had seen or imagined to be possible. It had one ship disassembled and reassembled upon another, with scaffolding supported by three masts, which rose above the height of the tower. The entire creation was wrapped in animal hide to repel attacks from the tower guards. It was, as von Salza declared it, brilliant. Rikard had done what was sarcastically demanded of him. He engineered a new kind of warfare, one never dreamed of anywhere or anytime in military history.

The priests and friars were set immediately to making copies of the plans. The copies were given to all who would take a part in the construction of this new floating siege tower. There were many hands at work — hands that had long been idle and were starving for employment. The floating tower was finished in three weeks.

On 17 August, Rikard's design was in full physical splendor. Many in the camp doubted its ability to float and sail, yet it did, with a full complement of knights aboard. Wikerus and Rikard were not among them. It had become clear that Wikerus' sword, though proficient enough, was not the primary tool of his contribution to the campaign. And Rikard, well, let me just say that his callused hands more often gripped a pencil than a forging hammer, after the physical manifestation of his brilliant imagination successfully set sail.

The tower guards clearly saw them coming and were as astounded as they were terrified by the massive brainchild of Wikerus' friend, for the tower was entirely abandoned when the crusaders arrived. Not a single arrow flew in their direction. The guards retreated into the city walls. The tower was taken without another drop of blood spilled in its attack or defense. The crusaders dropped the chain that blocked entrance to the harbor, and Christian ships poured in.

Possession of the tower and harbor meant that the crusaders could choke off all supplies to Damietta. Its inhabitants were, for the moment, secure behind the substantial city walls, but they were trapped. The gates of the city were surrounded by crusader camps. Nobody could escape and nobody could enter.

Rikard had ended the fruitless attacks on the tower and saved the lives of countless knights. Now, new councils needed to convene, and new decisions needed to be made. The leaders drew together again. This time, Wikerus did not have to demand the presence of Rikard and Andreas. They were invited and given prominent seats at the table. But the table had a new head, one that would test the moral patience and obedience of this story's hero and his righteous friends.

In the days after the tower was taken, the Ayyubid Sultan, al-Adil, died. His son and military commander, al-Kamil, took his place as Sultan. Nobody knew quite what this meant, what sort of Sultan al-Kamil would be, or where his leadership would take the crusade. In response, the Pope dispatched Pelagius of Albano to take full command. Honorius did not want the crusade in the hands of local European nobles, and he did not fully trust the Grand Masters of his own military orders. Orders came from Rome that nothing is to be done until Pelagius arrived. In early September, he did, and sat at the head of the council, dressed in the latest and richest Italian fashions.

Francis of Assisi was there, and after leading the council in prayer, he was the first to speak, "Thank the Lord for our bloodless victory over the harbor tower. Now the city of Damietta may be taken without warfare. We must begin negotiations immediately."

"Negotiations over what?" Pelagius asked with a pompous tone of thinly veiled distain.

Francis answered, "The terms of the city's surrender. We hold the harbor. We decide what enters Damietta and what does not. They will accept whatever terms we offer. Life for the common people of Damietta need not be disrupted."

Pelagius grunted but said nothing. Hermann von Salza asked for clarification before Pelagius could voice his disapproval.

"The point of taking Damietta," Andreas jumped in, "is to protect our backs on the road to Cairo, to prevent enemy reinforcements behind us and to provide for our reinforcements and supplies. That is already accomplished. The families of Damietta need not suffer. Their homes and streets do not need to be a battlefield of this war."

Pelagius clapped his hands several times to draw the undivided attention of all in the tent, loudly, repetitively, and unnecessarily, then spoke directly to Andreas, "You know nothing of which you speak. If we are to take the Holy Land, we need to take Egypt. It must be entirely ours, entirely Christian, not Muslim land under Christian control, but Christian land comprehensively. If we are going to take Egypt, we must start here. The city will be ours, entirely clear of Egyptians. It will be a Christian city, full of Christian knights and merchants and their Christian families."

Wikerus asked hesitantly, "And if they will not leave their homes?"

Francis added, "Even if they choose to leave, where would they go? If it is our intention to hold all of Egypt, to which town do we send them that we will not later clear out as we will do with Damietta?"

With a slight, lopped-sided grin, Pelagius answered, "We send them nowhere, but back to their false god."

Wikerus stood and shouted, "No!"

Frances, who sat beside him, rose to his feet and pushed Wikerus down with a hand on his shoulder.

Hermann von Salza spoke up, "You will be hard-pressed to find a single knight willing to enter the city and slaughter the women and children, or for that matter, the innocent men."

"I would not put such guilt onto their blades," Pelagius responded, "I will bear that guilt. We will hold as we are…, starve the city to death. There is no reason to swing a sword inside the walls of Damietta, not while we hold this advantage."

Wikerus began to cough and gag, trying to hold his sickness in. Pelagius spoke eloquently about the blood spilled in the previous crusades, about the Pope's intentions to end the conflicts once and for all with a full and irreversible victory. He begged his fellows, in a much softer tone, to consider the future lives that would *not* be lost by following generations, following campaigns and counter-campaigns. This did nothing to convince Wikerus and his friends of the righteousness of starving Damietta to death. But the Grand Masters, those great men who weigh little over the lives of their knights, felt the power of the argument. They stood by Pelagius, as did all others in attendance. Only Wikerus, Francis, Rikard, and Andreas dissented.

The decision was final and had enough support to see it through. It would not have mattered either way. Pelagius had full command of the crusade. Wikerus continued to argue, but his words grew increasingly emotional as he realized the futility of dissention. He would have had a better chance of breaking down the walls of Damietta by throwing grapes at it, than of altering the will of the council. He cried all the way back to his tent. Although it was early in the evening, he went directly to bed. Had he known what sort of dream awaited him, he would have done all in his power to remain awake. The dream went as follows.

Wikerus walked alone down the woods and paths that surround his home. He was seeking Alawich, the brother of his rustic rescuer. At first, he walked leisurely. His desire to find the old man was not desperate. But as the trees grew thicker and the path narrower, panic set over him and he quickened his pace. Finally, the woods opened to a field, a familiar farm, filled with familiar faces.

He was on his father's field, and there, first among the workers, was his dear Alawich. His delight was short-lived. It dissolved entirely when he noticed their condition. They were emaciated, starving to death. Their cheeks were sunken in, their hair thinned, and their clothing barely holding to their slight, boney figures. They froze their labors simultaneously and looked to Wikerus — no words, no expressions, just motionless stares.

Alawich lifted one hand to Wikerus. As he did, the bones of his arm, from finger to shoulder, scraped together, sending to Wikerus' horrified ears, the most wretchedly painful, grinding, screeching sound. In a desperate desire to stop the pain and the sound, Wikerus ran to him. But he was encumbered, weighed down by a large sack strapped around his shoulder. He did not need to investigate. He knew what was in the sack. It was filled with fresh bread, and the aroma it put forth was delectable.

Wikerus ran to within arm's reach of Alawich. He reached into the sack and pulled out a fist-sized roll. He placed it in Alawich's still outreached hand. But the moment he released it to the old man's control, it was no longer a roll of bread, but a rock. Alawich dropped it and reached again for Wikerus, with the same painfully grinding sound. Wikerus pulled another roll from the sack, inspected it, sniffed it, squeezed it, verified that it was indeed bread, and placed it in Alawich's hand. But again, Alawich held only a rock.

Wikerus pulled a third roll. This time he bit of it. It was soft and delicious, and still bore an oven's warmth. Rather than handing it to Alawich, he held it toward the old man's withered lips. Alawich turned away.

"Eat it!" Wikerus demanded.

Alawich would not turn his face toward him. Wikerus looked around to the others. They had surrounded him, each of them facing their bodies toward him but turning their heads away. Wikerus threw the roll in his hand, with his one bite taken from it, to a woman in the crowd of farmers. In mid-air, it turned to stone and struck the woman in the head, gashing her scalp open and knocking her to the ground.

The other farmers turned on the woman and began eating her. Horrified, Wikerus screamed at them to stop, to come to him and eat his bread. He pulled roll after roll from his sack and threw it into the huddled mass of starving farmers. Roll after roll turned to stone in mid-air, each striking a farmer. In a mindless panic, Wikerus continued to throw the bread until his sack was empty. Once all motion had come to a dead silence, he realized that he had stoned them all to death.

Wikerus wanted to die. He wanted to be one of them — a poor, obscure farmer, dead on his father's field. He piled the bodies atop each other and crawled among them, burying himself beneath them.

He awoke from his dream in early morning, in his crusader tent, outside the walls of Damietta. He rose and stepped from the tent, looking at the city walls. In a vivid flashback from his dream, he heard the grinding, screeching sound of emaciated bones upon each other, followed by the wretched sound of the farmers devouring the woman. He forced all air from his body in a single, silent, but violent sob, then he lost consciousness and fell to his side. He napped outside of his tent, waking every few minutes to look at the city walls and imagine what nightmarish horrors await the families of Damietta.

Andreas and Rikard had similar dreams. They did not need to speak of them. With a single glance into each other's eyes, they bonded in mortification. In the following weeks, Wikerus broke regularly from his ranks, as his position as an adviser allowed, and joined his Meersburg friends for meals hardly touched and wine that grew sour without wetting their troubled lips.

CHAPTER 16
To the Brink and Back

THE NEXT SEVERAL MONTHS OF WIKERUS' LIFE were his most wretched to that point — a fitting rehearsal, I suppose, for the tribulations that give substance to the rest of this book. Poor Wikerus. The starvation of Damietta was sinful. It was ungodly and wholly unchristian. That is how he saw it, and he had no choice but to be party to it.

Al-Kamil held a camp near the riverbank, on the opposite side of the city from the crusader camp. There were skirmishes along the city walls. Swords swung. Blood was drawn. Enemy corpses were carried away on enemy horses, and crusaders were shipped back to their families to be buried on their ancestral estates. But such action was scarce and short-lived. Wikerus and his fellow knights spent most of their days encamped. The idle hours were not experienced identically by all. While most were bored or impatient with the conditions of encampment, for Wikerus, the hours were long, lonely, and painfully contemplative.

Each night, he took a mental tally of the miseries he knew were being suffered behind the city walls, miseries he failed to prevent, miseries that bore the mark of the Cross, the same Cross that was embroidered upon his chest. After the first week of the siege, he began flogging himself. It was his only way of surviving the guilt. Damietta was not a Pit of Starvation out of which the inhabitants would be pulled to live a transcended life. It was a graveyard for the still-living. They would die there, and Wikerus prayed that they would maintain their humanity and not turn to chaos and cannibalism.

Each morning, he awoke from the same dream. Each night, he delivered himself forty lashes upon his bare back. It did not take long for his friends and commanders to notice his bloody clothes. To occupy him from self-harm, they sent him to the front of each battle on the outskirts of the city. This did not have its desired effect. He and a small band of five fellow knights charged a pocket of about twenty-five Ayyubid foot soldiers. The seasoned war horses of the Teutonic Order rode straight through the poorly armored enemy. In the first pass, Wikerus slashed the life from three of them. The few that remained charged the mounted knights. Wikerus dismounted his horse and defended his comrades on foot.

Only six of the Ayyubid soldiers survived the initial charge of the mounted knights. Wikerus marched at them all while his brothers trotted to encircle them. In the throes of battle, he resorted to his training. His sword flew accurately and quickly. The potential recognized in him by his father and early tutors was realized outside of the walls of Damietta. The others watched as Wikerus dispatched the six. They cheered him, and when he mounted his horse without a drop of his own blood staining his white tunic, they applauded him and congratulated him. He did not appear at all like a triumphant hero. He did not feel like one. Wikerus had to kill with his own sword, and he was not prepared for the spiritual conflict. The immorality of human destruction by human hands confounded him.

These were not some imagined, theoretical enemies, going hungry behind tall and thick walls. These were faces, mere inches from his own. These were eyes that lost the sparkle of life at the end of his Teutonic sword, lips that gasped for their last breath as Wikerus withdrew his weapon from them. The sounds, the smells, the sights, and the sensations that traveled through his sword to his hand, and from his hand to his heart, wreaked cruel havoc on his morality. The wretchedness of his thoughts and dreams for having played a part in the starvation of the inhabitants of Damietta could not compare to what raged in him for having slaughtered men with his own hand.

He did not sleep a single minute of the night. His heart and his mind, in their dire attempt to reconcile what they were with what they did, battled each other day and night in violent internal debate. It drove poor Wikerus mad. Every few days, as the dust in his head began to settle, he was sent into battle again, with each kill compounding the conflict within him. He responded in the only way that could keep him in one piece. He became angry, and with the rallying cries of his comrades guiding the way, he shifted that anger toward his opponents on the battlefield.

Although he maintained his nightly vigil for the people of Damietta, it became hollow. His routine of nightly flogging turned habitual, performed without the intense emotions that initiated the practice. He sang the songs of his order, strapped himself into his crusader's armor, and rode at his enemies in a habitual recitation of the previous battle. He went into battle angry, and he took it out on his enemies, only to torture himself later for the lives he had to take.

On the battlefield, every lesson and every instinct came together when he drew his sword. Plus, a secret ingredient stirred inside of him — inherited blood that neither of his parents knew about. He would not discover its secret for a few more years, when it turned his life upside down. But the sands surrounding Damietta, in late 1218 and early 1219, is where the skills that were dormant in his blood bubbled to the surface. Wikerus fought like ten knights. His body moved as quickly as his sword. The soldiers of the Sultanate were fatally wounded before they gained any sensual perception of him. Rumors quickly spread throughout the Ayyubid ranks that the Teutonic Knights were invincible, that they conjured abilities through unnatural means, and that the first among them was, as they called him, "The Tanhuter".

As the weeks went on, Wikerus' spirit was more securely shackled to its new identity. During the day, he caught the occasional hour of sleep. But in the quiet hours of the night, when his consciousness lost its firm grip on his thoughts, those deepest parts of him roamed tentatively through his head, and the battles inside of him raged on. Some nights he wept in despair. Some nights he seethed with fury. He spent little time in between, and nobody who was not there to witness the changes in him would have recognized him as someone they once knew — not Father Stefan or Count Konradin, not his brothers, his sister, or his father, and certainly not his good mother.

Wikerus was heading in a dangerous direction, in serious peril of losing himself entirely. He continued to flog himself each night, but he no longer felt the pain and he no longer did it for same reasons. What initially kept his sensations fresh and compassionate, only further numbed him. Before he knew it, he did not care for the merchants and their families starving inside the blockaded walls of Damietta. He no longer cared for the fathers, husbands, and sons he slaughtered by the dozens with his own sword.

In the rare moments when he spoke, his words were violent, his tone abusive, and his demeanor was as hateful as any of the uncouth commoners that were recruited into his Order. And he only worsened with each encounter. After several weeks of fighting, he rose in the morning with the single ambition of killing. He flung blood from his sword as if it was filthy and disgusted him, not as if it was sacred. The change in him was bold enough for all to see. But few commented on it. Wikerus was the most efficient killer in the entire crusade. His tally was uncountable, and with each kill, he lost more of himself.

Andreas and Rikard noticed. Of course they did. How could they not. It was as plain to them as the sun that rose in the east. But they dared not interfere. His anger made him ferocious. He did not have that look of transcendence in his eyes that he had so admired in Andreas and Rikard. In fact, the flame in his eyes was unlike that of any camped outside of Damietta. Wikerus was brutal and inhuman, but he returned to the camp alive after each battle. He was the only knight fighting in every skirmish, and his friends waited daily for word of his death.

"God, just let him live," they prayed, "His spirit is not irretrievable. When this is over, he can be returned. He can be redeemed. But let him live."

He had become a bloodier version of Meinrad, the cocky young initiate that Father Stefan ran from Mainau Island, equally heartless and ten times as vicious. That same wrinkled old sage, Wikerus' oldest and dearest friend, was exactly what he needed to expel the "Meinrad" within him. Andreas sent for him with a brother's concern and with vivid descriptions of his friend's transformation.

In February of 1219, Father Stefan arrived at the Teutonic section of the crusader camp. The Sultan had lost enough men from the constant crusader attacks and he abandoned his position on the riverbank. Small bands of Ayyubid soldiers, with loose leadership, remained in defense of Damietta. Father Stefan found Wikerus on the morning before an offensive. They were to attack and wipe out the remaining soldiers, clearing the perimeter of the city of all enemies. And they counted on Wikerus' sword to lead the slaughter.

Father Stefan saw Wikerus strapping his armor in place, with a fury in his eyes that brought chills to the stoic old priest. Oh he had seen passion in Wikerus' eyes before, but a bright passion, a pious and righteous passion, nothing at all resembling what shot from beneath his lowered eyebrows that morning. Stefan's influence was put to the test. He requested that the deadliest sword in the crusade be left out of the offensive — left in his hands, to counsel, to nurture, and to retrieve from its place of darkness the bright soul that had once served so many, so well.

Wikerus looked directly at Father Stefan, but showed no signs of recognition. He simply continued to secure and prepare his accoutrements of war. The old priest began unstrapping the knight's armor. Wikerus grabbed him defensively by the wrist, squeezing and wrenching the old man, as if he held the arm of an enemy. But Stefan did not flinch. He simply plastered his signature scowl into Wikerus' eyes. The look struck the knight deeply, jarring free those tender memories that had been imprisoned under the hardening shell of hatred and violence.

The soft boyish voice that had not broken air in weeks fought its way through the gruff, knightly tones of a warrior, cracking his voice as he simply said, "Father?"

"Yes, my brother. I am here with you, and we will spend this day together."

The slight softening of Wikerus face regained its harshness as he responded as if shouting at a stranger, "No! The sand is dry and thirsty, and I will wet it."

Father Stefan grabbed Wikerus by the shoulder plates of his armor and shook him. Their eyes locked firmly together, and Stefan's seemed to swirl like a whirlpool in a raging storm, a storm under his control.

He shook Wikerus, held him still, then shook him again before saying, "No, brother, you are staying with me today."

"I am a knight at war!"

"You are a monk!" Stefan shouted, "a man of God, a disciple of the Gospels, and my brother of the cloth."

Stefan released his grip on Wikerus' shoulders and continued calmly, "Look around you. This camp..., this entire coast is filled to its limits with *knights*, all trained with the sword and lance. Yes, you are a knight..., one of thousands. Yet your place in this is entirely unique. What you alone bring has less to do with that blade at your side and more to do with the Cross on your chest and shoulder."

Wikerus' warrior's scowl returned and Stefan slapped it with the will of a disciplining parent and the force of a fellow warrior, speaking to the startled face at the end of his hand, "You are here for the True Cross. Have you forgotten that? What are a few bands of disorganized enemy soldiers beside the Blood of our Lord? How dare you jeopardize your destiny. Yes, you are a knight. Kill when you must kill, and only when you must. Keep your mind and your heart on your destiny and keep your actions focused clearly on that end."

Father Stefan continued to speak, but Wikerus heard little more than muted echoes. He had fallen into a deep trance of thought. Stefan's words had reached deeply inside of him, grabbed those truths that were richly and purely Wikerus, and shook and yanked them from their crusty cage. Wikerus' eyes, turned entirely inward, and watched this action within himself. He encouraged his true self to fight itself free, then slapped at its hand and demanded obedience.

Stefan continued to talk. His voice landed softly on Wikerus' skull, like a gentle rain on a high roof. It was enough to soothe his harsher nature. With a powerful narcotic effect, the priest's voice lulled the violent knight inside of him to sleep, and the holy monk rose to prominence over Wikerus' consciousness. He remembered the young recruit with idealistic dreams of righteousness in battle.

162

Stefan's voice rose to clarity, as if a door between them had been opened. Wikerus lifted his head and looked at Stefan with an expression of gratitude and awe. Stefan continued to speak, unaware of the transformation, until they locked eyes, and the churning ocean of brilliant blueish green that was so endearingly familiar to the old priest revealed itself, washing over Stefan and bathing him in a warmly welcomed greeting.

Wikerus' face lifted and shone for a few seconds, then grew dark and mournful as his actions over the previous weeks slammed in conflict with his reawakened sensibilities. The wrenching squeeze on his spirits clutched more ferociously as his thoughts turned to the city of Damietta and the people who had not entered his thoughts in weeks. How much worse was there condition since last he thought of them?

His knees buckled. He dropped to the floor, pointed in the direction of the city, and whimpered, "The children. The mothers and fathers."

Father Stefan lifted him to his feet and helped him into a nearby tent, where he took the anguished knight's confession. He cleansed Wikerus of his confessed sins, giving only one penance — to keep foremost on his mind his true purpose in the Holy Land. They prayed together for every soul caught in the conflict, Christian and Muslim, child and adult, knight and merchant. But inwardly, one prayer to God billowed most profusely from Stefan's heart. It was a prayer of thanksgiving. He knew how near Wikerus had come to losing himself irretrievably. He thanked Christ for maintaining his anchor to the young man until an old friend could take ahold and bind him to himself. Stefan found Andreas' tent and described with relief to both him and Rikard how Wikerus' true self immerged from the darkness. Stefan thanked Andreas for saving Wikerus from Satan's grip with his timely appeal for help. It was no exaggeration. Andreas saved Wikerus, and not for the last time.

CHAPTER 17
The Rancid Stench of Remorse

THE OFFENSIVE WAS SUCCESSFUL. The Teutonic, Templar, and Hospitaller Knights rode together. A massive wave of horses swept the perimeter of Damietta, eliminating the ragtag bands of enemy soldiers, without the loss of a single Christian knight. The towers and walls of the city were still. Not a single arrow flew toward the massacre. It was clear that al-Kamil had given up on Damietta, and Damietta had given up on itself.

Within a few days, Cardinal Pelagius, the Pope's emissary, received an offer from al-Kamil. The crusade appeared to be over. It was a generous peace offering, little less than an absolute surrender. Al-Kamil offered Jerusalem and all of the surrounding lands, with the exception of three Muslim fortresses. He promised thirty years of peace, guaranteeing no attempts to retake the Holy City in that time. In exchange, the crusaders were to return Damietta and leave Egypt.

The offer so favored the Pope's ambitions that few imagined it would be rejected. The point of taking Egypt was to keep Jerusalem secure once it was captured. The treaty secured Jerusalem for almost a third of a century. It did not seem that any reasons remained to fight in Egypt. The war-weary Duke Ludwig of Bavaria rejoiced at the news, as did Hermann von Salza and his Teutonic Order. But Pelagius was not satisfied, and he convinced the Grand

Masters of the other two Holy Orders to press al-Kamil for more.

Whether the first deal offered by al-Kamil was accepted, most believed that the fighting was over. Many leaders of the crusade, including Leopold of Austria, took their armies and returned home. The crusading forces weakened, but so did the Ayyubid Sultanate. Word reached al-Kamil that a Kurdish plot against him had come silently close to taking his life. He abandoned all fortresses and encampments between Damietta and Cairo. This development swelled Pelagius' ambitions. He refused the offer and ordered the crusaders to take all of the land abandoned by a-Kamil.

Templars and Hospitallers walked into the abandoned fortresses, as if by invitation. Al-Kamil held up in Cairo, which put Pelagius' eyes on that grand prize. Despite the crusader momentum, Cairo was a daunting prospect, which if obtainable, would come at the cost of thousands of crusader lives.

Al-Kamil sent another offer, this time including the three fortresses around Jerusalem that were denied in the first offer. That was enough for the Templars and Hospitallers, who only refused the first offer because Jerusalem would be difficult to defend without the fortresses. But Pelagius still refused. He wanted all of Egypt.

Wikerus and his Teutonic brothers were left out of the advancements toward Cairo. Pelagius knew where von Salza stood and was in no mood to be contradicted. But there would be no hope of taking Cairo without his knights, so Pelagius invited him to consult with the other leaders. This time, it took place in one of the abandoned fortresses on the way to Cairo. Pelagius chose it intentionally, so that his argument would ride the waves of their momentum. Of course, Wikerus was brought along. Francis came, and with Father Stefan.

Cardinal Pelagius argued, "The Ayyubid is on its heels. Cairo will fall to us."

Francis contended, "We already have all that was designed by the Fourth Lateran Council. Jerusalem is ours in peace for thirty years, as are all fortresses around the Holy City."

"But," Pelagius belted, "if we take Cairo and all of Egypt, Jerusalem will be ours for a hundred years."

Peire de Montagut, Grand Master of the Templars, being satisfied with the second offer, spoke, "In thirty years of peace, with possession of the surrounding fortresses, surely we can secure Jerusalem for a hundred years without throwing the bodies of my knights at the walls of Cairo."

Montagut's point was sound, and all but Pelagius agreed. Dozens of opinions flew forward in support of Montagut. The muscle of the crusade was for peace and Pelagius stood alone. But none of that mattered. In designing the leadership of the crusade, Pope Innocent III took all power from the secular leaders; and the orders of warrior monks, ordained by the Pope, were under the Papal authority.

Pelagius silenced the room and reminded all of the hierarchy of the crusade. It was Innocent's war, and Honorius' after Innocent's death. Pelagius was the Pope's emissary. He spoke with Papal authority. Ultimately, despite all the noble and powerful influences in the room, the decision was his alone.

"For God's sake, Your Grace," von Salza spoke up, "let us retreat to Damietta and wait for Duke Ludwig of Bavaria and the Imperial Forces."

Montagut continued as if of the same voice, "We have lost whole armies and their numbers must be replenished if we are to press toward Cairo."

The Grand Master of the Knights Hospitaller, Guérin de Montaigu, untied them all, saying, "The Holy Orders speak with one voice on this matter. Let us overwhelm Cairo with Ludwig and the German forces."

It was a compromise that Pelagius struggled to refuse. He agreed, for the time being, to regather outside of Damietta, with the fortresses in between remaining manned by the Templars.

Francis and Stefan tried to argue that the Sultan's offer should be accepted and the siege on Damietta should end immediately. Their words may as well have been directed to the rats, for all of the influence they carried.

Wikerus spoke, and for some reason, the entire room silenced and listened, "May we at least bring food into Damietta. If the city still lives, we hold a more powerful bargain against it."

Of course, Wikerus cared little for bargains and leverage. It was the people of Damietta he cared for.

Pelagius answered in terms and tone not to be refuted. He insisted that such a move would show weakness that would be exploited by the enemy, that the more desperate the conditions in Damietta were, the more powerful their position, and that all such points were ultimately moot, because no deal for Damietta would ever be accepted. They would keep Damietta and march on to Cairo as soon as Ludwig arrived with the knights of the Holy Roman Empire.

They did as Montagut prescribed. They returned to the camps around Damietta, leaving garrisons of Templars in the abandoned fortresses. They awaited Ludwig, who delayed as long as he could, hoping al-Kamil would present an offer that would be accepted, and he could return to his hidden Bavarian estate with his wife and son.

No more offers came, and the crusaders sat idly. Summer passed and Autumn came. Finally, on 4

November 1219, Andreas, with his band of Buchhorn knights, camped outside of a section of Damietta's wall, noticed that the nearest tower was unmanned. He mounted his horse and rode the perimeter of the city. It was as he expected. All twenty-eight towers and every inch of the wall was abandoned. The people of Damietta had given up, or had all died. The siege was over and the city could be entered without conflict.

The crusaders marched into Damietta without drawing their swords, led by the Teutonic Knights. Nothing in the darkest portions of their imaginations could have prepared them for what awaited them. In the months preceding, Wikerus tried to imagine the worst, but even his imagination could not dive to such depths.

They were not one full step within the walls when they were hit in the face by the wafting stench of decay. The smell of death was pungent, penetrating, and utterly sickening. Over 800,000 had called Damietta their home. But there was no sign of life as the crusaders trotted down the primary thoroughfare.

The mystery of the missing inhabitants was pondered by many, for Wikerus heard a lone voice behind him say through a nauseated cough, "Where are they? They must be somewhere."

Hermann von Salza answered, "They are in their homes. There was nothing left for them in the streets. They died in their beds."

Hermann was right. This came as a relief to Wikerus. There was no indication of chaos or cannibalism, no sign of rioting or break-ins, nothing to paint in his mind the dreaded images he feared the most — the loss of the people's humanity. But hell waited around the corners. The side streets, back alleys, and the homes themselves told a grizzly tale of a dying city.

The people of Damietta had too much dignity to die on the main streets, where they would be easily seen. The alleys were filled with bodies, half eaten by starving pets and vermin. The pristine exteriors of the homes told a lovely lie. The crusaders spread throughout the city, while the stench watered their eyes and closed their throats. Wikerus entered a house with a few of his Teutonic brothers. A dead mother held a dead child. There was no way to tell which died first. As Wikerus considered it, each possibility brought a different sort of anguish.

There were no other bodies in the house, only the mother and child, and nothing seemed broken or out of place. The bodies were intact and uncut. Yet blood was smeared on the walls and floor. Beside the couch where the bodies rested withered and sunken, were three musical instruments, two stringed and one flute. These were not polished decorations. They were well-used. Their wear spoke of joyful times, of dancing children and walls that were gleeful to echo back the celebratory melodies. The instruments created such blissful imagery in Wikerus' head, which contrasted wretchedly with the sights and smells around them. In his mind, he wept. But his chest was so constricted by sorrow and stench that the cries remained inside of him. His eyes had to do all the crying, which they did in abundance. His neck was thoroughly drenched by the time he took his eyes from the instruments.

Not all the homes were like the first. Some showed signs of violence. Things were smashed and bodies were not only emaciated, but also lacerated and bruised. The shops in the main market were empty. The finest fabrics, gilded trinkets, and wares from far and wide sat unwanted, unhoarded, and completely useless.

Wikerus continued searching the market, not having the stomach to enter another home. From an alley behind him, he heard laughter. The sound was so strangely unbefitting the atmosphere around him. He followed the laughter down the alley to its owner. A strange man, withered and parched, huddled over a pile of rich fabrics. He laughed with what little air he could force from his weakened body. It was a bizarrely devious sounding cackle, one that did little to betray the emotions behind it.

Wikerus stood directly against the man. In a high-pitched, crackly, prickly, abrasive voice, the man began shouting sentences in his native language. They blended in and out of the laughter and sounded like he was barking commands. Wikerus startled and took a quick step backward. The man squeezed his arms more tightly around the mound of rich fabrics.

Wikerus took another step back and assured the man, "I am not going to take your—"

At his new distance he realized that the mound of fabric was in fact a slightly greying, middle-aged woman dressed in her finest. The man barked another command, then his laughter transitioned to clear and pitiful cries, as he squeezed the woman more tightly and spoke something that sounded rather apologetic to her.

Wikerus stepped forward, knelt down, and lifted the veil that covered the woman's head. She was dead and appeared to have been for many days. Wikerus' pity swelled well beyond his terror. He stroked the man's hand, then grabbed it and ran it along the woman's hip. With great difficulty, the man turned his head to Wikerus. Wikerus lifted the dead woman's hand, removed the ring that his mother had sent to him on Mainau Island, placed the ring on the woman's shriveled finger, and set her hand back in the hand of the man.

The man ran his thumb over the ring and seemed to smile. Wikerus pulled some dried berries from a pouch at his side and tried to hand them to the man, who looked at Wikerus' hand then turned his attention entirely to the woman, without a gesture toward the food. He clearly had no desire to survive. But in the few moments when he looked into Wikerus' eyes, our dear hero saw no hate — tremendous sorrow, great loss, but no hate. The man's love of the woman, the lack of vengeful hatred in his eyes, and his warm reception of the ring were all beautiful to Wikerus. It was a stinging and sorrowful beauty, one that cannot be beheld for long. But it was a moment that remained with him for the rest of his life.

The crusaders had a job to clear the city, to remove the bodies, gather the survivors, and outfit Damietta for their own purposes. But Wikerus was not the only one hesitant to do so. Every alteration seemed wrong. They had stepped into the lives of these once happy people. Disturbing their belongings and gathering their dead grated against their sensibilities. Nevertheless, they did what had to be done.

Of the 800,000 inhabitants of Damietta, little more than 3,000 survived the siege. Those were gathered and fed. Some ate and recovered. Some ate and died. Many refused to eat or drink, too mournful for the loved ones they watched starve to death. Of the 3,000 they found alive, perhaps half saw the end of the crusade.

One of the primary strategies in taking and keeping Damietta was to make of it a war hospital, to tend to wounded knights as the campaign for Cairo, and Jerusalem beyond, raged on. Damietta *had* an impressive medical center, and few alterations needed to be made. About three weeks after they entered the city, when the city was clean and the hospital complete, Wikerus assumed its first patients would be the recovering survivors of Damietta. But that was not the plan. Pelagius demanded that the survivors be sent upriver alone, to be found and rescued, if they were so lucky, by their own people.

The demand received little resistance from the Holy Orders, until Wikerus stood tall among them and shouted the slogan of his Order, "Helfen - Wehren – Heilen" (Help – Defend – Heal).

Instinctively and without thought, the Teutonic brothers around him repeated the slogan. Then heads began to turn toward each other as the profound application of the sacred slogan became clear.

"That's right," Wikerus shouted, "let us not forget who we are… *The Order of Brothers of the German House of Saint Mary in Jerusalem.* We are healers first and foremost, monks of Christ. Did Christ not die for the weak and ungodly, or did he die only for his seventy-two disciples?"

He ran to the nearest steps, leading to the entrance of a large building. He climbed the steps and turned to face a growing crowd of knights, from different orders and different armies. They were drawn to him, and only the quietest murmurs floated between them.

Our righteous hero pointed to a band of Knights Hospitaller and asked, "Have you forgotten your Lord, or the foundations of your Order. And you," he pointed to some Templars, "remember your vows. Which is your more powerful weapon, the sword at your hip or the Crucifix in your heart?"

Wikerus went on for nearly half an hour in this manner, quoting scripture in ways that the most hardened warriors could not refute. Even Pelagius himself had no choice but to fill the hospital with the victims of the siege. Had he demanded otherwise, after the righteous rally of our good hero, he likely would have been run back to Rome.

Wikerus' words swelled the hearts of the crusaders into full and righteous zeal. They remembered their vows. They rekindled their faith. They were still knights, still warriors at war. But they were Christians first, and the Teutonic Knights, the Knights Templar, and the Knights Hospitaller were again what they swore to be before they wore the signature cloaks of their orders. They were monks, holy men in service to Christ and the Church. The sickly victims of the siege were tended to by Christian hands, caring hands that wished them well, and faces that smiled at them, sang for them, and gave to them of their finest stores of food and drink.

CHAPTER 18
Elusive Redemption

BY THE TIME THE CRUSADERS CELEBRATED CHRISTMAS 1219, Damietta was very much *their* city. If one could ignore the stylistic architecture, it would be easy to convince one's self that Damietta sat in the heart of Europe. Christian symbols hung on the walls while European conversations were held in European languages. The Holy Sacraments of the Church assumed their common schedules and formats, as clergy arrived from all over Europe to tend to the religious needs of the crusaders. The Christmas celebration was attended by priests and bishops. The mass was given by Cardinal Pelagius, and a message directly from the Pope was read aloud.

There were hymns in the mornings and concerts at night. Most adapted to this "Little Europe" they were to call home until orders to move out were given. Wikerus alone did not see a "Little Europe". He alone saw Damietta for what it was — an Egyptian city, where Egyptian families died in the arms of loved ones, while crusading armies surrounded the city, eating, laughing, and carrying on as the city starved to death.

Fortunately for Wikerus, his routine gave him little time for contemptable contemplation. He worked before the sun and well into the next day, sleeping only long enough for a few torturous dreams, before waking and working again. There was a seriousness to Wikerus that few others seemed to carry about them. Those ordered knights who worked the hospital were stripped daily of any jovial air by the sights and sounds of their patients. The survivors of the siege, those who recovered, came along nicely and affixed their affections to the knights who cared for them. Wikerus came to call many of them brothers and sisters. The work should have been satisfying, fulfilling his spirits in accordance with his morality. But he was haunted — not by his experiences in the city, but those from his time outside of the city, when he nearly lost himself to rage. His brand of sadness and guilt was uniquely his.

When the work on the city structures completed, the Teutonic Order and their fellow warrior orders found the leisure to resume their peacetime routines. Despite the morbid association with the progress around him, Wikerus found great relief in his return to a monastic life. The ways of the Military Orders took firm root in the revitalizing Damietta. The city halted for The Liturgy of the Hours. The Psalter and the Vespers Hymn echoed in exquisite chants off the city's walls and filled the crowded spaces between the buildings. The Orders lived in communes similar to what Wikerus experienced on Mainau Island.

A significant portion of the day was for solitary, sequestered prayer. For this, Wikerus went to Damietta's old mosque. It was a magnificent structure, a glorious testament to the Muslim devotion to God. The Christians outfitted it for their own services, with an altar and Crucifix behind. The remarkable feature of the old mosque was an anomaly like none Wikerus had ever experienced. It was an acoustic wonder. The center of the floor was marked with a crescent in mosaic marble, centered beneath the domed ceiling. If one stood on the crescent and spoke, his voice would reverberate with the richness and fullness of ten voices.

Wikerus was not the first crusader to discover the phenomenon. But he was the first to utilize it to the glory for which it was designed. During sequestered prayer, on an early Thursday evening in March 1220, he found his way to the mosaic crescent. He was not stopped by any force of that symbol. It was the Crucifix hanging on the wall beyond the altar that commanded him. As he approached it, he believed he saw the head of Christ turn to face him. He froze on the spot and dropped to his knees, precisely on the crescent.

Christ had something to say to him, and he begged the Lord for instruction, beginning, as he began every prayer, with a hymn of thanksgiving. On this occasion, he chose an ancient hymn, *Of the Father's Heart Begotten*.

He began singing low, almost beneath his breath, but as his devotion swelled, so did his voice. The genius design of the church's ceiling took Wikerus' angelic voice and exalted it. He sang.

Corde natus ex parentis
Ante mundi exordium
A et O cognominatus,
ipse fons et clausula
Omnium quæ sunt, fuerunt,
quæque post futura sunt.
Sæculorum sæculis.

(Of the Father's heart begotten,
Ere the world from chaos rose,
He is Alpha, from that Fountain
All that is and hath been flows;
He is Omega, of all things,
Yet to come the mystic Close,
Evermore and evermore.)

Seldom in the course of human affairs do a construct of man and a creation of God coordinate in such splendor. But when the Egyptian architecture of the old mosque worked with the throat and tongue of Wikerus, those lingering near the church thought that their crusade was being blessed by a host of angels. The sound that swelled and crested through the arched double doors and onto the main street of Damietta drew the attention of a gathering crowd of enamored listeners. They trickled into the church but dared not disturb the melodious prayers of the kneeling knight. They scooted silently along the walls until they stood heel to toe in a wall of flesh and armor at least ten men thick. Those who could not get in remained outside, where Wikerus' song was little less moving.

Tears flowed and Christian faith swelled inside of Christian hearts. They saw only half of what Wikerus saw. For them, it was a Christian experience. Continuing to sing, Wikerus took his eyes upward, not upward to God, and certainly not away from Christ. He looked at the engineering wonder above him, the Muslim wonder that took his Christian hymn and transcended it into something truly divine. This cooperation that he alone pondered pinched cruelly at his heart. God placed him there. Christ dropped him to his knees upon the crescent, and in a communion of cultures and faiths, divinity erupted in Damietta.

He could not deny it. The brilliant scientific wonder of the mosque was a result of Muslim devotion to God, and Wikerus imagined that the Muslim songs to God in that same mosque could not have been very unlike the devotional he sang. He wished he could have visited Damietta before the siege, and witnessed their celebrations in the mosque, their use of the genius acoustics. In that moment of clarity, he thought of the enemies he slaughtered outside of the city walls. He saw himself in them — devoted soldiers of God, fighting for their faith and in defense of their homes, separated from himself by the fact that they call God by a different name, and view the same God through different lenses. He imagined that they attended services in the same mosque, and perhaps even stood on the crescent where he knelt and sang their praise to God.

"Now they are dead," he thought to himself as his throat continued to sing, "Now their prayerful songs are silenced by my hand."

By the fourth verse of the hymn, many had joined the singing. Wikerus rose to his feet in mid-verse, weighed by guilt heavier in his heart than anything he had felt. Those in the church with him watched him rise and they stopped singing. The chanting silenced in a wave that washed from the mosaic crescent outward. Wikerus, with his head down and his knees bent awkwardly low, so his Teutonic cloak dragged on the floor behind him, moved in struggling steps toward the church entrance.

They made way for him, wanting to embrace him but not daring to disturb his trance-like saunter. He went to bed without passing a word to the crowd around him. The others, that besotted audience still packed in and around the mosque, wanted to carry on where Wikerus left off. But not one of them could bring himself to sing. The evening was Wikerus' to carry on or extinguish. He extinguished it and the city went to bed. Within half an hour of Wikerus' head hitting his bed, the city of Damietta was silent and thoughtful.

The next morning, when the knights gathered to give their weekly confessions, Wikerus' usual confessor was removed from his post. Wikerus entered the confessional and found his friend, Father Stefan.

"Forgive me Father, for I have sinned," Wikerus recited habitually.

Father Stefan interrupted the weekly routine, placing his hand on Wikerus' knee, saying, "You are haunted by something beyond your sinful thoughts from the past week. Something dark has rooted deeply into you. Speak to me, Brother."

Wikerus leaped at the opportunity to settle the tumult within him, "I have murdered," he blurted out.

"One of your patients?"

Wikerus shook his head.

"One of our brothers?"

Wikerus shook more wildly and impatiently.

"Whom then? Whom did you murder?"

"The men on the battlefields, outside of the city walls."

Stefan sighed deeply in relief. He patted Wikerus repeatedly on the knee and replied, "You have not murdered. You are a knight, a warrior. You killed in battle, *as did your enemies.*"

"What you say would be true, had I killed as a warrior monk should kill, with mercy and respect, with the love of Christ in my heart. But that is not who I was on the battlefield. I killed with ungodly fury, and try as I have, I do not remember the faces of the men I slaughtered. I *know* why my sword was forged. It was forged to end lives, but in the hand of a Christian knight, one who looks into the eyes of his enemies and prays for their souls. I did not fight for Christ. I fought for the satiation of my own fury. That is not what a *warrior monk* does in battle. That is what a murderer does. I have murdered... in numbers far more than I can recall."

Father Stefan wanted to contradict Wikerus' self-loathing portrayal of his battles outside the walls. But the truth was plainly and honestly argued by the lips of the guilty. Wikerus did *not* fight like a monk. He slaughtered

180

with hatred in his heart. He murdered. And his immortal soul was in great peril.

Father Stefan placed both hands, palms up, on Wikerus' knees, inviting a grasp. Wikerus responded and took Stefan's hands.

"Bow your head, my *Brother*," Stefan calmly commanded.

They bowed together and Stefan spoke barely above a whisper, "Through the Lord, there is mercy, and fulfillment of redemption."

Wikerus squeezed Stefan's hands more tightly and raised his shoulders to his ears. He paused his breath and waited for some sensation of forgiveness. It did not come, and his spirits dropped even further.

He lifted his tearful face to Stefan and spoke, "I feel no redemption. Am I lost to God?"

"Of course you are not, nor will you feel redemption while you are here. Did Andreas' hunger go away while he was still in the Meersburg pit? The pain you feel inside of you must continue to burn. It was placed there by God and it will guide you through this war and beyond. Without it, you *are* lost to God, to me and to yourself…, and to your destiny. Redemption will come to you, my dear friend. You will be pulled from your Pit of Starvation, but not until you are all but broken. Cling to your shame. Let it guide you. And in the last moment, look for God to lower his rope and extract you from your pit."

He let go of Wikerus' hands and took him by the cheeks, adding, "You will know bliss before you die, and your soul will be rested and grateful when you come face to face with the Lord."

With Stefan's hands still holding Wikerus' face, the two friends prayed together. Wikerus left the confessional with no less pain in his heart. But he did not cower under it, nor did he scorn it. He held it to the deepest parts of his inner self, and looked for it to guide his behavior. His passions swelled well beyond what it had been, fueled by that infernal speck of shame, smoldering in its own designated kiln, in the center of Wikerus' chest.

With his first step outside of the confessional, his eyes saw everything differently. The lesson of the mosque remained with him, still burning him from within. Each knight he beheld, each wall, each recovering Egyptian, each star in the sky added air to that kiln, like Rikard's giant bellows cramp, surging within him an ever increasing passion to be what he truly was — the son of Methildis, the friend of Alawich, a brother of Father Stefan, a warrior monk, a Helper - a Defender - a Healer, and a knight.

CHAPTER 19
Inside the Warrior's Heart

WORK WAS STRENUOUS AND CONSTANT during the first few months in Damietta. But once the work on the city was complete, and there were no battles to fight, no walls to repair, and no churches to build, tensions began to rise between the various factions occupying the city. Idleness and weak leadership united dangerously. The three Military Orders of the Church maintained their good humor. Tensions between the other knights were bound to arise. Many of these very warriors were entangled in domestic disputes before the Pope brokered peace so he could focus all of Europe on the crusade. They were antsy. They were bored. And their old rivalries reared their heads.

Little blood was shed, but fights were common and the unified spirit that was so masterfully mustered during the years since the Fourth Lateran Council, through all of the sermons and indulgences, was at risk of falling apart. It was heart-breaking to see the spaces of the Damietta hospital filled with injuries suffered by Christian knights at the hands of Christian knights. Thank God the vices of debauchery were not at their disposal, that fights and small brawls were all the sinfulness that excessive ennui could bait them with.

Father Stefan took weekly confessions. They were filled with repetitive episodes — "Father I have been vain",

"Father I have allowed my temper to navigate my actions", "Father I struck my Christian brother."

Stefan prayed for an active and common enemy, whether sword or sickness, to adhere their common ambitions and make use of the idle energy that threatened the crusade.

Relief came in the form of an Ayyubid attack on a Templar fortress in the town of Atlit, on the northern coast of Israel. Château Pèlerin, as it was called then, was built two years earlier. Sitting on the Mediterranean coast, it could be easily supplied by sea. It was built to hold 4,000 knights. Its strategic proximity to Jerusalem worried al-Kamil, who knew he would be facing a mixed Crusader army coming south from Damietta. He did not want to allow such a large Templar force in Atlit.

When news of the attack reached Damietta, the Templars immediately dispatched a response. This was a Templar fortress and a Templar problem. They sailed from Damietta alone. There was such valor in their rallying call to support their brothers in Atlit, that they inspired every sword in Damietta. When the Templar Knights sailed from Damietta, every Christian in the city, knight, soldier, and servant, wore a small red cross on his shoulder in honor of the brave Templars.

Pelagius was impatient to take all of Egypt by force. He had no choice but to wait. The Templars were gone and the assault on Cairo could not proceed without them. The rest of the knights in Damietta dug in and waited, hoping either for a quick return of the Templars, or for the long-promised forces of Emperor Friedrich. The Imperial Knights were of notorious skill, and Friedrich had promised a sizable force, under the command of Duke Ludwig of Bavaria.

That is how the rest of 1220 went in Damietta. Nightly vigils were held for the Templars engaged at Atlit, and morning talk was of the Imperial Knights expected at the docks each day. But the Templars did not return. The Imperial forces under Ludwig did not dock, and secular armies were departing for home by the week.

Wikerus spectated the ebb and flow of morality and unity from a lofty perch, well above the petty disputes that erupted and dissolved around him. As a Teutonic Knight, he was uninvolved in the secular discord of local feuds. And despite the fact that the Holy Orders cloistered themselves to their own sections within the city, Wikerus managed to use his unique position as a leader in the crusade to move about the city like the Grand Masters, or like the kings, dukes, and counts who commanded their own armies. He shared three or four meals a week with Andreas and Rikard. He ended every meal, every conversation, and every encounter with a prayer for their Templar brothers. As he moved his way through Damietta, as few but he could, he reminded all he encountered of their shared interests.

Pelagius' impatience did not suffer past the spring of 1221. Although the Templars left a force in the recaptured Château Pèlerin, they returned a few dozen of their best knights. This coincided within days of Ludwig landing at the docks of Damietta with more than three hundred Imperial Knights. It was far short of the number promised by Emperor Friedrich, but as Ludwig explained, Friedrich's rise to the throne was tumultuous, and maintaining it promised to be no easier. Pope Innocent had guaranteed the protection of the Church to anyone who sent an army to the crusade. Honorius was less reliable on that front. So Friedrich kept most of his army in Germany.

Pelagius did not have the numbers he had when they entered Damietta. But the swords they had were in more capable hands. The Imperial Knights were worth ten of those regional knights who had abandoned the campaign and returned to their homes. It was enough for Pelagius' ambitions to push them forward. Before he did, he received another offer of peace from al-Kamil, offering the True Cross to Pelagius himself. Again the offer was rejected, and the crusader forces left the walls of Damietta and gathered to the south of the city, led by Pelagius, who was so greedy for a total victory that he would have sacrificed every knight in his army to achieve it. Ludwig relayed his orders from Emperor Friedrich, which was to make no advance until the Emperor himself arrived. Pelagius would not wait. Friedrich would command too much authority. His very presence in the crusade would weaken Pelagius' position. The Pope's man had to act quickly.

On the evening before they marched, Wikerus visited Father Stefan. He was frustrated by Pelagius' refusal of the peace offerings, particularly with regard to the True Cross. But Stefan reminded him of the strong sensation they shared — that Wikerus was destined to win the True Cross and return the Blood of Christ to the Christian people. The conversation was brief, but it succeeded in refilling our hero's faith in his destiny and his belief that the entire affair was in the hands of God.

Wikerus desired greatly to meet Duke Ludwig. The morning they departed Damietta, they left 450 knights to maintain the city, mostly comprised of the small secular armies, including Andreas and the Buchhorn Army. The rest gathered outside the walls to be led by Pelagius. The 300 Imperial Knights, with all of their squires, servants, cooks, and blacksmiths, were a small city in themselves. They were easy to find, and Wikerus knew Ludwig would be among them. Wikerus was so often away at some secret council, or conferring with some notorious figure or another, that his superiors in the Teutonic Order thought little of his absence among their ranks.

He made his way through the Imperial Knights, wearing the white cloak and tunic of the Grand Master's sect. Assuming he was on some urgent errand, a corridor of interested spectators opened for him as he parted the crowd. He froze when he saw Ludwig. The Duke cut a peculiar figure. His armor was old, quite antiquated in design, perhaps even Roman. He did not wear the cloak of an Imperial Commander, or the standard red, black, and gold of the Imperial Knights, rather the blue cloak of Bavaria, with his family insignia on the shoulder. It was the Wittelsbach crest, only it was different. It was still a shield with helmet atop. The shield still had upon it the blue and white of Bavaria, offset diagonally by standing lions. But crowning the helmet, rather than the lion, was a brilliantly white swan. The image of the swan intrigued Wikerus. It was neither a symbol of Bavaria, nor the empire. Nevertheless, it stood tall upon the image of the helmet, in regal dominance over all beneath it.

Ludwig gathered the attention of his knights, who swarmed around him, closing Wikerus' corridor and allowing him no nearer. Wikerus sat on his horse, among the Imperial Knights, perhaps forty or fifty feet from the Duke. Ludwig could not have seen him among the swarm. But Wikerus did not care. He lost all interest in *meeting* Ludwig. He knew the Duke was about to speak, and he cared only for the words that were about to billow over the mass of polished armor. Ludwig reared his horse high. With a piercing whinny and a thunderous landing of its front hooves, the Bavarian horse silenced the crowd. Ludwig spoke.

Most of you have been in constant war. For years you have been knights, not husbands, warriors, not fathers. You miss your homes and you miss your families, as I miss my wife and son. We find ourselves again on the verge of battle, not called by Friedrich von Hohenstaufen or Otto von Welf, but by our Holy Father.

I may fight in the Pope's war, but I fight for my wife and child. I fight for your wives and children, for your families and your homes. I fight for the songs you will sing in the peaceful days of your future. We will draw our swords in the name of the Pope, and we will fight. But let us fight for the right reasons... for the right people... and end this war as quickly as possible, with as many of us still perched proudly on our horses as possible. Let us fight to bring each other home, to the peace and the love that I pray will define the rest of our lives. Look around you and tell me, will you pay your own blood so those men can return to their families and live in peace?

The Duke gave them a cause they could see and hear, not just some ideal, out of reach of their earthly senses. In battle, the clang of the swords beside them was their reason to fight. The holler of their brothers and the image of those knights beside them again embracing their wives and children would be a reminder of why they fight — one that would not evaporate but strengthen as fighting grew intense and bloody. The response from the Imperial Knights was so overwhelmingly uproarious that they could be heard from the ships docked on the far side of the city. Wikerus, inspired to ecstasy, cheered so loudly and shook his arms so forcefully above his head that he nearly fell from his horse. Pelagius was nowhere near. He heard none of Ludwig's sentiments. That is a shame indeed. Had he heard, and took to it to heart, perhaps he may have learned why men rally to war. Perhaps he may have grown into an effective leader and altered the tragic events that pierce the following pages.

As it was, he knew nothing of the men he led. Oh they may have been recruited by the promises of Holy Indulgences, or inspired to train by sermons in their local churches, or been paid well by the Emperor to sail to war. But they ride into battle for other reasons. They draw their swords and clash their mortal bodies against their enemies with very different thoughts in mind. Ludwig understood this and he spoke to that part of their spirits that was most enlivened in the moments before battle, when fear and hope lose that border between them and embrace each other.

When the crowd settled from their exuberant response, Ludwig concluded.

> Then I tell you, my brothers, I am ready
> to fight with you. I am ready to fight for you,
> and if I must, I will die for that song you will
> sing to your child when you return home.

There was no holler of men's voices on those last words, just a silent and thick, almost tangible commitment between them all to exert everything within them to see each other through the battles ahead and safely to their homes.

Wikerus entirely dismissed his eagerness to meet Ludwig. His heart swelled with those same sentiments shared by the Imperial Knights. Although he had no family of his own, he felt that same determination to fight for his Teutonic brothers, and for the Templars and Hospitallers who would ride beside them, to fight for the songs they would sing in the peaceful days of their future.

Pelagius attempted a rallying speech before the three Military Orders. He spoke of the sacred sites of the Holy

Land, which bore little weight since he denied three offers to take Jerusalem without bloodshed, and the campaign in Egypt for which they were about to embark had nothing to do with the holy places of Christianity. He spoke of Pope Innocent III, assuming that the knights would rally around his memory. He reminded them of the indulgences that they would receive, securing their place in heaven. He did not speak of their homes or families. In fact, he rather spoke as if none of them would survive — that their lives were being exchanged for the ambitions of the Pope. The crusading fervor that had swept through Europe tastes differently in the mouth when one is upon horseback on the eve of battle.

Pelagius raised his voice only once to yell the threat, "Hurl yourselves at the enemy, with no concern for your flesh, or lose your promised reward in Heaven."

The knights gave their obligatory hurrahs when they were prompted to do so by the meticulously placed pauses in Pelagius' speech. But the hollowness of the sentiments stood in stark contrast to the authentic vigor that swept through the Imperial Knights while their Bavarian commander addressed them. Wikerus would later tell Ludwig that it seemed like he spoke directly to him that morning, addressing him as a man with a future beyond war, not as knight whose life had already been purchased for disposal.

CHAPTER 20
The Lovely Dead

LATE THAT MORNING, ON 1 JULY 1221, at the brink of their march southward, King John of England arrived with an army, delaying the departure. Six days later, Cardinal Pelagius led the massive army south along the Nile, toward Cairo. He departed Damietta with 5,000 knights, 40,000 foot soldiers, a corps of more than 900 archers, and a few hundred unarmed pilgrims. Small bands of enemy soldiers were spotted in the distance, almost immediately upon their departure. This was threat enough for the Cardinal to drop from the head of the march and take a position among the ranking officers of the Knights Hospitaller. The bands of no more than fifty Ayyubid soldiers, mostly on foot, posed no threat to the advancing crusaders. Nevertheless, the three dozen Templars set themselves as scouts, scattered evenly along the caravan.

They were not far from Damietta before the rigid divisions broke down. The mounted Teutonic Knights rode in impressively ordered formation. But the Halb-Brüder (the half-brothers), in their matching grey mantels, marching on foot between the knights, slowly dispersed and blended into the Imperial Army and the Hospitallers. The Halb-Brüder were not monks. They took no monastic vows, but received every honor that came with the black cross on their chests. They were all Waffenbrüder (Brothers-in-arms). The Halb-Brüder and their Hospitaller equivalents made up half of the 40,000 foot soldiers. Friedrich's imperial contribution may have led the advance, but this was an Ordered army in its numbers, even with the scant attendance of the Templars.

After Pelagius fell back, the head of the army was Ludwig. For each mounted Imperial Knight, there were ten trailing behind on foot — soldiers, servants, squires, cooks, and blacksmiths. Between those belonging to the Hospitallers and those of the Teutonic Order, around forty priests rode among the warriors. Father Stefan was not among them. He remained in Damietta, tending to the spiritual needs of the remaining knights and overseeing the hospital.

The contrast in leadership between Cardinal Pelagius and Duke Ludwig was plainly before their eyes. Pelagius was the leader of the Crusade, the Pope's man. Ludwig commanded only the Imperial Forces. But it was Ludwig they all followed. The caravan rode on his heels, led by him, drawn to him. There was something indescribable about him, something much more than a military commander, or even a duke. During the course of the crusade, that secret stayed scrupulously locked inside of Ludwig's head. But it would come out one day, to an unexpecting Wikerus, precisely when it would serve our hero the best. But I get ahead of myself. There are many things I must cover before we get to that.

The army arrived at Fariskur, one of the fortresses abandoned by al-Kamil when he retrenched to Cairo. It was held by a band of 40 Hungarian knights. Pelagius assumed control. The fortress was not nearly large enough to house the army. They filled it to capacity, mostly with Ludwig's knights. The rest camped outside of the fortress walls. The Teutonic Knights took the southern perimeter and kept the night watch.

At dawn, a messenger arrived by sea at the docks of Damietta. He bore a letter from al-Kamil. It was addressed to Cardinal Pelagius. Father Stefan eagerly received it. Assuming it to be another offer of peace, he opened it, and prayed that it would concede enough to tempt Pelagius' consideration. The truth is, though Stefan had great faith in Wikerus' destiny, and believed his own words when he prognosticated the blissful days of his future, he worried incessantly for his friend. He hoped the letter might be an offer that could end the Crusade with a resounding victory, without the loss of Christian blood.

The letter had no offer. It had a confession. The Sultan wrote.

Cardinal Pelagius of Albano,

I have made several generous offers to save the lives of your people and mine. I will insult neither of us by making another. I wish only to offer the one thing all men owe each other, honesty.

In my last attempt to prevent the death of thousands, I offered the return of your holy relic, the True Cross, which was taken by Saladin in the Battle of Hattin. I cannot continue under the eyes of God to deceive you on this matter. The True Cross is gone. After your King Richard of England slaughtered the captives from Acre, Saladin destroyed the True Cross. He melted the gold and minted it into coins to pay for his attack on Jaffa. The remnants of wood that were embedded, were destroyed in the process.

Whatever may come of this conflict, let our gains and losses come honestly.

al-Malik al-Kamil Naser ad-Din Abu al-Ma'ali Muhammad

Father Stefan's heart sank. For so long he had truly believed that Wikerus would return the True Cross. Beyond that, he knew that Wikerus believed it too. Without that assurance of Wikerus' destiny, Stefan had no faith in his friend's survival. In fact, he was certain of his death.

He dropped the letter on the ground. Before it finished falling, Stefan was overwhelmed with a panicked desire to retrieve Wikerus from the army, to lock him away in the heart of Meersburg Castle until the last blood of the crusade was spilled. He mounted a horse and rode south from the city.

Andreas and a few Buchhorn knights witnessed the delivery of the letter. They saw Stefan's frantic response and his flight from Damietta. Without pausing to investigate the contents of the dropped letter, they strapped into their armor, readied their horses, and rode after the old priest. They were only a few minutes behind him. But it was enough for Stefan to be overtaken by one of the bands of Ayyubid fighters along the Nile, the same men spotted and ignored by the marching crusader army. Eight Ayyubid soldiers broke from their band and captured Stefan.

Andreas rode faster than the others. He caught up to Father Stefan alone. He found the priest in wretched circumstances. Stefan was on his knees. One of the Ayyubid soldiers stood behind him with his sword drawn. Andreas arrived mere seconds before an intended beheading. Father Stefan was bleeding from the abdomen and from his left thigh. He was bent forward, buckled over his wound. His horse was nowhere to be seen.

The soldier was screaming at him, even as the sound of Andreas' approach drew the attention of the other seven

194

in their party. Andreas dismounted and drew his sword. The sound of his fellow Buchhorn knights could be heard in the distance. But Andreas knew that whatever would happen here would reach its conclusion before their arrival. The seven soldiers came at Andreas, while the one rested the tip of his sword on Stefan's shoulder and watched. The executioner wanted *two* Christian heads to return to his camp, and fully expected to have them.

Rather than encircling Andreas and demanding his surrender, they came directly at him in clusters. With a flick, Andreas sent the first one's sword flying from his grasp. He slashed the knee of the next, dropping him to the ground. A moment-by-moment description of the ensuing battle could never do justice to the eloquence of Andreas' sword. It sang a love song to his wounded friend, as it performed extraordinary acrobatics through the early morning Egyptian air. Within twenty seconds, the seven soldiers were dead on the ground, while the one who hovered over Father Stefan stared in amazement.

Andreas walked with steady determination toward Father Stefan, yelling at the soldier to drop his sword. The soldier did not appear to understand German. But lost all interest in Father Stefan's head. He shook the tip of his sword at Andreas while taking clumsy, wobbly backward steps away from him. Andreas walked right by Stefan in a steady pursuit. The soldier caught his heal on a rock. It did not drop him, but simply took the man's attention downward for a second. When he returned his eyes to Andreas, a German sword was poking him in the chest. Andreas wasted no time with words, no precious seconds on ceremonial revenge. He pushed his sword through the man's heart and turned his attention immediately to Father Stefan.

The other knights arrived as Andreas was throwing Stefan across his horse. They rushed back to the hospital of

Damietta, pushed from behind by a wind that seemed as concerned for the wounded old sage as the knights who cared for him.

When they arrived and took Father Stefan from the horse, the old man showed no signs of life. The amount of Stefan's blood that drenched the horse did little to proliferate their dwindling hope in his survival. But Stefan did not die that day. By that evening, he regained consciousness and even spoke to Andreas, albeit weakly. The physicians were astonished at the old man's strength. The gash across his left thigh cut into the bone. The wound in his abdomen came from a deeply plunged sword. It did not pierce him through, and the depth and damage were impossible to know. But the bleeding slowed, and the intensity of pain was not what was expected. Unable to attribute it to anything their science could explain, considering the nature of the wound, the physicians credited prayer for what was promising to be a quick and imminent recovery. They foolishly yielded their craft to the clergy, and prayer alone replaced medical attention.

That same morning, at the very moment Father Stefan received the letter from al-Kamil, an Ayyubid force of about 120 soldiers, more than 40 on horseback, assaulted the Teutonic camp on the southern side of the fortress at Fariskur. The majority of the Christian army still slept. But the knights of Wikerus' order were in full armor and high alert. They engaged an enemy with similar numbers to their own. It is difficult to imagine the strategic advantage of the assault. The Ayyubid soldiers stood no chance of inflicting considerable damage on the Christian army. The alarm was sounded, and everyone in and around the fortress rushed to arms.

They could have rallied twice as fast and still would have seen no action that morning. The Teutonic Knights, led by the notorious blade of The Tanhuter, dispatched the attackers with the loss of only four of their own soldiers. No full-member knights died in the defense of Fariskur. It is a shame that no chronicler was present to record the heroics and valor of Wikerus and his brothers. Had it been set to poetic tale, the battle would have been represented in art and song for centuries to come. They flowed like a silent breeze through the attacking force, dropping them to the ground the moment they brushed them.

From horseback, Wikerus was frustrated by the tempo of the battle. He dismounted and dispatched his enemies — four for every one dropped by his fellow knights.

For Wikerus, time seemed to slow to a tenth its natural flow. Despite the speed of Wikerus sword, each kill was a free-standing monument in his life. He fought like a warrior monk, and experience the battle, not as he did outside the walls of Damietta, but as he did in the dining room of Castle Tannhausen, with the imaginary enemies of his childhood. Even as he slashed his sword across his enemies, or plunged it into them, they struck his as beautiful. The rich depth of their deep brown eyes, and the shiny, copper complexion of their faces constricted his lungs while jolting his heart with their intense and magnificent beauty.

As he heard their final cries of anguish, he easily imagined those same voices singing to their children. He did not see them merely as enemies, like his Teutonic brothers saw them. He saw them as human, as sons and fathers, husbands and brothers. And he saw them as lovely creations of God. He saw their fear. He saw their passions as reflections of his own. Each drop of blood that ran down his sword was precious to him, and despite the rate at which he killed, he mourned each victim of his skills. He mourned them, prayed for them, and in that flash of a moment, when their eyes locked with his, he prayed *with* them, to his God, their God — it was all the same to Wikerus.

He saw them as the creators of the acoustic wonder in the old mosque of Damietta, as devotees of the same God that spoke to him as he knelt on the crescent and sang. He placed each face that lost the light of life at the end of his sword firmly in his memory, determined to carry them with him for life. As he fought, he thought about the people of Europe, and their collective zeal for holy war. He visualized the cheers, parades, and prayers that erupted under crusading fervor, and he wondered how differently they would feel were it their hands on the hilt of his sword, their eyes looking into those of the enemy.

Despite this, he killed all the same. Ludwig's entire speech rang in his ears with each swing and thrust of his sword. As he fought to secure the peaceful return of his Teutonic brothers, for the song they would one day sing in their own homes, he tallied the songs that would never be sung by the lifeless lips that dropped to the ground around him. These ponderings did not slow him. But they did weight him — a substantial spiritual burden heaped upon him each time he withdrew his sword from another man.

The battle concluded quickly, well before assistance could come from the encamped army. The quickly readied army wasted little time regathering into ranks and resuming their march south, but not before Wikerus secluded himself and relived the battle, moment by moment and kill by kill. The burden on his heart was extreme, but the weight was not nearly as debilitating as the shame he had felt before. The ponderous density of his compassion for his enemies revived his faith in his own redemption. The chain around him was heavy. But he carried it with the lightness of hope.

It is for the best that Wikerus had no knowledge of the blood that was lost just down river, at the same time that he was battling the attackers. Father Stefan's peril would have been too much to add to the weight already upon him. He surely would have broken. And it is unlikely he would have continued to march toward Cairo. He would have sped back to Damietta and joined his friends Andreas and Rikard at the bedside of his most cherished friend. Such would have changed the course of this tale, and the pages that follow would be unrecognizable to any who know this story well.

CHAPTER 21
The Sage's Final Prayer

THE CRUSADER ARMY CONTINUED THEIR MARCH SOUTH.
The forces of al-Kamil advanced from Cairo and took a
firm position at Sharimshah. They sent scouts to tally
Pelagius' army. When the scouts saw the size of the force
marching toward them, and reported back to Sharimsah, al-
Kamil knew that his position would not hold. He
abandoned Sharimsah and retreated to a more defensible
position in Talkhah. But al-Kamil would have no need to
defend Talkhah, and he knew he would not. He chose that
position for a reason other than its man-made defenses.

Between Talkhah and Sharimsah was a canal from a
different branch of the Nile. It was due for its annual
flooding. Ludwig and King John also knew the river would
soon flood. They strenuously advised that the army keep its
position and not advance to the abandoned fortress at
Sharimsah, and wait out the flood season. Pelagius, greedy
out of his wits for his total victory in Egypt, would not
listen to the more stable-minded. He took the bait — the
irresistibly tempting Sharimsah, just waiting empty to be
taken. On 20 July, the crusaders settled into Sharimsah. It
was masterfully played by al-Kamil. With their first steps
into Sharimsah, the crusaders doomed their campaign, and
all of the efforts since Pope Innocent declared his
intentions during the Fourth Lateran Council.

As the canal began to flood, al-Kamil's brother took a force across it and settled near Lake Manzaleh, north of Sharimsah, cutting off the now inevitable crusader retreat back to Damietta. By Thursday, 26 August, the floods had become the equivalent of a million-man army surrounding Sharimsah. There was no breaking through it. Pelagius had to face the fact that retreat was his only option. But it had even become too late for that.

The weakest point surrounding the crusader retreat was al-Kamil's Nubian forces to the southeast. It was the wrong direction for a retreat to Damietta, but a direct retreat was out of the question. What awaited them along the path that took them to Sharimsah was knee-deep mud and waist-deep water. They had to attack the Nubian forces and try to open an avenue of escape. It was likely to fail. Surrender seemed the most probable outcome. But this last effort to escape had to be made. It was likely to be a suicide mission and volunteers were difficult to find. Of course, Wikerus volunteered, still convinced of his destiny to retrieve the True Cross. Ludwig volunteered, and rallied several dozen of his Imperial Knights to join. Wikerus' heroism inspired his fellow Teutonic Knights from Mainau.

Ludwig gave another impassioned speech, which drew several Knights Hospitaller, along with a few hundred foot soldiers, squires, and servants into the mission. The volunteers left Sharimsah on Saturday, 28 August 1221, and worked their way through the flood toward the Nubian force.

If the volunteer force was successful, the rest of the army would need to move quickly through impassable conditions. The stores and supplies they brought from Damietta could not be carried in retreat. On the night of 27 August, just hours before Ludwig and Wikerus were set to leave, Pelagius ordered that everything that could not be carried in retreat needed to be consumed or burned. He

201

gave the order to the Ordensmarschall, the ranking marshal of the Teutonic Order, who carried out the command. He ordered the Teutonic Knights to burn their supplies. The fire alerted al-Kamil of the retreat. After evaluating the situation, al-Kamil determined that his Nubian flank was the most probable point of an attack. He bolstered the Nubian forces with his own guard. Wikerus and the volunteers trudged into a doomed offensive. They were surrounded and captured.

Those who had remained in Sharimsah resolved to retreat north, along their path to from Damietta. Despite the conditions, they broke through the force of al-Kamil's brother. But the battle in the flood waters and mud took days, and al-Kamil had time to bring more warriors between the retreating army and Damietta. The Templars took the rear of the retreat, and this small band of mounted knights fended off numerous attacks from the south.

Pelagius and the bogged down army received another offer from al-Kamil. This one was not nearly as generous as the previous offers. But the crusaders were still astonished by it, and Pelagius had no choice but to accept it. His knights were dying in the flood, without drawing their swords. The knights and soldiers on the perimeter of the retreat were not faring well against the enemy. They would have been annihilated if they continued to push toward Damietta.

The offer declared that Damietta would be returned to the Muslims. There would be an exchange of prisoners on both sides, and an eight-year truce. Hermann von Salza of the Teutonic Order and Peire de Montaigu of the Templar Knights were sent to Damietta with the news of the accepted offer and its conditions. Count Henry of Malta had just arrived with forty ships. His army was deeply disheartened, as were many of those who had remained in Damietta when the seemingly undefeatable crusader force traveled south. Defeat was not well-accepted. There was rioting in Damietta.

By 8 September, Pelagius and the retreating army, as well as all who had remained in Damietta, were aboard their ships in the Damietta harbor, and Sultan al-Kamil entered the city. He supplied the crusaders with food and provisions for fifteen days of sailing. There was one exception to the comprehensive retreat onto the ships. Father Stefan would not leave Egypt while Wikerus blindly pressed on toward an impossible destiny. The injury to his abdomen worsened. The internal damage proved more extensive than hoped. The cut to his leg festered. Infections set in and fevers spiked and retreated. It was increasingly unlikely he would survive the voyage home.

Regardless of his prospects at sea, Stefan had no intention of returning to Europe. In the bustle of departure, he demanded his horse.

"I hope you do not intend to ride back to Germany," his physician stated in a scolding tone.

"I know what fate awaits me," Stefan responded with acceptance, "which is why it does not matter whether I sail or ride."

It *does* matter. You can be attended and honored, dying in comfort, or you can die alone in a strange land, in excruciating pain."

The physician's air turned grave, and he added, "There are still Ayyubid soldiers in the area. You have earned a death in a bed. I weep to imagine you dying on your knees, at the end of a Muslim sword."

Stefan attempted a deep inhale, which stung him deeply and threw him into a seizing cough.

"Easy, easy," a priest sympathetically begged him, "Be still, be comfortable."

Stefan tried to sit up, but he failed so early in the attempt that his movement appeared as little more than a twitch, which threw him into another stabbing cough.

"Help me up," he demanded of the nearest priest.

The physician pushed the priests aside, and said, "I am afraid you will never leave this bed. Your wounds are fatal. Be still. Pray. We will make you as comfortable as possible, and carry you and the bed to one of our departing ships. With any luck, you will survive long enough to die on German soil."

The news that his death was soon did not distress Stefan. It was the manner of his death he could not abide — reclined in the lush bedding of some dead Egyptian merchant, while Wikerus, Duke Ludwig, and the other crusaders on the Nubian offensive faced an unknown fate.

Stefan looked beyond the physician, again to the priest, and demanded in a sterner voice, with much greater energy, "Help me to my feet and find me a horse."

The priest stepped forward to obey, but the physician slapped at him and scolded Stefan, "You have suffered two wounds. You are dying."

All tension dissolved from Stefan's figure. Even the harsh wrinkles of his stern face softened, as he responded dulcetly, "My Lord suffered five wounds for me, before he yielded to death. I will not die until I receive my fifth."

The speech rallied the faith of the priests in the room, who swarmed Stefan's bed, shoving the physician aside. They lifted him to his feet and helped him from the building and onto a horse, wearing only his pants. One of the priests tried to hand Stefan a sword.

He gestured the gift away with his hand and responded, "I ride out to die, not to kill. I will have no use of a weapon."

The physician would have nothing to do with it. He left the building and boarded the ships with the others. The priests walked Stefan and his horse to the gates of the city. They backed away, all but one, who slapped at the horse and sent Father Stefan rushing from town, weakly and unsteadily bobbing on the back of the horse. Once aboard a ship, the physician spoke with great frustration of Father Stefan's unmitigated obstinacy. Word came to Andreas and Rikard, who left the ship, returned to the city center, and asked al-Kamil himself for a horse to retrieve their friend. The Sultan granted the horse, along with a fervent prayer that Father Stefan be recovered quickly and easily.

Stefan's horse ran from town with uncommon fierceness. Each time a hoof touched the ground, Stefan was rattled throughout. His pain was constant and intense. It felt as if mighty fists grabbed at his wounds and pulled him apart by them. He escaped the pain with thoughts of Wikerus and projections about the glory his destiny would bring to God. So far was his mind from his body that he did not feel the arrow that flew from some unknown direction, from some distant bow, and grazed his arm, opening his skin and sending a gentle brook of blood to his elbow. He was not so distant as to not sense the second arrow, which struck him in the top of his right shoulder as he hunched over the horse's mane.

Stefan pulled hard on the reins and the horse came to a halt. Andreas flew at top speed toward him, on the fastest horse the Sultan could spare. As he approached, he hollered at his old friend. Stefan's horse spooked and bucked. The old priest with the forbidding scowl, the oldest and dearest friend of this story's beloved hero, fell from his horse, struck his head on a stone, and died on the spot. His final thoughts, his last wishes, prayers, and ambitions were for Wikerus. Poor Andreas witnessed Stefan's end, but not so near as to share in the moment of death and bring any brand or degree of comfort. There was no way for Andreas to get word to Wikerus, and it is best that he did not. Wikerus and the other prisoners had many months of misery ahead of them without being weighed further by news from outside of their prison.

Wikerus and his fellow prisoners were not well treated. Those who kept the prison were given orders by al-Kamil to treat the prisoners fairly, and to feed them abundantly. But the Sultan was in Damietta, far from the prison, and the prison guards were soldiers, who had fought, bled, and lost friends in the battles of the crusade. They were cruel. They were not just keepers of the imprisoned, but were punitive in every effort. The prisoners could not be kept in any building without fear of their escape. They were kept in an old sewage and drainage system, no longer in use. There were no doors or windows out of which they could escape, or through which fresh air could enter.

The peace offer was written before the capture of Wikerus and Ludwig. The prisoner exchange did not include them. Once in the prison, they were stripped of all indications of rank or station. Servant, knight, duke — they were all treated the same. But inside of the prison, among the prisoners, ranks remained intact. The monastic knights, soldiers, servants, and priests were accustomed to scant provisions. The noble knights of the Imperial Army were not. They were sons of barons, counts, even dukes. They expected to be treated well, and they expected to eat well. They were certain to maintain the thick border between them and the lower ranks.

Among those in the Teutonic Order, all were brothers. The lower ranks remained subservient to the knights, but there was nevertheless a brotherhood, and the welfare of the lowest remained on the minds of the noble-bred. When feeding time came, the lion's share went to the top of the ranks. When bellies were full, what remained filtered downward. The Teutonic Knights ate more sparingly than their Imperial counterparts, wishing to spread the food further. Still, it began at the top, and for most meals, little or none remained by the time it passed from the lowest of the soldiers to the servants. Men starved.

The servants of the Imperial Army had it much worse. Their noble knights stuffed themselves well beyond what was necessary to survive. Some even grew fatter, while the lower ranks went without. Almost nothing served to the Imperial Knights passed to the ranks beneath them.

Duke Ludwig was the sole exception among his army. He was the Emperor's man. Nobody in the prison ranked above him. Yet he ate little more than was required to maintain the strength to move about. He rationed his consumption admirably, but passed the rest through the knights, to go no further. Although his sacrifices did little to benefit the starving men among them, word quickly spread of his meager consumption. His reputation in the prison elevated. Ludwig lost weight at a rate to be expected. His sacrifices had a bold visual display.

After only a few days in the prison, Wikerus saw the inequality of food distribution among the prisoners. He began to claim all that his rank as a noble knight, as the son of a baron, entitled him, which was much more than he had been eating. He did not taste a morsel of it, but carried it around, beginning at the lowest ranks, feeding them and asking them to eat no more than is needed to survive, and begging them to pass what remained upward. Of course, nothing ever remained. In fact, Wikerus' portions only fed eight or nine servants.

Wikerus saw the servants gratefully eat his food, and it brought him some satisfaction. Nevertheless, he could not help but see the countless horde of men he could not feed. When they began to die, he felt none of his own hunger. It was the Imperial servants who suffered the greatest, and it was among those ranks that Wikerus distributed his own rations. He may not have noticed his own deterioration, but somebody else did.

Duke Ludwig joined the crusade late, after Wikerus' heroics gained renown. He did not hear any of the impassioned speeches, made in the secret councils of crusade leaders. In the battles since leaving Damietta, Wikerus' skills had caught the duke's eye, but our hero was mostly unknown to the Imperial Commander — until a week after Wikerus stopped eating. While his own knights grew fat, Ludwig could not help but notice the rapidly diminishing figure that moved about the lower ranks every day distributing a knight's meal among the servants. He observed Wikerus closely for a couple of days and saw that he did not spare a nibble of his nobleman's portion for his own palate. Ludwig was deeply moved by such Christian behavior.

The duke wanted to meet Wikerus, but much more, he worried for the good knight's health. One evening, he watched Wikerus give away his food. Ludwig did not eat that day. He saved bread from his own meager meal, and when Wikerus had made his rounds, and returned in weakness to his own dirty place against the wall, Ludwig came to him with an offering.

"Please," Ludwig begged with his fist full of bread extended forward, "Please take this bread."

Wikerus responded exactly as Ludwig expected, "No, My Duke, you must keep your strength."

Wikerus' predictable goodness brought a smile to Ludwig's austere expression. It was the first time that Ludwig saw Wikerus so closely. The skin of his face appeared to be stretched over a dry stone. He was amazed that Wikerus could stand, let alone walk throughout the prison, feeding others with brightness in his face, and love and hope in his voice. If Father Stefan's final wishes for his young friend were to ever come to pass, Wikerus would first need to survive the Egyptian prison. He would need to survive his own selflessness.

Ludwig took Wikerus by the wrist and turned his palm upward, trying to place the bread in his hand. Wikerus pulled away and again told the duke to eat his bread.

"I would sooner feed the rats with this bread," Ludwig declared, "than eat it while such a holy and noble knight as you starves before my eyes."

Ludwig retook Wikerus' arm and put the bread in his hand. Wikerus turned with the bread to offer it to a servant.

"No!" Ludwig demanded, "They are already better off than you. You must eat this bread."

Wikerus shook his head, but Ludwig continued, "When we leave here, I will need you, a selfless knight, for the perils of the journey home."

Wikerus was still reluctant to feed his desperate stomach, so Ludwig promised to give the entirety of his next three meals to the servants, but only if Wikerus would eat the bread. The calculations spoke for themselves. The duke's next three meals would save many more than that one handful of bread. Wikerus agreed and he ate the bread.

For the next few weeks, similar deals were struck between Wikerus and Ludwig. Word of the arrangement spread quickly. Wikerus survived and Ludwig grew rapidly thin. It immediately inspired the brothers of the Teutonic Order. The knights ate no more than the lowest servant. All of them were weak, all slowly dying, but together, at the same rate.

Since it was mostly the Imperial servants who benefited from the actions of Ludwig and Wikerus, it was among the Imperial ranks that the heroism resounded most loudly. Soon, some of the noble knights of the Holy Roman Empire began to more scantily ration their portions, and pass more to the ranks beneath them. Within weeks, all of them succumbed to the example of the Teutonic Order. The noblest blood in Germany, sons of the greatest names in the empire, ate no more than their servants.

It was still not enough. Servants died, but knights died beside them. In all of my surveys of history, I cannot think of a time or place where such Christian brotherhood wrapped so tightly together men of such varying social ranks. The ranks were still recognized, still strictly adhered to, but they ate the same. They attached their fates to an understanding of equality under God, and they placed it in the hands of their Lord. Many died miserably. But hundreds lived — because of the morality of one young man, and because of what his actions inspired in the heart of a great leader.

The conditions of the prison were hellish. Disease swept through, taking dozens of lives of every rank and title. There was no sanitation. Water that was hardly fit to drink came into the prison in no larger portions than what was required for drinking. The stench compared to the opening waft of Damietta air after the siege. Those who died were not quickly taken away. No money was wasted on lighting the prison. In the daytime, light bled through the various tunnels and provided enough for the prisoners to identify the faces nearest them. At night, the prison was entirely dark, and the prisoners dared not roam. Wikerus grew dear to Ludwig, and Ludwig to him. They remained near each other, partly through their mutual desire to protect the other, but mostly because their shared morality provided a desperately needed sense of familiarity. For every pound lost on their bodies, an equal portion of admiration swelled them.

CHAPTER 22

Caravan Home

AFTER SEVERAL MONTHS OF COMMUNAL LIVING in the prison, the release of the prisoners was negotiated by the Pope. When he gave the order, al-Kamil came to oversee the release. Ludwig's reputation preceded him into the prison and grew more potent in the months that followed. The Sultan wanted to meet him, so he attended the release personally. He was appalled to see the condition of the prison and its prisoners. Not only was he an honorable man who saw no honor in cruelty to the defeated. He feared that reports of their treatment would return to Europe with them and jeopardize the fragile peace. A trial was held to determine blame, and many heads were separated from their shoulders in response.

The Sultan ordered all of the crusaders' property that could still be accounted for to be set in piles outside of the prison, for the Christians to sort though and claim as they could. Most of the servants grabbed whatever tunics, belts, boots, and tools befitted their ranks and positions. Teutonic Knights mostly found the cloaks and armor of their order. Imperial Knights rode away in the red, black, and gold of their army.

Many painstakingly sought specific items, such as hereditary swords and particular heirlooms. Wikerus found a white Teutonic cloak. He found a Teutonic Knight's sword and dagger, and a belt that needed extreme adjustment to function aboard his dwindled frame. He sought his particular tunic. It bore the blood of those he had killed. He knew each stain, and he knew each face, each pair of eyes, and each final cry that associated with each stain. He found it, and knew it at a glance, as particular and familiar to him as his mother's face.

Ludwig sought desperately for his unique armor. It was not among the things returned. At the very moment he abandoned the effort, he dropped to his knees and cried. The armor had been in his family since the founding patriarch of his bloodline, more than 700 years earlier. He deeply regretted taking the heirloom with him on the crusade. His grief was relieved when he raised his head and saw all of the men sifting through the accoutrements of war, withered but living. His pride in his own contribution to their survival swelled within him, as did his love of the young Teutonic Knight who sparked the Christian fervor within him.

Rome ordered Venetian ships to land west of Damietta. Ludwig led the men along the western bank of the Damietta Branch of the Nile. Along the way, he rode along a master knight of his Imperial Army and inquired about Wikerus. The bargain that was struck — the fistful of bread in exchange for the duke's next three meals — had become legend among the survivors of the prison. But Ludwig realized, as he watched Wikerus riding ahead in the distance, that he did not even know the name of the hero who saved so many.

He rode alongside his marshal and asked, "That Teutonic Knight, the one with whom I struck the bargain, who is he? What estate does he call home?"

"I hear he descends from the Lords of Tannhausen, in Northeast Swabia."

Once in Europe, no ties would bind a Teutonic Knight with a Bavarian Duke and the former Commander of

Imperial Forces. Wikerus would return to the strongholds of his order and Ludwig needed to go quickly to Kelheim, the ducal seat of Bavaria, to oversee long-ignored affairs of state. After that, he intended to retreat and recover, with his beloved wife and son, to a small and secret valley, where a humble lodge with a magical and divine history waited to greet him. There would be nothing to throw them into each other's path without some effort on Ludwig's part, and he was not ready to relinquish the association.

He rode ahead, drawing nearer to Wikerus and yelling, "Tannhäuser! Tannhäuser!"

The Tannhäuser slowed and allowed the duke to ride beside him.

"When you can, come to me in Kelheim," the duke begged, "and you will be honored for every life you saved in that prison."

Wikerus responded, "All honor and praise should go to you, my Duke. When the other nobles were growing fat in prison, you nearly wasted away. It was your leadership that saved lives."

"My holy friend," Ludwig humbly retorted, "Any good I did, I did by your example. If ever you find yourself able to benefit from what I may offer, please come to me. I would love to know you outside of war…, no cloaks, no armor or swords, no prisons and no armies. Our kinship may have been forged in that kiln, but it now reaches into the deepest parts of me. And I will never forget you."

Wikerus promised that he would come to him someday. In truth, his humility forbade him from taking the duke's earnest sentiments to heart. He bowed his head to Ludwig and rode ahead to mingle among his Teutonic brothers.

On the morning before they reached the shore of the Mediterranean, and the Venetian ships that awaited them, a messenger from the north converged on the caravan. He came from the ships. He was sent from Mainau Island, by Hermann von Salza, for one purpose — to inform Wikerus of the death of his cherished mentor, Father Stefan. Hermann knew how close they were, and he did not want the news to reach Wikerus haphazardly. The messenger carried a letter from the Grand Master, with an order to read it with the greatest compassion to Luitpold Wikerus von Tannhausen, Teutonic Knight. The messenger found Wikerus and the letter was read. Wikerus made no response, gave no thanks for the effort. He did not acknowledge the messenger in any way. He stared forward for several minutes, then looked to the sky and cried loudly.

Duke Ludwig rode near the rear of the travelers, from which perspective he could observe the many moods of the retreating company. Many heads hung — some in longing for loved ones back home, others in embarrassment and disgrace for the failed crusade, but some still in mourning for friends and brothers lost in battle. Those heads hung the lowest, and were accompanied by sorrowful cries and prayers. One cry rang most wretchedly of all, near the middle of the pack. The Duke rode to investigate and soothe his suffering brother.

The wretched cry, of course, was Wikerus.

Ludwig rode beside and said, "Talk to me, my righteous brother. How can I comfort you?"

Wikerus turned slowly to Ludwig and answered, "Forgive me Duke, but the reconciliation I require cannot come from mortal lips. I have failed Father Stefan and I have failed God."

"I don't know your Father Stefan, but I struggle to imagine what offense you may have committed against God that has not been purged by the indulgence you have earned by crusading for the Pope and by your efforts in the prison."

"Father Stefan was my dearest friend. He fell in the campaign."

"If he was dear to you, I am certain he was a good man."

Wikerus whispered so lowly in response that Ludwig had to read his lips to understand, "The very best of us all."

"Then take comfort in knowing that he is proud of what you have done."

"No sire, he is not," he rebutted with harsh self-loathing.

Ludwig was hesitant to pry. He continued to ride alongside Wikerus, waiting for the broken man to say more.

After a long pause, filled with the most pitiful cries, Wikerus elaborated, "He had a vision from God. I was to retrieve the True Cross. God told him that. I was to return it to the faithful."

With keen and vivid memories of Wikerus' heroics in the prison, Ludwig pondered his words. In a sudden swell, the duke's face grew bright and he scanned his eyes across the ocean of survivors.

"Tell me," the duke implored, "What were his words, this Father Stefan of yours. What exactly did he tell you?"

Wikerus took a minute to recall being at the breakfast table in the main hall of Mainau Island. His vivacious memory placed him easily in the moment. He could feel Stefan's hand in his, reaching across the table.

The words came back to him and he answered Ludwig, "You are to retrieve the Blood of our Lord and deliver it to His faithful. That is what he said."

Ludwig grinned and giggled, which intrigued Wikerus, much more than it offended him. He turned his head squarely to Ludwig, whose bright face heralded a sublime message.

"Don't you see?" Ludwig asked with a laugh in his voice, "My dear, holy knight, don't you see? You misinterpret your friend, or he mistook the words of God. Look around you."

Believing the directive to be rhetorical, Wikerus continued to stare at the duke.

"Look, my friend!" the duke demanded.

Wikerus obeyed and passed his eyes across those riding and walking around him.

"These people are the Body and Blood of God, his children, his own Flesh and Blood," Ludwig spoke in a deep guttural whisper, "Many of them return to their families only by your sacrifices. Don't you see, you have delivered the Blood of Christ and returned it to the faithful? You have fulfilled your friend's prophecy and completed the task given to you by God. And you have done this with noble self-sacrifice. Most importantly, you did not realize at the time that you were fulfilling your holy quest. You did it not from any sense of obligation to your friend or God, but because your own pure heart demanded it of you."

The tears that were running down Wikerus' cheeks stopped in their tracks, like they were trying to swim back to their place of origin, embarrassed for having exposed themselves in such a way. Ludwig watched the young knight's face brighten, and the corners of his mouth rise to form a broad, delighted smile. Wikerus looked up to the sky and smiled at God. The truth of Ludwig's words was undeniable to his heart and senses. The fact is, many of the footsteps, the prayers and sighs, even the mournful cries around him, still came from living limbs, and weary but vital and subsistent lips because of the humble heroism of the Tannhäuser.

As he allowed those sounds to infiltrate his deepest self, Wikerus felt them all to be what he now understood them to be — the Body and Blood of Christ, delivered back to the faithful by his own hands. He reached one of those hands to the sky, as if holding the glorified, angelic face of his fallen friend, Stefan. He whispered words of gratitude and love to his oldest friend. And with that, all weight of sorrow lifted from his weary soul.

Wikerus rode away from the duke, determined to continue his duty to Stefan and God, tending to the servants and lifting the spirits of the vanquished army until he delivered them back to the faithful friends and families awaiting their return. Ludwig left him to pray and ponder. But he knew where he could always find the Tannhäuser — among weak and suffering souls, in the finest traditions of his order, Helping – Defending – Healing.

Later that day, the ships, and the sea behind them, came into view. Wikerus' reaction to the sight was in the harshest contrast to those who rode and walked around him. His jaw clinched and he grabbed the hilt of his sword, not from some teeth-grinding desire to kill again. No — he did not wish to *spill* blood. He wanted to bleed. He realized as the sails came into view, those billowing sheets that would push them all home, that he was not done suffering, not yet transcended and ready to be pulled from his pit.

He was the only one in the company who dreaded the sight of home, who loathed the feeling of a soft bed, the taste of a cool beer, and the sound of a full plate of meat hitting the table before him. He did not understand the sensation stirring wildly inside of him, as he trotted lazily at a slug's pace toward the ships. An inferno of passion churned in him, and the numbing comforts of home were to him a violent abhorrence.

He wanted to bleed for Stefan, for those who died on both sides of the line, and for God. Despite all that he had suffered in Egypt, his wounds were neither deep nor permanent enough for him to board a ship with peace in his heart. But he was a lonely raft in a mighty river, flowing back to Europe. This is not to say that he missed Egypt or would ever miss Egypt. He dismounted his horse and boarded a ship with feelings of complete emptiness, with a million echoes reverberating off the walls of that lonely chamber — the sounds of death and of life, of swords clashing and men hollering, of victory and loss, of growling stomachs, of final wishes, of consternation and of praise. But they did not echo dulcetly, like a delicate chant in a sacred chapel. They rushed hungrily and furiously inside him, begging for something they could not reach.

Wikerus did not sleep a wink before arriving in Venice. He twitched like a frightened child with a mad man's musings. The Pope demanded an audience with the released prisoners. Instead of heading north, to their own stronghold, to their own beds, they went south from Venice, toward the Lateran Palace and residence of the Pope. Family members of many of the Imperial soldiers met them along the way. As Wikerus continued to follow the rushing river of men, as they caravanned to Rome, he experienced little of the goings-on around him. The echoes within him were too loud, and they drowned out the most dynamic events of celebration, and the many marvelous reunions that were experienced by other members of the company. Like Andreas years earlier, he refused that "roll of bread". His spirit placed it ceremoniously on the ground and walked out of sight of others.

CHAPTER 23
The Home Fire Burning

IT WAS A LONG WAY TO TRAVEL FROM VENICE for such a small to-do. Wikerus refused to wash or change his bloody tunic. Something deep inside of him forbade it. Some small but strong portion of his morality hungered for what remained undone in the failed crusade. The others were all too quick to shed the miseries of the previous years and changed much more than just their clothes the very moment it was possible.

The Pope spoke briefly, thanking the warriors for their sacrifices, but primarily dispersing blame for the failures of the crusade to recipients all over Christendom. He gave a final blessing and dismissed them. The whole thing lasted less than an hour. When it broke, Wikerus began thinking about his friends, Andreas and Rikard. In the Egyptian prison, and during the caravan to Rome, Wikerus was the ranking Teutonic Knight among them. Duke Ludwig had no authority over the members of the Teutonic Order. Of course, it was not in Wikerus' nature to assume control over other men. He yielded the authority that would have been his to the Commander of Imperial Forces, a man whose judgment he respected over his own.

In Rome, the Großkomtur of the Order (the deputy to the Grand Master), awaited the return of his brothers. He took command of the returning Teutonic Knights. After the Pope's blessing, they all retreated to the Teutonic stronghold of Trazperch Castle, in the Tyrol region of Austria. Most of the Imperial Knights took advantage of all that was owed to them by Rome. The noble German knights slept in plush beds, in opulent houses, and ate abundant meals, as their ranks afforded. Duke Ludwig, whose position as Duke of Bavaria and Commander of the Imperial Forces would have brought him the most luxurious accommodations in Rome, remained only briefly, dining humbly with those few Bavarian members of his army who had been imprisoned with him. After that, he rode home to Kelheim, hoping fate would put the Tannhäuser in his path again.

It had been years since Wikerus had been among a concentration of his Teutonic Brothers, in a fortress of their own. Zeal for the Order was abundant in Trazperch Castle, where portraits of their leaders and heroes adorned every wall and hallway. Armor that saw action in the earliest battles of the Order stood hollow, keeping ornamental watch over the entrances to gathering halls. Even Wikerus, with all he had done and seen, could not help but swell with pride in his order. The prisoners were lauded and praised with every lift of a glass. The heroics of Wikerus, both on the battlefield and in the prison, both with his sword and with his bread, were told by every knight who served with him. He *felt* heroic, and he took the words of Ludwig to heart, seeing each of his surviving brothers as the Blood of Christ, brought home safely by him. He did not forget those he had killed. He removed his bloody tunic of war, folded it neatly and stored it among his things. It was not the fabric he idolized, but the blood stains upon it. He pulled it out several times a day to refresh in his heart and honor those beautiful eyes and copper faces he destroyed.

As the next weeks passed, the atmosphere in Trazperch Castle did much to numb Wikerus of the lingering pains of the war. He was becoming exactly what his father wished he would be when he secured his son's admission into the Teutonic Order — an admired Tannhäuser, whose exploits in war brought prestige to his family and father. Unlike the chaos in Acre, or the mixed armies in Damietta, or the conditions in prison, Trazperch Castle provided a strictly Teutonic environment, with all of the secret rituals and monastic regimen of the Order. It was not much unlike his time at Mainau Island, only this time he was not a recruit or a young untested knight. He was a seasoned warrior and a wise counselor who had earned the respect of anyone he might pass in the halls of Trazperch Castle.

On the first evening in Austria, the Großkomtur awarded Wikerus the Marian Cross of Saint Mary. It was a sword with the symbol of the Marian Cross of Saint Mary emblazoned on the pommel. Only a select few in the history of the order had received the honor. It raised Wikerus to a point of prestige among the elite knights in all of Europe. For a very short time, Wikerus was proud of the honor and envisioned a long and illustrious career in the Teutonic Order.

The Order had similar plans for Wikerus. Tensions grew between the Teutonic Order and the Templars and Hospitallers. Acre was the capital of Christian control in the Middle East. The Teutonic Knights needed to break from Acre and secure their place in the region with a strong fortress of their own. In 1220, they bought the Monfort Estate in Palestine. Plans were in the works for a Teutonic Castle, and Wikerus was to oversee its construction and take command of the fortress upon its completion. Everything was happening in accordance with the bargain his parents had made years earlier.

Methildis' son was a monk, serving God and the Church under vows of chastity, poverty, and obedience. Luitpold's son was an honored member of the aristocracy, toasted at gatherings by some of the most hallowed lips in Germany. Wikerus took pride in both, but his later influences haunted his solitary moments. Father Stefan, Francis of Assisi, Count Konradin, Andreas, and Rikard — the spirits of these men held a measuring stick beside Wikerus each night before he went to bed. He determined to accept the commandership of the Monfort estate and the Teutonic fortress. He went to bed with glorious plans of a true monastic fortress, securing a Christian presence in the region, but also serving the local population by the scared vows of the order.

After almost five months in Trazperch Castle, on the very night before he was to leave for Palestine, a messenger came from Castle Tannhausen. The Baroness Methildis von Tannhausen was dying. The letter was not dated and the messenger, being the third recipient, could not testify to its age. Wikerus was given permission to depart immediately. Perhaps his heart refused to accept more misery, or perhaps his faith in his mother's strength was exaggerated, but Wikerus did not rush home. He did not believe his mother would die before he arrived, and the larger part of his mind thought she would not die at all, but recover completely under his care.

He was in no hurry to leave. He slept at ease, participated in the morning prayers, sang the Psalter, ate, put on his ceremonial tunic and mantle, along with his Marian Cross sword and a winged, ceremonial helmet, and rode west with the intention of stopping at Mainau Island and Meersburg Castle first. In a sack, along with some humble provisions, was his blood-stained wartime tunic. He rode for several days, resting only briefly, until he arrived in Lindau, on the eastern edge of Lake Constance, where he secured lodgings with a friend of his Grand Master. He ate well and fell quickly to sleep.

He dreamed that night — a dream that shook him terribly and changed the plans and pace of his travels. The dream began with him back in Trazperch Castle, kneeling before the altar of the castle's chapel. His eyes were closed but he sensed someone kneeling beside him. He assumed it to be one of his Teutonic brothers, until a soft arm interlocked with his. He opened his eyes and saw his mother praying with him, and the chapel of Trazperch became the chapel of Castle Tannhausen. He was home. The warmth he felt encompassed him body and soul.

A voice called from behind them, ordering Methildis to rise and follow. Wikerus knew the voice but could not immediately place it. He turned to look behind them, but the room was dark and the voice came from deep within the blackness. As it drew nearer, Wikerus recognized it. It was the voice of Father Stefan, still calling Methildis to come to him. He was torn in half. He wanted to see Stefan, but did not want his mother to see him. Methildis stood from her knees and turned toward Stefan's voice. Wikerus tried to stand with her, but his knees would not leave the kneeler. Methildis began to walk into the darkness, toward the voice. Wikerus grabbed at her, but she slipped through his hands. He screamed at her to wait, to not go without him, struggling with all of his might to disengage from the kneeler and follow her. But he could not stand. He only twisted his body unnaturally to look behind him at the back of his departing mother.

Just before Methildis left the light, the figure of Father Stefan came visible — shadowy, ghostly, and bleeding from head to toe. Although Stefan did not appear to be in pain, his image was so gruesome that it conjured in our hero the most pathetic compassion. But all thoughts of Stefan evaporated when Methildis looked back at her son, smiled slightly, turned to Stefan, and followed him into the darkness. Wikerus hit at the kneeler. He drew his sword and tried to hack himself free. When that failed, he hacked at his own legs, while screaming for his mother to stay with him and begging Father Stefan to bring her back. He awoke in a full sweat with a pounding heart and a pressing desire to see his mother. He did not eat, or even pass a word to his hosts. He bolted before dawn and rode directly toward Castle Tannhausen, with his brilliant white Teutonic cloak flapping frenzied behind him, trying to keep pace.

In the afternoon of his first day of travel, he rode into a small strip of a village, with fourteen humble buildings on one side and nine on the other. Farmland surrounded the buildings. These were the simple dwellings of the workers and their foreman.

As Wikerus passed the first house on the right, a man ran out in distress, followed by his young daughter.

"You are finally here. Please, hurry and help them."

"Who needs my help?" Wikerus asked confused, but clearly willing to act.

"Did Valentin not warn you what you would be facing?"

"I do not know your Valentin. But if I can be of use to you, please, tell me what I must do."

The man explained that their little farming community was set upon by a gang of twelve bandits. The people of the village offered every bit of wealth they owned for the bandits to leave them in peace. But the scoundrels were not interested in wealth. They wished only to terrorize. They took over the town, allowing nobody to leave, not even to work the fields. They walked in and out of the homes as they pleased, beating down all who stood against them. They ate what they wanted, drank what they wanted — took whom they wanted.

The man explained in tears that the leader of the gang took an interest in his wife. She had been a prisoner at his side for more than a week. The leader made the villagers call him "Herr Bürgermeister" (Mister Mayor). Most of the gang was scantily armed, with just a few knives and clubs among them. The leader carried two short swords, strapped to either side of him at all times.

With the information provided, Wikerus asked, "Where are they?"

"Most of them are in that building," the man answered, pointing to the third house on the right, "but the rest..., I don't know."

Wikerus rode forward, to the house indicated by the man. He pulled on the reins and his horse reared up and whinnied loudly. He dismounted and pulled the Teutonic shield that was strapped to the left side of his saddle. He put on his ceremonial helmet, with its large wings bowing upward from the sides. One bandit stepped out from a house on the left. He whistled shrilly. It echoed off the buildings and drew another four men from a building on the right. The other seven soon followed from here and there.

Wikerus counted them, to be sure that none closed in from behind him. There they were — eleven of the most abominably wretched scoundrels Southern Germany had to offer, with a twelfth, superior to the others in all ways, standing in the center of them. This twelfth, this leader of theirs, had a keen intelligence in his eyes. He was not wild like the rest. He stood taller by a head, had his two short-swords strapped to his waist, and wore much fancier clothes.

None of the eleven had any armor. But the leader wore a single strip of hardened leather, strapped around his neck and hanging to cover the center of his chest. Facing a lesser opponent, I'm certain that strap of leather made him feel invincible. As he stared down Wikerus, gleaming in his ceremonial white tunic, with its large black cross from belt to neck, and his dazzling white cloak, with matching black cross on the left shoulder, with his shining armor and helmet, and his massive white shield and cross, the man must have felt completely naked.

Wikerus took one step toward them, as they huddled more tightly together. Those villagers being held captive in their own homes dared to come out, one by one. They must have thought they had fallen into a legendary tale, like the ones they recited to their children.

Wikerus took a few more steps forward.

One of the dirty men hollered, "Let's take him together. He cannot defeat us all."

The leader, who had not drawn his swords, slapped him across the head and scolded, "Of course he can! If we were twelve of me, instead of one of me and eleven of you, we might stand a chance."

He recognized a decorated Teutonic Knight when he saw one. The Teutonic Order had greater affairs, global affairs with which to concern itself. The sight of a sole knight like Wikerus, straddling the center of the road like it was his own horse, terrified the leader. He stepped toward Wikerus, still not drawing his sword. He doubted their ability to get to their horses, untie them, lead them from the fences, mount them and escape before Wikerus could strike them all down. He also knew they would likely all die in a direct assault. So he stepped forward, thinking that he would rather die on that street than be wounded, tried, and executed. He signaled for his men to remain in place. He drew his two swords, and he walked alone toward our hero.

Wikerus sure did cut an impressive figure. He looked almost magical as he marched to meet the leader. His cloak opened behind him, making him look twice his size. He drew his sword and met the leader face to face. They stared each other down for half of a minute, before the bandit swung the sword in his right hand, in a large arch toward Wikerus' head.

Wikerus swatted the man's striking forearm with the broad side of his sword, so as not to draw blood, and knocked his hand to his leg. With a flick of his wrist, he swung his sword back and thumped the leader in the ear, again not drawing blood. The man dropped the short-sword in his right hand and held his ear, whining and wheezing in pain. He looked up to see Wikerus swinging his sword from high above his head. Wikerus' ceremonial sword, that beautiful instrument with the Marian Cross of Saint Mary on its pommel, struck the scoundrel on the top of his head with its flat side.

The leader of the bandits dropped his other sword. His eyes rolled back in his head and he swayed in small circles. By now the entire town watched, as the tall brut who had terrorized them for more than a week dropped to the ground as if all bones had been suddenly removed from his body.

Wikerus looked up to the other eleven. They stood frozen in fear and disbelief.

"Go and never come back," Wikerus belted.

The eleven ran together to the fences that held their horses.

One of them mounted his horse and Wikerus yelled, "What do you think you are doing?"

The man answered pleadingly, "But these are our horses. We brought them here."

Wikerus replaced his sword, and strapped his helmet and shield to his horse, and answered casually, "Not anymore. Now they belong to these people."

In flawless unison, the eleven walked from the fenced horses, turned away from Wikerus and began walking from the town.

"Haven't you forgotten something?" Wikerus shouted.

The bandits froze in their tracks and turned around together, as if grabbed by the neck and spun by force. They saw Wikerus standing over his defeated opponent, pointing down to him. Two of the bandits ran to their leader. One grabbed him by the back of his collar, the other grabbed a pant leg, and they dragged him in contorted awkwardness to the other nine. Several of them assisted in lifted their unconscious leader and the gang left town together.

Wikerus watched until they were out of sight. He mounted his horse, turned it, and trotted back to the man he met as he entered the village.

"Why did you let them leave?" the man asked in distress, "I told you what they did to us. Why did you not kill them?"

"I fought one without spilling his blood," Wikerus answered with conviction, "I could not have arrested them all. Had I fought them all, I would have had to kill, and your street would be covered in blood."

Wikerus reached into his bag and pulled out his wartime tunic, stained with the blood of the slain. He held it up for the whole village to see. They understood. Wikerus wore a face with a thousand violent and bloody memories. They could read it in him and they could see it on the bloody garment. Wikerus folded his tunic and placed it gently back in his bag, needing no further justification for the cleanliness of his ceremonial sword.

"They will not come to this village again. Of that I am certain," he assured them.

The people offered all means of gratitude. Wikerus accepted their praise with humility, swore to them that no debt was owed to him or the Teutonic Order. He promised to be of further assistance to them, and he rode out of town, to his home and family.

After days of rushed travel, he finally arrived at the large doors of his home. It was early in the afternoon. He knocked as a guest or a stranger. A servant he did not know answered and led him to his father's study. The Baron lit with joy to see his son dressed and decorated as an honored knight. There was no sign of sorrow in Luitpold's face or words. Wikerus was relieved and inquired about his mother. The Baron, ignoring the request as if he did not hear it, insisted upon hearing stories of the crusade.

"Take me to my mother!" Wikerus demanded with the authority of his current, not his previous station.

Baron Luitpold cowered under the voice of his son, with his dazzling white crusader cloak.

He timidly replied, "All right… ähm, follow me."

Not a word passed between them as the clang of Wikerus' squared, metal sabatons thundered through the empty hallways. As they approached the entrance to the gardens, Luitpold began to speak the kindest compliments of Methildis, in terms that sent Wikerus into shivers. They entered the garden and the Baron pointed to Methildis' grave. The first glance at the grave did not elicit tenderness toward his mother, but harshness toward his father. He turned to the Baron ready to strike him across the face. But his father's eyes were forward, to the grave of his wife, and his eyes swelled with dewy tears. All anger left Wikerus. He embraced his father and they wept together.

The two of them sat together in the garden and told stories of Methildis. Wikerus had never seen such powerful sentiment from his father, and he began to believe that perhaps there is greater depth of spirit in the ambitious man than he had ever imagined before. He even began to consider that a life as a Baron von Tannhausen, living in the family estate and managing the good but simple farmers who work the land, might be a path he could stroll for the rest of his life. They cried and they laughed and they cried again. They remained near the grave for at least two hours. The sun went lower in the sky and Wikerus asked to use the chapel. His father excused him from his company with an embrace that swelled with warmth.

Despite the years of absence, Wikerus knew his way well to the chapel. He could have walked in blindfolded and drunk. So familiar was the walk that his mind gave it no consideration, freeing it to swim through the flood of memories that the familial walls poured on him. He thought of his brothers, of his thin memories of his sister, and of course, of his mother. That comfortable feeling of being cradled by familiarity to the senses was slashed violently as he entered the chapel and found a stranger kneeling where his mother used to kneel.

She was a young woman, or older girl, appearing, in glow and complexion, to be in her mid to upper teens. The altar candles placed a warm, orange halo around her head. Her hair was down. It cascaded, thick and auburn, down her back, over her shoulders, and along her arms. It was so richly diverse in color and texture that Wikerus believed he could reach the entire length of his arm into it without touching the back of her neck. He stared at her for a moment. In doing so, he realized that she appeared to belong there. He imagined that if a painter were to capture the chapel in oils, he would be obligated to paint this girl into the picture. The little room would be lonely without her. As he pondered this, she began to whisper her prayers. The whispers became vocalized, then rode the scales of an elegant chant.

Her voice was not so pure as Wikerus', nor was it as harsh as his Teutonic brothers. But there was a distinct piety and extreme depth of emotion in the subtle cracking of her notes. Her purity was undeniable, as was her devotion to God. Wikerus was intrigued. His attraction to her was in no way sexual or romantic. It was academic. He could not fathom why a creature like the one before him would be praying alone in his family chapel. Her song beckoned him. It drew in his spirit and demanded his voice as accompaniment.

Wikerus knelt beside her. She gave a slight turn of her head, seeing from that angle no more than his left shoulder and a portion of his forehead. When he started singing with her, she turned forward again and committed herself comprehensively to the prayer. His beautiful voice drew from her even richer emotion. Their voices had two very different qualities, which should not have worked so well together. But the duet was truly exquisite in its harsh differences, like a bright red rose against a worn grey stone, complimenting each other to perfection.

The chant, well known to them both, concluded with a sustained harmony that emptied from them the last of their air. After the moment of silence that followed, they comically inhaled together. They both laughed and turned to face each other. It was the first view each had of the other's full face. A sparkle was in her eyes that adorned the old castle beyond its merits. She looked at him with a smile that remained from their shared comical moment. But it quickly dropped when she saw the expanse of sorrow in his eyes. Readers, I tell you this, it is a remarkable teenager who can recognize that in the eyes of another. Wikerus noticed her loss of countenance, and attributed it correctly — to her penetrating vision of the horrors inside of him, horrors she could not possibly fathom, but could see nonetheless.

Momentarily losing his well-bred decorum, he asked in wonder, "Who are you?"

She had been locked to his eyes without a blink, but with his question, she blushed, batted her eyes several times, cleared her throat awkwardly and answered, "I am the Baroness von Tannhausen, new wife of Baron Luitpolt."

Needless to say, Wikerus was stunned. Ten thousand thoughts went through his mind, each giving a single, sharp jab at his heart. This girl knelt in his mother's chapel, ate at her seat at the table, wrote at her desk, and slept in her bed. He could make no sense of it. It was impossible. Methildis had so recently died. In the tenderest, most honest moment he ever shared with his father, there was no mention of this girl. Wikerus wanted to believe her to be a liar, but he knew better. There was nothing of deceit in her address, and only the most righteous purity in her eyes and in her voice. She had to be, as she said, his stepmother.

Those ten thousand thoughts tried to force their way through Wikerus' throat simultaneously. The result was a bumbling, "Where..., when..."

He stood from the kneeler but remained facing her. She stood and stepped her toes to his. She placed her delicate hand on his shoulder. He could not feel it through the hard mail that covered him. He wished he could. He wished it desperately, hoping that something in her innocent touch would clear the chaotic tumult inside of him.

She interrupted his clumsy interrogation with the answer she assumed he sought, "I am Aleidis von Vollrads, daughter of Konrad von Vollrads of the Knights of Vollrads."

A few years earlier, this would have meant nothing to Wikerus. He learned much as he mingled with the aristocracy of the empire. The Knights of Vollrads ranked beneath the Lords of Tannhausen, but their political connections were stronger. Above all else, Baron Luitpold wanted an electorship in the empire. Konrad von Vollrads had close ties to the Teutonic Order. Castle von Vollrads had been used by the Order during their earliest years. The family von Vollrads also had intimate ties with the Electors Palatine on the Rhine. It was clear to Wikerus that his own fame had secured this hasty marriage for his father, who had to make his political strike while the irons of his son's notoriety were still hot.

Wikerus saw the lovely young woman in front of him as a helpless victim of his father's ambitions. As much as he wished he could despise her for replacing his dear mother, he could not help but pity her and wish her well.

Aleidis asked him, "You are a Teutonic Knight. Did you fight in the Holy Land?"

Being forced by the question to consider what had been far from his thoughts, he lifted his chin and opened the doors of his mind for vivid flashbacks.

Seeing the wincing and twitching of his face, Aleidis changed the subject, "Are you a friend of my husband?"

Wikerus snapped from his violent recollections and returned his focus entirely on her, "I am perhaps his oldest remaining friend... I am his son."

He took one large step backward and bowed low, continuing, "Luitpold Wikerus von Tannhausen, son of Baron Luitpold von Tannhausen."

He rose from his bow to see her bright eyes glassed over and unnaturally wide.

Now it was she who clumsily stumbled to speak, "I…, I am…, what I mean to say is…, I am so sorry."

"Sorry for what?" he replied, truly unable to imagine what offense could be haunting her conscience.

"I am sorry you have lost your mother. And I am sorry to be standing here in her —."

He interrupted her, with far more compassion than bitterness, "The movements that placed you here happened well above your head. I may never come to see you as my stepmother, but I most certainly pray that I will call you my treasured friend."

She squinted her eyes and tilted her head in amazement, saying, "You do not hate me for replacing your mother?"

Her blush grew to outshine the candles.

"I knew nothing of your marriage to my father, not until you introduced yourself to me. It will take me some time. But when we knelt and sang together, you felt as family to me. I would not have imagined that we are, well, mother and son, but a connection was clear, and I will take it how it comes. As for my father…, let us say that he and I have some strong words to exchange."

She blushed more deeply, so he assured her, "Whatever comes of that, it will not change how I see you."

She curtsied lowly and slowly to him. He left the room in silence while she looked to the floor, and her eyes raised to a barren wall in front of her.

CHAPTER 24
Cut from All Tethers

HAD WIKERUS IMMEDIATELY MARCHED TO HIS FATHER, after meeting his new stepmother, it is possible that the relationship could have been salvaged, even nurtured into something stronger than it had ever been. That is not what Wikerus did. He strolled around the castle and surrounding grounds trying to clutch the spinning thoughts inside of him. When he encountered his father, he passed the lightest and most peripheral of pleasantries, ignoring that one subject that stood in the way of reconciliation.

When he saw Aleidis, there was awkward warmth, but it *was* warmth. He did not know what to call her. She was several years younger than he. And he tried mightily not to envision her among his mother's favorite places and things, like sitting and reading beside her bedroom window. It was a near certainty that Aleidis did those things, but the thought of it would stir a resentment for the innocent young woman that Wikerus did not think she deserved.

The three of them, Wikerus, his father, and Aleidis, skated each morning through evening on the thinnest layer of ice, each waiting for the wrong word or gesture to shatter it. It was not shattered by any of them, but by a visitor to the castle. Alawich, the simple farmer and brother of Methildis' rescuer, knocked late one afternoon on the thick doors of Castle Tannhausen.

Still standing in the doorway, Alawich declared, "It is true. You have come home."

Wikerus invited him in, led him to the sitting room, lit a large fire in the fireplace, and called for two mugs of beer. When the fire was roaring and the beer was served, he sent the servant away and bolted the door.

The moment their privacy was secured, Wikerus closed the space between him and Alawich with four or five long, quick steps. He threw his arms around the old man, and in that embrace, only then, he realized how impactful Alawich had been in sculpting the man he had become. The room had no windows to the outside. The candles that lit the room were muted by the brilliant blaze of the fire. It was a tremendous fireplace, about shoulder high on Wikerus and three times as wide, capable of burning half of an ancient linden tree at once. Two old chairs sat before the fireplace since it was christened centuries earlier. Bulky dark wood arms framed the deep red upholstery of the chairs. Embroidered into the backs was the Tannhausen crest. Between the chairs sat a simple, understated three-legged side table, where the mugs of beer awaited their masters.

The men released their mutually affectionate embrace and took seats in the chairs. Nothing was spoken between them for several minutes. Alawich stared into the fire with a face displaying deep and not particularly pleasant contemplation, hardly sipping at his beer. Wikerus, believing the visit purely social, stared at his old friend with a grin he could not subdue.

Alawich took several deep gulps of his beer and turned to Wikerus, maintaining the expression of dread and trepidation. The buoyant grin on Wikerus face sank as if made of lead.

Alawich spoke gravely, "I must speak to you of your mother."

Not imagining the conversation could be more distressing than what his time in the castle had already provided, Wikerus begged, "Please. I want to hear."

"While you were in the Holy Land, your mother was active. She wanted the entire estate in constant prayer for your victory and safe return. She came to us every week, sometimes in the fields and sometimes in our homes. She fed us and made gifts of things too rich, too opulent to grace our humble walls. When weather shortened our day, she plowed and sowed, and harvested with her own hands, so that we could finish before the storms rolled in. She joined us, often staying overnight in our houses, graciously and thankfully. She ate with us and kissed us goodbye like we were her family. Many of us wondered when she was home, when she was warm and rested in her own castle, and tending to her own needs."

Wikerus' eyes dewed so that when he blinked, a single tear rolled down each cheek. "That sounds like her," he replied with a choking giggle.

"There's more," Alawich continued, leaning toward Wikerus, "I don't know how much you have heard of her final days."

Wikerus shook his head to indicate that he had heard nothing of how his mother died.

Alawich perched himself on the edge of his chair and reached across the table between them, placing his hand on Wikerus' and continuing, "When word came that you had been captured and imprisoned, your good mother set to raise the money for your ransom. She was prepared to travel there herself to pay the Sultan and beg on her knees for your release."

Wikerus shivered at the thought of Methildis riding the wilderness alone, and sitting below boards with Venetian sailors, or dropping to her knees before al-Kamil and his soldiers.

238

Alawich squeezed Wikerus' hand and added, "She rode to every household that had coins to spare. Many of us tried to accompany her on the roads, but her horse was fast, and she drove it hard."

Alawich paused, and his voice went quieter as he spoke, "I feared for her health, and for her safety. And my fears were well warranted. One afternoon, not many weeks ago, I awaited her on the road, not very far from here, to escort her home. She did not come as expected, so I walked in search of her. I found her lying against a tree, on the side of the road."

Alawich began to cry and had to pause between words to remain intelligible, "There was blood in her hair and on her dress. Her horse was gone. She rode back and forth with the money she raised. Everyone in the region knew she did. This is why I feared for her."

Alawich broke into full sobs, covering his eyes with one hand and rubbing at his temples with the tips of his thumb and index finger. Clearly he tried to smear away the horrible image dominating his inner eye.

Wikerus left his seat and knelt in front of Alawich's chair. With both hands, he took the old hand that had held his. Wikerus sobbed as profusely as Alawich. But he did not want to disturb the tale, so he swallowed the cries. He could not swallow the shaking of his body as he tried to clamp down and cage his boiling emotions.

Alawich calmed in response to Wikerus' rubbing of his hand, and continued, "I did not expect to find her breathing when I lifted her. But she was not dead. The bandits must have assumed she was. She did not respond to me when I lifted her into my arms and begged for her words. She was so..., she was so cut up and bloodied that I would not have known her but for her hair and dress. I carried her here and gave her to your father's servants. I wanted to stay by her side, but I was pushed away, so I returned to the village and gathered them all in prayer for her recovery."

Wikerus took Alawich by the back of the head with both hands. He pulled the weathered old forehead to his lips, pressed him hard against his face, and said between kisses, "Thank you. Thank you."

Alawich pulled away, sat against the back of the chair and continued, "Many of us came, every day, to look for signs of her recovery. Three weeks after I found her, I knew that I had failed to rescue her as my brother did, when I heard that your father was to remarry. There were no announcements in the village of the death of our Baroness, no funeral for us to attend and praise her goodness as we were all so desperate to do. We saw the caravan of six knights escorting the Baron's new wife through the village and toward the castle."

Wikerus, who had been high upon his knees, sat back onto his heels and lowered his head.

"I tried," Alawich told him, "I ran as fast as I could carry her. I tried. I just wanted you to know that I tried."

"Of course you did."

"I have cursed my weak old body every day since."

"Cursed it?" Wikerus retorted defensively, "I praise it. I praise you. My mother would have died alone, dirty and bleeding on the side of a road. She died in her bed, with her own physician and priest by her side, warm and clean and surrounded by prayer. You could not save her from death, but you saved her from a terrible death, and granted her a peaceful departure from this world. I thank you for it. I praise you and bless you for it."

Despite Wikerus' insistence, Alawich did not want to linger in the castle. Wikerus walked him to his father's stables and sent the noble old farmer away on one of the Baron's finest horses, with no intention of collecting it later. The Baron would have protested had he ever found out. Wikerus knew that Luitpold paid little attention to such things, and he paid the stable keeper to keep his secret. He wondered how much Alawich and the other poor farmers gave to Methildis for his ransom, and took great satisfaction in the idea that the fine horse could be sold for more money than Alawich had possessed in decades combined.

Over the next several weeks, Baron Luitpold was as he had always been — distant and ambitious, with thoughts on the wealth and prestige of his future household, certainly not on the son and young wife who shared his roof. Wikerus and Aleidis found comfort and company in the only available resource — each other. Their formal pleasantries slowly grew and transformed, one small encounter at a time, into conversations complex and profound.

Aleidis' faith was that of a young person. In no way did she replace Methildis' spiritual contributions to the household. But she was an industrious scholar with a ferocious appetite for learning. Wikerus, not being so far removed from his life as an ordered monk, maintained his vows, not indulging in lavish meals with his father and stepmother, devoting his lonely hours as a monk should, praying in the morning and chanting his devotion in the evenings.

Aleidis, who had the natural propensity for devoutness, and who yearned for a more dynamic life than that of a baroness, was drawn to Wikerus' routine. She noticed his absence from the dining table, especially when noble visitors came and were indulged according to their rank. One evening, after the table was cleared and the servants retired for the night, Aleidis made her way to the quiet dining room. It was very quiet, but not unoccupied. While the smell of tender meat, fresh off the bone, was still in the air, Wikerus sat alone with a small bowl of soup, a piece of bread, and a small glass of wine.

Her heart leaped, not for Wikerus, but for his lifestyle, and for his intangible, indescribable richness of soul, depth of vision, and commitment to a code she found alluring. She joined him and offered to serve him in the absence of the family servants. Aleidis was the lady of the household, the Baroness von Tannhausen. It was her station to be served, not to serve. She knew that. Wikerus knew that she knew it, which made her offer intriguing to him.

"Join me if you wish," he told her, "Please join me. But nobody serves me, not here or anywhere. *I* am a servant, a servant of God and of all his people. Please sit and let me serve you."

Inspired to the point entrancement, she declined in like terms, saying, "Who am I to be served by you in this dining room? I have learned so much from you these past few weeks. You are unlike anyone I have ever known. I want to continue to learn from you. It is I who should serve you, and call you master."

A wise and profound reply came to Wikerus' mind, but he did not speak it. He simply stared at her and compared her to all of the young recruits to Mainau Island that he encountered there, including himself. He was about the same age when he left his home with Father Stefan. She understood more than any of them. An opulent life of leisure and pleasure was hers to enjoy, yet she craved sacrifice and spiritual enrichment. Her mind and her heart appeared immensely beautiful to him. As it did, and he continued to stare speechlessly at her, her face struck him as immensely beautiful. Her lovely spirit glowed from within and cast a magnificent hue on her otherwise mildly lovely face. He blushed deeply and turned from her.

She undoubtedly noticed, but could not have known the exact nature of his thoughts. She dispelled the awkwardness by asking him to describe his routine as he prepared for war. He recovered quickly as he considered the request, slipping easily into the role of teacher. He spoke and she inquired, then he inquired and she spoke. They both served themselves and each other, while their conversation skipped with the slightest of guidance through varying topics both mundane and sublime, comical and tragic, personal and public.

After that evening, Aleidis joined Wikerus in the chapel every morning. She sat with her husband at dinner time, but ate no more than she knew Wikerus would eat. After dinner, Baron Luitpold retired to his own study to read and drink. Aleidis used the time for solitary prayer, but she joined Wikerus in the chapel for his nightly chants. His influence on her was as profound as her natural ability to absorb what he offered. With pride and pleasure, and some confusing, mixed feelings, he watched her quickly grow wise and righteous. He had faith that her older years would yield a truly admirable woman.

As Aleidis' company did more and more to enrich his life, Wikerus began for the first time to doubt his desire for a monk's life. The time was coming quickly for him to leave his family and rejoin his order. His brotherhood had many knights of rich spirituality. But it was not the same. Feminine spirituality is different than that of men. Wikerus began to realize that he derived as much enrichment from Aleidis as he ever offered *to* her, a gift that the strongholds of the Teutonic Order were entirely without. He had no sexual attraction to his young stepmother. That is not to say that he did not revel in her physical beauty and the sound of her voice. He allowed himself to take pleasure in her appearance. But he would have been just as drawn to her if he had been blind. The attraction was academic and spiritual, still, it was a powerful attraction that cast the road before him into the darkness of doubt.

Several weeks went by in this way. Their friendship grew tighter, and in Wikerus' mind, less conflicting. An event, not surprising, but entirely unexpected by Wikerus, destroyed their enthralling symposiums. Aleidis expected a child. Wikerus knew that she was the wife of his father. There was nothing unnatural or unholy about her conceiving the Baron's next child, Wikerus' sibling. Still, her capacity as the wife of his father had been far removed from the topics they discussed, and the news came as a shock to him.

Baron Luitpold finally viewed Aleidis as the mistress of the household, and not some surrogate to fill the hole left by Methildis. He drew her into his days and away from Wikerus' tutelage. He flirted with her in front of his son. Wikerus withdrew from both of them, hoping that his lessons would stick, and she might make the Baron a better man.

Aleidis had lived among Methildis' things and Luitpold had done nothing to make the castle more hers. After news of the pregnancy, Luitpold began clearing out the things that had belonged to Methildis. He doted upon Aleidis as he should have done all along. Wikerus knew the rightness of the change, but was still deeply disturbed by it. His conflicting feelings swelled over one morning when the Baron made a pile of Methildis' books, to be discarded or destroyed. Among them were her sketches, her journals, and her poetry.

Wikerus yelled at his father, "What are you doing with these?"

"It is time to let them go, son, time to let *her* go. Take them if you wish, but they cannot stay here."

Wikerus began piling the books in his arms, but realized that he cannot take them all back to his simple lodgings with the Order. As he watched his father continue to make trash piles of Methildis' treasures, he broke down.

Finally, he mourned the loss of his mother as he should. He stumbled to the chair by the window, where Methildis used to read. He sat and he sobbed. Luitpold, not sure how to behave, left the room.

After a few minutes, Aleidis came in. Wikerus stood and Aleidis took him in her arms. He cried on her shoulder.

She whispered this prayer into his ear. "May the Lord grant mercy to this man, for he often refreshed me, and was not ashamed of my chains, he sought me diligently, and found me."

Wikerus thanked her for the prayer and told her that their time together was at an end.

"We cannot continue as we have been. Your role in this household has changed and I can no longer be a part of it."

Aleidis let go of him and stepped back. She begged him not to leave, citing all that he had done for her and all that she still must learn. Wikerus took Methildis' journal and prayer book from the pile of her treasures.

"You are beyond what I can assist," he assured her, "read these and learn from a much wiser person than I."

She took Methildis' books and held them tightly to her.

"Do not let your husband part you from them," he told her. "With them, you are in the hands of the person who raised me."

Wikerus took the book of his mother's poetry, kissed Aleidis as a son and friend should, retreated to his bedroom, assembled no more than the book and those things which accompanied him on his journey home, embraced his father, wishing him well, and he left Castle Tannhausen for the very last time. As he reached the threshold of the courtyard, Aleidis yelled to him from the castle doors. He turned his horse around to face her. She promised him that her home will always be his and begged that he will think of her fondly. He nodded his head, turned the horse, and rode away.

He decided to ride the path he took with Father Stefan and the two knights who escorted him to Meersburg Castle, hoping the memories would focus him. The ride certainly took him through some pungent memories. Although he rode much faster than he did in the cart years ago, he stopped and rested in the same villages, with the same friars, receiving the same paltry accommodations. It was plenty for him.

His trip was different than the last time he had made it. He was a decorated knight and a hero of the Teutonic Order. Every person he encountered between Tannhausen and Meersburg honored him, but no place more than his destination. Count Konradin kept abreast of all of the happenings during the crusade. When Wikerus and the others were captured and imprisoned, the Count fasted, eating only one meal before sunrise each day, and one after sunset. When he greeted Wikerus on the same old bridge, he was a much thinner man. He may not have been as hearty in the center, but his voice was the same — the same happy, booming, rich, oily voice.

Count Konradin had hosted many members of the Teutonic Order, being so near to Mainau Island and so well connected to its leadership. He knew how the knights ate, slept, and prayed. When Wikerus was in his home, despite the ceremonial dress, Konradin did not see a Teutonic Knight, a warrior monk. He saw the son of his dear departed Methildis. He kept Wikerus up in conversation, when the hour of day demanded his prayers. He gave him more food and drink than any monk in any holy order was accustomed to consuming.

The seasoned knight in front of Konradin was the loyal man's last living connection to his lifelong friend. He tried to milk each drop of Methildis out of the few conversations they had together. Wikerus stayed for three days, and sent word to the island that he would be returning to Trazperch Castle as soon as the Count could spare him. Wikerus' time in Meersburg did nothing to adhere him to the ways of the Order. Life as a Teutonic Knight seemed half a world away, and his conversations with Konradin only pulled him further.

On Wikerus' last evening in Meersburg, after the castle had gone silent and dark, except for a small fire in the library, where a count and a knight spoke openly and honestly, Konradin asked, "From what I have heard, you have faced your Pit of Starvation, as Stefan said you would. Our little hole here must seem like a laughable little thing next to your experiences of war and imprisonment. But I see in your eyes something very different than the shine of the transcended."

"You are correct," Wikerus replied with no brightness in his expression, "I was put in my own *Pit*. Only, I have not yet been taken out. I am waiting for someone to lower a rope and elevate me to that life of blissful understanding, where I am above the pains of life, like I see in Andreas and Rikard."

"Yes, I can see that is true, my boy. You are still starving, being kept in painful preparation for something. Perhaps the Order is not where you will find that rope."

Wikerus dropped his head and sat in silence for several minutes. Konradin's suggestion was not new to his thoughts. They rather hardened a thought that he had worked to keep pliable. When he raised his head to reengage in conversation, there was little to say. He embraced his friend and excused himself to bed. His sleep was short and disturbed regularly by thoughts that shook him awake. He left as the sun rose. Konradin was already up, dressed and ready to see him off. After a lengthy and covetous embrace, Wikerus rode east from Meersburg, toward Trazperch Castle.

By midday, Wikerus' horse must have been desperate for a good gallop. His rider did not care for speed. Wikerus' mind wandered, and he kept his pace slow with hopes that he could clear his thoughts before arriving, and join his brothers in the right state of mind. A breathless sprint would have been more conducive to that end. His mind drifted from subject to subject.

He thought of his mother, of Father Stefan and the many close associations he acquired in training and war. But it was when he thought of Aleidis that his mind drifted no more. He missed her. He missed the depth of their connection. He missed the influence of her feminine spirituality, and the thought of cloistering himself with the other knights and their wafting masculinity repelled him. He thought of his mother's books and wondered if Aleidis was reading them.

He drew his horse to a sudden stop, afraid that a single step closer to Trazperch Castle would take all air from his body. He dismounted his horse, sat against a tree and opened the book of Methildis' poetry. The verses had two primary themes — the goodness of God and the beauty of God's creation. Methildis saw beauty in everything under the sky. Where beauty was not immediately apparent, she looked more deeply. She peeled and pried until the beauty within was evident. Her poetry expressed the beauty of many things and many people. Hills and grass, stars and streams, men and women and children of all ages, buildings and animals, swords and vases — all of these things were described in her verses. Reading them, Wikerus saw through his mother's eyes, and the world around him was more colorful. He wondered why he had not seen so clearly before, why the world and everything in it was not as beautiful to his eyes as it was to his mother's.

Wikerus read a poem about a single tree, just one tree outside of the Tannhausen courtyard, a tree that Wikerus had glanced over thousands of times. After reading the poem, he chastised himself for not noticing the lovely complexities, the intricate architecture of the trunk and branches, the color dynamics from leaf to leaf, and from leaf to branch. Through the words, Wikerus was able to clearly visualize the old tree. He did not recall some image that had been filed away since his childhood. The poem painted something magnificent.

"Hers was an amazing world," he said out loud, "How is it that others can't see?"

He looked up from the pages, to a tree across the road from him. He tried to see it as his mother would have. The lines and angles, the geometry of the branches, clusters and spaces, bright green against deep brown, and the whole thing contrasted against the blue sky beyond, the coarseness of the bark and all of the detailed images it cut — it all sprang into his eyes at once.

"My God!" he exclaimed, "It is exquisite."

He turned his attention to another tree, the magnificence of which exploded onto his senses. He scanned his eyes ravenously until he settled on a small stone. He drew near to it and studied it closely. There were dozens of colors speckled around it. Its pits and bumps played a coy game of hide and seek with each other. Its uniqueness was only rivaled by its beauty.

Wikerus looked to his horse. It was such a handsome horse. Any passer-by would say it was a handsome horse. But they would not see it as Wikerus did then. The coarseness of the hairs, deepness of the dark brown eyes, even the highs and lows of its whinny had complexities he had been blind to before.

"Is the whole world like this?" he asked himself.

A tree, a rock, and a horse, three of the most commonplace things to pass a human eye, bedazzled him and intoxicated him with their intensity of expression, expressing praise for the God that made them.

"The world must be like this," he whispered to himself as his face lit, "everything and everyone."

Hungry to see more through his new vision, he mounted his horse, but he could not prod it forward. Everything about his previous life, his previous blindness, as he considered it, was drab to him. How could he lock himself into a chapel and pray, or be shipped to command a new castle, when there is a world of wonders all around him? He dismounted the horse and took only a pen, his mother's book, the bag with his wartime tunic, and the Marian Sword at his hip. He left the pouch of money strapped to the saddle. He slapped the horse and sent it trotting away to Trazperch Castle. He turned neither up nor down the road, but stepped into the woods beside it.

He walked at a snail's pace, his eyes darting left and right, up and down, fixing on the depth and complexity of beauty, peeking shyly from the most mundane objects. As he walked without aim, he tried to picture Aleidis through his new vision. Had he been numb to *her* hidden beauty? Of course he had. He wanted to see her hair and her skin, her eyes and the tiny wrinkles on the back of her hand with his newly opened eyes. But he knew it was best that he could not. His new vision would have erased that precious thin line of appropriateness that stood between them.

Wikerus could have traveled to Trazperch and requested dismissal from the Teutonic Order. After his accomplishments in war, it would certainly have been granted. But he would not take a single step in the direction of his former life. So, he was a deserter. He had taken vows of chastity, poverty, and obedience. He remained chaste. He remained poor. He violated his vow of obedience to the

Order. He abandoned his brothers in the Cross. He didn't care. He wanted nothing but to see more of the world through Methildis' exquisite eyes. So he roamed. There had been many chapters of his life, from birth through training and fighting, starving and recovering. He turned the page on all of it without regret or retrospection. As he stepped into those woods, he walked into a new life, one that in very few ways resembled anything known by him or anyone else.

CHAPTER 25
The Spear of Antioch

READERS, PLEASE PARDON ME, but I must stray from our narrative. I will bring us back to Wikerus in good time. I beg your indulgence as I return your thoughts to the Middle East, to the docks of Damietta, on the shore of Egypt, when the crusaders retreated into the Venetian ships that were to take them home. Our hero's friends, Andreas and Rikard did not return with the Buchhorn army to the shore of Lake Constance. They involved themselves in an adventure, which will play its part in the later pages of this story and others.

They boarded the last ship departing Damietta. This ship was filled with knights of Cyprus, Croatia, and Hungary. The ship sailed to Cyprus, where it was to remain docked for a week before sailing to Croatia, and later to Venice. During the voyage to Cyprus, weather was placid, and the wind was gentle. They sailed slowly, and with little enough worry for conversations of the most fantastical nature to rise and tickle the boards.

In light of the most recent events, it is not surprising that top among the stories were tales of the early crusades, the Holy Land, and sacred holy relics. One particular tale from the First Crusade seduced Andreas' attention. It was a relic of the most sacred order, for it had touched the Blood of Christ. One crusty old Hungarian knight told the story of the Holy Lance. It sparked our two travelers into the most unexpected adventure, which in time would impact the fate of millions.

The ship was crammed well past its intended capacity. Backs were stiff, legs were jittery, and hearts came in every design from elation to despair. Stories kept their minds off of what ailed them. The old knight cleared a path to pace back and forth in front of his audience, with eager ears on both sides of him. He cleared his throat several times, until he knew he had their attention.

He began loudly, almost too loudly, but settled into an appropriate volume, "On a hill, just outside the northern gates of Jerusalem, called Golgotha, or Calvary by others, three bloody bodies were nailed to their crosses. One, of course, was our Lord. The sun was sinking on the eve of the Sabbath, and the business of executions had to finish quickly. To be certain that our Lord was dead, a Roman Centurion named Longinus thrust his Roman spear into the side of Christ. Blood and water sprayed from the wound and ran down the spear. The Spear of Longinus, like the True Cross, bore the blood of Christ and was imbued with divine powers."

He stomped his first step without speaking, then his second, as he began again, "The spear went back to the armory, where it sat among a thousand other spears, until the year 66. A great Jewish rebellion against the Romans drove the Roman governor, Gessius Florus, and all of the Roman officials, out of Jerusalem. In the chaos, the Christians of the city set to finding the Holy Lance."

The knight's paces quickened as he rolled on. There was little room below deck, and the feet and legs of the seated knights listening to the tale spread across the Hungarian's path. Still, he strode dramatically, stepping over armored limbs and thundering on. He would stop face to face with one listener, or grab another by the shoulders.

Although they knew the story, they were enamored by the dynamic retelling, and the Hungarian continued, "They brought a small child into the Roman armory, a little girl no more than five… who could not walk. They set her on the floor and began touching her with every spear in the armory. They were hurried and desperate, and cut the girl several times with the failing spears. Finally, a neighbor of the crippled girl approached her with an ordinary spear. He slipped as he drew the spear to touch the child. He drove the tip onto the girl's chest with his full weight falling down. Everyone who watched thought she was dead. But the spear did not pierce the child. Where the tip struck her, there was not a mark. They lifted her and examined her, and all of the cuts made by the other spears were gone. The girl demanded to be set down. They placed her on her feet and she ran from the armory to her home."

Eyes were wide and breath was held as this master storyteller built the suspense.

"What happened to the spear?" a fellow passenger shouted.

"The Christians removed the wooden shaft from the head. They took the spear head to Antioch and hid it in that Christian city, and there it remained. In 637, Antioch was taken by the Rashidun, and all knowledge that the Holy Lance was ever there died in time. In 969, the city was retaken by the Byzantine Emperor Nikephoros II, and rumors began to arise about a great Christian relic hidden in Antioch. Some took the rumors seriously and dedicated their lives to finding it, not knowing what sort of relic they sought. In 1084 Antioch was captured by the Sultan of Rum, and was once again outside of the reach of devout Christians. But only fourteen years later, while the rumors were still fresh, our great crusade took control of the Christian city of Antioch."

Those few crusaders who did not already know the Hungarian's version of the spear's story, most assuredly knew of the First Crusade, and the details that would soon thunder from the Hungarian's lips, "The holy knights took Antioch, but were immediately surrounded, and the walls they had just overcome, became their only protection. They were outnumbered. They were hungry. There was no escape without engaging a superior army. They could sit and starve, or they could attack and be slaughtered. The great crusade was doomed before ever reaching Jerusalem."

He told the story with such gloomy foreboding in his voice, that his audience almost forgot what happened next, "The enemy was going to breach the walls and the crusaders prepared for death. One lowly monk named Peter Bartholomew went to bed with no expectation of living through the next day. But in his dreams, he was visited by Saint Andrew the Apostle. Saint Andrew told him that the Holy Lance that pierced the side of Christ and bore his Sacred Blood, was buried in the Church of Saint Peter, in the center of Antioch. The crusaders dug where Saint Andrew said the spear tip would be. They found nothing until the monk leaped into the hole and the Holy Lance appeared."

A round of cheers and applause from below the deck could be heard from the crow's nest, shaking the boards. The Hungarian had his audience swelling with Crusader pride, forgetful of their recent defeat, and he thundered on, "With the Spear of Longinus in hand, the crusaders rushed from the city gates. They demolished the army that encased them, sending the few survivors retreating in confusion and chaos. The spear marched triumphantly into the holy city of Jerusalem. It saved the crusade and won back the Holy Land."

The Hungarian hushed his zealous audience and told the sad ending of his story, "In 1187, when Jerusalem was lost to Saladin, the Holy Spear of Antioch was bargained and traded between Muslim leaders in their constant struggle for supremacy among themselves. We don't know where it is today, but it is outside of the Christian world, waiting to be found and wielded again by Christian hands."

"It is said," he concluded, "that the spear can pierce any armor worn by the unrighteous, and can do no harm to the innocent. That is why the crippled child was unharmed, though the Lance struck her with its sharp tip and the full weight of a man behind it. The loss of the True Cross is tragic. But the Spear... if we could retrieve the Spear, the armies of Christ would march triumphantly, as they did when they rode out of Antioch."

The Hungarian's story blended into other tales, told by other knights. Andreas' thoughts remained on the Spear of Antioch. The ship was loud, with multiple simultaneous conversations and eruptions of laughter and song. It was hard to hear the nearest person. Rikard was trying to listen to a Croatian's story of his family estate and one mysterious visitor who came selling relics from the Far East. Andreas tapped him on his shoulder to get his attention.

Rikard turned to him and said, "The Spear of Longinus is in Syria."

His voice was haunting and echoed in Andreas' ears. It did not sound like Rikard, but the ship was noisy and voices blended in and out of each other.

Andreas asked him, "How do you know it is in Syria?"

Among all the noise, Rikard answered in confusion, "What is in Syria?"

"For heaven's sake," Andreas scolded, "the Holy Lance. Who told you it was in Syria?"

Rikard, a little offended at Andreas' tone, shouted through the voices, "The Hungarian said nothing about Syria. Weren't you listening? He said that no Christian knows where it is."

"Then why did you—," Andreas stopped himself short and compared the voice he heard when Rikard spoke of Syria with the one yelling at him then, the one he had known for years. They were not the same voice. He looked quickly around him, but nobody was addressing him. Nobody was looking at him.

"When I tapped your shoulder, and you turned to me and spoke," he inquired, "what did you say to me?"

"I asked you if you believed the Croatian, when he spoke of the magic beads. Weren't you listening?"

Andreas took Rikard by the shoulders, drew him to his face, and asked, "You said nothing of the Holy Lance, nothing of Syria?"

Rikard just stared at him and shook his head. Andreas grabbed his old friend by the wrist and dragged him onto the deck, where the only noise was from the sea.

Andreas stood toe-to-toe with Rikard, draped his forearms over the blacksmith's shoulders, and said, "You turned to me and said that the Spear of Longinus is in Syria. It came from your mouth. Your lips were moving, but it was not your voice."

"I tell you, friend, when I turned to you, I spoke only of the Croatian's tale of the magic beads. If you heard about the spear, it did not come from me."

Andreas stood confused, still staring into Rikard's eyes.

Rikard pondered for a moment, then suggested, "If you say the voice came from my mouth, but was not mine, and it spoke words I do not remember saying, perhaps, like Peter Bartholomew, you are hearing from Saint Andrew.

The two old friends walked to the rails together and leaned over the gentle sea for several minutes, not saying a word, but both considering what Rikard said. The silence was long, but not awkward, for both followed similar trains of thought. Rikard finally looked at Andreas and placed his hand palm up on the rail.

Andreas grabbed his hand and they spoke together, "We go to Syria."

They nodded to each other, then shared a tight embrace. They did not rejoin the other knights with their stories and songs, but isolated themselves as well as possible until they landed in Cyprus. From Cyprus, while journeys to the west were being arranged and organized, Andreas and Rikard found other accommodations. They found a ship going east. After four days in Cyprus, Andreas and Rikard sailed back to the Middle East, to upper Galilee.

They landed near the Monfort estate, held by a standing contingent of Templar and Teutonic Knights. The knights welcomed their two visitors. Rikard was well-famous for his design of the floating siege tower that took the harbor tower at Damietta. They had a home at Monfort as long as they wished to stay. They did not wish to stay, and after securing provisions for a blind expedition, they dressed themselves as simple pilgrims and set out toward Syria. The Templars offered themselves as escorts and tried to pry from them the nature of their mission. They denied the offer, and only revealed that, like their monastic hosts, they worked for God.

Andreas and Rikard sought the local trade paths and kept their ears alert for any cryptic hint of the sacred spear. They worked and they traded. They bargained and they worked some more. Long days of toil, just to survive, often brought them to the sunset no nearer to their quest. For more than a full year they worked their way together, to and around Syria, sometimes getting separated for weeks at a time. Rikard worked his trade, carrying always on his belt a small forging hammer, while Andreas found a talent for whittling wood into figurines. It was a living that received more of his labor than the search for the Spear of Antioch. It received more of his labor, more of his time, but not more of his mind or heart. The voice of Saint Andrew, gliding sweetly and mysteriously from Rikard's lips, branded itself to the deepest layer of his soul. It was there with his first breath each morning, and all that echoed in his silent ears when he put his head down each night.

Finally, after more than a year in Syria, Rikard found himself in the employment of one of al-Kamil's generals. He hired Andreas to fashion the woodwork of their weapons. Rikard's position as blacksmith allowed him to mingle with soldiers of all ranks. They talked and he listened. They were planning to defend an attack from the Sultan's brother, al-Ashraf. The soldiers in al-Kamil's army were frightened. They heard that al-Ashraf was in possession of a powerful Christian relic. Trying not to appear too eager, Rikard pressed for details. By the descriptions that reached him he was confident that they had found the sacred spear.

Each night, he passed to Andreas all that he learned that day. When al-Ashraf's army approached their encampment, they knew their time to act had come. They left the Sultan's army at sunset and snuck into al-Ashraf's camp. They set their aim on the largest and most decorated tent. There, beside al-Ashraf, was a small chest with a lock. Andreas knelt beside the chest and prayed to Saint Andrew for guidance. He heard nothing but the rustling of men outside. He took the chest. He and Rikard left the tent and snuck their way to the outskirts of the camp.

They were seen by a guard, who recognized al-Ashraf's chest and called for his fellows to pursue them. Twenty soldiers followed them. They could not retreat back to al-Kamil's army. The truth would serve them no better there. They broke for the wilderness, for some dry and lonely hills, too forbidding for civilization. The band of soldiers caught up with them. Andreas fell and dropped the chest. It broke and a piece of metal fell from it. It was about the length of his arm from elbow to fingertip. Rikard grabbed him by the hand and yanked him to his feet, away from the treasure.

The soldiers surrounded them. One of them picked up the spear head and held it in his hand like a knife. The soldiers rushed them. Andreas and Rikard fought valiantly, Andreas with a short sword and Rikard with nothing but his forging hammer. Rikard was slashed across his right arm and left thigh. While he staggered, the soldiers laughed at him and mocked him, limping in circles. One kicked him in the wound on his leg and knocked him to the ground. Five others seized Andreas, took his sword, and held their swords to him.

The leader of the soldiers came at Rikard with the relic in his hand. He held it high and asked, "Is this what you came for? Would you like me to give it to you?"

Rikard struggled to his feet. He ripped the front of his shirt and exposed his chest, looking up to the light pink of the rising sun.

The soldiers rightfully assumed that Andreas and Rikard came from the al-Kamil camp, but their true identity was revealed when Andreas shouted in German, "Nein, bitte nein (No, please no)."

Rikard looked peacefully at his friend and recited from the old Hungarian's tale, "Kein Schaden für die Unschuldigen (No harm to the innocent)."

Andreas' faith swelled and he prayed not for Rikard's life, but that they would deserve to be carriers of the Holy Lance. The leader bore down on Rikard, driving the tip toward his heart. It hit the blacksmith's chest and sent a spark into the dim sky. The spear head flew from the soldier's hand. The soldiers did not follow the relic as it went over their heads and into the sand. Their attention was on Rikard, whose chest showed no marks from the forceful thrust. And they watched the wounds on his arm and leg seal shut, without a scar. Those who had held tightly to Andreas let their arms fall flatly at their sides.

Andreas ran unnoticed to the relic and wielded it against his enemies. The soldiers were more afraid of Rikard, who was still standing bare-breasted to them. They did not attribute the miracle to the weapon in Andreas' hand, but to Rikard himself. They backed away from him, all twenty soldiers, fearing the powerful sorcerer they believed Rikard to be, until Andreas slayed the first one with the Holy Lance.

The others turned on Andreas and attacked. Any wound he might have suffered while wielding the relic surely would have healed immediately. Those services were not needed. The piercing power of the relic against the unrighteous soldiers coupled exquisitely with Andreas' skill. Sixteen of the soldiers were dead before the other four decided to retreat back to their camp.

As the shy sun slowly brightened the sky, Andreas and Rikard fled to the hills, knowing that a force much larger than twenty would soon be in pursuit. There would be no way to reach the coastal plains of Israel, and crusader held land, while carrying the notorious relic. Al-Ashraf had spies in every town and village, all on the lookout for the distinct relic. Rikard gathered stones and built a kiln, while Andreas gathered fuel. The blacksmith forged the Spear of Longinus into two simple knifes, not remarkable in appearance. They appeared as an ordinary tool, like one might see on any belt on any wandering merchant or pilgrim.

They both wore a simple knife with divine powers at their hip, while they worked their way as humble travelers, much as they had for the previous year, staying by the other's side through wilderness and village, in caravan and alone, until they came to the Monfort Estate. Neither the Templars nor the Teutonic Knights at Monfort would have allowed them to depart with the Holy Lance. But they didn't have a Roman spear head, did they? They bore only simple knifes, and the Pope's knights arranged their passage back to Germany.

Andreas did not trust the relics in the hands of the Pope. He had to place them in the care of someone powerful enough to protect them, yet righteous and pious enough not to be tempted by their powers. They decided to hide one knife buried beneath the Pit of Starvation in Meersburg Castle, under the watch of their good master, Count Konradin. They had to decide on another. Only one man came to mind. They agreed. The other half of the Holy Spear of Longinus would go to Ludwig von Wittelsbach, Duke of Bavaria. They waited for him in Kelheim. Friends of Count Konradin von Buchhorn were welcome in any decent household. Andreas and Rikard were treated as family. When word came that the Duke was in town, they met with him at the ducal residence. They had an interesting, complex, and fascinating story to tell, beginning with Rikard's flamboyant reenactment of the Hungarian knight's tale, with vivid descriptions of their year-long attempt to locate the relic, a dramatic telling of the fight in the Syrian hills and Rikard's bare-breasted faith, and ending with their arrival in Kelheim.

Duke Ludwig was honored beyond expression to be chosen for the responsibility of caring for the Holy Lance. He was well used to shouldering such a weight. He held another title, one infinitely dearer to him than the *Duke of Bavaria* or *Commander of Imperial Forces*. Like his father before him, and the long line of his ancestors back to the year 515, Ludwig was the Swan Knight, the keeper of an ancient and sacred secret, which Wikerus would soon stumble upon quite accidentally.

CHAPTER 26
The Swan Knights

As I promised, I return our story to Wikerus. He wandered with no notion or concern of direction. His senses stung with the sharpness of beauty to which he had just awakened, like ripping off a callus and exposing the hyper-sensitive skin beneath it. The colors of the world were almost painfully vibrant. Flavors of the most mundane items, like bread or wine, exploded in his mouth with intricacies he never noticed before, spinning his head to identify, categorize, and appreciate each sensation. Smells seemed to fill his face, waft through his head, and occupy every space beneath his skin.

His whole life, Wikerus' sleep had been disturbed by raucous dreams, pleasant and unpleasant. But during this sensual renaissance, walking and roaming endlessly, his mind, body, and spirit were exhausted by the end of the day, and they collapsed in each other's arms each night. His sleep, although usually on hard ground or against a tree, was deep, sound, and undisturbed.

Every sensation was magnified, and in its own way, deemed pleasurable, even hunger. Wikerus felt much hunger. He left his money on the horse when he sent it away without him. He fed himself by singing. His own poetry, those attempts to capture his new world in his own words, was clumsy at first. His mouth and pen stuttered together as they tried to cram the world's complex beauty into the narrow chamber of written language. So, he sang from the book of his mother's poetry. His voice and her words combined to bemuse people wherever he roamed. He was paid modestly but often fed abundantly.

He was offered steady money for his talents, but was loathed to remain in one place for more than a day. He awoke each morning eager to experience the smell of dirt, or the sight of a new stranger's hair in the breeze. In the days that it often took to travel by foot, from one town to the next, he generally did not eat. It was a strange existence for a decorated Teutonic Knight and the son of a baron. He continued to wear his full armor, with his Teutonic cloak and bloody wartime tunic as he traveled and performed. It drew just enough attention to guarantee him an audience — and a meal. For two months he moved about southern Swabia and Bavaria in this way.

One afternoon, after walking for hours along a path through a forest, he was caught in a storm. He sat under a tree to wait it out. After falling asleep comfortably, he awoke in the middle of the night, chilled to the bone and excessively hungry. A weak and fruitless attempt to find food, shelter, and warmth followed. Wikerus collapsed in the mud of an empty path in the wee hours of a dreary night.

He opened his eyes to a warmly lit room. By the furnishings and décor, it was plain that he was in house of substantial means. He had been found by a servant from Werdenfels Castle, north of Garmisch-Partenkirchen. Construction of the castle was not yet completed, but sections were complete and already lavishly furnished. It was to be a fortress of the Teutonic Knights. The castle never made it into the possession of the Order. It fell later to the Prince-Bishopric of Freising, but that is neither here nor there. When Wikerus awoke in the opulent setting, construction was under the control of Count Gottfried von

Löwenstein. The land was donated by the family von Vollrads, Aleidis' cousins. That connection was never discovered by anyone involved in this story.

The Teutonic cloak and armor, and more importantly, the prestigious Sword of the Marian Cross, guaranteed Wikerus the finest treatment in what was meant to be a Teutonic Order stronghold. A priest of the Teutonic Order attended Wikerus, and when our hero awoke, informed him that word was sent to Trazperch Castle of his discovery and recovery. The monk assured him that he would be fully recovered and with his brothers again soon.

Wikerus was tired of hunger, and the incident numbed him temporarily to the sensual eruptions he had experienced. He considered returning to the Order and pursuing the life for which, until recently, he had praised God. As he waited for knights of the Order to come get him, he rested and he thought. Flashbacks of battles in Egypt mixed toxically with his new vision of human beauty and melted away any temptation to reclaim a warrior's life. He forced himself wobbly to his feet and left Werdenfels Castle on his own, claiming a desire for fresh air and a walk. He moved quickly for his condition, wanting to be far gone from the castle before the knights arrived to retrieve him.

Wikerus went north, to the eastern edge of the Graswang Valley. The valley was open, warm, green, and welcoming. He followed it west and prayed for the return of his keenly receptive senses. But it was not as before. It was tainted by his flashbacks of war, and run through the filter of physical weakness and the memory of extreme hunger. He feared being caught and tried for desertion. He begged God for direction, for any sign of God's will for him. A soldier, a poet, a monk, or a lover — he would have obeyed any hint from heaven, any subtle sign that told him where to point the tips of his boots.

After hours of walking, he was hungry again, for he had taken no food with him in his hasty retreat from the Teutonic fortress. Near the western end of Graswang Valley, he looked north. His eyes beheld the most picturesque scene he had ever encountered. A small, wooded valley ran north from the wide and sparse Graswang Valley. The mountains beyond crowned it regally. Something much deeper than the pleasure of his eyes called him to the little valley. It felt as if the very blood inside of him pushed against his skin in that direction. He turned north and explored.

Through a shielding of linden trees opened a magical place, a golden-green, wooded hill with a single rustic lodge. Wikerus walked to the lodge in hopes of finding its proprietors. He knocked on its door. The lodge was empty. It was well lived in. Stores of food could be easily seen through windows. It looked like a happy place, a family place with a thousand blissful memories. Something about it also spoke of trials and dark times long past.

The pantries of breads and vases of spirits tempted Wikerus. He was hungry and thirsty, and worn to the bone, having far from recovered from his night in the cold storm. There was a strong temptation to enter the lodge, eat, drink, and rest himself. He would never do so without invitation, so he walked around to explore the other side of the quaint little valley.

Wikerus hiked several labored paces up a hill from the lodge when he was shocked out of his wits by the strangest noise, of which he could not imagine the cause. It began as a low crackling sound, like of glass breaking under a thin layer of water. The sound quickly emerged loud and crisp, a piercing, wicked crackle, like sustained thunder, but higher pitched and frighteningly near, and was accompanied by the appearance of a large circle in the air in front of him.

The terror of the sound was dwarfed by that of the menacing circle. Its outer edge was discernable, but inside it was indescribable. It was a circle of nothing, as if some huge beast took a bite out of the alpine air, ripped it from the scenery around it, and swallowed it out of sight. Wikerus could see nothing on the other side of the circle. Its edges wavered, like seeing it through vapors. It was simultaneously forbidding and seductively inviting.

Wikerus thought for a moment that he had died in Egypt, that his spirit returned to Germany, thinking itself still attached to his body, and that the circle of nothingness in front of him was there to pull his spirit away. Becoming keenly aware of his senses, he dismissed the idea. At any rate, it was quite unearthly and Wikerus did not know if it meant him harm. He drew his sword, waved it at the circle, and shouted for it to either attack him or leave him alone.

The circle did not attack or retreat, nor was it still. It continued to growl with its menacing crackle. Wikerus heard the slap of horse hooves to his left, behind him. They grew louder, obviously charging toward him at full gallop. His instincts told him to look, but his eyes refused to release the terrifying phenomenon in front of him.

A voice shouted from the approaching horse, "Who are you? Who are you?"

There was a violent, angry, desperate edge behind the words. Still, Wikerus could not turn away from the circle. The horse came to a stop directly behind him. Over the continuing crackle of the circle, he heard someone dismount the horse and walk toward him. He prayed it was help, someone of a righteous heart who could stand beside him against the faceless demon. Wikerus raised his sword higher, pointing the tip directly at the center of the circle.

He yelled, "Come at us! Do your best!"

The voice beside him laughed. It was not a maniacal cackle, with malicious intent, but a warm laugh, like a parent seeing endearing comedy in the antics of a young child. There was no fear in the laugh, which relaxed Wikerus' fears enough to turn his head. To his astonishment, he saw the warm and welcoming face of Duke Ludwig.

Seeing the former commander, and a face from which the most inspiring words had come to rally Wikerus' heart on more than one occasion, bolstered Wikerus' courage.

"Get behind me, my Duke," he shouted, waving his sword defensively at the circle.

The duke laughed more heartily, and obeyed, moving to stand directly behind the knight. Wikerus poked his sword forward tentatively, not at all sure which sort of assault would best damage this strange enemy in front of him. He felt Duke Ludwig grab him by a fistful of belt and tunic. Ludwig pulled him slowly backward. Wikerus took one long step away from the circle, and with a crackling snap, the circle disappeared, diminishing from the outside in, in a flash, until it was out of sight and sound.

Ludwig reached over Wikerus' shoulder and pushed on his shaking forearm until the tip of his sword rested on the ground. He turned Wikerus by the shoulders to face him. His wide grin and sporadic chuckle told our hero that all was well and there was nothing to be feared in that little valley. Wikerus stared at Ludwig, and he thought about the cozy lodge. He knew — somehow he just knew that the lodge and the valley, and probably the crackling circle, belonged to the dear and respected Duke of Bavaria.

Ludwig cupped the side of Wikerus' face with his palm and said, "Come, eat and drink with me. Your life is about to change."

As Wikerus walked beside Ludwig toward the lodge, he thought about his prayer to God, walking along the Graswang Valley, that some subtle sign of direction might guide his lost life. Well, a crackling circle of nothingness

269

and the sudden appearance of an honored duke saying, "Your life is about to change" is not exactly what he would have called *subtle*. So he accompanied Ludwig in absolute faith that his prayer was resoundingly answered.

They settled into the lodge. Like a humble servant, Ludwig waited on his young friend. Wikerus was worn and thin, pale and weak. Ludwig's concern was unhidden. Once the duke was satisfied that he had tended to the knight's needs as well as could be, he sat across from him at the lodge's dining table.

Ludwig told Wikerus things that would have made a normal person faint, or scoff in disbelief. Wikerus was by no means normal, and in the immediate wake of the experience with the circle, his tender spirit was ready to except anything the good duke told him.

"You have just shown me," Ludwig said in an earnest tone, while taking him by the hands, "that you and I are cousins."

"Cousins?" was the simple and confused response.

"Yes, we are both descendants of an ancient line of knights, sworn to the protection of the portal."

"The p…, p…," Wikerus could not get the word from his lips.

"The portal," Ludwig finished, "The portal to the Sweeter Realm. The crackling circle of nothingness you just encountered is a doorway to another world, to a wonderful place, filled with good and wonderful creatures, and you opened the portal with the blood in your body."

Wikerus' eyes peeled from the duke's and drifted to the table in front of him. He stared downward and tried to come to grips with the words he just heard.

After a few seconds, he asked, "Is it my father's blood or my mother's?"

"I cannot answer that," Ludwig replied, "I do not know of any connection my family has with the Lords of

Tannhausen. Perhaps your enchanted blood comes from your mother."

At the words "enchanted blood", Wikerus shivered from scalp to toe.

"I should have known," Ludwig continued, "in the prison and on the roads of Egypt, I should have known that our blood ran through you. It was on brilliant display and I failed to see it. Had I known, I would have taken you directly here from Rome."

Wikerus' eyes rose again to lock with Ludwig's, and he asked, "Who are we? What is special about our blood? Does your blood open the portal as well?"

"Yes, it does, as did my father's, my great-grandmother's, and also my son's. I am the Swan Knight. Each generation, for seven hundred years, has had a Swan Knight, just one from our family, who is responsible for the safeguard of the portal and its secrecy, for the protection of the creatures we allow to pass through it, and for maintaining goodly relations with the Queen of the Land and Shallow Waters."

"The Queen of…?"

Ludwig squeezed Wikerus' held hands, released them, patted the table a few times, and said, "I have told you enough for now. I must consult with a friend before anything else can be said or done. Rest today. Sleep tonight. Tomorrow you will take my horse and fetch supplies for the lodge. When you return, I will have more to tell you."

CHAPTER 27
Inhabitants of the Portal Valley

WIKERUS LEFT EARLY THE NEXT MORNING, after a light breakfast and easy conversation. He had so many questions to ask the Swan Knight. Ludwig was particular to avoid any discussions of the mystical secrets of his little valley until after consulting with his friend. The breakfast conversation was warm in affection, but awkward in content. Wikerus' burning questions grew in flame as he mounted Ludwig's horse and rode from the valley.

Once Ludwig was alone in the valley, he opened the portal and summoned his friend — a giant swan who stood eye to eye with the duke, when his neck stretched high. He was known to the line of Swan Knights as *The Ancient One*. Except for the Queen of the Land and Shallow Waters, he was the oldest creature anyone on either side of the portal knew. The swan had been the teacher of the Swan Knight's children since the legendary Lohengrin. It was he who dubbed the Swan Knights and swore them into their lifelong commitments. It was after him that the title derived its name.

Ludwig and The Ancient One had much to discuss in Wikerus' absence. The swan knew all about the Tannhäuser. Ludwig spoke often and highly of him since returning from war. Although only the Swan Knight and his immediate family knew the secrets of the Portal Valley, the sacred blood sat ignorantly across southern Germany and beyond. It was inevitable that a special wanderer would someday enter the valley and trigger the portal to open. They both agreed that they were fortunate the wanderer was Wikerus, one who not only had the goodness to share in the duties of the valley, but who also had the openness of heart and the trust in God to serve the Portal Valley faithfully.

Ludwig had told Wikerus only the minutest wonders of the portal and the Swan Knight lineage. His discussion with the swan was to determine how much the Tannhäuser should know. There was no sending him away in complete ignorance. He had opened the portal. He had seen it and heard it. The full truth behind the magical little valley was not only grander. It was sacred and of the utmost consequence to God's people. Its secrets had been guarded, often viciously, for seven hundred years.

The first Swan Knight was none other than Parsifal, the Knight of the Holy Grail. It was Parsifal's blood that first opened the portal. He was stabbed in that lonely Bavarian valley. He drank from the Grail and his wound sealed. Before it did, a single drop of his Grail enchanted blood hit the floor of the valley and the portal to the Sweeter Realm opened on the spot. Parsifal was the first to befriend the swan. Parsifal, the Grail Knight, placed the Holy Grail of Christ, the cup of the Last Supper, in which the first consecration of the Holy Eucharist occurred by the hands of Christ himself, into the safe possession of the Queen of the Land and Shallow Waters, in the Sweeter Realm, on the other side of the portal. That is what was at stake — not only the secrecy and protection of the Sweeter Realm, with all of its lovely, magnificent inhabitants, but the Cup of Christ and its powers, which had been fruitlessly sought by hearts both good and evil for centuries.

The Ancient One swore Parsifal into the service of the Queen of the Land and Shallow Waters, for the purpose of protecting the portal. Parsifal swore the loyalty of his descendants. To aid him, the Queen dispatched the swan to teach and train the children of the Swan Knights and prepare them for their hereditary duties. The swan raised and taught the descendants of Parsifal, from the Grail Knight's son, Lohengrin, all the way to Duke Ludwig of Bavaria. The swan had a current student — Otto von Wittelsbach, the only child of the duke.

The swan taught Otto in a broad range of subjects, even in military matters. But both he and Ludwig agreed that a seasoned holy knight might be a good addition to Otto's education. After debate, disagreement, and finally consensus, it was decided. Wikerus had Grail Blood. He was a lost descendant of Parsifal. He could remain in the valley, living in the lodge with the Swan Knight's family, teaching Otto and serving the Swan Knight as a steward of the portal. As to the full depth of the portal's secrets and the family's history, Wikerus would learn no more than he needed to know. The swan feared intensely the proliferation of the secrets. Ludwig was afraid that the weight of responsibility would be too much for the troubled knight. So, for different reasons, they settled on a prescription for the immediate future.

When Wikerus returned a few days later, Ludwig met him at the door of the lodge, while the swan hid inside. The Swan Knight could compose no speech to prepare Wikerus for the wonders he would soon meet. What he did not know was that Wikerus had already been primed for such wonders. Through his mother's poetry he was ready to receive any degree of mystic beauty that could possibly be put in his path. With no words of preparation but a warm and affectionate greeting, Ludwig took Wikerus inside and introduced him to the giant talking swan.

Wikerus did not stumble. He did not gawk or stare. He only smiled wide, and in the most comfortably cordial terms, he introduced himself to The Ancient One. Ludwig and the swan were both relieved at the reaction, and did not hesitate to bring Wikerus back to the portal and present to him more of the Queen's loyal subjects. The Ancient One swore Wikerus to a life of service and secrecy as an official Portal Steward. Wikerus recited his oath without trepidation.

Ludwig retrieved some casual clothing from his own wardrobe, handed it to Wikerus said, "You may remove your armor and your warrior's clothing. You are a Portal Steward now. You have no need of armor or your sword with the friends you are about to meet."

Wikerus changed, and the three of them walked to the back of the lodge and up the gentle slope to the portal point. Ludwig led the way, but it was not *his* enchanted blood that opened the portal. Each descendant of Parsifal has a unique trigger point, a specific distance from which the portal responds to the Grail Blood. The portal opens at a different speed and with a different crackling sound for each of them. Ludwig had not yet reached his trigger point when the portal opened from Wikerus' blood. There was no doubt at all in the Swan Knight's mind. The sound, the speed, the number of paces from the portal point, none of these were his. Wikerus had a powerful connection to the portal. It was more alert to his presence than to the duke's. Ludwig did not mind. It was not in his nature to be jealous. He took it as proof of Wikerus' goodness.

The creatures of the Sweeter Realm, who often waited at the portal point on their side for the Swan Knight or his son Otto to allow them into the valley to play or train, knew that the portal did not react to Ludwig or Otto. They stepped through tentatively, with keen eyes darting around. The first through was a pair of Scheriers.

The Scheriers are the Sweeter Realm's most playful and social breed of creatures. They walk on four legs. At the end of each is a hand-like claw with three fingers and a thumb. They are covered almost entirely in white fur. On all fours, they stand only halfway to the Swan Knight's knees. Their bodies are no wider than a human thigh, but are flat, not much thicker than the hearty wooden doors of Castle Tannhausen. Despite their tiny pointed faces, they have mid-range voices, with the females a little higher than the males. The Scheriers are fine conversationalist. They are witty yet polite — the most pleasant company anyone may wish to keep.

The first to step through was Rei'mund. The second, Mercedes, followed halfway up Rei'mund's back. At first, Wikerus thought that a second head protruded from the back of the first. He stood in disturbed amazement until he realized that it was two separate creatures he beheld.

"Be at ease, my friends," Ludwig told the Scheriers, "We have a new Portal Steward. This is Tannhäuser. He was with me in the Egyptian prison. He has been my dear friend, and now he is yours."

The Scheriers stepped away from the crackling portal and walked to Wikerus' feet. They closed their eyes, twisted their heads sideways, and pressed one ear to the ground — the traditional bow of the Scheriers.

"We are pleased to meet you," Rei'mund declared with the utmost pomp and pageantry a Scherier can muster.

Mercedes opened one eye toward Wikerus and smashed the formal atmosphere, speaking forth with clumsiness, "Uh…, yes…, just what Rei said. That's me too. I mean, I am also pleased to meet you."

Wikerus bowed low to his two new friends, tickled and half-giggling.

He returned upright and said with delight, "You speak German."

Mercedes answered quickly, still pressing one ear to the ground, "Of course, I mean yes. The swan taught us.

Well, he did not teach *us*, Rei and me. He taught the Sweeter Realm so we could speak with the Swan Knights. He taught our teachers, a few from each breed, and, well…"

Never particularly patient for rambling communication, The Ancient One interrupted, "With the approval of the Queen, I spread German through the Sweeter Realm centuries ago. Now they all learn it. It is their only common tongue."

Wikerus grinned wider with delight and asked, "Everyone in your world speaks German?"

Rei'mund began to answer, "Everyone in the Land and Shallow Waters, all of the Queen's subjects. The creatures of the Deep are —"

Ludwig stomped his foot on the ground beside the Scheriers and spoke sternly, "That is the Queen's business. Let us not burden Tannhäuser with everything at once."

The Scheriers raised themselves from their Scherier bow. Rei'mund nodded to Ludwig. Mercedes drew a deep inhale and opened her mouth to speak, but Rei'mund threw one claw over her mouth and asked Wikerus, "Will you be staying in the Portal Valley or traveling here?"

The swan answered for him, "He will be staying in the lodge. He is a Portal Steward now. There is no reason for him to be anywhere else."

He said it warmly, making Wikerus blush. But he meant it very differently. The swan feared humans. Recent events in the valley had given him *more* reasons to distrust. He loved the Swan Knights and their families, more than anything else, on either side of the portal. But he was terrified of the world beyond the Portal Valley. He had no intention of allowing Wikerus to leave the valley with such precious secrets in his head.

With all formal introductions behind them, the Scheriers were eager to play with their new friend.

"Come to the wrestling tree," Mercedes invited.

She sprinted into the woods behind the portal, away from the lodge. Rei'mund's grin nearly wrapped around the back of his little head. He darted after Mercedes. Wikerus looked at Ludwig, who nodded to him and gestured one hand in the direction of the Scheriers. Wikerus ran after them.

When he cleared his trigger point, and the portal was held open by the blood in Ludwig's body, the portal assumed the familiar crackle of the Swan Knight's presence. Three more creatures walked through from the Sweeter Realm. They were Unicorns.

The Unicorns are tall, goat-like creatures, with cloven hooves and long, wiry beards. Their shoulders sit higher than their hips, so that their backs slope downward. The horns are as individual as a human face. They spiral from skull to tip. Some spirals wrap loosely, two or three times around as it travels the length of the horn. Some wrap tightly, with fifteen to twenty circles around the horn from base to tip. The horns are generally white, regardless of the Unicorn's coat. Some have colors peeking through from the deep recesses of the spirals.

The Unicorns speak little. They can pass thought through a gentle touch of their horns, usually to the chest, back, or head of the recipient. To communicate with each other, they do not need to make contact with the horns. These three Unicorns stepped through and greeted the swan and Ludwig with gentle nods of their bearded heads. The first of them touched her horn to Ludwig's chest and in mere seconds received all there was to know about the new Portal Steward.

Three Unicorns, one giant swan, and Ludwig watched as Wikerus chased the Scheriers to their "Wrestling Tree". The Scheriers stopped at the base of a wide linden tree. Wikerus was too tall to stand upright under its thick lower branches. He stood at a distance and watched the game. Rei'mund gave Mercedes a kiss on the nose and began running around the base of the tree. Mercedes was right behind him. Together, they were just a flash of white fur circling the trunk.

Mercedes leaped forward and grabbed Rei'mund by his back legs. They careened away from the tree as a single ball of Scherier fur. When they stopped rolling, they wrestled each other for several minutes. It looked quite violent, and Wikerus' sympathetic heart wanted once or twice to break it up. But the Scheriers released each other, rolled to their backs, and laughed heartily.

Wikerus laughed with them, and he could hear Ludwig's rolling chuckle behind him. Mercedes wiggled to her feet, took two steps to Rei'mund, kissed him on the nose, and bolted toward the trunk of the Wrestling Tree, starting the next round of the games. Wikerus could not remember his heart ever being lighter than while watching the Scheriers play. After the second round, they invited him to join.

Wikerus had to bend low to avoid the branches. The Scheriers could make seven laps around the trunk for each made by Wikerus. So, Mercedes jumped on Rei'mund's back and Rei'mund carried her up Wikerus' leg and chest, and held to the collar of his shirt. Mercedes stretched forward and kissed Wikerus on the nose. Rei'mund released his grip on Wikerus and he plopped his flat body to the ground, with Mercedes still on top of him. He galloped with his passenger, around the base of the tree, and two Scherier heads peaked around the other side at Wikerus. Wikerus hunched more lowly and chased after them.

It looked more like the Scheriers chased Wikerus. They were right on his heels as they all circled the trunk. Finally, Mercedes slid back on Rei'mund so that her back half dragged on the ground behind them. Wikerus caught up and grabbed her legs. He plopped to his side and rolled away from the tree with both Scheriers on his chest. They all wrestled together for several minutes. The Scheriers climbed all over the steward's body, under his arms, around his neck, onto his shoulder. They tugged on his ears and pushed against his nose until Wikerus laid himself out flat on his back. The Scheriers sat side by side, perched on his chest, staring into his eyes.

Rei'mund let out a long and pleasing sigh, which Mercedes followed with, "We love you, Portal Steward. We love the Tannhäuser."

The Scheriers' eyes glowed with earnest affection and authentic goodness. There was nothing of deceit about them. They saw through Wikerus' eyes, to the spirit inside of him, and what they witnessed, those things only seen by the most discerning, they truly did love. No eyes had looked at him like that since the last time he saw his mother.

Rei'mund and Mercedes spent the night in the lodge, with Wikerus, Ludwig, and The Ancient One. During the course of the evening, many tales were told of the long and storied history of the Swan Knights and the Portal Valley. Ludwig and the swan interrupted when the tales dove too deeply into the secrets that were not for Wikerus to share. The stories, and the way they were told by the Scheriers, Ludwig, and the old teacher, did much to adhere Wikerus to his new life. With every fantastic story, the bonds of connection to his old life further dissolved. The magic of the valley, the portal, the Swan Knights, and the creatures of the Sweeter Realm felt more like home to him than any place he had ever been or any company he had ever kept. His prayers were answered. Wikerus found purpose and direction in his stewardship of the portal and in his friendship with the lovely creatures.

Ludwig gave Wikerus a room in the lodge, with a bed of his own. But it was not disturbed that night. Wikerus stayed in the main hall, in conversation and play with the Scheriers, until they all fell asleep on the floor. The next day, the Scheriers returned to the Sweeter Realm to tell others in the queendom about the new steward. During the next few weeks, more creatures came through the portal to meet Wikerus. Zweigwesens, Eulesängers, and a host of Sweeter Realm nomads from near the Queen's Lake, all unlike anything Wikerus had ever seen, read about, or imagined, came to pay their respects and represent their breeds.

All of them took quickly and warmly to the steward — all except for the Unicorns. They sensed something in the knight that unsettled them. Wikerus was usually first to rise, and first to rush to the portal point and open the gate to visitors from the Sweeter Realm. The Unicorns were usually the first to step through. They posted sentries at the portal point on the other side. They were uneasy and distrustful of Wikerus. They did not doubt his goodness. There was something else, something they could not articulate to the Swan Knight when he asked.

One morning, when Wikerus opened the portal with his Grail Blood, a tall, grey Unicorn, with a darker grey beard and mane, and a long, sharp horn, with loosely wrapping spirals and a hint of deep burgundy peeking from the depths of the recesses, stepped through alone. Her name was Tiefhorn. There were no Scheriers, no Zweigwesens, no other Unicorns, only Tiefhorn. The Unicorn lowered her horn and touched it to Wikerus' chest. Wikerus could feel his thoughts and memories flowing through that tiny point. Tiefhorn stomped and huffed through her beard as she received Wikerus' thoughts. She saw deeply into him, more deeply than Wikerus could see in himself. She did not speak to Ludwig of the experience. She knew how the duke adored his steward. The other Unicorns came to know, and although they remained cordial and respectful, they kept a cold distance from that morning on.

The Unicorns patrolled the perimeter of the valley. Fast, stealthy, and viciously loyal to the Swan Knight, they kept a constant presence. They were the first to spy Wikerus when he wandered to the lodge on his fateful first day. They watched and they prayed that he would simply pass through, as so many had done before. They met the duke on the nearest ridge that day and told him that a stranger had opened the portal. They, and Ludwig, were prepared to kill the intruder, until the Swan Knight realized his identity.

That initial suspicion never subsided for the Unicorns, as it had with all others. They remained ready to defend their homeland and the valley secrets should Wikerus prove untrustworthy. The horn connection with Tiefhorn did little to ease them. They saw that he was honest. They saw that he was faithful, and they saw that his affection for Ludwig and the creatures was genuine and pure. But they saw much more — weaknesses and a distinct unrootedness that troubled them exceedingly.

The Ancient One, who spoke often with the Unicorns and treasured their wise counsel, came to share their feelings. He too saw no dubious intentions in the increasingly care-free daily frolicking of the Portal Steward. What he saw that unsettled him was a lack of seriousness. He did not believe that Wikerus would remain in the valley for the rest of his life. And he would not be allowed to return to the normal world should he ever decide that the life of a Portal Steward was not for him.

Alone in the lodge together one afternoon, the swan relayed his concerns to Ludwig, telling him, "Of course he is good. Anyone can see that. He would give his soul for the creatures."

"What then?" Ludwig challenged him.

The swan answered, "He shows me no interest in the seriousness and responsibilities of his position. He wishes only the pleasures of the Portal Valley."

Ludwig assumed a soft and compassionate tone as he thought of Wikerus and said, "His heart is finally light. I will not burden it now with more than he needs to know. We should let him play. Let him come to adore the valley and the creatures. In time, he will take it seriously enough.

"I am not alone in my concerns," the swan added.

"I know," Ludwig said defensively, "the Unicorns—"

"No, it is not just them," the swan spoke gravely, "the Queen has her own fears."

"It is her duty as the Queen of the Land and Shallow Waters to fear for her queendom," Ludwig spoke with authority, "and it is my duty to safeguard the portal. I am the Swan Knight, like my fathers and mothers, back to your friend Parsifal."

The Ancient One lowered his head, mortified for challenging the Swan Knight as he did.

Ludwig, who loved the swan dearly and had trusted his advice and teaching since childhood, regretted his tone, and he added softly, "He has had a difficult life, but I have never seen such selfless righteousness outside of the family. Please be patient with him. He will come around. Until then, I am with you. We should watch him closely and guide him, shape him into a steward that Parsifal would have been happy to have at his side."

He knew that the swan loved his first human friend, and referencing the founding patriarch of the Swan Knights would soften the old bird's heart. The Ancient One squinted in mock distrust, knowing well the game Ludwig played with his heart. He bowed, lowering his long neck until it ran along the floor of the lodge, raised his head, smiled, and waddled forward to receive an embrace from his former student.

Fortunately for the steward, the opinions of the Unicorns, the swan, and even the Queen were not the only opinions that mattered. The Swan Knight's son, Otto, was soon to marry, and would bring his new bride into the family secrets, and assume his position as Wikerus' student. Perhaps more importantly still, the Swan Knight's wife, Duchess Ludmilla, the matriarch of the Portal Valley, would join them.

CHAPTER 28
A New Family

WIKERUS SPENT A FEW WEEKS IN THE PORTAL VALLEY, alone with Ludwig, the swan, and the visitors from the Sweeter Realm. The Swan Knight was particular not to place more of the valley wonders on his young friend than could be handled. He did not understand. With Wikerus' appetite for beauty, he could not consume it at a fast-enough rate. The creatures trickled in a few at a time, some in the course of their usual business with the Swan Knight, some invited by Ludwig or The Ancient One, and others sent by the Queen to gather information on the new Portal Steward.

Word spread quickly throughout the Scherier homeland that a new friend awaited them in Parsifal's valley. They were light of heart. Both playful and philosophical, their time with Wikerus was delightfully spent and adoringly observed by Ludwig, who had seen him during his darkest moments. The Scheriers who came regularly quickly came to love Wikerus — truly love him. On occasion, some would accidentally refer to him as a Scherier. The Swan Knight loved all subjects of the Queen. He had grown up with them, trained with them, and learned from them. He had been riding Unicorns around the surrounding woods since he was nine years old. Seeing Wikerus take so closely and tenderly to the creatures of the

Sweeter Realm further hardened an already binding affection he had for this story's hero.

One sunny morning, about two and a half weeks after Wikerus roamed into the valley, he went to the portal point to allow some friends through to play and study with him. On the other side, a family of five Eulesängers flew around a nearby tree, in a game similar to the Wrestling Tree. They were some of the Sweeter Realm's few flying breeds, ankle-high birds, with hooked beaks, and a bushy tail they dragged behind them when they walked. They spoke in high-pitched whistles that none of the humans understood. The swan understood them, as did a few of the more well-traveled Scheriers. The Eulesängers understood German and responded to the commands of the Swan Knight.

The family of five flew at an increasing rate, and in increasingly larger circles around the tree, as the game became more spirited. Wikerus arrived at his trigger point precisely as the Eulesängers flew at the portal point in the Sweeter Realm. The portal opened and the birds passed through unexpectedly, crashing in rapid succession against Wikerus' chest. The startled steward let out a shrill cry far higher in pitch than any note he had struck in all of his glorious chants. He fell to his back with the Eulesängers gripping to his shirt.

There they sat, five Eulesängers on Wikerus' chest, staring at him and awaiting his reaction. Three Scheriers who had already been in the woods of the valley heard the cry and galloped to the scene. A Zweigwesen, very serious in nature passed through the open portal to seek the counsel of the Swan Knight on matters concerning the Zweigwesen homeland. Two Unicorns came through to relieve the two that were patrolling the perimeter of the valley. All stood or sat still, staring at Wikerus.

One of the Eulesängers, youngest of his family, released a shrill whistle that imitated to perfection

286

Wikerus' cry. They all continued to stare. The little bird repeated the mocking whistle. The Scheriers began to chuckle. Wikerus lifted a broad smile. When the other Eulesängers saw that all was well and the mood was light, all five of them whistled in imitation of Wikerus. The Scheriers rolled with laughter. Wikerus laughed so hard that the Eulesängers struggled to steady themselves on his shaking chest. The Unicorns tried not to laugh. When the chuckling began nevertheless, they tried to hide it, but their wiry beards shook and pops of giggling air shot from their noses. Even the serious Zweigwesen, there on his serious errand, folded over in laughter.

Ludwig and the swan observed the scene from an anonymous distance. They too giggled slightly, but with a deeper sensation than the frivolous moods of the others. The fine feathers on the swan's neck rose. In his centuries with the Swan Knights, he had seen many people join the life of the valley as adults. He could recall none who took so quickly to the lovely spirit of the Queen's subjects. Wikerus looked at home there, on his back at the open portal, with a host of Eulesängers on his chest, accepting with joy the good-hearted mocking of his new family.

In those weeks, Ludwig and the swan spoke often of Wikerus. The swan was afraid that Wikerus was *too* light of heart. None of the sober darkness that should come with the secrets they shared were apparent in his daily interactions with the creatures. Somewhere deep in his heart, Ludwig agreed, but was strenuously reluctant to allow those thoughts near the forefront of his contemplations. Battles had raged in protection of the portal's secrecy. Blood was spilled, often under morally ambiguous circumstances. It was a darkness faced by almost all who had called the Portal Valley their home. Life in the valley came with that burden, and the swan was not confident that Wikerus would rise to such an occasion.

Ludwig had seen so much misery in such a young and righteous man, he could only delight in the absence of it now.

"He has not removed his darkness," the swan reminded him, "he has only stored it deeply, to fester and swell. He is a child, hiding within him the horrors of nine lifetimes."

Ludwig knew his old teacher was right, but continued to excuse Wikerus and promise that all would be right in the end.

"The Unicorns see it clearly," the swan warned, "that deep darkness. He does not let it breath. He does not show it light. And when it is ready to escape him, the consequences could jeopardize all that your family has protected for seven hundred years."

The opinions of the swan were always weighed heavily, but Ludwig was the Swan Knight. The title, the valley, and all of its precious secrets were his by inheritance to protect.

The Swan Knight spoke, "Soon Otto will return with his wife, and my own dear wife will join us. Tannhäuser will have new considerations, new influences, and new family. I know him. He will rise to the responsibilities we have placed on him."

With a gnawing apprehension in his wise old heart, the swan had no choice but to yield to the Swan Knight. He began to exercise greater control of the flow of creatures through the portal.

"So much time with the dear Scheriers, God bless them, is not good for the steward," he thought to himself.

Other creatures, those with more serious natures, became the numerous guests in the valley. With Ludwig's reluctant approval, the swan closed passage one day to all but the Zweigwesens. They were thin, like a branch of a tree. They looked much like branches. They were covered entirely in soft, orangish-brown hair, soft to the touch, but course in appearance, resembling thick and rough bark. They stood less than shoulder high to Wikerus, on short, bowed legs. Their voices were high, like of a young boy. They loved to sing, but were not particularly pleasant to hear.

The Zweigwesens were botanists and healers. Their homeland hosted several medical centers to which creatures from across the Land and Shallow Waters would travel for care. They carried in their stout hearts a tremendous sense of responsibility for the care of others. Although they were as quick to laugh as the Scheriers, they were not playful. Although not as sternly stoic as the Unicorns, whose fierceness sparkled from them like the midday sun off of their brilliant horns, the Zweigwesens carried always about them an equal intensity to serve. Since the Unicorns would not stiffen Wikerus with their influence, the swan hoped that the Zweigwesens would.

A corps of six Zweigwesens spent a night in the lodge. They dined with Wikerus and told stories of their homeland and traditions. The swan's plan paid some dividends. Wikerus was eager to throw his heart at any noble being. The signature nobility of the Zweigwesens was no exception. Ludwig and the swan observed with satisfaction as Zweigwesen sensibilities infiltrated Wikerus' mind and displayed itself in his thoughtful contributions to the conversations. As healers, as keepers of hospitals, their code of life was not unlike the true mission of the Teutonic Order. The six Zweigwesens who came to see Wikerus would have been perfect additions to the hospital in Damietta. Wikerus considered this many times as they spoke.

The next day, Rei'mund and Mercedes were allowed through the portal to visit. They were the lone exceptions to a Zweigwesen-rich company. Wikerus spoke lightly and playfully to his small white friends, but with a coating of Zweigwesen austerity over his words. It seemed that some balance was achieved. Wikerus was openly in love with his new life as a Portal Steward, but turned a corner toward a more serious embrace of the role he needed to play. The sacrificing knight with his chivalric code showed itself in our hero's complexion. By the time the Swan Knight's family returned to the valley, Wikerus had met many different breeds of Sweeter Realm creatures, each influencing him in their own ways.

One late morning, the familiar tap of a Unicorn horn vibrated the door of the lodge. Ludwig and Wikerus were alone in the lodge. All of the Queen's subjects, except for the Unicorn sentries stealthily on duty, were gone from the valley. Ludwig answered and received the report. The Swan Knight's wife, Ludmilla, was over the first ridge, returning home with Otto and his bride. Otto married Agnes, daughter of Count Heinrich V Palatine of the Rhine. Her father was a shrewd politician. He and Ludwig had been on opposing sides of many German conflicts. The marriage had political benefits. The couple's meeting was arranged, but their love was their own. Agnes was as keen of mind and as politically aware as her father. She knew why she went to Kelheim, why she was introduced to young Otto von Wittelsbach.

What her father could not see and could never understand was the tender portions of Agnes' heart. She was a striking beauty, but it was her love of music, not any political considerations, that drew Otto and Agnes together. When they met, she was instructed to sing for him, to entertain him and please him with her voice. For Otto, the experience was beyond pleasurable. She reminded him of the lovely Brunnens, who came through the portal to sing for him and teach him music since he was a child. Agnes, who sang dutifully, did not realize how deeply her song penetrated into Otto, until he began to sing with her.

Their voices blended together and their unity lost all political considerations for both of them. They fell in love. Otto saw in Agnes that rare sort of woman whom he could easily picture as a Swan Knight, sharing his inherited responsibilities and loving the creatures of the Sweeter Realm. The family secrets would be hers. One of their children would someday be sworn into the service of the Queen of the Land and Shallow Waters as the Swan Knight and protector of the Portal Valley. When Otto's voice blended with Agnes', the image of the stiffly propped daughter of a politician melted away to reveal everything he had ever hoped to find in love. They sang their vows of love at their wedding in Kelheim. The ceremony was opened to the public and heavily attended. The vows were so romantically professed, and so tenderly infectious, that weddings in Kelheim doubled in the following year.

Otto was right. Agnes was everything the Portal Valley and the Swan Knighthood needed her to be. But the transition from her life at Heidelberg Castle to her life in the valley lodge was not without turmoil. While they traveled from Kelheim, Otto and Ludmilla tried to prepare Agnes for what awaited her. Agnes thought that her new husband was trying to entertain her with fantastic fiction. She giggled at the stories of Scheriers and Unicorns, of scaled Queens with immense powers, perched on thrones in lakeside palaces. Her heart accepted the stories giddily, but her mind refused them flatly.

When the Unicorn told Ludwig of their approach, the Swan Knight summoned Wikerus. Otto and Ludmilla did not know that lost Grail Blood had wandered into the valley, that Wikerus was sworn into the service of the Swan Knight. It was the first time anything like this had ever happened, and the introduction had to be sensitively administered — Wikerus' introduction to Otto and Ludmilla, and Agnes' introduction to the magnificent and unearthly wonders of the portal. All of Ludwig's scripted preparation for that moment evaporated.

Wikerus stood beside his master at the entrance to the lodge. Otto, Agnes, and Ludmilla dismounted their horses and walked together to greet the Swan Knight. The initial introduction was as warm as imaginable. Both Ludmilla and Otto had heard the stories from Ludwig, about the noble Teutonic Knight, the Tannhäuser, whose goodness saved so many lives. They were delighted to meet him, but were astonished to find him beside the Swan Knight in Parsifal's hidden valley.

Wikerus did not wait for Ludwig to explain the truths behind his presence there.

Wikerus put his hand on Otto's shoulder and said, "Come here. Watch this."

He ran around the lodge and up the hill toward the portal point. In instinctive defensiveness, Otto pursued him, not as a friend and brother, but as a young Swan Knight-in-Training, ready to fight, and kill if he must, in accordance with the oath his father had taken and would someday be his to take.

Wikerus ran at inhuman speed, followed directly by Otto. Agnes followed curiously behind, with no reason to imagine what she would soon experience. Ludwig and Ludmilla, being older, came up well behind them. Wikerus reached his trigger point to open the portal, and the family secret revealed itself to Agnes, in all of its crackling and terrifying splendor. Otto froze in place, seeing that Wikerus had opened the portal. Fury enveloped his eyes. He drew his sword.

Ludwig caught up and jumped between his son and the naively giddy steward, with his back to Wikerus and the portal, facing his son, and he shouted, "Tannhäuser is a lost cousin. He knows about the portal... *only about the portal.* He will serve the Swan Knight as his steward."

Otto's furious features relaxed. He put his sword away, knowing what his father meant but could not say, that Wikerus knew of the portal but not of the Holy Grail. Several creatures were waiting on the other side. When the portal opened with the Tannhäuser's unique crackle, they expected to talk and play with the Portal Steward. The swan came through as well. He greeted Ludmilla and Otto, who showered their old friend in affection. The Scheriers jumped on Wikerus. They knocked him to the ground and rolled on him. Their love for him was blazingly evident. Even the old swan, critical as ever, outstretched a wing and placed it affectionately on Wikerus. Otto knew that all was well.

He offered Wikerus his hand, helped him back to his feet, and told him with a smile, "Welcome to our wonderful valley, and thank you for being with my father when I could not."

Agnes, on the other hand, almost forgotten in the excitement by all but Otto, stood in shock. Her world turned upside down in those moments of reunion. She knew her husband had a fanciful imagination. She came to the valley expecting to hear more of his wild tales, not to see them spring from a portal before her eyes. She fainted. Otto caught her and carried her to the lodge.

There was a good reason Ludwig had scripted the introductions so painstakingly. Agnes came from a practical and political family. Her music was her only escape from the rigid and formal decorum of her political life. In Wikerus' excitement to have a family again, he shocked poor Agnes out of her wits. Ludmilla dismissed the creatures, pouring her affection upon them but asking that they return to their homes until Agnes was prepared properly to meet them. Ludwig held the portal open until all but the Unicorn sentries were gone from the valley.

Agnes awoke in the evening, still shaking, and wondering if it had all been a dream. Her husband was real enough. Otto tended to her with all of the care of a Zweigwesen and all of the nurturing tenderness of a Brunnen. After she had eaten, she sat at the dining table with Otto and his parents. Wikerus was asked to give them their privacy. He obeyed and strolled around the perimeter of the valley. The Swan Knight family took turns telling Agnes all of the family's secrets, including those kept hidden from the steward. She learned of Parsifal and the Grail, of the Sweeter Realm and the Queen of the Land and Shallow Waters, and many of the heroic Swan Knights who had lived in that valley since the year 515.

There was no giggling this time. The stories and the truths were told with the utmost sobriety. A few times each minute, Agnes startled and looked sharply to one side and the other for mystical creatures to spring from behind every chair.

"They are all gone from the valley. We sent them home until you are ready to meet them properly," Ludmilla assured her.

No assurances could calm her nerves. Her shock was extreme, and apparently far more lasting than any of them had hoped. The newlyweds did not sleep much that night. Agnes jolted awake in sweats, and trembled in Otto's arms until drifting into another short, shallow, and disturbed sleep.

In a few days, Agnes' condition was not much improved. Only the swan was let into the valley. Otto's lessons resumed. He studied with the swan and began his training with Wikerus. Agnes, who was to someday mother a Swan Knight and become the matriarch of the Portal Valley and a keeper of Parsifal's secret, sat in stone silence, watching her husband learn the ways of war from a veteran crusader. In the evenings, when Wikerus and the Swan Knight's family retired to the lodge, Agnes warmed slightly. She spoke very little and did not sing at all. Little by little, creatures from the Sweeter Realm were brought back into the valley. Agnes would not interact with them. She would not look at them. With the sight of each, or the sound of their voices, she turned away as if they hurt her eyes.

Something had to be done for Agnes. Otto hatched a plan. They would hold a concert. Ludwig's father, Duke Otto I, had built a small, intimate theater in the Portal Valley, to the southeast of the lodge. A musical concert in the theater, featuring the innocent voices of the creatures, could be just the key to unlock Agnes' heart as Otto had done with *his* singing. Wikerus was named Master of the Ceremony, responsible for gathering the creatures and arranging the acts. There was one act Ludmilla insisted upon. She demanded a choir of Brunnens. Theirs were the softest voices in the Sweeter Realm. In fact, they were the softest in every respect.

The Brunnens were a breed of Sweeter Realm creatures as mysterious as they were adored. The entire breed was of one gender, or perhaps it would be more accurate to say that they were without gender. They were generally referred to as women, because they bore such feminine features. They all, old and young alike, appeared as young women, pale blue or grey in color, covered in an inch of water. They were not covered in water. They were as dry as any creature. But if you were to reach out and touch one of them, you would expect to bring back a dripping hand. They had a thick outer layer of flesh that was clear, and it rippled like a stream in reaction to their movements and emotions. They did not have hair, but a flowing hair-like appendage draped from their heads and wrapped around their otherwise bare form.

When the Brunnens were perfectly still, and their watery Brunnen skin did not ripple, they faded from sight and appeared as wispy phantoms. But their water-like skin and their feminine figures were not their most notorious quality. The Brunnens had dual throats. Two throats, each with its own unique voice, allowed them to speak and sing in harmony with themselves. The Brunnen language was a musical language, with notes depicting tense and conjugations. The softness of their physical features held nothing to the dulcet tones of their singing. Their choirs were the highlight of every festival and celebration in the Sweeter Realm. They were slow to love, but their love, once achieved, was pure and eternal. They were devoutly pious and spiritual, and adhered religiously to a strict code of decorum, particularly as they related to the Swan Knights.

The Brunnens did not reproduce sexually. In fact, there was no need for physical contact at all. They were deeply spiritual and they reproduced spiritually. When a love developed between two Brunnens, infinitely deep and eternally committed, and both desired a child of the union, they were capable of spiritual reproduction. Only in a moment of profound adoration and spiritual closeness, can a Brunnen child be conceived.

Wikerus had never met the Brunnens, and was excited to hear them, after Ludmilla bragged so of their hypnotic voices. He arranged all of the acts, beginning with stories and games by the Scheriers, and concluding with the Brunnen choir. He and the Swan Knight's family were confident that the beauty and sincere innocence of the creatures in performance would melt the shocked and frightened casing around Agnes' heart. The Queen gave her permission. The program was set. The invitations went

296

out. And even the old swan skipped around with uncommon lightness of foot in anticipation of the rare event.

CHAPTER 29
The Brunnens

WHEN THE MORNING OF THE CONCERT ARRIVED, the valley was filled with magnificent creatures. The Eulesängers were there. They came to the valley that day with their own act prepared to display. Agnes did not find them as unsettling as the other creatures, and she smiled when they sang for her, as long as they did not get too close.

Evening came and Wikerus was as a schoolboy. During their lessons, Otto expressed his frustrations with Agnes' reclusiveness. Wikerus came to love Otto and was excited to master a ceremony that might bring Agnes' bright smile and sweet voice back to her husband. He lit candles in the theater, warming it to perfection and giving it the yellow glow of a summer sunset. Ludwig remained at the portal point, holding it open while the performers flowed into the valley. The swan directed the creatures into a line behind the theater. Once they were all in the valley, Ludwig and the swan joined Ludmilla, Otto, and Agnes in the theater.

The theater itself was a wonder to behold. It was fully enclosed, but designed to imitate the outdoor theaters of Ancient Greece. The ceiling was painted black and speckled with stars. Columns shot upward to support the ceiling, but appeared to rise endlessly into the night sky. It was a small theater, with seating to hold around thirty people very snuggly.

It was no wonder which act the Master of the Ceremony would choose to begin the night. The Scheriers gleefully took the stage first. Eight of them danced interpretations of the oldest stories in Scherier lore, while Mercedes stumbled through as narrator. Each time one Scherier bumped into another, an impromptu wrestling match interrupted the story. They wrestled until they laughed too hard to move, then sighed in concert and resumed their performance. It was hardly informative, if the point was to educate Agnes on the deepest pages of Scherier legends and lore. The point was to warm her and teach her to understand and appreciate Scherier joy, which the performance did in abundance. The silly antics and infectious laugh of the Scheriers spread like a happy plague.

The Eulesängers performed next, with daring aerialist swoops and dives around each other, all while whistling some fascinating tale that few in the room could understand. The swan tried to translate, but the act moved too quickly for his skills in their language.

The Zweigwesens followed with a skill that none of the Swan Knights of the Portal Valley ever knew they had. They stood upon each other, seamlessly connecting one to the next. Agnes was fascinated. She could not tell where one Zweigwesen ended and the next began. Their fur seemed to grab the fur of the next. The Zweigwesen constructed themselves into intricate architectural formations, imitating the drawings of famous buildings of antiquity, as they had seen in the Swan Knight's books and sketches. Once in a particular shape, they held it until the applause died down, broke from each other, and formed quickly into the next formation. For their finale, they connected themselves into a tall and wide formation, balancing with only a single Zweigwesen toe touching the floor of the stage. The geometric perfection spoke well of the scientific nature of the breed.

The Ancient One took the stage and read a letter from the Queen, welcoming Agnes to the Swan Knight Family. The acts warmed her well for the letter. By the time the swan unrolled it and began to read, Agnes wore a wide smile and flush cheeks. After the letter was read, the swan recited some of the most dramatic stories from the Swan Knight history. He was careful not to expose what Wikerus should not know, but there were plenty of dramatics to fill his hour.

The last act of the night was the eagerly anticipated Brunnen choir. They entered the theater in formal procession and worked their way to the stage. Wikerus, who had been light and jovial all night, struggled to introduce them. He had yet to meet a Brunnen, and he was struck to the bone with admiration of their beauty. As the Brunnens began to sing, doubling the depth of their song with their dual Brunnen throats. They sounded like a choir of forty, gracing a tall cathedral.

Wikerus seemed focused on one particular Brunnen. His jaw hung open and his eyes glossed over. Her name was too complex to write, and impossible to say through a single human throat. For the sake of the Swan Knight's family, they referred to her as Caris. Attention was drawn from the performance of the choir by the thick, tense air between Wikerus and Caris. She seemed equally besotted with him. The song continued, but every eye in the room was on Wikerus and Caris.

Still singing with her sisters, Caris stepped forward from the choir and walked toward Wikerus. This did not appear to be a conscious decision. She probably did not even realize she was walking. Her arms did not lay flatly at her sides, as she rode a ghostly wind across the floor, nor did they jig and jerk in spastic agitation. They swayed, but

300

not in unison with her steps or each other, rather separately, as if blown by the whims of nature, from different parts of the world, haphazardly, like dried leaves floating atop a flustered pool of water, giving her movement a complexity that intoxicated him.

Across the length of her entire body, there was not one rigid line or harsh angle. As his eyes scanned her from scalp to toes, they rode a swooshing, cascading path of gently rounded slopes and curves. Each inch of her toyed with his attention and was loathed to release it to the next. He stared, encased in a fit of frozen ecstasy. His body locked in fitful stillness, as if embedded in a glacier impatiently for a thousand years. Although he could hear his own pulse as it sent his fiery blood screaming through his veins, to the others in the room he was as still as stone.

Ludwig and his ancestors had known the Brunnens since the earliest days of the Portal Valley. The Swan Knight and his family were intimately familiar with each member of the Brunnen choir that night. Yet, even Ludwig was struck by the peculiarity of her movement toward the Tannhäuser. It was apparent that his effect on her was as profound as hers on him. She moved toward him like an unearthly specter, simultaneously savage and serene. Her hair-like appendage stirred in wild animation, seeming to be blown by a violent wind, though the air in the room was placid. To those in attendance, her hair appeared to react to his gaze and the undeniable, almost tangible energy that passed between them.

This all happened so suddenly and without prelude, that the song of the choir continued throughout. Caris' voice rose above the others, fueled by something deep and arcane, and burning infinitely more intensely than that which lifted song through the dual throats of the other Brunnens.

Caris continued to close the diminishing gap between her and Wikerus. She looked as if she would walk right through him. But she stopped with her face immeasurably near his. He remained frozen, except for a slight drop of his lower jaw, which parted his lips. He looked like he wanted to drink her soothing voice directly into his parched soul. In fact, that is precisely what he desired. Her nose made small circles around his, never quite touching him, as she sang directly into his open mouth. His chest began to heave as he tried to draw her into him. His throat seized as it tried to grasp the dulcet melody that leaped gleefully from her lips and through his, where it echoed around his head.

Through this, the choir continued to accompany her voice, in a supportive role, suddenly thrust into the background behind the mystical phenomenon that had taken command of the celebration. But all attention, every eye was on Wikerus and Caris. The song came to its natural conclusion. It settled into the rehearsed, complex harmonies of the many Brunnen throats in the room. The music faded into absolute silence. Not a breath, not a sigh, hardly a blinking eye broke the stillness that followed. All were captivated by the utterly unexpected and seemingly tyrannical spiritual grip they had on one another. Only one slight sound dared defile the silence. It was Caris' continuing exhale. Breath that had been abandoned by song continued to pour from her lips through his, while her circling nose slowed to barely noticeable, but still orbiting his, as if time itself had gotten drunk and lethargic.

The Brunnens stared in confounded mortification. The Swan Knight feared what might happen in each slowly passing second, but he, like the others, was kept in stillness and silence by some beguiling curiosity. The scene before them bore such an arcane aroma of bizarre exoticism that nobody, not even the playful Scheriers, dared to interfere. Only one member of their party was able to portion some of his attention elsewhere. Otto held the hand of his wife. And through that clutch flowed a love, while not nearly so mystical, enigmatic, and esoteric, was as pure and richly authentic as any that had graced the sacred valley in its long and storied history. So it was Otto who crashed the scene and snapped Wikerus and Caris from the strange and distant place of their spiritual rendezvous, back to the crowded little theater they shared with their friends.

The evening was about Agnes. The concert was for Agnes. And Otto would see it return to its purpose. He thanked the Brunnen choir for their lovely music. He thanked Caris in particular. The mortified Brunnens reached for their sister, whose skin rippled toward the clustered choir, seeming to drag Caris backward while her attention remained locked on Wikerus. She moved without grace, without the signature elegance of her kind, yanked reluctantly by her own skin until she stood among her Brunnen sisters. They wrapped their arms around her — not an embrace of affection, but one of confinement. Their skin rippled in a myriad of various colors and shades. It was the only outward sign of embarrassment that their reserved manners would allow on display in front of their revered hosts.

Otto was successful in returning the celebration to its designed agenda. But strangeness lingered in thick, pungent clouds that seasoned every inhale for the rest of the evening. Wikerus tried to return to normal. But he stuttered and stumbled across his words. He shook as waves of chills ran rapidly and unannounced across his body. The Brunnens maintained a crowded wall of sisters between Caris and Tannhäuser. Caris tried in vain to steer her eyes around them. But the room was small and the company shifted. Although there remained for the rest of the evening bodies between the lovers, their eyes found one another. And each time they did, Wikerus felt perilously in danger of repeating the episode that changed the course of the evening's events. Whether he locked his eyes squarely on hers or he only caught the swiftest glimpse of the tiniest portion of her body, it shook him mercilessly and destroyed the façade of normalcy he struggled to construct and maintain.

At last, Otto took the stage and began to sing the song of his wedding vows. Agnes, whose feelings of having been transported to another world were in no way lightened by the strangeness of Wikerus and Caris' connection, was brought back by her husband's voice and his bold but sweet proclamations of love and eternal devotion. Hairy little Scheriers, branch-like Zweigwesens, owl-like Eulesängers, a giant swan, Unicorns, rippling, dual-throated Brunnens all bore a glow of the familiar under the light of Otto's adoring gaze and rich, billowing voice. She saw nothing but the man she loved. And all that accompanied that man was good. She smiled — the smile of their earliest encounters, beneath the exact wink she gave him at their wedding. Then she joined him on the stage, merged her voice to his, and sang her vows to him.

Otto and Agnes were no Brunnens. Their voices did not sound like a full choir in a grand cathedral. It sounded like two young and idealistic people, very much in love, singing from the depths of their hearts in the family's little theater. There was not the arcane mysticism of Wikerus and Caris' connection, only the sort of genuine human love that goes mostly unsung in the tales of great romantics.

Such innocent love, such untarnishable and pious adoration washed the peculiarity from the air. And for all but Wikerus and Caris, laughs were genuine. Wishes of welcome to Agnes were authentic and without the diluting effects of divided attention. Agnes laughed. She told stories of her childhood, stories of meeting Otto and getting married. She even told with light-heartedness of her shock upon seeing the portal and the creatures for the first time. It seems she did not need a concert to adjust to her new life. She needed only Otto, and to bathe in his simple song of love and devotion.

The remainder of the evening was about the newlyweds, as it should have been. The Scheriers jumped on Agnes and embraced her. The Zweigwesens presented her with a gift of medicine, some concoction of Sweeter Realm herbs and spices known to enhance the senses. They also connected with each other into a large throne and hoisted her upon themselves. A hairy throne with blinking eyes spoke of tender commitment to her. This bizarre incident would have shaken her out of her wits a day earlier. But she delighted in it, in all of it — this strange new life of hers, as young mistress of the Portal Valley.

When the jubilee in the theater concluded, it was time for the creatures to return through the portal and leave the Swan Knight's family and their steward to celebrate more intimately in a quiet lodge. Ludwig escorted his friends to the portal and held it open with the Grail Blood inside of him. Ludmilla stood beside her husband, and Otto and Agnes beside her. Wikerus followed the performers to the portal. The creatures bid their congratulations and farewells, one by one. The choir of Brunnens were the last to step through. Caris lingered to the rear of them, just in front of Wikerus. As he walked directly behind her, her rippling skin sang a siren's song to his hand. The skin of his palm thirsted for her tenderness. But he could not lift his arm. Something inside of him forbade it, and his arms remained at his sides.

The Brunnens said their goodbyes with an old Brunnen custom. They rubbed their soft thumbs across the eyelids of their human hosts, then kissed them on the forehead. The Brunnen just in front of Caris took her by the hand, afraid that she might refuse to leave Wikerus behind and return to her homeland. She bid farewell with her one available hand. Caris walked as if in a dream, and paid no attention to the line of humans seeing her off.

When Caris stepped through the portal, leaving none of the Queen's subjects in the valley, except for four Unicorns and six Zweigwesens guarding the perimeter of the valley, Ludwig stepped quickly to his side, almost knocking his wife to the ground, in order to close the portal as soon as he could and put the strange business of Caris and the Tannhäuser behind them. When the portal snapped to a crackling close, Wikerus dropped to his knees. It appeared to the lookers on like the spiritual connection between the two of them was all that held Wikerus' skeleton erect. When that connection was severed by the closing of the portal, the poor knight lost his ability to stand.

For all but Ludwig, the evening was Otto's and Agnes'. They had almost forgotten what happened during the Brunnen song. Ludwig, however, still with strong feelings for his wartime comrade, felt great compassion for Wikerus' misery. He had seen starvation in his young friend's face before. But the withered, sunken, drawn, and deathly look that Wikerus wore in the Egyptian prison did not compare in torment or anguish with the expression he wore as he stared from his knees at the silent and empty portal point.

The others turned toward the lodge and skipped down the slope in light-hearted conversation. Ludwig remained behind.

Under a clear, starlit Bavarian night sky, the Duke stood before his friend, pressed Wikerus' head against his chest, ran his fingers nurturingly through our hero's thick black hair, and said, "Come inside, Tannhäuser. Celebrate with us."

The Portal Steward obeyed his master and followed Ludwig to the lodge. A much smaller, intimate, but radiantly warm and familial atmosphere filled the main hall of the lodge. They tried to include Wikerus as a full member of the family celebration. They asked him for stories of the crusade. To avoid bursting into sobs, Wikerus constricted his chest and bit on his lips. His answers were conspicuously brief and without passion.

Each time Otto and Agnes looked at each other, their love plumed outward from them, which only frustrated Wikerus further. Caris occupied every portion of his mind and soul, and anything that tried to work its way into him that was not Caris irritated him immensely. As much as he loved Ludwig and his new life as the Portal Steward, he could bear no company. Having exhaled completely, and feeling unable to draw new breath, Wikerus stumbled from his seat at the table, knocking over his chair. He excused himself to bed with a gesture of his hand and left without another word to any of them.

They had all seen the connection between Wikerus and Caris. They knew that their friend and steward suffered. No offense was taken. They spoke briefly of their compassion for the man, and turned the celebration back on course. Still, in the back of each of their heads, even Agnes', was their shared concern for what might come of this mystical and instant love between a human and a Brunnen. While conversations on a variety of subjects spun in free form through their celebration, in the darkest recesses of their thoughts, each of them housed a series of projected worst-case-scenarios, and each imagined what might be done to intercede.

CHAPTER 30
Unseverable Connection

DESPITE A LONG NIGHT, the Swan Knight and his family rose early the next morning. They were concerned about their steward. Their concerns quickly proved merited. They took turns standing near Tannhäuser's door. From there, they heard him alternate between pacing his room and weeping loudly on his bed. There was little doubt among them that the poor man had not slept. They maintained this cycling vigil over Wikerus' door until half the day had gone. Ludmilla convened them to discuss the matter, and determined that it had to be Ludwig to pull his friend from his state of misery.

Wikerus was a trained and seasoned knight. He was obedient. He also loved and respected Ludwig very much. Ludwig decided to approach the tender circumstance as the Duke of Bavaria, and as the Swan Knight, not as Wikerus' friend. Just after noon, Ludwig opened Wikerus' door and ordered him, with the authority of an Imperial Commander, to rise and begin his lessons with Otto.

Ever-dutiful, Wikerus gathered himself together, and with the strongest parts of his mind still at his disposal, he shoved his feelings downward and obeyed the Swan Knight. He took his Marian Sword and marched from his room. He walked right by Ludmilla, as if she was invisible to him.

She cleared her throat loudly and said, "Good afternoon, Tannhäuser."

Wikerus turned to see her and was instantly mortified by the impertinence of his behavior.

"Please forgive me, Duchess," he sincerely begged her, "Good afternoon to you."

Wikerus turned again to the front door of the lodge, but was stopped again in his tracks by Ludmilla's voice, "Not so fast, young steward!"

Wikerus turned to receive the chastisement he thought was coming. The matriarch of the Portal Valley gave no such thing. She stood statuesque as always, holding a dish of food.

"You have not eaten," her maternal voice broke through.

Wikerus noticed the food that she had held for him since before he left his room. He bowed low and reverently to her.

Ludmilla took his chin by two fingertips and raised him until he stood erect.

"We are not in Kelheim," she reminded him, "here we are family."

Ludmilla handed Wikerus the food, raised herself onto her toes, extended her face forward and puckered her lips. Wikerus lowered his head and received her nurturing, maternal kiss on the crown of his head. She winked at him and ordered him with mock formality to sit and eat every morsel given to him before he took a single step outside of the lodge. Wikerus blushed deeply. He felt the strong sense of kinship coming from Ludmilla. It honored him and motivated him. While he ate his breakfast, he set his thoughts on his duties to the Duke, the Portal Valley, and to Otto, whose training was the primary purpose for Wikerus' presence in the valley.

The next several days went by as if nothing at all bizarre had occurred at the concert. Wikerus spent the whole of each day training Otto as *he* had been trained, adding much of what he had learned in war. He swore Otto into an oath of fealty, not to Wikerus, as a servant to a lord, but to his training. Otto needed no oath to bind him. He had trained to be the next Swan Knight since he was nine years old, in accordance with the Laws of Ermenrich, a code of regulation passed down from the fifth Swan Knight. Even the Laws of Ermenrich did not hold Otto's devotion to his teacher more than sheer affection. Since his return from the crusade, Ludwig had spoken openly and with great enthusiastic praise of the selfless Tannhäuser, and of his exploits in battle. Otto was committedly his.

From the rosy brushes of the morning sky to the brilliant orange of sunset, Wikerus trained his student. The evenings were his to do as he pleased. He did not admire the beauty of the lush valley, or see the complex magnificence of nature around him. He did not read his mother's poetry or compose his own. He spent his evenings sitting at the portal point, holding the passage between worlds open with his sacred blood.

He sat and stared into the open circle of nothingness that had terrified him so when he first encountered it. Every now and then, creatures would bound through, hoping to share the same games and conversations as they used to share with the Portal Steward. Wikerus could not play. He could not converse. He sat, trying somehow to communicate with Caris through the portal. Sometimes he was still and silent, like a sentry at his post. Other times he cried or pleaded his love for her into the portal, conversing with the constant crackling. Ludwig and Ludmilla watched him closely, not at all sure what was to be done.

Since meeting Wikerus, Mercedes and Rei'mund spent more time in the valley than in their own home. After the concert, they still came, with the same naïve hope that they would cross the portal to find a light and playful Wikerus, ready to race them to the Wrestling Tree. Often, while Wikerus sat and cried at the open portal, his Scherier friends would snuggle tightly against him and rub and pat him with their affectionate little claws. They would hum to him when he was silent, and cry with him when he cried.

Despite his long and mournful evenings, Wikerus taught his student well. Otto's skills swelled beyond most of those Imperial Knights who rode into battle with his father. Wikerus was still a far superior warrior than Otto. But one day, Otto got the best of him. In a moment of distraction, Wikerus' guard fell and Otto's sword slashed him down the left arm, from shoulder to elbow. Wikerus let his arms fall flatly at his side. The tip of his sword rested on the ground in front of him, while blood dripped in rapid rhythm off the fingers of his other hand.

Otto dropped his sword and yelled, "I am so sorry, Master."

Wikerus just stared at his student until he saw Otto's focus on the wound. He looked to his arm as if the wound belonged to another.

"Come!" Otto belted as he grabbed his teacher by his sword hand.

Wikerus did not move. He wasn't resisting Otto's pull, but he wasn't assisting it either. The blood pooled at Wikerus' feet and Otto took his master's care into his own hands. He lifted Wikerus into his arms and ran him into the lodge. Ludwig was in Heidelberg with Agnes. Ludmilla was inside and saw that the wound was beyond her care. She took one long step past the threshold of the doorway and whistled loudly. Two Unicorns appeared from the thick linden trees like ghosts entering a room through its walls. They sprinted to the lodge and received Ludmilla's orders.

"Go into Zweigwesen land," she commanded, "Bring back who you can. Tell them it is a long and deep wound to the bone of the arm. Please hurry, our steward needs their help."

Otto grabbed a horn, and its owner raised his head forcefully, flinging Otto onto the pair of high Unicorn shoulders. They sprinted to Otto's portal trigger point. When the crackling circle sprang to life, Otto leaped from the shoulders and the two Unicorns flew through without retarding their pace. Otto did not move, but kept the portal open for about twenty minutes, at which point both Unicorns returned, each carrying a Zweigwesen. They did not pause to acknowledge Otto but ran directly to the lodge, where Ludmilla waited.

The Zweigwesens dismounted their rides in agile, vaulted acrobatics, each with a sack in hand. They brought herbs from the Sweeter Realm, gathered from far and wide and stored in bulk at the Zweigwesen medical centers. They quickly emptied one sack into a bowl, removing from the contents a pale-green bandage wrapped tightly onto itself. With their hard, splintery fingers, they mashed the herbs together. Once the herbs were ground together, one of the Zweigwesens made a tight fist. When she released her fist and extended her fingers forward, a thick, yellow sap oozed from her fingertips into the bowl. Otto helplessly watched.

Ludmilla joined, and the three of them kneaded the excretion into the herbs. When they were satisfied, the Zweigwesens each took a handful of the mixture and shoved it into their mouths. They chewed it, mixing it thoroughly with their own saliva, spat it back into their hands and took quickly to smearing it on Wikerus' wound. The steward sat on the dining table watching with lethargic curiosity as Ludmilla and the Zweigwesens worked frantically to mix and apply the substance. Once a thick coating of the medicine was applied, Ludmilla wrapped his arm with the green bandage.

Many thoughts worked their way unrestricted through his head. He saw the compassion and goodness of Ludmilla and Otto, and he pictured Ludwig high upon his horse outside of the walls of Damietta, speaking of his wife and son.

"He had this life to lose," Wikerus thought, "yet he rode into battle."

The gleaming, gilded image of Ludwig he held in his head gained an even brighter polish. He looked at the Zweigwesens and saw in them the magnificent Trinity of God's creation, the body, mind, and spirit united — the beauty of their narrow figures and deep orangish-brown hair and miraculous secretions from their fingertips, the masterful knowledge and skill put to such rapid employment, and the sincerest compassion and nurturing care with which they administered their craft.

And he thought of Caris. The whirlwind of love and care around him made him think of her. His air abandoned him in a sudden and forceful exhale, and he could not recall it. As all thought but Caris faded away, I don't think he cared to recall it. He shook in a cry that had no air to expel. The Zweigwesens knew, as all knew the source of his pain. It had nothing to do with Otto's sword. His hairy friends hoisted him into their arms and carried him to his bed.

With his bedroom door closed behind him, they returned to the table, and in a much slower pace and somber mood, the four of them, Otto, Ludmilla, and the Zweigwesens mixed the contents of the other sack, with the Zweigwesen fingertip sap and their own chewing, into another batch of medicine. When it was done, the guests shared from the lodge's stores of wine and returned solemnly through the portal to their home.

While he rested and healed, Wikerus tried to sketch Caris' image in his book, and whittle it into wood, but he failed. His skilled and talented hand could not produce what was vividly and implacably in the forefront of his mind.

Wikerus healed quickly. Two days later, the wound was little more than a deep red scar. He returned to his lessons with Otto. Otto knew his teacher was distracted. One evening after Ludwig and Agnes' return to the valley, Wikerus' mind was clearly not on his daily duties. Otto expressed his deep concern to his father. Ludwig stood behind the lodge and watched Wikerus sitting by the open portal. He did not sit still, but twitched and leaned toward the sacred passage. A few times, he rose to one knee and looked to Ludwig as if he might run through.

Ludwig went to him, placed his hand on the steward's shoulder, and said, "We cannot go through. It is forbidden."

Wikerus did not turn to look at his master, but continued to stare into the portal, saying more to himself than to his company, "I want to see her..., her home. I want to see her home and know her..., know it."

Ludwig squeezed Wikerus' shoulder so tightly that he could not be ignored, and he repeated slowly and clearly, "We cannot go through. It is forbidden."

Wikerus stood and took one sharp step toward the portal.

Ludwig grabbed him and turned him forcefully around to face him, and he spoke with gravity, "These are not *my* rules. Even as the Swan Knight I am subject to them, as my father was, and as you must be if you wish to remain here with us."

All of the weight of Wikerus' dutiful respect for Ludwig crashed upon him at once. He was again mortified by his behavior. He apologized and Ludwig patted him on the head.

"Come, my dear friend," the Duke told him, "I will help you through this. We will work it out together."

Ludwig tugged Wikerus toward the lodge and the steward followed. But seeing the creatures of the Sweeter Realm made Wikerus think of Caris, and seeing the daily interactions of the Swan Knight's family made him even lonelier. Many creatures had come through to spend time in the valley and perform their various duties for the Swan Knight. No Brunnens had made an appearance since the night of the concert. This was unusual and everyone agreed silently that it had something to do with Caris and Wikerus.

One morning, about four months after the concert, Ludwig and Ludmilla were in Kelheim on ducal business. Otto patrolled the outskirts of the sacred valley with the Unicorns. Agnes was busy with domestic affairs in the lodge. Wikerus stood alone near the portal point. He walked slowly to his trigger point, somehow fearful of the crackling opening. The morning was different, and Wikerus could not place his finger upon the inexpressible anger, fear, and agitation stirring inside of him.

He creeped forward apprehensively until he triggered an opening of the portal. To his surprise, The Ancient One appeared before him. The old swan was followed by a host of Brunnens. Wikerus watched the Brunnens with fevered anticipation. One by one they appeared on the valley's side of the portal. The last one came through and Caris was not among them. The Brunnens and the swan looked at Wikerus with sad but stern faces. It was clear to Wikerus the news they brought to the valley would crush him.

He did not give them a chance to speak, but turned sharply to the swan and demanded, "They are not allowing her to see me. Am I right?"

The swan shook his head and the Brunnens swayed side to side in chorus behind him. Their skin rippled with their movements and their beauty did nothing to ween Wikerus of his infatuation.

"Let her come to me," Wikerus demanded, "or take me to her!"

He took one step toward the portal. The swan stepped in front of him and stretched a wing out to block him from the opening.

"Step back, steward of the portal's protection," the venerable old sage commanded, "Step back and close the portal as you know you should."

Wikerus did not step back as ordered, but collapsed to the ground in debilitating sobs. The scene was pathetically mournful. The Brunnens cried for him. Their skin rippled downward with their tears, covering every inch of their fair figures, from their eyes to their toes. The swan's compassion was provoked. He sat beside Wikerus, enveloped him with one wing, and rested his cheek on the broken man's head.

The swan and the Brunnens were resolute. But they were not heartless. The display before them was that of a genuine but tragic love, and a man whose future, one way or another, would be sculpted by it.

The swan lifted his head from Wikerus, and Wikerus sat up and looked into the swan's eyes, as the old bird explained, "The Brunnens are creatures of rigid decorum. They are as pious as they are devoutly committed to the Swan Knight and his secrets."

They continued to stare at each other. Wikerus knew that the next words from the old beak would pierce his heart.

"She cannot come to you," the swan continued, "Her people forbid it. She has been exiled from the valley by her own kind and may never cross the portal again."

The Ancient One expected another episode of rabid sobs, but they did not come. Instead, Wikerus pulled himself from the swan's embrace and stood calmly, keeping a lock on the old bird's eyes. He seemed cured of his obsession, not at all bothered by the deep, penetrating infection that had gripped him so despotically since the night of the concert.

"I am sorry," Wikerus calmly told him.

"No, no, no, my good man. Your heart is pure and passionate. These things happen," the swan assured him with a few pats on the shoulder from the tips of his wing feathers.

Tannhäuser reached his hand forward and took the swan's head into his palm. He looked at the old sage with sincere admiration, and spoke in a low, dreamy voice, "Please forgive me."

He looked at the Brunnens, then again at the swan, took a deep breath, and ran through the portal. It closed behind him, leaving The Ancient One and the host of Brunnen leaders alone at the portal point in the valley, helpless, perplexed, and at an utter loss as to what could be done and what would come of this unprecedented breach.

CHAPTER 31
The Brunnen Wilderness

TRAVEL THROUGH THE PORTAL was not what Wikerus
expected it to be. All went black and quiet, but not silent.
The only thing perceivable to his senses was faint
swooshing sound, like wind through trees at a distance, and
the much fainter sound of voices that sounded buried, or
behind a wall. Light, sound, smell, and feel rushed onto
him at once. He was in a shaded forest. It was sparsely
wooded, with tall, thick trees, and minimal undergrowth.
Patches of short, thin grass grew sporadically between the
trees. The tops of the trees spread wide and dense, creating
a canopy that allowed the softest sunlight to the forest floor.

Four Unicorns stood in an arched line in front of him.
A single Zweigwesen stood between the middle two. The
Unicorns wore grimaces of severe disapprobation. Wikerus
had seen many Unicorns during his time in the valley.
Never had their horns looked so sharp or their eyes so
fierce. He had heard a dozen stories of Unicorn heroics in
defense of the valley, of the knights they had slaughtered
to keep the portal secret, of bands of wild men intent on
doing one Swan Knight or another harm slaughtered by the
fiercely loyal and protective Unicorns. Wikerus was aware
of the seriousness of his transgression and the depth of his
betrayal. Each shallow, faltering breath, he thought would
be his last.

A familiar voice cried out from behind the Unicorns. Rei'mund galloped, as only a Scherier does, between the Unicorns' cloven hooves, to sit upright an arm's length from Wikerus.

"They knew," he told his human playmate, "somehow the Unicorns knew this would happen. They have been waiting here for days. They said this would happen. I said no…, the Tannhäuser would not violate his oath. I said that, and so did Mercedes. But here you are. You did it, just like they said you would."

Wikerus dropped to one knee and hunched to be almost eye to eye with Rei'mund, and asked with resolute acceptance of his fate, "Are they going to kill me?"

"Kill you?" Rei'mund responded as if the notion was absurd, "No, they will not kill you…, not until the Swan Knight tells them to. But you will stay right here, until we hear from Ludwig."

The Zweigwesen, a kind and gentle healer, called Weichesholz, stepped forward and announced, "The Swan Knight is not in the valley. He is in Kelheim. We do not expect him back for many weeks."

Wikerus looked to the Unicorns, expecting some decision, some response to Weichesholz' declaration. They said nothing, but only stared directly into Wikerus' eyes.

Rei'mund broke the tense air, "Well, we cannot all stand here like this for many weeks."

The Unicorn on the far left of the four said in a gruff bark that ruffled her long beard, "Otto is in the valley. What he says, we will obey."

This was a surprise to none. Otto was close to the Unicorns and spent much of his time galloping around the valley on Unicornback.

"Come now, Helleklinge," Weichesholz reminded the same Unicorn, "We all know Otto. He might go days without opening the portal."

Helleklinge, tall, majestic, and matriarch of her clan, argued, "Someone would have seen him cross, or they will have guessed it, when he cannot be found. The swan is there. He will insist that Otto open the portal and deal with this."

"Or is it more likely," Weichesholz added, "that Otto would rather consult with his father first. He might already be on his way to Kelheim."

"Right, right," Rei'mund answered, "And we cannot stand here. What are we to do?"

"There is just one authority we must consult now," Helleklinge spoke with firmness, "We must go to Kandake. The Queen of the Land and Shallow Waters will decide."

Rei'mund shivered and spoke in a broken voice, "She will put him in her watery jail. I know she will."

Helleklinge reminded them all, "We are in her queendom. The Queen should decide."

"Wait a moment!" a high-pitched but scratchy voice rang from behind Wikerus.

Another Scherier walked beside him and stood low on all fours in front of the Unicorns. He tilted his head and placed his ear on the ground in a reverent bow to the noble beasts.

"You are not parading this man to the lakeside palace," the old Scherier demanded, "He has seen too much already. Is this not really a Brunnen problem? Am I wrong, or is he here because of a Brunnen? Rush him directly to Nährenstadt. The Brunnen council will be convened there. Let them serve the Swan Knight and the Queen by solving their own problem."

The Unicorns, and even the tender Weichesholz, were apprehensive, and shook their heads in subconscious unison. Only Rei'mund saw the wisdom in the suggestion, and nodded his pointy chin in agreement.

Rei'mund defended the old Scherier, "If the Old Digger says it, I think it is good."

The Old Digger was a legendary figure in the Scherier homeland, and throughout the Land and Shallow Waters. He designed and dug by claw most of the Scherier capital city of Eineklaue. He was well respected in every homeland. More importantly, he had the ear of the Queen.

The Unicorns closed their eyes and connected their minds, as only the Unicorns could do. They held council among themselves.

Their eyes sprung open together and Helleklinge spoke for them all, "Very well, Scherier. You are the bringer of the Old Peace. The Queen would take your suggestion, and so will we. But I will take him there, faster than any Unicorn has ever traveled. He will be blindfolded. And he must be muted as well. His voice cannot disturb the air. Old evils lurk in the wilderness of our world. You all have seen it."

Rei'mund ran up the leg of Weichesholz, and leaped from his shoulder to the back of one of the other Unicorns, and said in a tone uncommonly stern for him, "This is Wikerus, the Tannhäuser. He is a friend of the Swan Knight. You have heard the stories. I promise you." He looked directly at Wikerus and continued, "He will close his eyes and his lips, and he will keep them closed until he is well inside of the Brunnen capital."

Wikerus, half mortified and willing to take the remonstrance of the creatures, and half in anticipation of seeing the Brunnen homeland and possibly Caris, dropped to one knee and solemnly swore to do as Rei'mund said.

Helleklinge lowered his horn and directed Wikerus to grab it. Once the man had a tight grip, the Unicorn swung his head around effortlessly and tossed Wikerus high upon his shoulders. Wikerus looked to the Old Digger, who smiled and winked at him devilishly. He looked to

Rei'mund, whose expression was less friendly. He clinched his eyes shut with all his might. He bit on the inside of his lips, and Helleklinge disappeared through the forest, to the northeast, toward the Brunnen homeland.

Back in the valley, The Ancient One stood as he was when Wikerus ran through, passing confounded stares between the Brunnens and the silent, empty portal point. The Brunnens said nothing. They only dropped their heads, carrying the shame of their entire kind. The swan jumped up and flapped violently, taking to the sky in search of Otto.

He found the Swan Knight's son and told what had happened. Otto rode his Unicorn at full sprint to the portal point. He vaulted off of the beast and landed directly on his trigger point, opening the portal. Otto was furious and terrified. He feared what all Swan Knights since Lohengrin feared the most — that the portal would be breached, the Sweeter Realm destroyed, and the Holy Grail lost to evil on his watch. He sent the Brunnens home with his love and forgiveness but demanded that they move hastily and retrieve Tannhäuser to the valley. They disappeared into the Sweeter Realm with The Ancient One directly behind them.

Otto took his Unicorn by the horn and pulled the tip to touch the center of his chest. He thought the command, "You must oversee this. It is on your horn now. But first, go to the Queen and tell her what has happened. She must hear this from us."

The Unicorn thought his acknowledgement of the orders. But before Otto released the connection, he sent a thought from his heart through his friend's horn, "He is a good man. He is family. See that they are gentle with him."

The Unicorn pulled from Otto and ran through the portal. All of the yelling, wild flapping, and furious galloping drew Agnes from the lodge. She walked around the home to see her husband standing alone at the open portal.

She walked beside him, wrapped her fingers around the back of his neck, and asked, "He has gone though, hasn't he?"

Otto acknowledged the truth to her with a simple drop of his head to look down at their feet.

"Do you want me to stay with you?" Agnes asked him.

"Yes, my love. Please"

Agnes kissed her husband and stood tightly beside him, holding his hand. They both remained standing at the open portal, looking fruitlessly into it, praying that each moment would bring Tannhäuser back into the valley with no harm done, but fearing every imaginable disaster that could rise from the occasion— and there were plenty of those to consider.

Of all the terrible things Otto considered, none pained him as much as the inevitable duty of telling his father.

He turned to his stout bride and said, "This will wreck my good father, just as he is blissful again."

Agnes squeezed in tighter than before, and the two of them stared silently into the portal, while their united shadows grew long on the valley floor.

Several hours later, the swan stepped through the awaiting portal.

"He is gone," he told them, "deep into the Brunnen wilderness. Not even Queen Kandake could find him there, unless he desires to be found. He and Caris have been banished from the cities and forbidden to leave Brunnen land. The Brunnen wilderness is his home now, until he dies."

"Well," Otto said, happy with any report at all, "let us pray it comes to nothing."

When Wikerus and Helleklinge reached the Brunnen capital of Nährenstadt, the Brunnens already expected them. The council of sisters met them at the threshold of the city and escorted them into their most secret chamber. Wikerus' life was in jeopardy. Of course, he knew it was. But he did not beg for his life. He only asked that his eyes be allowed to swim once more in Caris' beauty, while his ears ride the cascading currents of her dulcet voice, one last time, so he can die truly blessed and content.

The Brunnens had no intention of killing their uninvited guest. He had mortified them and placed in great peril the ancient good-will between them and the descendants of Parsifal. Wikerus would not get off easily. But he was in no mortal danger while in their sacred homeland.

The Brunnens heeded his request and called forth Caris to stand beside her lover. Their embrace was something truly legendary, that sort of embrace one seeks for a lifetime and is so unlikely to ever experience, where unity, true unity of body and spirit occurs. Her skin rippled across her body toward him. He wrapped his arms fully around her and half again. He buried his face into her neck and drew an inhale that could have filled the lungs of seven men. He kept his eyes wide and made a study of a small portion of her neck and shoulder.

Wikerus released his love reluctantly, turned to face the Brunnen council, dropped to both knees, and said with a calm voice and a satisfied expression on his face, "*You will know bliss before you die, and your soul will be rested and grateful when you come face to face with the Lord.* That is what Father Stefan told me. He knew. Somehow he knew… Of course he knew. He was of God."

Wikerus looked upward, to the blackness above the mysterious Brunnen building. He raised his hand, as if to be grabbed from above, and whispered to Father Stefan, "Thank you. I love you."

The Brunnens were pure and pious, and they knew purity and piety when they saw it in others. Wikerus and Caris shared a pure and pious love, the sort that only comes as a gift from God. They would not be the ones to interfere. At the same time, great damage had been done by the lovers, damage the Brunnens were unsure could ever be remedied. They sealed off their borders, allowing nobody, man, woman, or creature to pass. They banished the couple to the savage depths of the Brunnen wilderness, where they were to live out their lives together, never again to be seen by another.

This was no punishment to either. It was not meant to punish, but to reward pure love while limiting the damage of the union. Without command or escort, Caris took Wikerus by the hand and led him from the building, out of Nährenstadt, and into the lush and untamed wilderness of southeastern Brunnen land.

Otto did not rush to Kelheim to tell his father about his treasured knight. Wikerus was gone to everyone but his lover. Nothing could be done. The Queen approved of the decision of the Brunnen council, and Ludwig was weighed enough with the politics of his duchy. Over the next few weeks, until Ludwig the Swan Knight returned to the valley, Otto received regular reports in his father's place, all saying the same thing, that there was nothing to report. Still, no news was a great relief to his ears, as he suspected that they had not heard the last of the Tannhäuser, and that the events that had just unfolded would somehow, someday impact them all, and perhaps the world.

CHAPTER 32
New Uses for Old Skills

CARIS AND WIKERUS TRIED TO SETTLE into the Brunnen wilderness. She found it more difficult than he did. Caris belonged to an exclusive order of Brunnen sisters called Die Engel des Mörsers (Angels of Mortar). It was the sworn lifelong duty of Die Engel des Mörsers to tend and repair the sacred shrines, churches, and holy sites of the Brunnen homeland. The position kept her in the populated centers and on the worn, pilgrimed paths and streams between. She was accustomed to company and the acclaim that her honored oath brought her. She was one of the few in the queendom trained to read, translate, and transcribe the archaic writings that adorned the older monuments.

After banishment, she found herself with only her lover and the whispered words of nature as company. The Brunnen wilderness provided plenty to eat and drink. Wild berries and fruit trees grew beside the many wild streams that striped the forests and fields. For the first few days, they sought no permanence, no structures to call their new and settled home. They scarcely broke eye contact and were constantly in each other's arms. After a few days, Caris longed for something, for anything that resembled her previous life. Oh, she was content to have given it up for her lover, and would do it again, a million times consecutively. But the romantic novelty of nights under the stars and days under the sun soon transitioned rather rudely to a desire for a settled home to call their own, where she could read to her lover and teach him of the Brunnen culture and traditions.

The challenge of building a structure was a tough one indeed. Caris forbade Wikerus to fell a single tree. The buildings of the Brunnen cities were a phenomenon difficult to understand. Their cities appeared to the unfamiliar as a simple forest or wooded field. Certain trees with a nearby twin were doorways. Walk between the twin trees and you find yourself in a building. Walk between the wrong two trees and you simply find yourself between two trees. A true intimacy of a Brunnen city is required to make one's way around.

Caris did not belong to the order of Brunnen architects. She could read ancient scribblings, but had not the first idea what strange science went behind the construction of a Brunnen city. At the same time, they could not destroy trees. Wikerus was forced to dig for clay and fill it with fallen leaves and branches to build the smallest hut, barely large enough to sleep the two of them. It was not the place of study and worship Caris and he both desired.

Help came their way in the most surprising form. While Wikerus scavenged for materials to repair their falling hut, he encountered another creature banished to that wilderness. It looked to him like a small, horned, winged rabbit with two long fangs jutting downward from its mouth. It was as peculiar to him as it was adorable and inviting. But that is not what kept Wikerus' attention. There was such an undeniable intelligence in the creature's eyes, eyes that spoke of joy and celebration, of a profound love of life, but of the deepest of sorrows and endless persecution.

The creature barely poked its head from behind a tree, until it stepped forward to get a closer look at its first human. No doubt it saw similar features in Wikerus' eyes. Forgetting himself, and fancying himself in his own world, not this creature's, he treated it as he would any adorable rabbit in the woods outside of Castle Tannhausen. He squatted down, whistled at it and snapped his finger, not imagining it capable of intelligent conversation. The creature raised its bushy eyebrows in disgust and ran away. Wikerus correctly interpreted its reaction and shamed himself for such narrow thinking.

"How foolish!" he said to himself, "After playing with the Scheriers and debating with the Zweigwesens, receiving their healing, after singing with the Brunnens and giving myself wholly to one, do I now still close my mind to this creature?"

He ran as fast as he could back to Caris and told her of the encounter, describing the creature in detail. Caris seemed more incredulous than *he* had been.

"You cannot have seen what you describe," she declared in disbelief.

Wikerus thought this to be strangely closed-minded for a creature who lived in such a magical place, until he heard her follow-up.

Speaking to herself but for him to hear, she added, "Unless it was a ghost that you saw. There are no ghosts. God's good creatures do not haunt. They are one with the Lord. So could it have been? Could they be here?"

"For Heaven's sake, my love," he demanded, "Tell me what you know."

Wikerus was in the right company for such a tale. Caris was well-versed in the dustiest old pages of Sweeter Realm legends and lore. She told him the tragic story of the Wolpertingers. Ages ago, before the reign of Queen Kandake, before the days of her predecessor, the great Unicorn Queen Achima, before the peace that united the Land with the Shallow Waters, the Land and the Waters were at constant war. The creatures of the Deep Waters were ruled by a tyrannical serpent. The Shallow Waters were not under the rule of the King of the Deep. But the King kept the Shallow creatures terrified and obedient just the same.

During the war, the serpents of the Deep captured thousands of the Land creatures. They tortured them before eating them, and developed a particular liking for certain breeds. Among the greatest Deep Waters delicacies was the Wolpertingers. After Achima secured peace and united the Land and Shallow Waters into one queendom under her reign, the wars ended, but the serpents' taste for

Wolpertinger did not. Hunting raids took them onto the beaches of every lake in the Land and Shallow Waters, into the woods, and across the homelands in search of the poor creatures.

The Wolpertingers were nomads. They roamed easily through each homeland, as friends to all. They scattered after the peace and sought protection where it was offered. Eventually, the last of them was taken to the Deep and eaten. No creature had seen hide nor soft little hair of them in the many long ages since.

It was more than the taste of their meat that drove them to death. The Wolpertingers were one of only a few known flying breeds in the entire Sweeter Realm. When the King died, and his infinitely wickeder son, Löwschock assumed the throne of the Deep, he wanted total dominion over the Waters. He was merciless to the border creatures between the Deep and Shallow Waters. And he wanted no creature living who could fly over the lakes and deep ponds and spy on his kingdom. He hunted the flyers with brutal zeal. First on his list were the old swans. He drove them to near extinction. Only The Ancient One and a few forgotten hermits remain of their kind.

The Wolpertingers enjoyed flying over the water and watching their reflections. They could not see the Deep Waters from above any more than I can see the core of the Earth from where I sit. Nevertheless, Löwschock hunted the poor Wolpertingers to extinction.

"Or so we thought," Caris concluded.

"If the Wolpertingers are all gone," Wikerus asked, "then what horned, winged rabbit did I see."

"No," she spoke resolutely, "they are not gone. They have come here *of course*. There is no place for them to hide that is better than the Brunnen wilderness."

She looked shyly to her lover and added, "This is where things are sent when they are not to be seen."

Wikerus raised his eyebrows as if to say, "Yes, well, that is us, my love."

"Take me!" Caris shouted suddenly, "Show me. Show me the Wolpertinger."

Wikerus took Caris to the spot, and there waiting for them was not the one Wolpertinger, but eight of them. They had been out of company with the creatures of the Land and Shallow Waters since well before the swan met Parsifal, long before the creatures learned German. Nor did the dear creatures speak Brunnen. One of them began to talk to Wikerus, in a high, melodic half-whisper. Wikerus gestured his inability to understand. It was clearly frustrating for both of them.

Wikerus turned in exasperation to Caris, whose eyes were wide and all aglow.

"The ancient tongue," she said in an ecstatic trance to no particular recipient, "They speak the archaic words, those written on the oldest of our shrines."

Caris took a step toward the half-circle of eight Wolpertingers. She sat on the forest floor and invited them to gather around her. They did not respond until Caris began reciting one of the prayers inscribed on one of the ancient shrines she had tended and studied since joining her order. At the first word, the Wolpertingers began whispering among themselves and gathering more tightly around Caris. They knew the prayer she recited. It was in their language — their very living and active language. They joined her, and Wikerus stood again in bewilderment of his amazing lover, as she prayed with the Wolpertingers in a language that maybe six or seven creatures under the Queen's reign, other than the Wolpertingers, could speak.

After the prayer, they struggled through Caris' limited knowledge of the language, to conduct the proper introductions and explanations. It was as she thought. The Wolpertingers united their nomadic clans in the wilderness of southeastern Brunnen land. They were far from the Queen's Lake, in the depths of which sat the throne of Löwschock. The only streams were narrow and shallow and difficult for the serpents of the Deep Waters to travel. Their new friends explained to Caris that the protections of the Brunnen homeland were not absolute. The serpents still found them. They still abducted them. It was rumored among them that those taken were devoured in cruel rituals, by the ancient demonic rites that Löwschock had revived from the lost pages of Deep Waters traditions. He was crueler than any who sat on the Deep throne before him. The Wolpertingers warned that the darkest of days would be coming to the Land and Shallow Waters.

Caris had no reason to believe that such dire warnings had merit. But then, she had no reason to believe that the Wolpertingers still existed and lived in numbers in the heart of the Brunnen homeland. They set such dark divinations aside for the moment. The Wolpertingers knew the area well and offered to help the couple in any way they could. Wikerus knew exactly what task to lay before their generosity first. He asked their help in building a home.

It was obvious that the Wolpertingers were uncomfortable lingering in one place. They spent a few days helping Wikerus and Caris build a nice home of clay and debris. But they rotated every few hours. No Wolpertinger was with the couple for more than a few hours. Their fear saturated the thick Brunnen air. The trees around them seemed to share in the apprehension. Less than a week after meeting the lost breed, the couple came to understand the fear.

In the evenings, before the sun set, the Wolpertingers would disappear from Caris and Wikerus' company. They did not say where they went. They rarely bid adieu. They scattered into the woods like their lives depended on it. One evening, just a few minutes after the last Wolpertinger left

332

their company, Caris heard a high-pitched scream with her keen Brunnen ears. She ran from their one-room house without a word. Wikerus followed. Her expression gave him just cause for concern.

They ran together into the dark woods and found a Wolpertinger, a dear creature with whom Caris had just finished singing and praying, clutched in the jaws of the foulest creature either of them had ever seen. It had two tusks extending from either side of its long, lower jaw. The tusks rose from the side of the jaws to the eye level of the beast, then circled backward like the horns of a ram. The equally long upper jaw was lined with foul, black, rotting, yet razor sharp teeth. The entire monster was covered in dark green, moldy, mossy scales that smelled of death. It crawled on four thick, stubby legs that appeared to be without joints. The ends of the stubby legs webbed out into fins.

The Wolpertinger held to a tusk and tried to hold himself above the lower teeth. He screamed in words that neither Wikerus nor Caris understood. The sentiment was plain enough. He was in pain and in fear of death. Just as Caris had amazed Wikerus when she recited the ancient prayers, Wikerus impressed his lover with a revival of *his* old skill. He attacked the beast like he attacked the faceless enemies outside the walls of Damietta. There was no pity, no compassion for the vile serpent. With nothing but his dirty clothes and his bare hands, he mounted the enemy and tore its scales from its body. He reached around to its left front leg and pulled it back until it snapped. The serpent howled and the Wolpertinger escaped its jaws.

The wounded little friend hid behind Caris. But that hiding place did not stand still. Caris joined her lover and attacked the serpent. She pulled on it and struck its hard, scaly head, while Wikerus pulled on a tusk. Caris grabbed the other tusk and pulled in the opposite direction. The beast broke like a wishbone. Wikerus rolled it onto its back, exposing its much softer under side. Both lovers struck the foul beast, forcing expulsions of rancid, gurgling, grunts, until it was dead.

When the battle was over, they noticed that their little Wolpertinger was gone. Who could blame him? The lovers dragged the carcass to their house and set it ablaze on a humble pyre. The odor was pungent and overpowered all of the pleasant smells native to their new home. As they watched the carcass burn and complained about the stench, they heard a small voice from behind them.

The Wolpertinger they just rescued from certain death stood among six or seven of his kind and informed the couple in his archaic language, "That is the smell of the Deep."

Caris translated and Wikerus responded, "It is the smell of death. I know it too well."

The little creature, seeming to already understand Wikerus' German, returned in Wolpertinger, "It is the same. The Deep Waters *is* death."

When Caris translated again, Wikerus had no response. He knew what his little friends faced, and the mantel of a holy warrior slipped over his spirit again, this time to a new Order, with no vows of chastity, poverty, and obedience. He was already chaste, loving forever-more his one true love. He was already impoverished, with nothing in his possession but what the wilderness offered. He was already obedient, captured with no desire for escape to a life he had no ambition beyond. A new identity was emblazoned upon his chest, one that blended his old with his new and raised a fire in him that made him feel that his own skin might ripple like the soft and nurturing skin of his only lover.

CHAPTER 33
IN THE FALL OF BLOOD

AFTER THE INCIDENT WITH THE TUSKED SERPENT, the Wolpertingers spent more time with Wikerus and Caris, and in greater numbers. The attack that the lovers witnessed was not an extraordinary occurrence. Sometimes months would go by without any sign of a monster from the Deep. On the other hand, weeks would drag by at a time when attacks happened every night. A Wolpertinger would drift to sleep with little expectation of awakening. They had reduced to a population so small that every surviving one of them could huddle into a tight mass and be seen in a single glance. Perhaps eighty lived, and their numbers dwindled each year.

Tales of their woes distressed Wikerus and bolstered his sense of duty to their protection. Caris committed to documenting their story and creating a dictionary of their language, scratched into the trunks of old, fallen trees. The Wolpertingers did not keep written records. They used to. But during their years of brutal persecution, writing was a leisure and luxurious accommodation they could not allow themselves.

"Why don't they fly above their attackers?" Wikerus asked Caris.

"Their wings are for long flights. They are migrational wings and not good for quick retreating. They have powerful legs for that, and are difficult to catch."

The Wolpertingers felt safer around our noble hero and his angelic lover. Never before had they defeated an attacker from the Deep. Running was their only defense. The glowing pyre of that smoldering carcass was a beacon of hope. They couldn't imagine Wikerus and Caris being defeated in a fight, not after word spread and their heroics grew with each retelling, as tales of that sort tend to do. They began to gather in larger numbers again, always in the vicinity of the couple. Over the next few weeks, they slowly revived their old rites, fell in love, returned to old customs and created new ones.

Five weeks went by without another attack. In that time, Caris took it upon herself to share with her lover and their friends the deeper truths behind Tannhäuser's blood. They were banished, never to leave the Brunnen wilderness, never to encounter another being, other than the Wolpertingers, who were as lost and isolated as the ostracized lovers. Caris thought Wikerus should know who he was and why the blood inside of him opened the portal.

Every loyal subject of the Queen knew of the Swan Knights. Many spent more time in the Portal Valley than in their own homes, especially the Unicorns and the Scheriers. The Brunnens were first introduced to the Swan Knight Elsa, the third Swan Knight and daughter of Lohengrin. They fought and died in the Portal Valley. In one rather recent incident, the Brunnens saved the valley from a band of Welf knights, luring them into the thick of the woods with their beauty and their song, to be ambushed by Unicorns, Zweigwesens, and Scheriers.

The Brunnens were great keepers of history, and Caris was one of their premiere historians. She was well-steeped in the Swan Knight history, from Parsifal to Ludwig. She pulled her lover into their house, pushed him to both knees, knelt in front of him, and told him what Ludwig and the swan would not.

"Have you wondered, my lover," she began, "why your blood opens the portal?"

"It is because I am a cousin of the Swan Knight," he answered like a student reciting his lesson.

"But who are the Swan Knights?" she asked while caressing his ear with her tender Brunnen fingers.

"They are the protectors of the portal to the Sweeter Realm."

"Surely you must know that there is more to the story than that," she hinted, "Something inside of you must be shouting at your open heart."

He sat back on his heels, took her hand from the side of his head, held it tightly on his lap, and answered, "This has to do with the Cup of Christ, doesn't it?"

"Yes," she whispered, "What else does your blood tell you?"

He closed his eyes and concentrated on all that flowed through his veins, reopened his eyes and proclaimed in wonder and delight, "The Holy Grail. It is here, here in the Sweeter Realm."

"Yes. And you?"

"I…, I am a child of the Swan Knights, a descendant of the keepers of the Grail."

Caris nodded her head and took his other ear with her other hand.

"Not just the keepers of the Grail…"

"Did we drink of it?" he asked her, "Is that why my blood is enchanted? Did I inherit Grail Blood?"

Caris told the story, well-chronicled in the Swan Knights history, of the founding patriarch of the Swan Knighthood, of Parsifal and his wife Gütel, how Parsifal was attacked in the Portal Valley, was saved by Gütel, drank from the Grail, and healed. She told him of the single drop of Parsifal's Grail enchanted blood that fell from his wound and opened the portal for the first time. She recited for him the oath to the Queen that has been administered by the swan to every Swan Knight, through Lohengrin and

337

Elsa, through Elsa's son and all the way down to Duke Ludwig. She told him many of the storied tales of adventure in defense of the portal and its secrets, and of the centuries of cooperation between the subjects of the Queen and the Swan Knights.

He delighted in the stories, but his face suddenly went sour and he pondered and asked, "From which Swan Knights am I descended? Where did my blood break from the Portal Valley?"

"I do not know that. I know that you come from Parsifal and the Grail Blood, just like Ludwig and Otto."

"Did I get the blood from my father or my mother?"

"What does your blood tell you?"

"… My mother, and my mother's mother."

"Yes, my treasure. I believe that as well."

Infatuated with his new-found lineage, Wikerus gathered as many of the Wolpertingers as were within earshot of his voice. He seated them around Caris and begged her to tell the story. They knew nothing of Parsifal and the portal, nothing of the Queen's agreement to protect the Grail. They wondered what sort of creature Wikerus was, unlike anything they or their ancestors had ever seen in the Sweeter Realm. Wikerus declared that they needed to know, that their reintroduction into the company of the Queen's subjects should begin with the Grail story. Caris told her eager audience, much as she told her lover, and they received it with similar intrigue.

Knowing of the sacred blood and heroic lineage of their new protector greatly bolstered Wolpertinger faith in their safety. They began to speak of a holy war against the Deep Waters. They feared little when another foul-smelling attack came to their little portion of the Brunnen wilderness. This time there were three serpents, one of the same kind as before, and two of another form. The two had no rear legs or fins, only two arms and a long, scaly tail.

They were crowned with a blade-like cone atop the head, which they slashed side-to-side in attack.

They came at night, as they always did. They knew nothing of Wikerus and Caris. They sought food in the Wolpertingers, as they had before, and were frozen in shock at the sight of a Brunnen and her strange companion in the refuge of the Wolpertingers. The hunted did not scatter, as was their common reaction. They rallied to the lovers' house and stood boldly and confidently behind Wikerus and Caris when they came out to investigate.

One attacker was a difficult enough battle without the addition of two more dangerous beasts. Wikerus took a firm step toward the hunters, and they squirmed backward in response. But their meal stood behind the defenders and the beasts were hungry. The blade-headed serpents came at them first. They whipped their tails and sent themselves flying at Wikerus and Caris. Wikerus parried the attack and sent one beast careening into a tree trunk. The other slashed Caris across the cheek and landed among the Wolpertingers behind her.

Not her banishment from the valley nor her exile into the wilderness had brought such a writhing wincing to her face, or such a painful screech to her throats. It sent Wikerus into a fury. Every moment of training with his father's tutors, every hour spent on Mainau Island, every swing of his sword in Egypt sprang from the memories locked inside of his bones. His blood pulled forth its sacred properties and conjured each conflict since Parsifal sipped from the Grail. His thoughts were unnecessary. His mind yielded navigation of his movements to the arcane heroism inside of him. Wikerus fought like fifty knights. The three intruders were grossly outnumbered by a single man.

He grabbed a coned beast by the tail and swung its bladed head at the other, slicing off one of its arms. He slammed his living weapon against a tree and knocked it unconscious. As he dropped it to the ground, the tusked serpent lunged at him. Wikerus wrapped his arms around its head. With one hand, he grabbed it by the nostrils. With the other, he squeezed its lower jaw. He hollered a raw, wild battle cry as he puffed his chest and pulled his hands apart, tearing its head in half like it was an old, worn, and weathered shirt. With his bare hands, Wikerus tore the moldy serpents into unrecognizable scraps of scales, blood, and bones. But his lover bled from her heavenly face, and one Wolpertinger died in the fight. No doubt they won the night. But the Wolpertinger faith that they were invincible in Wikerus' company evaporated with the sight of Caris' blood and the loss of their own.

The lovers and the Wolpertingers gathered tightly. They mourned their loss and they tended to the gash on Caris' face. Wikerus tormented himself.

"You fought like Saint Michael," Caris tried to convince him, "No creature under God's creation could have done better."

"It is not enough," he answered gravely, "We are not safe. That was three. What happens when we face four or six or a dozen?"

The question was a sound one, and it sobered the company with a heavy dose of the tragic truth. The Wolpertingers *were* safer with Wikerus and Caris. But they gathered in larger company than before and drew more vicious attacks.

With the deepest and richest of sorrow lining her dual throats, Caris said, "Maybe they are better without us, living as they did before, only two or three gathered in one place."

Wikerus shook his head, and many Wolpertingers reacted in kind.

"Are we the ones to bring salvation to these dear creatures?" she asked her lover with increased animation,

"We try to revive their traditions, to document their language, to bring them back to the glory of their ancestors. But is that worth their lives?"

The Wolpertingers had not been idle in their weeks of peace. With Caris' help, they were teaching themselves German. Caris was a proficient teacher and they were apt students.

One Wolpertinger stepped forward and reminded her, "We have lost one dear friend in two attacks. We have been used to mourning several after a single attack. We praise God for your banishment. You and the Grail Blood are God's answer to our prayers. Wikerus fought like a hero tonight."

"Not entirely," Wikerus interrupted, "A hero fights with his heart and his head. My heart fought. My head reclined. There is much that I know, much I have learned, things that cannot remain locked in my head while my heart defends us."

His words had a hint of optimism that drew closely the attention of all, particularly Caris'

"She pulled herself tightly against his side with both of her arms and whispered, "Go on."

"Weapons!" he told them, "We need weapons."

The Wolpertingers were confused. They did not know that word. They looked to Caris to translate, but she knew no Wolpertinger word for "weapons".

Wikerus explained, "The sharp edge of the serpent's head, that which cut Caris' face, I must make something like that for me to hold."

Their eager eyes showed understanding.

Wikerus' Latin schooling gave him a very different image of Saint Michael than that which was taught to young Wolpertingers. Wikerus returned the confusion, saying, "Like the sword carried by Saint Michael, which he used to slay Satan."

Caris explained to her lover that the old Wolpertinger images of Saint Michael were not like those in European art. The Wolpertingers, and most of Sweeter Realm religious culture, envisioned the archangel as a Unicorn.

Wikerus quickly adapted and amended, "Like the horn of Saint Michael, thrust through the serpent."

That was an image well-engrained in Wolpertinger culture. They applauded and vowed to assist in the construction of Wikerus' hand-held "horns".

One other measure of their defense was moved and seconded. Their stable target of a building and constant gathering place was a luxury they could not afford. They agreed to demolish the house. Wikerus and Caris left what little life they had allowed themselves to settle and build. They stripped themselves of all that was not essential and assumed alongside their friends the life of a nomad. Caris and Wikerus became Wolpertingers. Perhaps that is unfair to say. There was a proportionate blending of their ways. But the changes were more dramatic for the Brunnen and the human.

Wikerus shed his clothing and walked about like every other creature of the Sweeter Realm. His period of awkwardness was brief. Caris had no real notion of nakedness. Her kind occasionally adorned themselves with a garland of flowers around the waist, but wore no clothing. She saw the things that the Swan Knight wore and grew accustomed to seeing it on them, but never understood the purpose of it, other than the fact that the valley grew icy in the winter and the humans were not tolerant of the cold.

So, Wikerus and Caris lived with the Wolpertingers, as *they* had been living, while making Wikerus wooden weapons from the old fallen branches around the woods. Within days, he had a staff, a wooden short-sword, and a bow with a few arrows. They dared to continue gathering in larger numbers. Their desire for society grew hungry.

They disbanded for days at a time and reconvened in different areas of the Brunnen wilderness.

Wikerus and Caris enjoyed the days they had to themselves, away from their scattered friends. Their love continued to grow in their shared purpose. Caris taught Wikerus the languages of the Sweeter Realm, including the ancient words of the Wolpertingers. He came to understand Brunnen, but comically failed to reproduce the language with his single human throat. The society they enjoyed with their little friends made their time alone with only each other a cherished treasure. They spent the time getting to know each other intimately, binding their strange and instant love with the love of familiarity. She was the air he breathed. Her company, her smile, her smell, and the way her skin rippled, was all that kept his lungs filling and emptying. He became the daily spark that lit her passions for all that she loved. Without him, nothing was attractive. Nothing was worth seeing, tasting, or touching.

CHAPTER 34
New Life, New Plans

SEVERAL WEEKS OF PEACE FOLLOWED the destruction of the house. They limited the size of their gatherings and made themselves a more difficult target. Reports of Deep serpent sightings would come to them from the Wolpertingers they encountered. The reports were often third and fourth hand. One evening, just after the setting sun revealed the stars, after Caris had trained hard with the wooden sword, the couple found a spot near a stream. They held hands and sat with their feet soaking in the running water. Wikerus stared in awe at Caris as the ripples of the water appeared to ride up her legs, across her body, and onto his hand, as her skin imitated the stream. The hand Wikerus held was quite dry. But it soothed him like running water, and at that moment, he considered himself the happiest of creatures.

He giggled like a child, entirely encased in his adoration for her. She giggled in response. In an instant, her expression dropped, and her skin held still.

"What is it?" he asked.

She looked to her feet, released his hand and plunged herself hip-deep in the stream.

"The water speaks to me of violence," she said with horror in her throats, "Foul things are in this stream, and the blood of the innocent."

She sprang from the stream, took Wikerus' hand, and yelled, "This way, hurry. Grab your weapons!"

They ran upstream along the bank. Wikerus carried his staff and knife. Caris carried the sword with which she had been training. They left the bow behind. Within minutes they could hear the bustle of scrambling creatures, the hollers of Wolpertingers, and the grunts and growls of hungry Deep creatures. A few seconds later, they could smell the stench of the Deep. There were at least thirty monsters on the other side of the stream. Some were scaled and similar to the enemies they had faced so far. Others were fleshy, with human-like arms. Some were long and low, like a crocodile, others tall and standing on two legs. All were ferocious. There were plenty of fangs, tusks, claws, and hard, bladed body party among them. And all were hungry for Wolpertinger flesh. They knew to strike at the wings first, disabling flight and leaving the Wolpertingers with only their legs to escape.

Wikerus dropped the knife and used the staff to vault across the stream. He gave a war cry that was so blaring and piercing that it drew all attention from the scrambling Wolpertingers. In groups of three and four, the creatures of the Deep Waters broke from their pursuits and charged at Wikerus.

Caris crossed the stream and stood beside her love. "Too many," she warned in fear.

The couple took a concerted step backward. Wikerus stepped his bare foot on something that could not be mistaken. He looked down and saw the half-eaten corpse of a little friend. By the unique marking on her legs, he knew which friend he had lost. She had spent much time with the lovers, and had grown dear to Wikerus. Wikerus looked at the body at his feet, then looked up at the approaching monsters with a deep growl and face that told Caris that there would be no retreat that night. He gathered his heart *and* his head, recalling all that he knew of warfare and allowing it to ride the rushing wave of rage.

Weary from training and the hard run along the stream, the lovers entered the battle. They tried to remain near each other, but the enemy was too numerous, and the chaotic flow of fighting took them apart. Caris wielded the wooden sword like a holy knight. Wikerus performed magnificent fetes of violent acrobatics with the staff.

The Wolpertingers were gone from the bloody arena. They ran and flew in such terror that they did not realize Caris and Wikerus were there. By the time they realized that they were no longer pursued, no longer being snatched in mid-leap and severed in two by rancid and razor-sharp teeth, they were far from the scene of action. They regathered in small groups to search for their wounded and dead.

Caris and Wikerus were like harmonizing notes moving spritely up and down a scale, sometimes fighting back to back, sometimes hand-in-hand, and sometimes separated entirely. At one point. Wikerus threw Caris over a wall of four charging beasts. The first thing to land was the tip of her sword in the back of a serpent's neck. It squealed and arched as her feet followed the sword, landed on its back, and forced it to the ground so hard that foul air and liquid evacuated from inside of the monster like sailors from a burning ship.

There are no trees in the Deep Waters. Its violent citizens had no skill at utilizing them. Our hero and his lover on the other hand, they swung and vaulted, climbed and sprang from the trees around them. Their enemies could not tell where they went or from where they would appear next. Wikerus leaped from a low branch, onto the back of a tall, scaly, fish-like creature. It had thick legs and webbed feet. Its short, muscular arms looked almost human as they came from the shoulders. At the elbows, the arms flattened into sharp fins. It had a normal looking human skull, except for the long snout — more like the bill of a pelican, but scaled and filled with teeth. It was covered entirely in slimy, slippery scales. Wikerus slipped off of it and fell to his back.

The monster bore down on him, opening its long mouth toward his face. The mouth opened wider, and a circular, hose-like tongue flailed like a whip to the shrieking noise that came from its throat. Thick, webbed feet stood on Wikerus' staff and he could not dislodge it. Just as that wide mouth drew near enough to snap his head off, the tip of Caris' wooden sword appeared from the back of the monster's throat, above its tongue, and shot forward from its mouth like a second tongue. Coated in blood and slime, Caris' sword came within a few inches of Wikerus' nose. It retracted as quickly as it appeared as Caris withdrew it from the base of the monster's skull. It was dead before her sword fully cleared it. She kicked it aside and reached for her lover.

Wikerus took her hand and sprang to his feet, darting his eyes in all directions. Nothing around him moved except for the heaving chest of his lover, and her skin that rippled outward in response.

The Wolpertingers continued searching, cutting circles nearer and nearer the battlefield. They found dead and dying Wolpertingers. But they also found Wikerus and Caris, kneeling in an embrace, with carcasses of more than thirty monsters scattered about them. Every one of the monsters was dead. Not one of them twitched with the faintest sparkle of life. The Wolpertingers surrounded their rescuers and poured gratitude and affection upon them.

When they were recovered of breath enough to stand and help. Wikerus gathered the bodies of slain Wolpertingers, while Caris joined in the search for the wounded. The moon made the dead glow morbidly silver. Some lived and were carried away from the scene, only to die later that night. Some recovered to tell the tale of the battle. In the final hours before sunrise, Wikerus and Caris left their friends to mourn and recover. They found a secluded place to tend to their own recovery.

They were hidden inside of a large verdurous grove with a clearing in the center, about thirty feet wide. It was a living wooden grotto of sorts, with a thick wall of trees and growth encasing them like a cave with no ceiling. The tree trunks grew nearly atop the next. It was difficult to walk through and impossible to see through. There was one narrow path through the shell of trees to the clearing. Only the stars above had a view of our two lovers. Only after they found themselves inside of this natural barrier did the couple allow a healthy deep exhale and examination of each other for injuries. Some minor cuts and plenty of scrapes and bruises gave them discomfort, but little pain.

Wikerus dropped his staff and took Caris by the upper arms, "Thank God for you, my love."

She looked into him and saw admiration in his eyes with a brilliancy like she had never seen in him before.

"You were a valiant warrior tonight," he continued, "You saved many lives. You saved my life."

She tilted her head and began to cry. She buried her face in his chest and said, "You fought like twenty of me."

He pushed her away from his chest to look her in the eyes again, and said, "But I am a knight, a warrior. You are a Brunnen scholar, not made for war. Yet you rose to the occasion and fought beside me better than any knight of my order. You are always everything you need to be. I love you. I love you."

He drew her into his chest again and continued to repeat, "I love you. I love you."

They dropped to their knees, holding hands and gazing more penetratingly into each other. The victory and the losses, the warm profusions of gratitude showered upon them by the Wolpertingers, and their own heroics in battle further strengthened the already profound connection between them. They wanted for nothing but the company of the other. At that moment and onward, their most sacred purpose was to love and protect the other. They were equal individuals whose lives intertwined so tightly and complexly that their spirits had grown together and could no longer be distinguished individually.

They remained on their knees facing each other. Their eyes were bright *and* dark. Their touch cold and hot. When they met in the theater of the Portal Valley, they were drawn to each other by an arcane love. On their knees together in that secluded grove, they wrapped and bound that love in shared experiences that were sewn tightly through them both.

They knelt only connected physically by their held hands. But the chord of communion between their eyes and hearts was so thick and strong, it could not have been broken by every hard tusk and rancid, sharp fang in the Deep Waters. They leaned forward in unison and touched their foreheads together. With only those three points of physical contact, in the timeless tradition of Brunnen spiritual reproduction, their spirits united and Caris conceived their child inside of her. They both knew at the instant.

They cried and professed their love and devotion in the most sincere and binding terms. And since no combination of words, in any and all languages ever spoken or sung, could encompass the depth and width of their feelings, they stopped trying and simply hummed. They brought their sealed, humming lips to lightly touch the other's, then parted them slightly, just enough to sing their harmonizing notes into the other's mouth. Music, breath, love and commitment, and a shared future flowed back and forth between their open mouths.

The child was not conceived in a light and playful love, during a free-spirited time, in the lives of ordinary Brunnens. The child was extraordinary in many ways — the first of human blood conceived in spiritual reproduction, the first Brunnen of a non-Brunnen parent. But most profoundly, the child was conceived under a sort of love beyond what any other Brunnen had ever felt. There was darkness in their shared experiences and darkness in their love. There was darkness in the spiritual connection that brought the child into being. But there was a brightness of faith in each other and in God that balanced the darkness to perfection. At the moment of conception, both Caris and Wikerus knew that their child would be unique among all creatures, on either side of the portal. They did not know exactly what to expect. With their faith in each other, God, and in the child inside of her, they did not care.

Caris sang a lullaby to the new life inside of her. They held each other tightly, fell flat in that embrace, and slept together as a family. They awoke a few hours later determined to change the nature of their existence. They could not return to the Brunnen cities, or cross the Brunnen border into other lands. They chose that grove as their new home, determined to deliver the child from her mother in the exact spot where their united spirits created her.

They gathered some of their Wolpertinger friends, shared the news, and set immediately to fortifying the grove. No structures would do. They could build nothing that could not be breached by a force like the one they faced the night before. So they planted trees, thickening the verdurous wall that hid them so well that night. As only the Brunnens can, Caris nurtured the trees, and within weeks they slept behind a virtual fortress of trunks and limbs.

Caris designed a maze of trees, winding from the entrance to the clearing. The wide canopy of branches and leaves covered the maze. The center clearing was open to the sky, and the Wolpertingers could fly in and out as they pleased. It was unrecognizable as an intentional structure from the outside, and the perfect place for their little community to prepare for the birth of the child. Their labors in its construction served to bind their spirits to the child whose conception inspired it.

The child grew quickly inside of Caris. Within three months, she was in no state to fight. She roamed during the days, when the creatures of the Deep dared not attack. They walked along the streams together. Caris remained ankle deep so the water could communicate to her any warning of violence ahead or behind. During the night, she remained in the fortress grove, rubbing her belly and telling her unborn child the tales of her love for Wikerus.

CHAPTER 35
Eccentricity of Form

ONLY FIVE MONTHS INTO PREGNANCY, Caris seemed ready to deliver the child, especially when Wikerus was near. The child desired his company and leaped within the womb toward his voice and touch. Wikerus slept much of the day. At night, he climbed the highest tree in the grove, and posted a lookout. Although he could see her in the clearing from his high perch, she could not see him, and she was very lonely. She spoke loudly to him, shouting up to the treetops. Her voice called out to any monster within a mile, announcing the location of the secret wooden fortress and the expectant mother inside. Wikerus was aware of this, and he cringed when she spoke out to him. But he would not stop her. She needed him to hear her voice. So he let her call out, and he answered when she prompted him to.

The Wolpertingers saw him in the treetops, and heard their exaggerated conversations with their long and uncommonly keen ears. They offered to take his place. Wikerus recruited five volunteers, who maintained watch through the night so he was able to join his wife and expected baby and hold them both through the night.

Attacks continued. The Wolpertingers gathered the remainder of their kind near the fortress grove. They were still nomadic and roamed as their instincts demanded, but remained within a reasonable sprint to Wikerus and his weapons, and always within sight of the Wolpertinger

352

lookouts. When an enemy was sighted, the lookouts gave a whistle, and the hunted made their way quickly to the fortress. Serpents found the fortress, but never breached it. They were unable to squeeze their bulky bodies in the narrow spaces between the trunks. They followed their intended prey into the maze entrance. Nothing of the Deep Waters left the maze alive.

Security liberated their tongues to speak of other topics. Discussion and debate arose among the lovers and their friends about the sex of the child. Would it be a boy or a girl, or like its mother's people — without sex. How human and how Brunnen would the child appear? Secretly, Wikerus hoped that their child would take one form or the other entirely, hoping for his child what is not available to either him or Caris, a life among their kind.

One night, the full moon rose directly over the narrow clearing in the center of the thick canopy of the grove. Silvery light lit the interior of the fortress like a steely sun. Caris and Wikerus were alone. The lookouts held their positions with eyes outward. Caris recited Brunnen ecclesiastical poetry to her lover, in the Brunnen language, soulful and melodic.

When she finished, she kissed Wikerus and said to him, "The baby is coming."

"Now!" he belted in a panic, "What do I need to do?"

"No, my treasure," she responded calmly, speaking in German but harmonizing her throats as if speaking in Brunnen, "the baby comes tomorrow morning."

"How do you know?" he gathered himself and asked.

She looked at him with a slightly tilted head and a grin that spoke for her. It said without breaking the air between them, "Why do you ask me such things, when the answers are beyond explanation?"

He read the grin as only a dedicated scholar of her face could.

"Then I will see our child tomorrow, and it will be my turn to hold her," he responded with warmth throughout his chest.

"Her?" she asked probingly, "Do you say the child is as a human girl, or as a Brunnen, womanly but without gender?"

"She is a girl, like a human girl, but most certainly of your kind," he answered with confidence.

"How could you know that?" she asked sincerely.

He tried his best to imitate her telling grin. He failed. There was no muscle within him capable of imitating her delicate form in any way. But she understood and giggled at the turnaround.

For the first few hours after the next dawn, Wikerus asked five times per hour, "Now?"

She never answered. She only smiled at him, until mid-morning, while they leaned against the trunks of the grove interior, when he opened his mouth to ask again. She answered before the question could gather in his mouth, "Yes, love. Now."

She took him by the hand and began to lead him into the entrance maze.

"No," he spoke firmly while tugging against her pull, "It is safer in here."

She released his hand and turned to face him squarely, saying, "The sun shines, and the foulness of the Deep Waters hides where the brightness cannot penetrate. Come hold your child... your daughter."

He returned his hand to hers eagerly and followed her through the maze, to a clear, low, rounded hill nearby. Without ceremony and without words, Caris reclined in the short grass. She delivered their child directly into Wikerus' hands. The baby appeared quite human, with amber hair that mimicked the locks that flowed from her father's childhood head. Her skin was pale and silvery, like a mirror that gave no reflection.

Upon making first contact with her father, she opened her eyes wide and stared without a blink into Wikerus' face. With her first cry, she declared her Brunnen lineage in exquisite fashion. This was not the shrill pronouncement of a human baby's birth. Two steady, pure, and flawlessly harmonizing notes swam with easy conviction from the girl's twin Brunnen throats. Her song, like the sirens of legend, entranced her doting father.

Caris, while her chest heaved with exhaustion, fixed her eyes on her lover and her child. Her skin turned rosy-pink and began rippling in all directions. As her love and joy swelled, the ripples grew and crashed against each other. Of all the lovely sights in the Sweeter Realm, she had seen nothing that stirred and agitated her rich, tender, and abundant affection like the vision before her.

Wikerus sat with a gaping mouth, entirely embedded inside of his love for the daughter he held. Her first cry, which rang in his jubilant ears like a thousand choirs singing of the Resurrection of the Lord, faded to its elegant conclusion. Time seemed to freeze in the moment of silence that followed. Mother, father, and child were motionless, as if they were mere images, captured by oils long-since hardened to a canvas, but as vibrant as the day they were brushed by the artist.

The static scene was broken by Wikerus' giggle, a boyish, child-like giggle that would have struck Methildis von Tannhausen as intimately familiar. In contrast with the puerile sound blurting from his lips, his eyes expelled such a flow of tears that his cheeks appeared to ripple like a Brunnen. The baby imitated her father's laugh, in a crude but effective communication, while ripples rolled down her dry cheeks, in a reflection of her father's tears. Caris sat up on her own and enveloped them both in her soft, nurturing, loving, and maternal arms.

Caris named the girl Chryzanthoseude, a name when spoken correctly required two throats to say. The first two syllables were spoken with one throat, simultaneous with the other three syllables with the other throat. Wikerus accepted the formal Brunnen name, but declared that she would be called Zanthie, a version of the name that he could form with his human physiology. Caris fed Zanthie under the bright, open sky of the unwooded hill, while Wikerus crawled in circles spiraling outward around them, picking flowers and knotting them into a garland for his daughter's head. They spent much of the remaining day on that hill. The Wolpertingers watched from a distance, but gave the family their space, and neither did nor said anything to make the three of them remember that they were not the only creatures in God's creation.

Well before sunset, Wikerus whistled for his friends. Every living Wolpertinger bore down upon the hill, by foot and by wing. They paraded the parents and child down the gentle hill, twice around its base, and triumphantly through the maze and into the fortress.

There were so many more than five or six guards on the tallest trees of the grove that night. It seemed that every tree that surrounded the family boasted a pair of sharp, defensive Wolpertinger eyes, and many had more. Zanthie was as much theirs as she was Caris and Wikerus', at least that is how they felt. Every leaf that twitched in the light breeze drew fifty eyes to it, every rustle of the low bushes brought long Wolpertinger ears into a tremble. The new family saw nothing of it. Such things were not their concern that night. Wikerus and Caris formed a sort of cradle between their wrapped arms and intertwined legs, where Zanthie spent her first night in no less warmth, comfort, and security than she enjoyed in the womb.

Wikerus had a dream that night that remained with him in little less clarity through the following morning. He was back in the Brunnen capital, surrounded by their council of leadership. The council was not angry or embarrassed. A different sort of desperation molded the contours of their troubled faces.

They pulled at him and begged him to follow them. He looked to his left and right. Caris was not with him. The Brunnens led him to the outskirts of the city, where an ancient shrine sat statuesque and mossy. It was about four times Wikerus' height — a flat-topped cone, something like a spent volcano. Fountains sprang randomly and sporadically from its sides. But the water that came from the fountains was not water at all, but stone carved to imitate flowing water. The stone water was not still, but appeared to cascade down the shrine as water would.

A band of writing encircled the base of the shrine. It was in no language Wikerus could decipher. Still, the Brunnens begged him to interpret the writing. When he said that he could not, they shook him violently and begged again. Wikerus stared at the writing, walking slowly around the shrine in search of any single character he recognized or could make sense of. About halfway around, he saw a symbol that struck him. He could not say how he knew, nor can I, but he understood the symbol to represent Zanthie. He followed the writing, understanding bits of it. It spoke of Zanthie's future. A magic sword, endless fields of armed enemies facing her, the Holy Grail, pain, loneliness, fury, violence, and a new Queen, a human Queen of the Land and Shallow Waters, standing at Zanthie's side — these are the disconnected pieces of the monument's writing. Each word bit at Wikerus' lungs and made it painful to draw breath.

He made several laps around the shrine, looking for words to connect the images into some narrative he could follow. As the day went dark, the Brunnens left him. Wikerus continued to walk circles, straining his eyes to see the symbols. When he awoke from the dream, his legs were fatigued, and his lugs still felt the bite of panic.

His eyes opened to a warm and blissful scene. He still held his lover and his daughter exactly as they had fallen asleep. Wikerus needed rest to recover from his dream. So it is just as well that neither Caris nor Zanthie seemed inclined to begin their day. The early morning passed in care-free comfort. By late morning, Wikerus' active mind began to probe deep into his daughter's future, prompted by the lingering sensation of the dream, posing questions to him that needed answers.

"Where will she live?" he asked the mother.

"Right here, of course," Caris answered slightly perturbed.

"Yes, yes. I mean when she is grown. We have each other. Who will she have? She will be eccentric of form in any setting, any Brunnen church, or any human village. Where will she make her own life?"

"We are in exile, my love," she spoke in confusion, as if having to remind him of his own name.

"*We* are exiled. She is not."

She looked downward and considered his point, then responded thoughtfully, "She will always remind the sisters of our union, of our breach and their humiliation. I am afraid she can live no blissful life among my kind."

"And among mine?" he added, "She will be peculiar in all company. Trust me. My kind are not accepting of that which differs from them. There she would be unsafe."

They agreed that their current course of discussion led them down no fruitful paths. It was not a question that required an immediate answer. They prayed together that God would guide them, and guide their daughter when the time came. They canvassed the matter no further that day.

There was enough in the present to fill them to their limits with both joy and fear, but both continued to devote their silent musings to the distant future and the perplexing dilemma of Zanthie's adulthood.

CHAPTER 36
Visitors

PERHAPS THE MONSTERS OF THE DEEP sensed a new power in the Brunnen wilderness. Chryzanthoseude quickly showed herself to be something more than Brunnen, and much more than human. When she was hungry or desired attention, she sang out in her two voices — notes of magnificent purity, that were by no means painful to hear. So it was difficult to explain why it aroused such a desperate need in her parents to make it stop.

Her cry for attention was unlike anything else that came from her mouth, and it carried much farther, maybe beyond the fortress grove and the wilderness, past the Unicorn homeland and the Nomadic Belt, through the Shallow Waters of the Queen's Lake, to the throne of Löwschock. At any rate, Zanthie's birth began a period of peace, when nothing foul, nothing that reeked of death and the Deep showed its scaly form in the Brunnen wilderness.

The uniqueness of the child did not only reach out to what is foul. Without knowing why or what drew them out of the pockets of Sweeter Realm society and into the wild, visitors came to the grove. It began with a flock of seventeen Eulesängers. They did not land and converse, but only flew overhead and whistled their concern and well-wishes to Caris and Wikerus. They did not see the baby, but they knew that they were drawn to a new power, something beyond the notoriously arcane love of the most famous lovers in the Land and Shallow Waters. Caris understood the language of the Eulesängers, but could not sing back to them in their native whistles. She shouted her gratitude in German, which they seemed well to understand. They circled around the grove a few times and flew away in the direction of the Eulesänger homeland.

In violation of their laws, a single Brunnen ventured out into the wilderness to bring gifts to Caris. The Wolpertingers spotted the sister well off and soared to tell the couple. Caris met her far from the grove. Her name was Graféas, and she was of Caris' order. Graféas brought books. Some were dictionaries of the ancient languages. Others were filled with the legends and lore of the Land and Shallow Waters. There was one book of religious canon, and a single book of empty pages for Caris to fill with her own writing. The gifts were warmly accepted along with the tender greetings that were sent through Graféas by some of Caris' dearest friends. A long embrace was exchanged, complete with the skin rippling routine that was a sort of "secret handshake" of their order, and Graféas returned the way she came.

A couple of years went by with no more visitors and no attacks from the Deep. Our hero and his family spent the entire length of the day and night in each other's tight company. Zanthie's future may have still been a subject of consternation, but her present was more blissful than any young thing that had ever lived. She played with the Wolpertingers, who loved her as their own and praised her like a queen. The love in Wikerus' heart for Caris was in no way diluted as he doted on his daughter, but seemed to double with every hour.

The weapons they had made sat unused. Caris filled her idle hours with study and writing. Wikerus spent every second he could with Zanthie. There was no swordplay in those days, no training for battles, only peace and love. The child spoke in exquisite Brunnen and German by the time she was two years old. Before she was three, she wrote in many Sweeter Realm languages, including those ancient scribblings only known to her mother's order. Caris made games of Zanthie's education. She would bury rocks for the girl to find. With each rock Zanthie found, she would have to recite a verse from scriptures, translated into a different language for every rock, for every verse.

Soon after Zanthie turned three years old, she and Wikerus were playing much deeper in the woods, much farther from the grove than she had been before. The years of peace had faded all fear from the woods. Wikerus held Zanthie on his lap and napped against a tree. He awoke an hour later and his daughter was gone. Old fears resurfaced. Old memories came screaming back to the front of his mind with vivid vengeance. He yelled for her, and he ran without thought or direction through the woods.

He was brought to a halt by a wonderfully familiar sound. The cry of Zanthie's infancy bounced between the trees. Wikerus followed it and found his lost daughter. The cry penetrated the much thicker air of the Sweeter Realm and found its way to some curious ears. The Unicorn Helleklinge, the same that confronted Wikerus at the portal point when he ran into the Sweeter Realm, sensed the cry for help and responded. She was near the portal point, in the Nomadic Belt near Zweigwesen land. She fetched her old friend, the Zweigwesen Weichesholz, whom Wikerus had also met. Weichesholz mounted his friend high on the Unicorn's shoulders and the two of them raced toward the innocent cry.

Unicorns sprint at great speeds, but the cry ended before they crossed the border of the Zweigwesen homeland. With the keen Unicorn sense of direction, some prayers, and some luck, Helleklinge and Weichesholz found their way into the Brunnen wilderness. They both knew where they were, and they both knew who was in exile there. They suspected that the cry had something to do with the banished lovers. That is all they would come to know. With his faithful Wolpertinger eyes throughout the woods, Wikerus knew exactly where to head them off.

His previous encounter with Helleklinge was less than friendly. It would be fair to say that he was trepidatious. He stood in an open area in their path, intentionally conspicuous. The Unicorn found him easily.

"Tannhäuser," Helleklinge said with Weichesholz still mounted high upon her, "It is good to find you well. Please tell me quickly, how is Caris?"

"She is well," Wikerus answered dryly, "She and I are both well."

Helleklinge waited for words to be added, for some elaboration that could explain the powerful vocal beacon that drew her into the Brunnen wilderness.

Wikerus only added, "We are both happy and well."

The visitors understood Wikerus' tone and posture. He did not trust them.

Weichesholz broke the silent tension saying, "Thank God for that. We have prayed for you both every day since your exile."

Wikerus did not draw his eyes upward to the Zweigwesen, but kept them gripping tightly to the gaze of the Unicorn.

In the sort of bluntness that develops when someone spends too much time in intimate company, and none among others, Wikerus asked, "Would you have killed me that day, when I crossed through the portal? Would you have deprived Caris of her only lover, and…"

He stopped short, almost revealing his most precious little secret, that which beckoned the visitors to the wilderness.

Helleklinge did not read into the unfinished question, but defended herself, "I serve the Queen of the Land and Shallow Waters, and I serve the Swan Knight."

"So you *would* have killed me if you believed they wished it."

Weichesholz tried to soften the sharp air around them, adding, "We would have mourned you, all of us, in the Portal Valley and in the homelands of the queendom."

The sentiment was effective enough to allow Wikerus a tender reminiscence of the Swan Knight.

"How is Ludwig?" he asked softly.

Helleklinge answered, "Your transgression was hard on him. But the Swan Knight is a strong man, noble and pious, as stout as he is faithful."

"Yes," was Wikerus' answer, "Yes, I know he is."

He wanted to say that he was sorry for all distress he caused. He could not form the words. He knew, and they knew as well, that his love for Caris would have driven him to any deed, and would drive him again if fate demanded it.

Weichesholz addressed the obvious question, "There was a scream, or more of a song, a sad and desperate cry."

Wikerus put his hands on his hips, lifted his chest and lowered his chin, and responded, "It was not the first cry to ring in the wilderness, nor will it be the last, I imagine."

It was obvious that Wikerus knew what they did not, and had no intention of telling more. The Brunnen wilderness was his and Caris'. The Unicorns and Zweigwesens had no righteous duty to investigate further. Weichesholz yielded as much and begged his Unicorn friend to turn around and take them home.

"As you can see," he said to Helleklinge, "he is well and happy. There is nothing in these woods that needs our assistance."

Helleklinge lowered her head in a deferential bow to Wikerus. Wikerus saw the horn coming to his chest. He was not going to let the Unicorn probe his thoughts. He took three large steps backward and retuned a formal bow to the visitors. Helleklinge raised her head and lifted a half-grin, distorting the symmetry of her wiry beard. She huffed and trotted away.

Wikerus stood and watched, and as they diminished in his sight, he saw Weichesholz turn toward him as he yelled, "Our prayers are truly with you. God bless you, Tannhäuser, and God bless Caris."

Wikerus waved to him, and continued to wave until trees and distance obscured them entirely from his senses. When he turned toward his home, he saw dozens of Wolpertinger eyes observing him with defensive pride. They came out from the tops of trees and from behind rocks and bushes. They walked beside and behind their treasured friend, looking up to him, waiting for him to speak. He had nothing to report to them that they did not witness. They walked leisurely through the wilderness until they reached the fortress grove.

Wikerus told Caris of the encounter. Zanthie listened closely. She was uncommonly intelligent and contributed often to the deep, complex, and philosophical discussions that graced the grove, often surprising them with wisdom beyond their own.

The thoughtful little girl said, "It was my cry that drew them, wasn't it?"

Caris, not wanting to burden such a young heart, answered, "They came because of what your father and I did, not for anything you did."

Wikerus contradicted his lover and told the child, "As you have perceived, my precious one, they heard your cry. You are different than any living creature."

"We are all different," the child answered.

"No, my love. There are many like me and many like your mother, like there are many Wolpertingers. But you are the only one of your kind. You have abilities that we must understand and control."

Zanthie looked to Caris, who nodded her head in agreement, but added, "This is a challenge that belongs to all of us. It is yet another delight in our lives together, like any fun game or challenge."

Zanthie looked back to her father, who nodded his agreement while a single tear wiggled free of his left eye and took a casual stroll down his cheek.

"You are a delight to us in every way," he told his daughter, "Everything about you brings us pride and puts us in greater debt to the Lord. We do not fear your uniqueness, but it is important that we understand it."

Zanthie smiled, then giggled and slapped at her father's leg, saying, "You're the bird and I'm the worm," and she ran from him in a game they often played together.

She had never seen a bird *or* a worm, not like the ones that inspired the game her father taught her. That did not stop her from running in circles and looking back to see if she was being chased. He ran after her, of course, flapping his arms like wings, but not before placing a tender kiss on his lover's lips. The kiss spoke of their unity in all things, and their united commitment to their daughter.

CHAPTER 37
Lost in the Grass

IT WAS COMMON FOR THE CREATURES in the Sweeter Realm to make grand affairs of occurrences such as marriages, births, and deaths. It was not a general practice to recognize anniversaries of any kind. Other than the sacred Christian holidays of Christmas and Easter, influenced by their bond with the Swan Knights, their calendars were not marked with annual celebrations. Impromptu homage to some historical event or another was known to swell into large gatherings and boisterous celebration, but did so without rhyme or reason, and were held to no particular day.

Wikerus, however, was not from the Sweeter Realm, and although he abandoned almost all of his previous life in adapting to his new one, he kept with him a few stubborn sensibilities. For example, he insisted on the annual celebration of Chryzanthoseude's birthday. Preparations for her fifth birthday were so seriously and intricately planned by Wikerus that Caris swore it would rival the coronation of Queen Kandake.

The Wolpertingers were tasked with decking the fortress grove with an abundance of flowers, of all colors. Wikerus also made it clear that a gift would be presented to the child from her only friends and playmates. It was to symbolize the relationship between the Wolpertingers and "The Family", as the Wolpertingers came to call them. With their long front teeth, they whittled a staff, perfectly fitted to a five-year-old girl. From top to bottom, carved into the wood, were detailed figures, telling the stories from their history with Wikerus and Caris. In the very center was a likeness of Caris with her wooden sword, hacking away bravely at monsters from the Deep Waters.

Caris tore from her precious books a specific selection of prayers, and bound them into a new book made especially for Zanthie's unique spirituality. Wikerus took the clothes he wore when he crossed through the portal, clothes that had not covered his body in years, and fashioned them into a family of dolls — a father, a mother, and a little child.

Zanthie slept soundly on the eve of her birthday, while the Wolpertingers decorated. Wikerus made a large pile of dried grass on one end of the clearing. He hid the three gifts inside of it. In the morning, Wikerus and Caris rose to see their daughter gawking at the flowery grove. Wikerus whistled for their friends, and the Wolpertingers came pouring in, some through the maze and some through the gap in the canopy above.

When they were all gathered, the visitors lined up and processed by Zanthie, each standing tall on their back legs, only to bow low and wish the girl a "Happy Birth". She knew what they meant and she smiled and stroked each one of them between the long ears and down the back.

Once the wishes were all spoken, Wikerus drew her attention to the mound of dried grass.

"Three gifts for you are hidden in the grass, one from the Wolpertingers, one from your mother, and one from me."

Wikerus had a specific order in which he wanted them discovered, and he arranged them accordingly. The bottom tip of the staff stuck slightly out, and Zanthie saw it before she touched a blade of the dried grass. She pulled it out and her eyes nearly doubled in size.

"It is for your long walks," one of her friends told her, "and look, there is a story in it."

Zanthie allowed her eyes to trickle slowly down the staff and absorb the depicted stories in dramatic form. She gasped when the carving told of adventure, and sighed when it told of love. Wikerus was too eager, and he took the staff from her before her eyes reached the bottom.

"There's more," he reminded her, while pointing into the pile.

The next thing she found was the prayer book. Wikerus allowed her more time to examine it than he permitted with the staff. Zanthie stopped at one page, her favorite prayer, one which Caris recited to her every day since infancy. She read it precisely in her mother's tone and inflection, utilizing her dual throats to Brunnen perfection, while Caris silently moved her lips in perfect synchronization.

After handing the book to her father, Zanthie dove to the center of the pile. Buried completely out of sight, she let out a squeal of glee. She poked from the center like a jack-in-the-box, holding high above her head the three dolls, bound loosely together with twine.

"That is us," Wikerus informed her.

"Yes, I can see that," she replied with passion, "it is us, you, me, and mother."

Chryzanthoseude untied the twine and examined the dolls closely. She set the small one on the floor in front of her and held closely to her eyes those which represented her parents. Her skin turned rosy and began to ripple upward. Never had she felt so uplifted by love. He skin rippled larger and faster, until she grew lighter than the thick Sweeter Realm air and floated off the ground. Astonishment was universal. No Brunnen had such an ability. Caris walked to her lover and took his hand.

Zanthie's wide smile went wider, and she floated toward her parents, as she shouted, "Look at me! I am like our friends…, in the air like the Wolpertingers."

"You are in the air, child," one of the winged friends replied, "but not like us."

Wikerus nodded his head without breaking eye-contact with his daughter, and said, "He is right. This is not like them, or like anything. Come to me."

Wikerus held out his arms, and when Zanthie was directly above him, he told her to come down. With no transition, her skin stopped rippling upward and she fell at a normal rate into his arms. The Wolpertingers all hollered in applause. But Caris and Wikerus did not.

"This could prove dangerous," Caris commented, "if it cannot be controlled. Where could she fly and how far could she fall?"

"Yes, yes, my love," was his answer, "She must be taught to control it."

Where Caris saw disaster, Wikerus envisioned opportunity. His mind set immediately to devising ways to train and control this new-found ability in his daughter, to keep her safe, to facilitate her escape from danger, and to someday serve the family as her parents had, in violent defense of their friends.

One week after the birthday celebration, Wikerus took his daughter away from the fortress grove, to a sparsely wooded field. He sat her down, held her little hands, and spoke to her of the responsibilities that come with her uniqueness. He told honest stories of his own mistakes, and of the regret that gnaws at him from the inside. He told her of the oath he swore to the Teutonic Order, and of the Chivalric Code, by which all warriors for God must live.

The girl took well to the instruction. When Wikerus was finished speaking, she stood and asked, "Can I be a knight like you? I want to live by the code."

Wikerus' heart swelled with pride and relief. He told her to kneel before him. She did so with a gravity of mood that was beyond her years and bordered on the comical. Wikerus pulled his wooden knife from the band around his hips. He tapped it on her shoulders and swore her into a life in service to God.

"Do I get a sword like Mother's?" she asked excitedly.

"In time, my very dear one. First, let us see what you can do *without* a weapon."

There was one skill alone that he wished her to hone and control. It was her ability to float. They worked for hours. His goal was to see her float to the highest libs of a tree, safe from the monsters of the Deep, then float softly and safely back down. They were not without success on that first day of training. She raised herself on command, but no more than her own height from the ground. She did not come down softly, but fell at her full weight.

Wikerus delighted in the progress and showed no signs to his daughter of his frustrations and fears. They worked much later than he intended, and did not begin for the grove until the sun was low. It was fully dark before they reached home. To save time, and in conflict with his better judgment, Wikerus took them near a creek.

"Watch the water," he instructed his daughter, "Anything foul could spring from it. It drains into a deep pond where the King's subjects live."

They ran along the creek, with eyes glued to the water beside them. The attack came from the other side. Wikerus caught the odor of them in time to turn and see four slimy-scaled figures barreling at them. It was dark. The moon was still too low in the sky to assist their defense. All Wikerus saw was greenish scales and the flash of white teeth and tusks.

"Now!" he shouted to his daughter, "Float above them!"

She tried but could not. The monsters must not have considered the girl to be a threat. They focused all attention on the father. Wikerus was on his back, being bitten at and scratched at by all four attackers. Zanthie had just sworn an oath of obedience. She held tightly to her father's command. She stood as she was, straining and concentrating, rippling her skin upward to no avail. She did not float, nor did she see her father's battle beside her, for her eyelids were squeezed tightly shut in concentration.

She did not see, but she heard. The sounds of the fight terrified and infuriated her. Bones snapped loudly, grunts she knew to be her father's were followed by shrill and horrifying screams. The smells and sounds of the battle made her want more desperately to succeed as her father commanded. But her feet remained on the ground.

The creatures of the Deep knew nothing of Wikerus. None who encountered him had lived to tell of him. They came that night to hunt Wolpertingers, otherwise, they would have sent more and larger, attackers. They did not encounter their desired prey that night, but a knight and father. With his little wooden knife, Wikerus made quick work of them.

The sounds of battle that shook poor Zanthie's ears with fury ended with a crack and a squish, a deep and gurgling release of air, and the soft voice of her father saying, "It is over, my love. We have won."

Wikerus rose to find his daughter's Brunnen skin rippling with a vengeance, but not upward. It crashed in all directions. It seemed that only in lightness of heart could she raise herself. The desired skills would come only after she learned to control her emotions.

At the sound of her father's voice, and the sight of him standing tall and well, her skin reacted to her relieved emotions, rippling upward and lifting her off the ground. She went higher than she had all day. Her feelings were authentically exuberant. Wikerus caught her by an ankle and pulled her from the air and into his arms.

As he held her and kissed her, a rustling drew their attention to the pile of carcasses. One of the beasts was not dead. It wiggled and writhed its way toward the creek.

"Look father! One is getting away!"

Wikerus had too much in his heart to portion to his mind its share of control. He had fought alone and won. His daughter was safe. And he watched her float almost out of his reach. That was more than enough victory for one day. He did not pursue the beast, but held his daughter tightly and continued kissing her.

Chryzanthoseude wiggled in her father's arms until he placed her gently on her feet.

"What is wrong, little one?" he asked her.

"Why did you let that one live?" she demanded, with hands on her hips and a puzzled look on her face.

"It is wounded and unlikely to recover. I assure you, my love, that beast will never bother us again."

Wikerus knelt in front of his daughter, took her hands, and told her, "That creature was made by God."

She winced as if the very notion caused her pain.

He continued, "We did not give it life, and we should not be so determined to take it. God will hold us accountable for each life we take. We had better be justified."

His warning did not seem to move her.

"I am sure it is justified," she answered, "I'm sure it will not come back to fight us again, but it will tell its king about us. Right now, Löwschock does not know that you are here and that I am here. Soon, he will know. And Mother, dear Mother and the Wolpertingers, the fortress grove, now he will know."

Wikerus' heart sank under the weight of his daughter's foresight, and shivered at his own lacking. They rushed home and doubled the sentries over their home. They gathered the entire population of Wolpertingers within the stout trunks of their circled grove. Although Caris could not imagine the wounded creature returning by way of the creek to the Deep Waters of the nearest deep pond quickly enough to cause them concern that night, she still shivered in fear until morning. Nothing came to attack them that night, but preparations were made well into the morning for what might come the following night.

As soon as the Land was bright the next morning, Wikerus took Chryzanthoseude back to the same sparsely wooded field. They trained as the day before, for many uninterrupted hours. The results did not call for celebration, nor did they bring frustration. The child made some progress, using happy thoughts and memories to elevate her mood and send her skin rippling upward. She brought with her the three dolls made by her father. In holding them together in front of her, she found her lightest feelings.

One lesson was learned from the previous day, and it was not a lesson for the girl. Wikerus kept an eye on the sun and left the field shortly after midday. They would arrive at the fortress grove well before sunset. With enough success to put a little skip in their steps, father and daughter held hands and went home.

The tips of the grove trees were just barely in sight. Wikerus pointed them out, but Zanthie could not see them. He hoisted her onto his shoulder to give her a better view. The sight of home lifted her spirits higher. She turned rosy-pink and Wikerus had to hold tightly to her legs to keep her seated firmly on his shoulders. With his eyes upward, he did not see what lay at his feet. He stepped onto something warm, soft, and wet.

He looked down with his spirits still high. They fell at a dizzying rate when he saw what his foot had felt. It was the body of a slain Wolpertinger. By now, he knew them all well and cared for each individually. This one worked closely with Caris in her efforts to document the Wolpertinger language and culture. The child also saw the body, and cried the poor creature's name. Wikerus looked sharply around him, but saw nothing but the body of his friend. He walked gingerly forward at first, which slowly transitioned to a run, as he began to fear for his home.

As he ran, he saw the bodies of Deep creatures, scratched and gnawed by the teeth and claws of Wolpertingers. They must have fought well. For every slain Wolpertinger, there were three dead monsters. The sight of each dead friend quickened Wikerus' steps. With his daughter still upon his shoulders, he ran at full speed toward the grove, looking downward to the dead, but also to his right and left. It was daytime, the sky was bright, and their home was attacked by the dark monsters of the Deep.

Suddenly, Wikerus came to a halt at the sight of a slain monster. It was not the teeth and claws of their friends that killed the beast. It was lanced through the neck by Caris' wooden sword. His lover fought in the battle. Wikerus lost his mind. He forgot about the child on his shoulders and ran toward the grove, screaming Caris' name. Zanthie fell from her father, recovered herself, and ran after him as fast as she could.

The signs of Caris' heroism increased as he approached the thick wall of trees. Evidence of the proficiency of her sword lay strewn about in mutilated form. Wikerus ran around the grove, to the entrance of the maze. He looked inside. It was undisturbed, as if the day had nothing peculiar to boast. He left through the maze and ran out into a nearby field. There were no dead Wolpertingers, but the grass was disturbed by violence. He called for his lover but heard no response.

Finally, a faint breath rose above the knee-high grass. He followed it and found Caris. She bled from more places than Wikerus could count. He dropped to his knees and lifted her to his lap. Her eyes were closed with extreme and pathetic anguish frozen to her face. Her expression spoke of her own fear and physical pain, but also of her compassion for their lost friends.

"Caris," Wikerus begged his lover, "open your eyes. I am here."

He never saw her eyes again. She responded to his request by deeply and painfully drawing her last breath, and letting it go with a vocalized whimper. She was dead in his arms, still wearing her miserable grimace.

Wikerus screamed the most wretched sound to ever catch the wind of the Sweeter Realm. He pulled his lover's body to his chest. She went soft, as if her bones disappeared inside of her. It sent shivers through him as he relaxed his embrace and drew her from his chest. Her skin turned blue and began calmly rippling downward. She melted away, appearing to his eyes to turn to water in his grasp. But he remained dry as he held her. She fell apart, through his arms and his fingers, and into the grass at his knees. He clutched at what remained of her as she ran through his fingers, until nothing of her remained. There was no sign of her on his arms and hands, nothing of her on his lap, and nothing on the grass between his knees.

Chryzanthoseude caught up to him and stood behind her father, crying and holding tightly to her dolls. She called to her father, but he did not notice her.

He looked to the grass in front of him and said in a whisper of disbelief, "She is gone. I have lost her."

Wikerus stood and began walking forward, looking not where he was going, but down to the arms he held out in front of him, picturing Caris' body as he last saw it.

He walked mindlessly, varying his speed and paces with no pattern, saying in gradually increasing volume, "She is gone. I have lost her."

His daughter dropped two of the three dolls, clinging only to the likeness of her mother. She followed behind, calling to him more desperately as they went farther and farther from their home. Wikerus walked in this manner, repeating the same words, through the sunset and into the night. The desperate, hungry child followed behind, calling constantly to him. She followed her father through the night, out of the Brunnen wilderness and across the border into Zweigwesen land. They continued as the sun rose to their left.

The poor, brave girl! She watched her mother's last breath, and on legs that burned with fatigue, she continued to walk behind her father and cry for his attention. They were seen leaving Brunnen land and the Brunnen leadership pursued them. Word also reached The Ancient One. The Brunnens and the old swan found them as they approached the Nomadic Belt. Except for the brief visit from Helleklinge and Weichesholz, nobody had seen Wikerus in six years. They knew nothing of the child or the fate of Caris.

The identity of the child was no mystery. She was clearly the product of Caris and Wikerus' love. The Brunnens found father and daughter as they had been for more than a full day. Wikerus called in tormented despair, "She is gone. I have lost her," while Zanthie followed closely behind, begging for her father, and clinching tightly the doll made of his old clothes. The Brunnens surrounded the girl and tried to nurture her. She recognized them as her mother's kind, but it was her father and only her father that she wanted.

She had never met any creature but her parents and the Wolpertingers. No creature in the many homelands of the Land and Shallow Waters knew that the borders to the Deep Waters had been breached, and that the subjects of King Löwschock raided the wilderness for innocent flesh.

They found out when the swan wrapped the girl in his wings and asked her what had happened. She knew well of the swan. Both of her parents spoke well and often of the venerable sage. Chryzanthoseude spoke in Brunnen, and told the swan everything that had happened.

By the time they knew the truth, Wikerus was far in the distance and well out of sight. When they silenced their company, they could faintly hear his wailing. They followed him toward the portal point, where Wikerus' feet instinctively took him.

Otto and Agnes were in the Portal Valley. Ludwig had given them the Palatinate on the Rhine, where Agnes was raised. They had recently given birth to their second child, a son they named Ludwig, after his grandfather. Their daughter Elizabeth was two years old. At that distance, and with the affairs of the Palatinate in their hands, Otto and Agnes did not come often to the valley. They were there to celebrate the birth of baby Ludwig with the swan and their other friends from the Sweeter Realm.

Agnes wanted to see if the baby's blood would open the portal. She carried little Ludwig to the portal point, with Elizabeth toddling behind. A faint crackle stirred in the air in front of her, but no portal appeared.

"This is nothing to alarm," Otto told her, "Few have been able to open the portal during infancy."

Otto stepped forward and opened the portal himself, expecting to greet the swan. To his astonishment, the Tannhäuser walked through instead, naked and dirty, crying and calling out, "She is gone. I have lost her."

Wikerus walked right by his former student, brushing him like he was a mere breeze. He went into the lodge and closed the door behind him. Agnes held baby Ludwig. Little Elizabeth stood beside her mother. Otto stared at his wife in astonishment for a few exaggerated moments before turning to the lodge.

When Otto crossed his trigger point, the portal remained open by the blood of Elizabeth. Just as Otto reached for the door of the lodge, Wikerus busted through, wearing his old, stained Teutonic tunic, and carrying his Marian Sword, which had remained in the lodge as he had left them. He jumped onto Otto's horse and rode savagely out of the valley, south, into Graswang Valley. The Swan Knight's son and his family retreated to the lodge, letting the portal snap to a close behind them. They knew there was a story behind Wikerus' strange appearance through the portal. They saw in the strange occurrence the cover of a book whose pages were locked to them. It was nothing that could be resolved that evening. They went to bed confused and in a state of severe agitation.

CHAPTER 38
The Birth of the Legend

AFTER COMFORTING CHRYZANTHOSEUDE and gathering what information they could from the child, The Ancient One and the Brunnens followed Wikerus. They caught up with him in time to see him disappear through the portal. Just as they reached it, it snapped shut, leaving them in the Nomadic Belt with Wikerus' child. The swan kept a nest near the portal point in the Sweeter Realm. He settled the child into the nest and held her. He waited, with the Brunnen leadership and a growing crowd of Zweigwesens surrounding him and the child.

Otto rose early the next morning. While his wife and children slept, he strolled thoughtfully but aimlessly around the lodge, cutting larger circles with each pass. He had allowed Wikerus to carry precious secrets from the valley. He could have ordered the Unicorn sentries to stop him. Fretful regret chewed at him. He brought himself solace in the self-reminder that his father loved the Tannhäuser. That thought alone relieved his worries.

Otto strolled until he accidentally crossed his trigger point and opened the portal. It startled him. When he recovered, he sat in front of the crackling circle and stared into it, as he so often did as a child. He thought about The Ancient One. He needed, at that moment more than ever, to consult with the swan. He was startled by the sudden appearance of a Brunnen, followed by another, and

380

another, until the entire Brunnen leadership stood before him. They were timid and scared of Otto's judgment. From the moment they exiled Wikerus and Caris into the wilderness and sealed their borders, no Brunnen had left their homeland. They did not associate with the other creatures of the Land and Shallow Waters. They did not come into the valley and sing with Otto. The Swan Knight's family missed them during the years that followed, and prayed for a return to the old good-humor they had enjoyed since the Brunnens first presented themselves to the Swan Knight Elsa.

Otto smiled at the Brunnens with a face of love and eyes that begged for the sort of nurturing that only the Brunnens can provide. The visitors relaxed their timidity and returned Otto's smile back to him. Otto began telling the Brunnens how much they had been missed in the valley, but his words were cut short by a surprise far more shocking than the return of the Brunnens through the portal. The swan stepped through with Chryzanthoseude. Otto needed no hints to the identity of the girl. When she walked and her skin rippled, she bore the color and features of a normal human girl with Brunnen skin. When she stood still, she faded into the ghostly vapors of a still Brunnen. When she held herself perfectly motionless, she nearly disappeared entirely from sight.

Otto kept his eyes on the girl, trying to maintain a warm and welcoming calmness, while he asked the swan beside him, "This is Tannhäuser's child?"

The Ancient One extended his wing, pointing to the huddled crowd of Brunnens, knowing that their reconciliation with the Swan Knights required their participation, and he answered, "This is not my story. The Brunnens should tell you."

Before any word on the dire topics at hand were passed from mouth to ear, the Swan Knight's son embraced and kissed his Brunnen visitors, assuring them of his love and insisting that no blame or resentment toward the Brunnens was ever felt in the Portal Valley. Once that was completed, the Brunnens told what they knew. At points they spoke individually, at points in chorus. They sang, they spoke. They used one throat and both. They slipped into the Brunnen language until reminded that Otto did not understand Brunnen.

At the end, Otto knew all that the Brunnens and the swan knew. He told them that Wikerus went into the lodge, put on his old tunic, cloak, and sword, and rode south from the valley. They all brought Chryzanthoseude to the lodge. They woke Agnes and Elizabeth and introduced the poor girl to the only humans other than her father that she had ever met. She delighted at the sight of Elizabeth. She had never known another child. She was three years older than Elizabeth, who smiled and waved at her.

Elizabeth's smile warmed Chryzanthoseude, whose skin began to ripple upward just as Agnes lifted her into her arms.

"You are as light as an empty eggshell," Agnes noted, then asked, "What is your name, our dear one?"

Chryzanthoseude spoke her full name in the Brunnen pronunciation, using both of her throats.

"I am sorry, my sweet," Agnes said in a motherly tone, "I cannot say that. What does your father call you?"

At the mention of Wikerus, Chryzanthoseude dropped her head and thought about her father, still clenching the doll of her mother's likeness. Her mind went speedily through every warm and gentle memory within her reach. Her skin began to ripple upward. She turned lighter than air and raised slightly out of Agnes' arms. Her skin turned red and tears flowed down her face. Agnes pulled her in tightly and wiped her cheeks. The appearance of tears continued to flow, but the child's cheeks were dry. Agnes wiped and wiped again, but each time she pulled back a dry hand. It was the skin of her face that rippled downward and gave the appearance of tears. She was trying to tell Agnes that she was sad, without having to speak of her beloved father.

Agnes sensed this and told her, "My treasure, we are your father's family. We are *your* family. We love you very much. Now, we must give you a name that we can all say."

The swan spoke immediately, "I already have one in mind. She looks exactly like Hildemar at that age, the daughter of the Swan Knight Elsa and her husband Cunrad. She is half Brunnen and half Hildemar. I would like to call her Brunhilde."

Otto stroked the girl's face with his thumb and repeated, "Brunhilde…, it is perfect."

Agnes squeezed Brunhilde more tightly and announced, "Whenever you are in the valley, you are Brunhilde, our darling Brunhilde."

Agnes set her down among the Brunnens and told her, "You are welcome in the Portal Valley whenever the sisters would like to bring you."

The Brunnens timidly interrupted and informed Otto and Agnes that the child cannot return with them to Brunnen land. The exile of the parents extended to the child. They held no ill-will toward her, but Caris and Wikerus had brought humiliation to the Brunnens. Whether it was actual or only perceived was irrelevant. The laws of the Brunnens forbade Brunhilde's accompanying them back to their cities and shrines. They could not send her into the wilderness alone. That left just once option.

"We are sorry," the Brunnens sang in unison, "She must stay here."

The lodge was silent under the heavy pall of the proclamation.

"She would never be able to leave the valley," The Ancient One insisted. "She is peculiar in both worlds. She would draw attention wherever she went."

Agnes broke the following silence, looking directly at Brunhilde and saying, "So she will stay here with us."

To the swan's occasional resentment, the valley had been left empty sometimes for months at a time, when neither Duke Ludwig nor Otto could spend time away from their secular duties. He reminded Agnes that if the valley is to be the child's home, and she may never leave it, a member of the Swan Knight's family must always be in the valley with her.

"No,' Otto retorted sharply, "We will try to find her father. Until then, you must raise the girl."

The swan protested with a series of sound points. But Otto reminded him that Brunhilde is the daughter of the Tannhäuser, who is a descendant of Parsifal. Brunhilde can open the portal.

He told the swan, "While we are from the valley, the child will allow you to open the portal and refresh the sentries. Keep her at a wing's distance, old friend, but see the opportunity she provides."

There was wisdom in Otto's words. The old swan wrapped his long neck around Brunhilde's forehead and rested his beak on the crown of her head. He enveloped her entirely in his wings.

He poked his head from the dome of feathers and announced with more vulnerable affection than any had seen from him in years, "She will be mine as long as she needs a father... she will be mine."

The Brunnens were embarrassed for all the trouble caused by their sister and her lover. Agnes reminded them that Caris and Wikerus' love brought them Brunhilde, and that is to be praised. She absolved them of any sense of guilt and begged them to resume the old relations.

In her wisdom she spoke, "I am proud of whatever part I have played in those events. It brought us Brunhilde, our sweet treasure."

At that comment, Brunhilde's skin rippled rapidly upward. She gave a slight push off the floor and rose out of the swan's embrace, floated across the main hall of the lodge with the doll of her mother in her hand, and lowered herself with control into Agnes' accepting arms. Everyone gawked in amazement, even the Brunnens, who had never known such an ability among their own kind.

The swan did not gawk, but observed with satisfaction, and spoke quietly as Agnes caught her, "That is a talent I must develop in her. Agnes is right. She is a gift from God and she will do us good."

Wikerus was well into Austria before he regained his senses. He had no memory of walking through day and night, crossing the portal, and riding away on Otto's horse. He was confused to find himself on horseback in his old clothes, clearly not in the wilderness of Brunnen land. In a flash, the memory of Caris' last breath grabbed his consciousness and shook it violently. He thought about his daughter, his little Zanthie, and he fell from the horse in tears.

After a good cry, and some confused contemplation, he decided to go back to the Portal Valley, open the portal, and return to his daughter. He did not know that Brunhilde had followed him. He had no reason to imagine that she was lovingly accepted into the arms of Agnes and Otto. He thought that all hope for reconciliation with Ludwig was shattered the moment he violated the Laws of Ermenrich and ran through the portal. His horse took a few steady trots back toward Bavaria before Wikerus stopped again, stuck between chapters of his life.

"I cannot show my face in the Portal Valley," he thought. "My Zanthie, my sweet daughter, she will find her mother's people. I cannot take her here, among humans. Her future is in the churches and shrines of the Brunnens. They are better for her than I. I have nothing to give her."

Every potential scenario played through his head at a lightning rate. He could not return and live with his daughter in the fortress grove. Caris was dead and the Wolpertingers with her. He could not parade her on horseback through the towns of Europe. He could think of no place better for her than in the care of the Brunnen sisters. On that determination, he turned around again and rode for Rome, resolved to address the Pope and beg for reinstatement in the Teutonic Order.

He took the verdurous paths, those used more by the wildlife than by human travelers. No part of his mind was prepared to deal with human beings. Before crossing out of Austria, he came to a sudden stop. His path was blocked by a broken cart. One wheel was broken, and the horse that pulled it was gone. Poor but pristine clothes were strewn about, across the back of the cart and onto the path. Wikerus dismounted and investigated. On the far side of the cart, half buried in the thick brush, were four bodies — a man, a woman, and two young children. They were half stripped and slashed through the heart. Each one bore the face of anguish that held to their skulls as life left them. The wounds were precise, calculated with skill to hit their mark and end life quickly and efficiently.

The sight of innocent bodies, of slaughtered innocence, was too fresh in his most painful memory. Wikerus flew into a rage. He mounted his horse and rode down the path. Within half an hour, he came across a band of four men with sacks full of goods and pulling an unmanned horse behind them. He found the murderers. He tore off the path and cut a wide circle through the thick trees to meet with the path ahead of them. He rode directly to them, and while still well in front of them, recognized them. Their leader was tall, wore a single strip of leather armor across his chest, and carried two short swords. This was the marauder he defeated without spilling a drop of blood, and allowed to live and retreat with his gang.

"Why did you let that one live?" his daughter's voice rang in is ears.

It repeated and grew louder, piercing the side of his head and splitting his skull.

"Why did you let that one live?" louder and louder in Zanthie's voice.

He looked to his empty arms held out in front of him. In them, he saw Caris, exhaling her last breath and falling away into the grass. Her image was replaced with the anguished faces of the slaughtered family beside the cart.

"Why did you let that one live?" he began to speak aloud with the ringing voice of his daughter. He grew louder with each recitation, trying to drown out the splintering echo in his ears.

The four men were still about forty feet down the path when Wikerus and the voice in his head stopped shouting. The family's stolen horse stood orphaned beside the leader. Wikerus raced after the murderers. The men were still on the path. Each man for himself, they did not stay together, but scattered apart into the woods. Wikerus caught them one by one and struck with the same sort of precision used to kill the traveling family. One, two, and three — all but the leader were pierced by our hero's ceremonial sword and died before falling from their horses. Wikerus hardly disturbed his horse's stride.

He caught up with the leader, who now, in Wikerus' tormented and regretful imagination, bore the face of some foul creature of the Deep Waters. He knocked the man from his horse, drew his own horse to a stop, dismounted, and faced the murderer.

"I should have listened to Zanthie," he told the man.

The marauder drew his swords, not knowing or caring what Wikerus meant by his words.

Wikerus held his sword in front of him and marched slowly forward, saying, "I let you live and now my Caris is gone."

A sword swung at Wikerus' head from the side, which he parried with ease. He continued to march at the man, never swinging his Marian Sword, but blocking strike after strike, while the man backed at equal pace.

"Oh Zanthie," he said, staring the man in the eyes and flicking away the attempted strikes, "I should have listened. I should have saved your mother."

"I do not know a Zanthie," the killer shouted, "I have never heard of Zanthie!"

Wikerus disarmed the man's right hand with his next parry, and smacked him in the ear with the broad side of his sword as he had done years before, but harder, this time cutting the man across the cheek. He flicked away the other short sword and wacked the man across the top of his head, again with the flat side of the sword, as he did when he encountered the villain in the village. The man fell to his knees.

"I should not have let you live," Wikerus told him, "My Caris is dead, and so is a husband and wife, and their two small children. God knows what other lives I might have saved that day, if I would have angled my blade more viciously and killed you on the street where we fought."

"I—," was all the man could speak before Wikerus drove his sword through the villain's heart.

Through the sound of gasps, he added, "No, not the same as them, not for you."

He withdrew the sword quickly. Before a drop of blood could escape through the fatal wound, the man's head was severed from his shoulders and resting against Wikerus' right boot.

He felt great satisfaction, not for avenging the slaughtered family, or for some displaced revenge for the murder of his lover. He thought of what future misery and death was spared by his crusader's sword. The thought rallied his knight's blood within him. He rode with little rest to Rome, determined more than ever to see the Pope and gain reinstatement into the Teutonic Order

It was not uncommon for a Teutonic Knight to ride into Rome and demand an audience with the Pope. Knights of the Holy Orders came and went on various errands and with messages for His Holiness, from the mundane to the monumental. It was not at all common for a former Teutonic Knight, a defector, who disappeared from all knowledge, to ride into Rome in a blood-stained tunic and carrying a Marian Sword. This Holy audience would be more difficult to achieve. Nevertheless, Wikerus rode to the Lateran Palace, drawing every eye in Rome.

Fortunately for him, an old friend was there, a friar with the ear of Pope Gregory IX. Francis heard of Wikerus' appearance at the gates of Saint Peter, and ran to greet him. Such a reunion should have been warm and comfortable, but the circumstances were all but that. Francis asked no questions of his old friend, but let him through the gates and into his protection. Wikerus was a deserter. He had reason to fear a far worse fate than the Pope's refusal to see him. The influential Francis interceded on Wikerus' behalf, and secured for him the desired audience.

As Wikerus walked to the Pope, knelt before him and kissed the papal ring, he had three things in his favor — the word of Francis, the Marian Sword at his hip, and the bloody reminder of his heroics in the Holy Land stained across his chest. Pope Gregory softened and listened.

While Wikerus remained on his knees, too humble to lift his face, the Pope asked, "Where have you been, my son?"

"I was in —," Wikerus stopped short, not sure if His Holiness, the Pope was aware of the portal to the Sweeter Realm, the resting place of the Holy Grail, of the Swan Knights, and all of the wonders that Ludwig and his ancestors fought so long and hard to keep secret. He was not willing to take the chance, and threw out a metaphor he hoped the Pope would accept.

"I was in Venus' Lair, Your Holiness, living with a goddess of love and beauty."

To Wikerus, this was not untrue. To him, Caris was as lovely as Venus and the incarnation of love. Gregory recognized the statement as a metaphor for a truth Wikerus did not want to tell. But he interpreted it poorly.

"You have lived in sin and licentiousness, and now you come for forgiveness. You want to be reinstated into the Order of Teutonic Brothers."

Wikerus defended his devoted love, saying, "I have lived with one love, and with her, I had a child."

At the mention of Chryzanthoseude, the full weight of his love for her crashed upon him. On top of that fell the guilt of leaving her behind. He buckled under the load and collapsed, catching himself with his elbows on the floor. His sobs were so penetratingly soulful, they brought compassion to the Pope. Wikerus did not suffer the fate of a deserter, but he did not receive the absolution and reinstatement he sought.

"I do not doubt the purity of your love," Pope Gregory declared, "but you lived in sin and had a child from the union. Repent. Renounce the woman who lured you to sin…, this *Venus* of yours. Recommit yourself to your vows, and you will have your absolution."

He could not do it. His love for Caris was pure and Godly. Their life together was committed to prayer. Their child sprang from spiritual reproduction. He could not repent it and denounce that life as sinful. The lovely Caris was not the unwholesome harlot the Pope envisioned, nor was their union shadowed from God's light.

Wikerus raised himself to his former kneeling position of reverence and spoke with humility, "I am sorry..., I cannot repent a life I believe was blessed by God. It was the happiest time I have ever lived. Only God can give such rewards to his faithful. My Caris was pure and devout, committed to her faith in Christ, and to me and our daughter. My only regret is that I could not save her life."

Pope Gregory was furious. He had offered his conditional forgiveness and he expected Wikerus to take it with effusions of gratitude. He stood, holding his staff — a dried, gnarled, old branch of some tree long, long dead. It had been a full century since the cracked old wood flowed with life, generations since it had held a leaf or blossom.

The Pope hammered the end of the staff on the floor in front of Wikerus and proclaimed, "You want back into your Order, into MY Order? You want God's forgiveness, which I can give you? I tell you this. You will have absolution and acceptance when this staff blossoms with new and fresh flowers!"

Wikerus lowered his head and kissed the floor in front of the Pope's feet. He turned away, rose slowly, and left the Lateran Palace with no direction for what remained of his life, no tethers tying him to friends or family. In his mind, he threw away the love of the Swan Knight and his family. He severed his connection to the Church and the Teutonic Order. Castle Tannhausen had nothing to offer him. He could not go to Meersburg, not after abandoning the Order. He drifted, too embarrassed to look to the sky and ask the Lord for direction.

Wikerus' audience with the Pope had witnesses, simpler-minded priests and superstitious servants. When Wikerus spoke of Venus, and the Pope recognized the metaphor and did not refute it, the seeds of the Tannhäuser legend were planted. The Tannhäuser — the warrior who descended into Venus' Lair and lived in sin with the goddess of love. Like many such legends, it began with a few overheard words, and grew into a folk saga that found its way onto canvas, into stone, in immortal pages of lore, and onto the opera stages of the world. The truth was both simpler and infinitely more magnificent. As Wikerus fled Rome, the tale of his mythological exploits spread faster than Otto's horse could trot, and preceded him into many of the communities he encountered. The story and his appearance made him conspicuous in the extreme, only serving to further isolate the broken, lonely, and entirely disconnected man.

CHAPTER 39
Flight of the Minnesänger

THE MORNING AFTER TANNHÄUSER'S RETURN, Otto, Agnes, and The Ancient One gathered in deliberation. Otto suggested that Elizabeth remain in the valley with Brunhilde and the swan.

"The Laws of Ermenrich!" the swan reminded, "She cannot be brought in until she is nine."

Agnes grinned and reminded him, "Oh friend, she she has already seen the portal. She has seen you. What is more, she has seen Brunhilde. The Laws of Ermenrich must yield to the moment."

Otto supported his wife, adding, "She will not be the first to begin her training early. This is the decision of the Swan Knight, and I am certain my father would support us on this."

Although The Ancient One was rigidly affixed to tradition, he had to admit that it made sense. Elizabeth would be good for Brunhilde. They could play together.

Otto reminded him, "Agnes and I must search for the Tannhäuser with baby Ludwig in our arms. It is much better for Elisabeth to stay here with you."

"All right," the swan yielded, "but you must go first to Kelheim and tell your father what has happened."

Otto promised to leave immediately and stop nowhere until Duke Ludwig knew everything. It was settled. Otto and Agnes left later that morning for Kelheim. The swan, in strict accordance with his personality, set the girls to play while he planned and plotted, in the minutest detail, how his days in the valley with his two charges should be spent.

He really was the perfect guardian for Brunhilde. His capacity for love and loyalty had seen no limitations in his many centuries with the Swan Knights. As a scholar and teacher, he understood every language in the Sweeter Realm, and could speak Brunnen better than any one-throated creature that was. His German was exquisite. He also understood some Wolpertinger, having spent many years in study of the ancient shrines. Brunhilde lost everything she had previously known. Any familiarity the swan could offer her in the valley would certainly help the transition into her new life.

Brunhilde delighted in speaking Brunnen to him. She delighted more in improving his Wolpertinger. The old teacher made an admirable student to his five-year old master. Their bond developed quickly, and one of the strongest friendships in the entire story of the Swan Knights rooted well and blossomed under the Bavarian sun.

When Wikerus left Rome, Pope Gregory stewed over the impertinence and the insubordination of their audience together. He sent a message to the leaders of the Teutonic Order, explaining that the deserter had resurfaced. He demanded that Wikerus be captured to face charges of cowardice and desertion. He went to bed that night desiring Wikerus' head, but awoke the next morning to a message from God that turned his ambitions entirely.

The Pope's staff, the same old, dried, gnarled stick, was vibrant with life. Fresh, new twigs pushed out from the old wood. Leaves and blossoms of many colors sprang and shouted their brilliance. From top to bottom, the old staff was an orchard of life, color, and sweet aroma.

Gregory hollered for anyone who could hear him. Servants, priests, and cardinals rushed into his room.

"The Swabian..., the Tannhäuser," he shouted, "We must find him."

"We know, Your Holiness," a cardinal answered, "to answer for his crimes. Letters have already been sent."

"Unsend them!" the Pope demanded.

All in the room looked at Gregory as if he had lost his mind. The Pope held the staff above his head and shook it for all to see. He shook it harshly, but not a single leaf or petal fell from it. It remained as whole and lively as he found it. With the miracle before their eyes, they understood what Gregory meant. They scrambled to rescind the orders, and riders were sent in all directions to bring Wikerus back to receive absolution and reinstatement.

The Pope was not the only one whose intentions toward Wikerus were much gentler than Wikerus knew. Duke Ludwig still loved him, and when Otto told his father what had occurred in the valley, Ludwig felt none of the anger and betrayal Wikerus feared from him. The Swan Knight felt only pity, and rich, sorrowful, paternal compassion. Ludwig sent Otto and Agnes, and other trusted riders as well, to find Wikerus, not to bring him to justice, but to bring him home, home to the valley and home to his daughter. Wikerus knew that he was sought. He was too cunning to be easily found.

His renown often preceded him. Folks wanted to hear from his own lips his stories of Venus' Lair, and they paid him well for his time. He began composing a consistent version of it, of passing into the goddess' grove and living with her in love and pleasure. It was good theater, and it paid him well, but it was so far from the truth of his time in the Sweeter Realm. Wikerus set his story to song and rhyme, and traveled from town to town, never staying for more than a day, singing to the people what they desired to hear. Word spread quickly, and the warrior knight of the previous decades had a whole new identity. He was the Tannhäuser, a minnesänger and mythical lover.

His celebrity grew with each new town. What had been "a song for a meal" became lavish accommodations and performances in fine halls in front of rich and poor alike. Otto often arrived within days of Wikerus' performances, to hear with freshness from the locals' memories about the passionate minnesänger who enthralled them. Wikerus told nobody where he would go next. He generally did not know himself. Otto and Agnes felt the frustration of feeling the wind of his wake, with no idea in which direction to turn next.

Messengers from the Pope had no more luck than Otto and Agnes. The miracle of the staff made Gregory regret sending Wikerus away, and he feared for his soul if he could not make it right. In Wikerus' absence, Pope Gregory promoted him to the level of the Großgebietiger in the Teutonic Order, a position among the leadership usually elevated only by the Grand Master. Wikerus was made Marschall, the chief of military affairs. In his absence, the previous Marschall served in an acting role. Earnestly given, the promotion served as bait to bring Wikerus back as Gregory believed God intended.

Word of the promotion never reached Wikerus. It is unlikely the bait would have been tempting. Wikerus found liberty in his new life. He mourned Caris deeply, and used her Venus personification in his songs to praise her to many ears, as he knew she should be praised. He could speak of her without speaking of her, glorify her without breaking his oath of silence to the Swan Knight.

Wikerus did not just sing his stories. He wrote them down and sold the manuscripts at a royal price. Bavaria was not the ideal place to avoid Ludwig's eyes. He spent most of his time in Austria, and when he entertained in Vienna, he caught the attention of Duke Friedrich of Austria. Friedrich was fascinated with mythology and folklore. Before meeting Wikerus, he bought as many of the manuscripts as his servants could find. Finally, Friedrich secured a private performance. Wikerus' voice only grew richer and more luxuriously smooth as he aged. The dark depths of love and loss gilded his throat, and the purest of sounds passed through his lips. Friedrich was in raptures at the performance.

The Duke of Austria was a full thirteen years younger than Wikerus. He wanted Wikerus to stay with him, to live in the palace and perform for him daily. Wikerus was uncomfortable remaining in one place. He could sense Otto on his heels, and feared for his life if the soldiers of the Pope would find him. Friedrich sent letters to Rome and Kelheim, saying that Luitpold Wikerus von Tannhausen, the knight and minnesänger known as the Tannhäuser, was under his protection, and that all attempts to find him should cease immediately.

The duke was known as "Friedrich the Quarrelsome." Neither Pope Gregory nor Ludwig wished to cross him. The Pope placed the matter of the Tannhäuser into God's care and washed his own hands of it. Wikerus maintained the title of Marschall of the Teutonic Order as an honorary title. He learned of his reinstatement and promotion from the duke, and embroidered it into his growing public persona, wearing his Teutonic garb every day. Otto and Agnes went home, and Ludwig, still troubled with empathy for his friend and brother-at-arms, rested with the hope that Wikerus found some semblance of peace in the court of Friedrich of Austria.

The swan continued to raise Brunhilde in the Portal Valley. Her peculiarities grew with her size, first among them was a striking beauty that would debilitate in awe any viewer not accustomed to her. The swan decided that the valley was too dangerous a place to keep her. Travelers and wanderers, like Wikerus, had made a long history of stumbling across the valley and bringing with them many troubles and battles for the long line of Swan Knights. The Ancient One could not afford to allow Brunhilde to be seen, and he was not prepared to destroy every eye that passed innocently through their sacred valley.

With the Swan Knight's approval, construction began on a new castle. They chose a hill across from the ruins of an old fortress from the earliest days of the Swan Knights history. In its glory, it was a castle that Lohengrin himself had visited. The great Swan Knight Ermenrich was born there. Brunhilde's new castle sat on the side of a forbidding slope. The plan was to construct the castle while Brunhilde continued learning and growing in the valley. Upon its completion, she could hide away there, safe from eyes that could do her harm and jeopardize the secrets of the Portal Valley. It was to be Brunhilde's Castle, a name it held on the lips of the following Swan Knights into the nineteenth century.

Ludwig sent Otto to oversee the beginning of construction. When the foundation was level and the first stones were being placed, Otto returned to Kelheim to give his father an update. He arrived at the ducal seat in time to learn of his father's death. Duke Ludwig of Bavaria, Commander of Imperial Forces in the Fifth Crusade, the Swan Knight and guardian of the portal to the Sweeter Realm was assassinated while crossing a bridge in his hometown of Kelheim. The killers were immediately lynched by the Duke's adoring subjects before they could talk. History has never known why Ludwig was assassinated or who ordered his death.

Otto was devastated and did not immediately take the Swan Knight's oath, despite the swan's insistence. Oh, he was the new Swan Knight. He had served in that capacity for years. But to take the oath was to recognize his father's death, and he refused. He sent a letter to Vienna and informed Wikerus of the tragedy. In the letter, Otto told Wikerus that Ludwig never stopped loving him and blamed only himself for all that had happened. Wikerus locked himself away for days, not eating, not sleeping, and not singing. He spent those long hours in deep contemplation about the man he admired, the man who rallied his heart and the hearts of so many outside the walls of Damietta. In that isolated vigil, he drew all that was good in Ludwig and held it to his chest, pushing it into himself and making it part of his own character.

Wikerus immerged from his isolation hungry in body and spirit. A piece of bread or meat could easily soothe the one. The other required a more difficult form of sustenance. Ludwig's goodness bubbled inside of him, and Wikerus was determined to let it out, to portion it among every being within his sphere of influence. He had the precise tools to do so — a silver tongue and a golden voice.

Wikerus continued to write poetry of love, but imbued it all with the devout chivalry of Ludwig. The words he wrote and the songs he sang bore Ludwig's scent, and was familiar to the nostrils of anyone who had met the late Duke of Bavaria. Wikerus' own noble ideals of love and eternal commitment blended with it into a seductive alloy that rallied hearts and drew audiences to Vienna, from across Europe, from the coast of England to the Baltic Sea. It brought commerce to Vienna and wealth to Duke Friedrich.

Wikerus' new persona required a new look. He commissioned a wig to resemble the flowing amber locks of Methildis von Tannhausen. When he put it on his head, it brightened his face. His reflection resembled the boy he once was, before his hair darkened. Wikerus never left the

399

solitude of his own quarters without his wig well-fastened to his head.

Friedrich kept Wikerus close to him. In the poet he found not only a key to his duchy's influence and affluence, but also a personal inspiration. Friedrich was not immune to the rallying effects of Wikerus' morality. He became duke at only nineteen years of age, and the thirteen years separating him from Wikerus made it easy for the young duke to place himself in role of disciple. He had an elasticity of spirit that began to harden into the shape of Wikerus, albeit a thinner, more childish version, without the full depth of soul to truly grip the virtues of Wikerus' movement.

It *was* a movement. Let there be no doubt at all about that, my readers. Whether in the market or the church, the ducal palace or simple homes, where Wikerus often accepted the humblest of invitations, the minnesänger spoke, sang, and recited with inebriating passion. Merchants, lawyers, and beggars committed themselves to the Chivalric Code. Women and girls fell in love with him. Men fell in love with him. As he lived his life in Vienna, just being Wikerus, and speaking and writing those ideas that enflamed his heart, his image was raised to the pinnacle of Austrian society. Wigs resembling Wikerus' became an expensive but popular fashion in Vienna and beyond. Boasting his honorary title in the Teutonic Order, Wikerus usually wore his old Teutonic cloak over his otherwise fashionable but pedestrian clothes. His reflection was seen walking every street and alley in Vienna — normal clothes, a white cloak, and an amber wig, on merchants, lawyers, nobles, and anyone who could afford it.

The very air Wikerus exhaled made people want to be pure and pious, impassioned and active, and burn with righteous ambition. All art in Vienna was stained with

Wikerus' spirit. The city quickly became the center of spiritual expression in Europe. Poets and painters, musicians and sculptors, flocked to Vienna to stain themselves with the atmosphere. It grew well beyond one minnesänger. Each new artist to arrive and be inspired by the Viennese air added a pinch of spice. It was a glorious explosion of artistic expression, and it took the name of Luitpold Wikerus von Tannhausen. Pilgrims came to see, hear, and touch the Tannhäuser, and whatever transitions occurred within them were credited to him.

The social effects were profound. Each year Wikerus spent in Vienna brushed the area more vibrantly with his color. Scoundrels who were incapable of such lofty ideals were out of place in Vienna. The common talk in the markets was rich with romantic and chivalric notions, and even began to bounce with the meter of poetry. A cruel word to the lowly, or any slight against women and maternal sensibilities, or any greed or lust was met with harsh chastisement from all directions. Vienna became a knightly city, embodying all of the knightliest principles. People were said to either be like the Tannhäuser or not. The image of Wikerus, much more, I would say, that the man himself, was the measuring stick by which all people were gauged. And Wikerus did not need to pay expensive copiers to proliferate his poetry. Every literate person in Vienna with access to the tools copied bought, sold, and traded the manuscripts.

Success breeds resentment, ambition, and turmoil. Duke Friedrich made enemies. Chief among them was the Emperor. Seen as too powerful and too influential, Friedrich's run of rapid and steady gain had to end. In 1235, when Friedrich was just twenty-four, the Emperor banished him from Vienna and set the city as a Free Imperial City. Friedrich retreated to his home in Wiener Neustadt, south of Vienna. He ordered Wikerus to accompany him there.

But Wiener Neustadt was not a place of influence, and Wikerus was loathed to abandon what he had by this time spent the better part of a decade building. He enjoyed his notoriety, but not for the reasons a lesser man might.

He heard the noble talk in the markets. He bathed each day in the chivalry that flooded the streets. The people did not need the man, only the image he represented. But Wikerus could not help but fear that his departure might bring the whole thing crashing down. Fouler ideals waited tirelessly in the wings, and the littlest crack in the wall could be exploited. So Wikerus stayed in Vienna and remained the city's greatest talisman of virtue, beauty, and righteous love.

Friedrich's banishment did not last. Within a few years, he regained favor with the Emperor and returned to Vienna. By 1239, he had grown and strengthened, and become one of the Emperor's closest friends. Friedrich's wife was Agnes of Merania. She was more than four years younger than Friedrich and a good eighteen years younger than Wikerus. She admired the famous minnesänger. Unlike many who wore the wig and cloak through the streets of Vienna, she understood the poetry, the songs, and the spiritual message of the Tannhäuser.

Agnes had a substantial capacity for understanding. At half Wikerus' age, she wrapped her opulent mind around the full meaning of his poetry. In short, she got it, and it got her. Her mind blossomed during her years in Wiener Neustadt. Her return to Vienna was more joyfully undertaken than Friedrich's. She wanted the atmosphere of the city, but more importantly, she wanted Wikerus in her court, to learn from him in a much deeper manner than thumbing through manuscripts of his writings.

Agnes wasted no time securing Wikerus' company and attention. They spent many long hours together. Wikerus aged well into a beautifully distinguished older man, with a face and figure as alluring as his infectious spirit. He was the object of many an infatuation. Agnes' desire for him was not so shallow. Poems of eternal love and undying commitment to ideals beyond the reach of most humans were not means to an end for her, or fancy words to be flashed in gatherings then tucked away in private. She lived by them, and she knew that he did too. She saw in him a teacher whose contributions to her life were strictly spiritual. Wikerus saw in Agnes a student. He hoped to be her Father Stefan, Count Konradin, Francis of Assisi, and Duke Ludwig all rolled into one.

People of weaker intellectual and spiritual means saw their time together through dubious lenses, and began to plant seeds of suspicion in the ears of Friedrich. Prior to that, the Duke saw Wikerus as a purely altruistic teacher and artist, whose time with the Duchess could only bring benefits. Afterward, jealousy tainted his eyes with a putrid filter. Wikerus and Agnes spent many long and fruitful hours alone together. By 1242, the jealous whisperings in Friedrich's ear became explosive tirades. The situation was not mitigated by the undeniable fact that the most famous and loved person in the duchy was not the Duke, but the minnesänger working for the Duke.

Wikerus did nothing to avoid Friedrich's company, but the Duke avoided Wikerus, for fear that he would kill the social icon and spark a revolt. Amber wigs and white cloaks walking up and down every thoroughfare in Vienna did nothing to lessen Friedrich's jealousy. You see, readers, Friedrich fell well short of his wife's ability to understand Wikerus. To him, romantic devotion and the Chivalric Code were cards to be played in a game of self-promotion. Oh, he truly believed in it, as he truly loved Wikerus to the extent and depth of his capacity for love. But he had a feebleness of mind that forbade Agnes' sort of intimacy with the teacher.

Agnes did not abandon Wikerus. But she did not meet with him in the palace. That was too dangerous. She met him in the halls and taverns where mobs of his devotees secured their safety. Loud gathering places where Wikerus' celebrity allowed no intimacy were not the ideal classrooms for Agnes' learning. She had learned all that could be taught in the crowded halls of the city. One summer morning in 1243, Ludwig took her deep into the forest, southeast of Vienna. He sat her down against the trunk of a tree and began to speak of the things most cannot see or hear. He drew her perceptive ears the precise notes struck by the breeze, the depth of color in the dirt around her, the delicately sculpted intricacy of each piece of bark and each leaf, and nature's culinary masterpiece — the blend of natural smells.

Agnes' eyes opened, both physically and internally. She saw beauty as comprehensively and omnipresent as Wikerus did. In one pop of enlightenment, she gained at her young age what took Wikerus so long to develop. He was proud of his student and she held an eternity of gratitude for her teacher. They walked together from the forest as two of a very unique kind. Unfortunately, they were followed by one of Friedrich's spies.

When they arrived back in Vienna, the Duke arrested them both, charging Agnes with adultery and Wikerus with treason. Both were punishable by death. He removed Wikerus' wig, his cloak, and his Marian Sword. There is a sad irony here. Wikerus' heart could never stray from Caris, until his death and well beyond. This devotion was first among his lessons, and Agnes took it to heart. Because of Wikerus' influence, she could never love any but her husband. It was Wikerus who cemented her faithfulness to Friedrich, and Wikerus who faced capital charges for a crime forbidden by the deepest and most implacable pillars of his soul.

CHAPTER 40
One Eternal Love

FRIEDRICH COULD NOT AFFORD to hold a quick trial followed by immediate executions. He would have been lynched in his own streets. He held his prisoners for two months, in that time smearing Wikerus' reputation and producing debauched, repulsive poetry in his name. He cried every night. The deepest part of him knew that Wikerus was pure and that he was loved by both Wikerus and Agnes. But in the morning, there was always another poisonous tongue to lick venom into his ear.

Wikerus had faithful friends and followers everywhere, even in the Duke's palace. He was able to get one letter out. He wrote to Meersburg. The letter arrived to find Count Konradin long dead, but it found its way into even better hands. Rikard received the letter. He rushed it to Andreas and the two of them left immediately for Vienna.

While imprisoned, Wikerus wrote no poetry. He wrote personal letters never intended to be delivered to their subjects. He wrote to Caris and he wrote to Zanthie. Friends in the palace brought him an excess of paper, acquired in trade from the Middle East. He wrote love letters to his wife and daughter, allowing them to pile in the corners of his cell. His Caris was long dead. The letters to her were just his hand's way of trying to bridge the deep and silent ravine between a living lover and a memory that haunted his mind and flesh. The letters to his daughter bore, in addition to the scent of devotion, a distinct aroma of hope. Any casual reader of those letters would think that the writer remained in intimate contact with the recipient. But Wikerus knew he could not send the letters to the Portal Valley, to be carried through the portal by one creature or another and delivered to the heart of Brunnen land, where he presumed his daughter to be living.

In early September of 1243, Friedrich held the mock trial, with bloated testimony, slanted half-truths, and complete falsehoods, orchestrated by those ambitious advisors who had planted the evil business in the Duke's ear. Wikerus and Agnes were sentenced to death. After the trial, soldiers pulled Wikerus and Agnes into a crowded courtyard. The two of them were shoved together for all to see.

"Kiss her!" Friedrich demanded, "Let me now see what you both hid from me for so long."

Both Wikerus and Agnes felt guilt for bringing the other to this fate.

"Take my wife in your arms and kiss her!" Friedrich demanded again.

It was no use for Wikerus to declare that he had never kissed her, nor desired to, pointless to say that his heart belonged comprehensively and eternally to his one and only lover, lost to him these several years. Nor would it have borne any fruit for Agnes to scream into the crowd that Wikerus' influence over her only tightened her commitment to her husband and the solemn oath she swore at their wedding. So Wikerus and Agnes just looked at each other and smiled at the sight of one so admired. The smile alone was close enough for the maddened Friedrich. He declared the righteousness of the conviction and sentence, and sent them both to separate cells, on opposite ends of the palace to await execution.

Friedrich could not write with Wikerus' hand, nor could he reproduce his eloquence. The two months of rancid poetry and smearing fooled very few. At midnight, faithful followers came to Wikerus' cell, a man and two women. They freed him and bid him to follow them in silence.

Wikerus pulled away from them and demanded loudly, "I will not escape without freeing Agnes."

They shushed him and said, "We went to her first. She refused to leave her husband. She is a virtuous woman. She swore an oath to remain at her husband's side until death, and by your own noble teaching, she intends to do so. She will face her execution at dawn with a noble and innocent heart."

Wikerus laughed and cried simultaneously, and said, "Such valor in the name of virtue!"

Wikerus had sworn no oath to Friedrich and saw no breach of his virtues in a midnight escape from death. He followed his liberators through dark hallways and onto the palace grounds. They were spotted in the gardens and soldiers were clumsily gathered to pursue. Wikerus and his rescuers escaped the palace grounds and made their way into the silent streets.

"You must leave Vienna with haste," one of them told him, "You would be safe in one house and ransomed in another. Trust nobody until you are out of Austria."

Wikerus thanked them, blessed them, then snuck his way from shadow to shadow.

Andreas and Rikard were in Vienna. The whole city spoke of the execution and Wikerus' old friends were well-informed. They knew nothing of his escape and hoped at least to be there for him, to love him and support him when he dies. That is what they thought, and they were grateful for the opportunity. I can only imagine the surprise and delight when they caught a shadowy glimpse of Wikerus, hunched over and sneaking beneath a window across the way. They said nothing, but sprinted into the street and seized him by the shirt.

Oh what a silent but happy reunion it was! Andreas and Rikard did not know or care how the escape was managed. That was good conversation for a more liberated situation. With Andreas in front of him and Rikard at his side, Wikerus moved quickly through the streets.

A single scream in the night was followed by the thundering boots of a dozen soldiers. Andreas drew his longsword. Rikard held his short sword in one hand and his faithful forging hammer in the other. Wikerus was unarmed. They ran into a narrow alley. The soldiers plugged one end of the alley, shoulder-to-shoulder and three men deep.

Andreas pushed Wikerus behind them and demanded, "Go! We will hold them."

Wikerus ran to the other end of the alley. But with the first sound of a sword clanging against another, he turned. He saw the two bravest and most loyal men he could ever hope to call his friends fighting a dozen soldiers for no more glorious ideal than his welfare. Weapon or no, he would not abandon them. Wikerus charged into the fight.

Friedrich's soldiers got around and behind them. Blades flew so furiously it is amazing they did not all drop to the ground together. Wikerus dodged and pushed and punched and kicked. The fight drifted from the alley, into the wider street. More soldiers came. It was three against dozens, but not three ordinary men, not three palace guards or common foot soldiers. Three extraordinary men, fighting for each other, with mutual love as the war cry in their hearts, moved and slashed and kicked like they were giants from ancient myths. Soldiers fell with every flick of Andreas' wrist, with every drop of Rikard's hammer. But the most heroic figures of legend could not defeat such an army. There must have been fifty soldiers in the street, and their ranks thickened by the moment.

Wikerus felt a hard knock to the back of his head, which dropped him to his knees. He stood and swung his fist, spinning his assailant's head and dropping him. He felt a sting behind his left shoulder and saw the bloody tip of a sword extending forward out of him. Another sting to his right leg, and another to his side froze him in place. His faith would have completely abandoned him, except for the sounds of battle. With every clang and every thump, he knew that his friends still fought, and as long as Andreas and Rikard swung their weapons, Wikerus held hope.

He was struck in the face by something blunt. His vision blurred and he fell to his back. His eyes covered with twin pools of his own blood. Angry hands lifted him to his feet. He cleared his eyes and opened them to see a soldier square to him. He stared at the Duke's emblem on the soldier's chest, an emblem that once meant protection and sanctuary. The soldier extended his sword and ran it through Wikerus' abdomen. Wikerus walked forward, driving the sword through him and out his back side, until he was within arm's reach of the soldier. He drew back his fist but did not strike the man. Instead, he reached forward and removed the soldier's helmet. He looked at the man with sorrowful forgiveness and fell to the ground.

His eyes filled again with blood. The world around him was black. His ears focused and removed from the air every noise but those made by his friends. He heard Andreas' sword whistle through the air. He counted their breaths, which echoed loudly as if captured in a bottle and poured into his ears. Even those sounds slowly faded until he perceived nothing but his thoughts.

To Wikerus, time stood still, or rather it circled the universe until coming to a rest where it began. A flash of a second or half of eternity in that senseless blackness,

Wikerus could not tell. Suddenly, a speck of light pierced the center of his vision. It widened and brought with it the sounds of nature, those very sounds he taught Agnes to hear and obey. Now *he* obeyed those sounds. They told him to rise. His eyes opened fully and the light expanded to a full view of the forest around him. He was on his back, looking up to the tall trees that rose on all sides of him.

No buildings, no streets or alleys, only the wild nature of a forest surrounded him. He stood to his feet and examined himself. There was not a wound to be seen on his body. His clothes, with bloody rips and slashes, showed every place he was split open. His hair was still soaked with his blood and that of others. But not a scratch or scar, not a cut or bruise could boast of the battle on the streets of Vienna. He looked around him for his friends, and softly called their names. He was alone in the woods. Beside him was his Marian Sword, which had been taken by Friedrich when he was arrested. He had no explanation for any of it.

He thought about Agnes. The sun told him it was well past dawn and the execution would have already happened. He took solace in knowing that she not only found peace with her fate, but cherished it. She set herself on a narrow path, upon which few can tread without faltering. She remained on that path until the end. It would have pleased him to know that Agnes of Merania did not die that morning. And he would have been proud to know why.

At the execution block, Friedrich asked her, "Why did you not take your opportunity to escape execution with your lover?"

She looked at him with peaceful resolution and said, "Did you not learn anything from the Tannhäuser? I stayed because I am your wife. I swore my faithfulness to you before God and witnesses. I have always been faithful to you and I always will be. I would die a thousand times before I would diminish myself by breaking an oath of loyalty. Does that sound familiar to you? I learned it from *your* friend, from a man equally devoted to his only true love, a man you intended to kill because you allowed the spark that he brought to our eyes to be extinguished by those too thin of character to understand him. That is why I did not take my chance to escape. I love you. Like my teacher, I have one eternal love. When you execute me, I will die at your side, which is all I hope to do."

Agnes recited a few verses of Wikerus' poetry. Friedrich's sense of shame was too burdensome for his weak heart. He did not have her executed. She was innocent and a far truer companion to him than anybody who lived. He did not deserve her and could not share her bed while laden with such oppressive guilt. Against her vehement protestations, he divorced her and begged her to find a husband worthy of her virtue.

Much like Pope Gregory many years before, Friedrich wanted to have Wikerus before him to apologize for having not recognized his worth when it was there before him, and only seeing it clearly when he was gone from reach. Unlike Gregory, Friedrich did not send people in pursuit. He had no promotion to offer as bait. He had nothing in his entire duchy that he believed worthy of the Tannhäuser. Having come so close to executing the two noblest people he had ever known stabbed daily at his heart. He did not survive the guilt. Duke Friedrich II of Austria died three years later, at the age of thirty-five. Agnes did just as her husband begged. After Friedrich's death, she went on to marry Duke Ulrich III of Carinthia, where she inspired a duchy with the lessons she learned from Wikerus. Ulrich knew he was not her one eternal love. But he treated her well. He learned from her, and he honored her as she deserved.

CHAPTER 41
The Valkyrie's Castle

WIKERUS ROAMED THE WOODS in search of direction. He found the shore of Lake Neusiedl and knew where he was. Still in fear of Duke Friedrich, he followed the shore south, into Hungary. He imagined Andreas and Rikard would have done the same. Wikerus had no explanation for the miracle of his recovery. Most certainly he was as near death as a living man can be. But there he stood, pristine of complexion. Even the scars of his youth were gone. His body surged with youthful energy, but a heavy spiritual weight drew him downward in an inexplicable way. Light of body but infinitely weary of soul, he pictured his valiantly fighting friends, defending him in the dark streets of Vienna, like two personal angels dispatched by God on his behalf.

Wikerus strained his imagination to visualize how Andreas and Rikard could have escaped the battle in the street, and how they could have brought him all the way to Lake Neusiedl. He wondered what part they played, if any, in the miracle of his recovery. His feet pushed him south with the singular goal of finding his friends and the secrets they held. For months he made his way slowly through the rugged forests and hills of Hungary, into Croatia. He stopped in Zagreb. The city had been ravaged by the Mongols, and King Béla IV of Hungary was there to personally witness the reconstruction effort.

Wikerus took a lowly job hauling stone. He worked himself to the bone for three months, pushing his physical limits for eighteen hours a day and aging ten years in that short time. His glorious complexion turned weathered and wrinkled. He did not look like the son of a baron, like a knight, or a royal poet. He bore none of the glorious air that followed him covetously through his brightest years in Vienna. He looked exactly like the life he lived as a hauler of stone for the masons. It was still, however, peculiar to see a laborer in tattered, bloody clothing with a Marian Sword at his hip. King Béla saw him and accused him of stealing the sword. The king's men seized him. King Béla was a friend of the Teutonic Order and a supporter of Christian efforts in the Holy Land. He knew well of the Tannhäuser, but had no reason to suspect the dirty, tanned and weathered laborer in front of him to be the same man.

King Béla took the sword from Wikerus as if recovering a treasure from a thief, to which Wikerus immediately shouted, "That is my sword! I have earned it."

The king replied scornfully, "You have earned it by stealing from the knight who owned it. I am certain you could not have killed him for it."

Wikerus said that he killed no one for the sword, nor did he steal it. He continued, describing in detail the ceremony and the presentation of the Marian Cross of Saint Mary. He included names, places, and secret rites that only a Teutonic Knight, or one intimately familiar with them, would know. King Béla was familiar with them, and he knew Wikerus to be truthful.

"Good God, my brother," he said in astonishment, "How have you come to this fate?"

Wikerus identified himself, "I am Luitpold Wikerus von Tannhausen, son of the Baron von Tannhausen and Knight of the Teutonic Order."

Pope Gregory IX was dead, as was his immediate successor. A friend and confidant of Gregory, Cardinal Sinibaldo Fieschi, was the new pontiff, under the title Pope Innocent IV. Innocent IV continued Gregory's efforts to recall the miraculous Tannhäuser. He carried the still-blooming staff. King Béla arranged Wikerus' travels to Rome, to receive the honors awaiting him.

Béla fed Wikerus, and offered every royal accommodation. Wikerus received them all with gratitude — all but one. He refused an exchange of clothing. His torn and bloody shirt reminded him of his friends, Andreas and Rikard, and the mysterious miracle that brought him unscratched to the shore of Lake Neusiedl. For many months, it refreshed his memory and kept him from sinking irretrievably into a new identity as a humble laborer.

The caravan traveled west to Italy and rested on the northern coast of the Adriatic Sea, at the Venetian city of Bibione. In Bibione, Wikerus received a king's welcome. He was offered every indulgence imaginable. Each consecutive offering — the food, the clothing, the jewelry, and the women increasingly sickened him. He refused them all. He wanted only to find his friends. The contrast in character between those who surrounded him and those he sought aggrandized in his eyes until he could not stand it. Andreas and Rikard had been in the Pit of Starvation. They lived lives so far above and beyond the petty trinkets being offered and coveted around him. Wikerus had lived a miraculous and extraordinary youth, and his years in Vienna were not much more rooted to normalcy. Regardless of what company he kept in the caravan or in Bibione, he was a stranger among strangers, more isolated in a packed room than he was in an empty forest.

Wikerus broke from his caravan in the middle of the night heading north, and taking nothing with him but his battle-torn clothes, his Marian Sword, and enough food to humbly sustain him in his travels to Meersburg, where he hoped his friends were awaiting him with answers to his burning questions.

He planned to travel into Bavaria, to Füssen, where the Bishop of Augsburg lived. The Lords of Buchhorn had maintained a strong political and military alliance with the Bishops of Augsburg. Wikerus hoped to secure lodgings and refreshment, and safe carriage to Lake Constance and Meersburg. It took him three months to cross the Alps into Tirol. He avoided towns and well-traveled paths, working slowly through the thickest forests and most forbidding mountains. When he reached the northern foothills, there was little left of him. His body was worn as thin as his heavy and tattered soul. If Duke Ludwig could have seen him, there would be a figure frighteningly familiar to his eyes. Wikerus was an older, grey and weathered reflection of the young knight who starved himself in the Egyptian prison.

With each starving step, his consciousness gave way to his sweetest memories. He longed for the fortress grove, his lover and daughter, and the company of the Wolpertingers. Those things which his senses beheld, the mountains, snows, trees, and rocks of the alps became increasingly alien to him. His eyes saw no beauty in his surroundings. And his surroundings were cruel — cold, sharp, and unforgiving.

As he rested his body against the cold ground at night, if it can in any way be called rest, his mind tried to think of the soulful prayers and chants he used to sing. Across Christendom, monks and clerics sang the Vespers Hymn. Wikerus' parched throat could not produce the sound. But that was not the worst of it. His tattered mind could not even conjure a clear memory of every having produced the prayers. He was a man comprehensively worn, and neither body nor spirit had the strength to lift the other. If the beat of his heart or the expansion and deflation of his lungs had been controlled by the strength of his will power, he would have died each night when he collapsed his body on the hard and cold alps between Bibione and Füssen. As his eyes closed, his conscious mind released all that is in this world. His vital functions continued without his care for them, and he awoke despite himself every cold and lonely, hungry morning.

It had been several days since he had eaten. Night was falling, but Füssen was mere hours away. He was so near his destination but knew that his legs would not finish the journey. A single speck of a light twinkled low in the sky in front of him. No, it was not in the sky. A steep and jagged hill framed it. Wikerus followed the light and saw that it came from a castle window. It was a steep climb to the walls. He gathered the last of his strength and hiked the unforgiving slope.

The ground around him was lit by a full, silvery moon just above the castle walls. He looked up and admired its beauty. The moonlight silhouetted the castle wall, creating a magical scene. His stomach grasped ravenously at his throat, desperate for food. His legs stabbed at the bones within them. His chest was tired of the perpetual volley of give and take with the alpine air. He asked himself why he continued to suffer, why he wanted to find Andreas and Rikard. Was is just to answer the mystery of his miraculous recovery, or to thank them for coming to his side?

His friends were not the sort of men who required praise, and Wikerus had known mystery. He had witnessed miracles and lived comfortably without their secrets. Why now did he press on? He had lived for many things, none so petty as a thank you or an answer to a single question. So why press his weary legs? He asked himself that question and could not give an answer.

He whispered to himself, "If Andreas and Rikard wanted my company, they would have stayed with me or brought me with them. They left me for a reason."

He considered closely his situation. Every place in the world that he had proudly called home was closed to him. He could not return to Castle Tannhausen and live with his father and Aleidis. He could not breach the portal again and live in the Brunnen wilderness. His Wolpertinger friends were slaughtered to extinction in the battle that took his only lover. He assumed that his daughter was living in the Brunnen cities with the sisters, where he was forbidden by their laws to go. Regardless of the sentiments in Otto's letter, his shame forbade a return to the Portal Valley of the Swan Knights. Even if he could return to the valley, what sort of Portal Steward could he be. Otto had no need of his training. He would be there only to be taken care of, not to serve. He could not go back to Vienna, where happy and glorious days collected dust in his past. He truly floated without anchor, with no place to call home and nobody to call family.

There he was on that slope in the night, with no imaginable reason to press on. He decided that he knew enough, had seen and done enough. He was sleepy. He knew if he laid himself down and closed his eyes, he would sleep and never awaken, and he took a brief moment to content himself with that fate. He looked at the castle that had beckoned him. It promised mystery and adventure. Wikerus desired neither mystery nor adventure. He wanted only the nurturing arms of Caris. They were not to be found among the living. He took one last look at the full moon, resting above the wall of the castle like a shiny head on broad shoulders. The glow and color reminded him of Caris' belly, when she was in a contemplative mood, pondering subjects deep and dark. He often held his cheek against her when she was like that. He pretended to do so then.

He held his hands in front of him. It looked to his eyes like he was palming the moon. He half believed it *was* Caris he held. He recited loudly to the night sky his last verse of poetry

Da sol nieman sin vnfro
Da der Tannhäuser
Rieget mit der Lieben so

(None shall be unhappy
When the Tannhäuser with such fire
Dances with his love again)

He let the verse roll from his tongue like sweet nectar, truly reveling in the feel of the words in his mouth and the sound of them in his ears. He was ready to join Caris wherever she awaited him.

He could not have explained it, but he had a desire to take one last look at the dark castle before falling to his side and closing his eyes. Suddenly there appeared on the wall of the castle a figure that glued his eyes in place and paralyzed his features. It was the image of a giant bird, a swan, standing regally with outstretched wings and a long neck that seemed to rise above the troubles of the world. Wikerus could not say if the swan rose from the castle or fell from the moon. It shone silver, as if it were *born* of the moon.

The swan tilted his head and nodded. The familiar gesture struck Wikerus' memory. It was The Ancient One he saw, whether real or imagined. Wikerus reached his hand to the bird and curled his fingers in invitation. The swan flew from the wall and landed in front of him. It *was* the swan, The Ancient One and teacher of the Swan

418

Knights since Lohengrin. Wikerus was forty-eight years old, but looked twice that age. It was not his weathered skin that the swan recognized, nor was it the Marian Sword. The eternal fire that burned in Wikerus' eyes since the days when he vanquished imaginary enemies in the dining hall of Castle Tannhausen, still lit the air around him, even as he planned a cold but peaceful death on the side of a Bavarian hill.

The swan stood directly against his weary old friend. Wikerus threw his arms around the bird and held him tightly, communicating only in the form of choppy sighs. Another figure cut the descending moonlight, a magnificent figure. Brunhilde sailed like a cloud from behind the wall and floated with perfect grace and control down to the ground behind The Ancient One. Her bare, pale silver, rippling skin appeared as living armor, polished and giving off as much light as the moon she reflected. She landed on a single toe, then grabbed the dirt beneath her with her bare feet. She swayed gently and rippled her skin in order to remain visible to her father. Her powers had blossomed in her many years living with the Swan Knight's family.

Brunhilde landed so silently that the sharp senses of the swan did not perceive her. It was Wikerus' reaction that told the old sage that she was behind him. Wikerus released his embrace of the swan and leaned backward with a stunned expression of disbelief.

"Chryzanthoseude," he whispered in his best attempt at a Brunnen name.

She responded, "I am called Brunhilde now."

Her voice was a little deeper than the child he left behind, but it was most certainly his daughter's voice. Wikerus lifted the edges of his thin lips and formed a smile of the most authentic delight. He began speaking to her in Brunnen, as well as his single throat could.

"I don't remember those words," she interrupted. "I have been raised in the valley by the Swan Knight Family. Now I live here in this castle, in my castle, built for me by Ludmilla."

Standing awkwardly on the difficult slope, The Ancient One began explaining some of the events since Tannhäuser returned from the Sweeter Realm.

Brunhilde interrupted, sounding much more like her younger self. In the voice of a crying five-year old, she spoke, "I called for you, father. Why didn't you stop? Why didn't you answer?"

What little strength in Wikerus' body gave out under the emotional strain. He fell to his knees, and in a broken voice, half-crying, he told her that in all of the years that passed, he could never remember anything between finding Caris' body and finding himself on Otto's horse, riding for Rome.

"I had nothing to offer you," he cried, "You are of the Sweeter Realm and I am not."

The swan suggested that the unexpected reunion take place in the more appropriate setting of the castle interior. Brunhilde obeyed and bottled her questions and comments for safe keeping. She rippled her skin upward and with a tiny push of a single toe, sent herself floating through the trees. Her movement in the air obeyed the changing currents of her Brunnen skin, and she floated over the castle wall and out of sight. From the inside, she opened the narrow door to the castle, and the swan helped his old friend inside.

Wikerus was in awe of his surroundings. The castle that the Swan Knights built to conceal Brunhilde from the world was elaborate in the extreme. It was no bunker. It was as unique as the creature for whom it was built. It was a home for one but could have held with opulence an entire royal household. Elizabeth grew up and married. She still

420

visited her childhood playmate as often as she could. Ludmilla came to the castle and spent weeks at a time, until her death a few years earlier. Otto was the Duke of Bavaria, the Count Palatinate on the Rhine, and the Swan Knight. He and Agnes had little time to spare for trips to Brunhilde's castle.

Otto came only once to her castle. As a homecoming gift, he presented her with a knife. She could not hold a sword or axe and still float easily. The knife armed her with a weapon she could hold in her hand while drifting with the breeze. It was no ordinary knife. It had been given to his father by two brave crusaders, by Andreas and Rikard. It was one of the twin blades forged in the hills of Syria from the Spear of Antioch. Brunhilde held the lance that pierced the side of Christ, with all of its dynamic endowments.

The only frequent inhabitants in the castle were Brunhilde and her truest friend and teacher, the swan, whose affections for her grew powerful. Yet, the castle compared to any in Europe, in scale and opulence.

Brunhilde's abilities did not stagnate after her father left her walking through the Sweeter Realm. In addition to her now highly honed ability to float through the air, she became a skilled fighter under the tutelage of the swan, and still one more. In a single glance at a person, Brunhilde could sense the goodness or badness of the human heart. It was this talent that required the swan's attention and guidance. For whenever she sensed evil in a person, she turned furious. Her silent and deadly skills made her treacherous for every evil heart that stumbled into her vision. While still holding his ancient post as the teacher to the Swan Knights' children, the swan's first concern was to protect Brunhilde from the world, and the world from Brunhilde.

No expense was spared in the construction of her castle. The greatest artists in Bavaria were brought in to adorn it with beauty — stone and paint reminders of her sacred heritage and the holy responsibilities that come with it. Wikerus was slow to move through the courtyard. His eyes held tightly to the ornate carvings in the masonry. Brunhilde took him by the hand and pulled him from one dazzling spectacle to another.

At last, she managed to drag her father into her favorite room. It was a study, rich in accommodations, yet plainer to behold than any other room in the castle. In the revelations of the well-lit room, Wikerus was able to see his fully grown daughter. She was the most magnificently beautiful thing he had ever imagined. Her face was his and Caris' blended in equal proportion. Her eyes were the deep but calm oceans that highlighted her mother's face, with the churning fire that drove her father through a heroic life.

As a child in the Portal Valley, she wore clothes, like any human child. But in her own castle she lived as free of such vanities as any Brunnen. Clothes weighed her down and obstructed the free rippling of her Brunnen skin, preventing her ability to take flight. The only things upon her, other than what God had given her, was a thin belt around her waist, made of her own hair, and the special knife that it held to her hip.

Brunhilde placed Wikerus in her favorite chair, a piece capable of easily sitting two, upholstered in a deep blue tapestry, with white swan figures scattered about it. Wikerus sank deeply into the chair. It was an apt physical manifestation of what was in his mind and heart. He felt as insignificant as he was impressed — by the castle and its furnishings, by the affection showed to him, and by the extraordinary beauty and power of his daughter. Yet he did not sink deeply enough for his own liking. He anticipated a furious scolding from Brunhilde, whose first five years contrasted greatly with the rest of her life.

Wikerus told the swan what he had never known, that Caris had revealed to him the true secrets of the Portal Valley and the Holy Grail. Brunhilde and the swan alternated in explaining to Wikerus all that he did not know about the valley and the Swan Knights, about The Ancient One and Brunhilde, including their reasons for hiding her away in her castle.

"If this castle is to keep you isolated, why didn't you kill me the moment you saw me coming?"

"Your daughter has a unique ability," the swan answered with the pride of a father and teacher.

He looked at Brunhilde and gestured for her to elaborate.

"I can sense the hearts of men, good, evil, or otherwise. Your heart is good. I saw that even before the swan's keen eyes could identify you."

The Ancient One, in a sharp turn from his earliest opinions, added, "You are a sworn steward of the portal, we trust you. What is more, you are her father, and your return to her life is welcomed and celebrated."

Wikerus sheepishly protested, "You are more of her father than I."

"My old friend," the swan said softly, while placing the tip of a wing on his shoulder, "do not underestimate your influence on her. My God, I see you in her every day. You and Caris sculpted the major contours of her character. I have been working on the finer details."

The truth is, the swan had been fearfully watching Brunhilde's fury outpace her ability to control it. He knew that Wikerus was a compassionate and loving man, a reluctant warrior who went into battle as a Christian should. She was quickly slipping from the grip of his feathers and Wikerus' appearance in her life came on the edge of too late.

Wikerus recovered from his slouched position at the swan's words.

He looked at his daughter as he did on her fifth birthday. The expression reminded Brunhilde of her only heirloom. She opened a small drawer in a side table and pulled from it the Caris doll that her father made of his old clothing. Wikerus had long forgotten the birthday gifts. The recollections erupted inside of him. He sobbed heavily, with a heaving chest and a torrent of tears.

"Oh my sweet Zanthie!" he forced through the tears, "What have I done to you, my sweet Zanthie?"

The mention of her childhood nickname plunged deeply into her and dislodged a current of long-buried memories. They reached the surface with vibrancy, having fermented and magnified under the weight of many years.

She grabbed tightly the little doll of her mother and held it to her nose. Her fine senses could still detect the smells of the Brunnen wilderness, and those of her father's old clothing.

"Zanthie!" she declared, "You used to call me Zanthie."

"You were my little Zanthie," his broken voice forced out through his dried lips, "Now you are Brunhilde, a woman like none that has ever been."

"You are right. I am Brunhilde now. And Brunhilde is Zanthie…, her father's little Zanthie."

She sat on the large chair with her father. Her rippling cheeks mimicked his tears.

He wrapped his long fingers around the back of her head and gruffly whispered, "I look at you, my daughter, grown into a beauty that outshines everything, and I love you. I love you more now than I ever have. There is nothing in this world of more value to me than you."

Brunhilde curled tightly onto his lap, diminishing herself to the proportions of a child. She held a few strands of grey hairs around his temple in her fingertips and caressed and twirled them. She lifted her head and planted her nose into the side of his head. She inhaled deeply and invited the heavy flow of memories to wash into her by the scent. She spoke a few long-forgotten words in Wolpertinger and in Brunnen. The swan was delighted. He left the room, and flew east from the castle to the Portal Valley, leaving the tender reunion to its exclusive members.

As Brunhilde coiled tightly again on his lap, she repeated, alternating between rubbing his face and squeezing his shoulders, "Father..., my father..., my father is here," until she fell asleep in his arms.

Wikerus lived for many more years in his daughter's castle. He passed to her the calm wisdom of her grandmother, Methildis. He told her everything to tell about her mother and the intense spiritual unity that brought Brunhilde into existence. His influence over her grew. They took long walks together around the nearby Alpsee. Brunhilde would venture out to the well-worn paths, hiding high in the trees, still and virtually invisible. She returned to him and described what she felt from the hearts she encountered. With the vision of a lover and poet, he helped her process the feelings. The swan was right. Wikerus was exactly what she needed, bringing her calmness in ways no other teacher could. In turn, she reminded him of the happiest years of his life, of the fighter and knight, of the lover and father that he was.

Their daily prayers were of nothing but thanksgiving. Neither Wikerus nor Brunhilde asked God for anything but the company of their only family. The swan visited often and stayed as long as he could. In 1253, Duke Otto died and young Ludwig took the title and the Swan Knighthood. Politics and turmoil shadowed over the affairs of state, and Duke Ludwig was much more Duke than Swan Knight.

The old bird managed the Portal Valley in the Swan Knight's absence, but he was happiest when he was with Brunhilde and Wikerus.

One warm night in 1267, Wikerus breath slowed and grew shallow. Fatigue weighed his limbs beyond his ability to lift them. Brunhilde held her father day and night. She sang to him and told stories of her early days in the fortress grove with her mother, father, and faithful Wolpertinger friends. As his eyelids became too heavy to open, the loss of Wikerus' sight was more than compensated for by the tender and adoring caress of Brunhilde's half-Brunnen fingers. A few days later, the swan visited Brunhilde's castle to find the furnishings broken, torn, and strewn about in violence. The Tannhäuser was dead. He lived to be nearly seventy years old, spending the last two decades in love and bliss — a fact that the swan had to remind Brunhilde, who alternated between sobbing in an infantile ball in the large chair where she slept in her father's arms on the night of his return to her life, and rampaging through the castle destroying all that was not made of stone. She was in furious mourning, and without the moderating effect of Wikerus' guidance, her perception of the evils of the world put her in peril of falling irretrievably into a deep pit of anger and violence.

She screamed at her old teacher, "Why does goodness wither and perish... while evil grows and perpetuates? Evil and cruelty fill the air around me. It seeps into my home from bad people everywhere. I smell it. I breathe it in... It fills my throats..., God, it is rancid!"

The swan knew that the castle would not contain her, that evil people would perish at the edge of her little blade, and there was nothing he could do about it. He sent her away, far to the north, where she could not draw attention to the Grail Portal. When he bade her farewell, he reminded her that her father lived his most peaceful years in her company, that among his last sensations in this world were her songs of love to him and the loving stroke of her tender Brunnen fingers.

She left the swan, her castle, and Bavaria, determined to use her gifts as she believed God intended. In the fields and fjords of the north, she descended into battles, perceiving the good hearts from the bad. Her silvery skin reflected natural light like polished armor. Stunned by her beauty, she brought battles between armies to a halt. She killed the evil-hearted and spared the good, giving rise to the legend of the Valkyrie.

Her father's passion for goodness flowed through her veins. Where she appeared, righteous warriors lived, regardless for which side they fought. Her fury toward evil was unchecked. She grew in speed, power, and skill. She aged very slowly, and witnessed generations go by in front of her. She would save a man in battle, only to destroy his great-grandson many years later. As the centuries followed her through time, and she manipulated battle after bloody battle, she invoked her father's name with each draw of her sacred relic.

"Father," she would pray, "your Zanthie goes into battle. Guide me. Thrust my knife as you would have it thrusted, and stay it as you would have it stayed."

He had poured all that he was into her, from the earliest influences of Methildis, to the advice of Count Konradin and the wise guidance of Father Stefan, from Friar Francis to Andreas and Rikard. In his daughter's blood and deeds, Wikerus' life continued, and affected the good and the evil of the world on a scale beyond anything a mortal man can hope to accomplish.

Incidentally, my readers, the letters that Wikerus wrote to Caris and Zanthie when he was imprisoned by Duke Friedrich in Vienna have yet to be discovered. Such an addition to the literary trove of mankind waits in some dusty chamber for eyes deserving enough to swim through the most eloquently and devoutly passionate words ever scribbled by human fingers. When they are found, I hope to read them myself, and allow my spirit to be galvanized in righteous goodness by the signature morality of the Tannhäuser.

GLOSSARY

(Warning: Plot points revealed in definitions)

Aachen, Germany [a: x ə n] – A city near the French border, between Luxembourg and Düsseldorf, Germany. It is where Emperor Friedrich II held his re-crowning as King of Germany. Duke Ludwig I of Bavaria, Swan Knight, gave an impassioned speech at the re-crowning. Afterward, Friedrich asked him to lead the Imperial Forces in the Fifth Crusade.

Achima [a x ɪ m a] – A Unicorn and Queen of the Land of the Sweeter Realm, before the Land and the Shallow Waters united. She is credited with the treaty that united the Land and Shallow Waters.

Acre, Israel – A strategic port city on the coastal plain of Israel. In 1104, in the wake of the First Crusade, after a four year siege, Acre fell to Christian forces. It served as the primary port and stronghold in the Crusader held Holy Land. In 1187, the Christian lost the city to the Ayyubid Sultan Saladin. In 1191, during the Third Crusade, Christian Crusader under King Richard I of England retook the city.

Adolf VI von Berg, Count –Ruler of the County of Berg in old Swabia. He headed the Pope's forces during the

Albigensian Crusade. Adolf died of plague in Damietta during the Fifth Crusade.

Agnes of Merania – The wife of Duke Friedrich II of Austria. Like her husband, she became a student of the Tannhäuser during the years he spent in Vienna.

Agnes of the Palatinate on the Rhine – Swan Knight's wife who married Duke Otto II. The two enjoyed the closest, most tenderly romantic Swan Knight marriage since the first generations of Swan Knights. Agnes grew particularly close to Brunhilde, Tannhäuser's daughter, assuming a maternal role in her upbringing in the absence of her father.

Al-Adil, Sultan – Leader of the Ayyubid Sultanate at the beginning of the Fifth Crusade, until his death on 31 August 1218. He was succeeded by his son, al-Kamil.

Al- Ashraf – Brother of Sultan al-Kamil, he rallied his army against al-Kamil in an attempt to take control of the Ayyubid Sultanate. He had in his possession, locked in a chest, the Holy Lance.

Al-Kamil, Sultan – Leader of the Ayyubid Sultanate from the death of his father, al-Adil on 31 August 1218. He was a general for his father until rising to sultan. He offered several generous peace terms to end the Fifth Crusade with minimal bloodshed. All were rejected by the crusader leadership until poor strategy and weak leadership demolished the chances of a crusader victory. Even after all was lost for the crusaders, al-Kamil's peace offer was more generous than it needed to be.

Alawich [a l a: v ɪ ʃ] – A farmer and tenant on the land of Baron Luitpold von Tannhausen. He and his brother Wikerus moved to Tannhausen after a series of personal tragedies. Wikerus rescued the Baroness, Methildis von Tannhausen, from bandits and delivered her child in the back of a cart. The baby became the hero of this story. When the Tannhäuser was fifteen years old, he met Alawich while searching for the brother, Wikerus. In their brief encounter, Alawich's humble goodness influenced the Tannhäuser greatly.

Albigensian Crusade – Also known as the Cathar Crusade, it was a crusade called by Pope Innocent III against the Cathar heretics in Southern France. The crusading forces were led by Count Adolf VI of Berg.

Aleidis von Vollrads [a l aɪ d i: s f ɔ n f ɔ l ʁ a: t s] – Daughter of Konrad von Vollrads of the Knights of Vollrads. She married the aged Baron Luitpold von Tannhausen when she was still a teenager, becoming the stepmother of the Tannhäuser. The Knights of Vollrads had strong political connections and close ties to the Church and the Teutonic Order.

Alpsee [a l p s e:] – A lake in the Hohenschwangau area of southern Bavaria, near the city of Füssen.

Andreas, Knight of Buchhorn [a n d ʁ e: a s] – The son of a Baron from the area around Ravensburg in Upper Swabia, he joined the army of Count Konradin of Buchhorn. In the Buchhorn army, he fought in the Fifth Crusade. After the crusade, he traveled with his friend and blacksmith, Rikard, but always wearing the Buchhorn colors proudly.

Andrew II, King of Hungary and Croatia – Strategic leader in the early stages of the Fifth Crusade, Andrew presided over the war council in Acre that included the Tannhäuser. Andrew left the crusade early and did not take part in the siege of Damietta. It is rumored that he was poisoned and returned to Hungary due to illness.

Ayyubid Sultanate – A royal dynasty of Sunni Muslim leaders based in Egypt. Its founding patriarch was Saladin. It established a system of family rule where members of Saladin's family were given rule of areas within the sultanate's control, with the sultan reigning over all of them. The Ayyubid Sultanate suffered in-fighting as the Syrian and Egyptian branches fought for supremacy, sometimes colluding with Christian crusaders against the other. It could be said that the Crusades were not Christian wars against Muslim control of the Holy Land, but a centuries-long war of vendetta against the Ayyubid Sultanate.

Battle of Bouvines – A battle on 27 July, 1214 in near the city of Bouvines in northern France, between French King Philip Augustus and the Holy Roman Empire under Emperor Otto IV of Welf. Philip won the battle and thus weakened Otto's tenuous hold on the empire.

Battle of Hattin – A battle on 4 July 1187 and part of a campaign led by the Ayyubid Sultan Saladin to retake Jerusalem and the other Crusader States in the Holy Land. The battle was a resounding victory for Saladin. More than 1,000 Christian knights were killed or captured. Most notably, the Christian relic, the True Cross, was taken by Saladin in the battle.

Bavaria – A state within Germany. It was a duchy during the Holy Roman Empire and a kingdom when the empire dissolved.

Béla IV, King of Hungary – Hungarian king who oversaw his country's recovery from the Mongol invasions. He recognized the Tannhäuser by the Marian Sword at his hip, and arranged for this story's hero to travel by caravan to Rome.

Bibione, Italy – A city on the coast of the Adriatic Sea. It was one of the lucrative ports of the Republic of Venice. It was from that city that the Tannhäuser broke from his caravan to Rome and headed north.

Bishops of Augsburg [aʊ k s b ʊ ɐ̯ k] – Prince-bishoprics of the Holy Roman Empire. They were powerful electors of the empire and enjoyed significant autonomy from both the empire and the church.

Bohemund IV, Prince of Antioch – Member of the ruling family of Christian Antioch. Contentious successions in Antioch made Bohemund seek Muslim alliances in the region. This proved useful in the Fifth Crusade when his previous partnership with Kaykaus I, the Sultan of Rum proved fruitful in the Christian campaign against the Ayyubid Sultanate. Bohemund was involved in the war council in Acre where the Tannhäuser spoke.

Brew Master – A highly skilled foreman of a brewery. During the period and places covered in this book, the position was usually inherited. Every region, town, and many private estates had their own breweries and the position of Brew Master was one of local prestige.

Brunhilde [b r ʊ n h ɪ l d ə] – The daughter of
Tannhäuser and his Brunnen lover Caris, born deep in the
Brunnen wilderness and raised alone with her parents
until her mother died and her father abandoned her. She
was adopted by the Swan Knight family and raised by
The Ancient One. Among her amazing talents is the
ability to jump high into the air and float weightless, and
to sense the nature of human hearts. Duke Ludwig I built
the castle for her, over the ruins of which King Ludwig II
built Neuschwanstein Castle. (See also Valkyrie).

Brunhilde's Castle – A castle commissioned by Duke
Ludwig I and overseen by his wife Ludmilla to be a home
and hiding place for Brunhilde. Later Wittelsbach referred
to it as Vorderhohenschwangau, after a second, twin
castle was built behind it.

Brunnens [b r ʊ n ə n s] – Creatures of the Sweeter
Realm, with tall, feminine figures, and almost clear
bodies that ripple like water when they move. They have
two throats through which they speak in sweet melodic
tones. They are intensely spiritual creatures and maintain
ancient shrines in their homeland that are visited by
pilgrims from across the Land and Shallow Waters.

Caris – A Brunnen and part of the choir that performd at
Agnes' concert. She fell in love with the Tannhäuser and
they lived together in the Brunnen wilderness, in the
Sweeter Realm, where she gave birth to Brunhilde. Caris
was a member of an ancient order of Brunnen clergy
called Die Engel des Mörsers that maintained the old
shrines and monuments of the Brunnen homeland. She
was one of the few in her order responsible for learning

and keeping the old languages, whose inscriptions covered the old shrines.

Castle Saarbrücken [z a: b̰ b ʁ ɣ k ə n] – A castle in Saarbrücken Germany, on the Saar River, near the border of Lorraine France. Holy Roman Emperor Friedrich I ordered the castle destroyed in 1168. By as early as 1205, efforts began slowly to reconstruct the fortress for the protection of the surrounding areas. In May of 1210, the construction efforts were paused as Count Adolf VI of Berg used the ruins as the gathering point for his forces in the Albigensian Crusade. The castle became a functioning fortress again in the 1270s, and was refortified in 1459.

Castle Tannhausen [t a n h aʊ z ə n] – Family estate of the Lords of Tannhausen, barons and landlords in northeast Swabia. The original structure was of bulky grey stone, with rounded towers and heavy wooden double doors. It stood in the heart of a forest of mostly linden trees. West of the forest were the fields and villages that supported the estate. It is the childhood home of this story's hero, The Tannhäuser.

Cathars – A branch of Christianity centered in Southern France, condemned by Pope Innocent III as heretical. They believed in two gods, one of the Old Testament and the physical world, and one of the New Testament and the spiritual world. It stood in the face of the Church's teaching of one God of all creation. Attempts were made to convert the Cathars. When those attempts failed, the Pope called the Cathar Crusade, also known as the Albigensian Crusade.

Cathar Crusade – See Albigensian Crusade.

Château Pèlerin – A Templar fortress on the coast of Israel, near the city of Atlit. It was also known as the Pilgrim's Castle because it was a secure land place for Christian pilgrims to Jerusalem.

Chivalric Code – This is a tricky one. The term "chivalry" has been so diluted since the time of its inception that it might be easier to say what chivalry is not. It is not simplistic acts like a man opening a door for a woman, or paying for her meal. Please don't call these actions chivalrous. It is a code that governs every thought and every action, down to the core of an individual, and holds its practitioners to the most devoutly pious, respectful, and generous life. First and foremost, it is a code of self-control and subduing our baser instincts. The code is spelled out in various works of medieval literature. Although they differ slightly, they all speak of faith in God, temperance of behavior, honesty, generosity toward the less fortunate, protection of the weak, and self-sacrifice for the greater good. The vows sworn in knighthood included these precepts, though the code was adopted by many less lauded individuals, male and female.

Chivalry – See Chivalric Code

Christ Ist Erstanden [k ʁ ɪ s t ɪ s t ɛ ɐ̯ ʃ t a n d ə n] – The unofficial anthem of the Order of Teutonic Knights. It translates literally to "Christ is Risen".

Chryzanthoseude – See **Zanthie**, see **Brunhilde**.

Church of the Holy Sepulcher – A Christian church in Old Jerusalem, still a place of Christian pilgrimage. According to tradition, the church rests over two sacred sites, the place of Jesus' crucifixion (Calvary) and the empty tomb where Jesus was laid before the Resurrection.

Cologne, Germany – City in northwest Germany. It was the seat of the prince-bishops of Cologne who had an electorship in the Holy Roman Empire.

Crucifix – Any image of Jesus crucified upon the cross. It is most commonly associated with three-dimensional artistic renderings of Jesus nailed to the cross.

Cunrad – Swan Knight's husband. He is the husband of Elsa and the father of Bechtold, Diterich, Hildemar, and Birgit. He built the first lodge of Linderhof.

Cyprus, Kingdom of – A European island and Crusader state in the Mediterranean Sea, ruled by the French Lusignan Dynasty. Its strategic location in the eastern Mediterranean made it the ideal naval launching point for crusading armies to the Holy Land.

Damietta, Egypt – A city in the Nile River Delta, where the Damietta branch of the Nile meets the Mediterranean Sea. It was a hotly contested piece of real estate during the crusades for its access to the river. Once controlled, Damietta could receive and supply crusaders with goods and reinforcements from Europe. The city had massive walls dozens of high towers, and a protective moat. Its most formidable feature was a harbor tower with a chain that blocked entrance to the harbor. There was no taking the city by sea without first taking control of the tower.

Deep Waters – A kingdom of the Sweeter Realm consisting of the deep parts of all bodies of water. It is ruled by Löwschock, whose throne is in the deep center of the Queen's Lake. There is a tangible border between the dark, cold waters of the Deep and the bright, warm waters of the Shallow.

Die Engel des Mörsers [d i: ɛ ŋ ə l d ɛ s m œ ʁ z ɐ s] – Literally "Angels of Mortar", they were a revered order of holy Brunnens dedicated to maintaining the ancient shrines and monuments of the Brunnen homeland. They learned the old languages that were inscribed on the shrines and kept them alive inside the heads of a few select members. Caris was one of those members.

Egon von Urach, Count [e: g ɔ n f ɔ n u: ʁ a: x] – The father of Methildis, Baroness of Tannhausen, and the grandfather of this story's hero. He ruled the wealthy and prominent region of Urach from his estate at Hohenurach Castle.

Elisabeth von Wittelsbach [v ɪ t ə l s b a x] – First-in-Training and first child of Swan Knight Duke Otto II and his wife Agnes. Elizabeth was raised in the valley by The Ancient One, along with her childhood companion and dearest friend, Brunhilde, the child of Tannhäuser and Caris. Elizabeth married Conrad IV of Hohenstaufen, King of Germany and later Count Meinhard II of Tirol.

Elizabeth von Zähringen, Countess [ts ɛ: ʁ ɪ ŋ ə n] – Wife of Count Egon von Urach and mother of Methildis, Baroness of Tannhausen. It was through Elizabeth that the Tannhäuser inherited the Grail Blood of Parsifal.

Elsa – The third Swan Knight and the daughter of Lohengrin and Nethe. She was the greatest Swan Knight until Verena, the last Swan Knight. Until Verena, Elsa was the only Swan Knight to fully control the behavior of the portal with her mind. She developed telepathic communication with the Unicorns without having to make contact with the horns.

Ermenrich [ɛ r m ə n r ɪ ç] – Fifth Swan Knight, the son of Hildemar and the Welf prince Aldwin. He was the grandson of Elsa. His royal obligations and his concern over the proliferation of Grail Blood led to the Laws of Ermenrich.

Eulesängers [ɔʏ l ə s ɛ ŋ ɐ s] – Creatures of the Sweeter Realm, brown, ankle-high birds, with awkwardly large wings, a bushy tail, and a hooked beak like an owl's. They communicate in high-pitched, high-spirited whistles.

Fariskur – A fortress town south of Damietta, abandoned by al-Kamil when he retreated his army to Cairo.

Fifth Crusade – An attempt by the powerful Pope Innocent III to take the Holy Land. When Innocent III died, the crusade was continued by his successor, Pope Honorius III. The crusade failed and resulted in the capture and imprisonment of many crusaders. In the Egyptian prison, the Tannhäuser met Swan Knight Duke Ludwig I.

Flagellation – Self-whipping of flogging, usually for the reparation of past or future sins. It is a denial of the will of the flesh that is used to gain favor with God and relieve the practitioner of guilt.

Fourth Lateran Council – A council assembled by Pope Innocent III in the Lateran Palace in Rome on 11 November 1215. Because of the span of time since the previous council and the important topics covered, attendance was high. In attendance were 71 Patriarchs, 412 bishops, and more than 900 Abbots and Abbesses. It was in this assembly that Pope Innocent III officially called for the Fifth Crusade.

Francis of Assisi – A canonized saint of the Catholic Church. Francis founded the Friars Minor and the Order of Saint Claire. He went to Acre during the Fifth Crusade and counseled with the leaders. To avoid the horrors of war, Francis tried to convert the Muslim population in the Holy land. When he failed to do so, he along with the Tannhäuser urged the most peaceful possible approach to the goals of the crusade.

Free Imperial City – A city in the Holy Roman Empire not under the control of local nobility. Answering only to the Emperor, they were favorite locations of the Emperors and were commonly the home of Imperial palaces.

Friar – An Ordered member of Catholic clergy. They abandoned the monastic life for a more practical Christian lifestyle, living in urban areas or traveling, tending to the poor and evangelizing. Their vows include poverty.

Friedrich II, Duke of Austria [f ʁ iː d ʁ ɪ ç] – Austrian Duke known as "The Quarrelsome". He gave shelter to Tannhäuser. After Tannhäuser fled Rome, Friedrich was enamored by his passion and poetry, and kept the poet as a member of his household, before falsely suspecting him of adultery with Agnes, the Duchess of Austria.

Friedrich I von Hohenstaufen, Emperor [f r iː d r ɪ ç f ɔ n h oː ə n ʃ t aʊ f ə n] – Known as Friedrich **Barbarossa**, Holy Roman Emperor saved at the Battle of

Verona by Otto of Wittelsbach. He rewarded Otto the Duchy of Bavaria.

Friedrich II von Hohenstaufen [h o: ə n ʃ t aʊ f ə n] – Holy Roman Emperor and King of the German, friend of Duke Ludwig I of Bavaria, Swan Knight.

Gessius Florus – Roman governor of Israel in 66 AD, during the great Jewish rebellion that liberated the Spear of Longinus from Roman control.

Gottfried von Löwenstein, Count [g ɔ t f ʁ i: t   f ɔ n l ø: v ə n ʃ t aɪ n] – Bavaria count tasked with overseeing the construction of Werdenfels Castle, a donation to the Teutonic Order by a collective of Swabian and Bavarian noble families.

Graféas [g ʁ a f e: a s] – A Brunnen, member of the Die Engel des Mörsers, and close friend of Caris. She violated Brunnen law to visit Caris in the wilderness. She brought presents when beckoned by Zanthie's cry.

Graswang Valley [g r a s v a ŋ] – A long valley in southern Bavaria. It runs near the Austrian border. Its western end in just south of the southern tip of the Portal Valley.

Gregory IX, Pope – Catholic pope from March 1227 to August 1241. He was Pope when Caris died and Wikerus emerged from the Sweeter Realm. The legends of the Tannhäuser attribute the story of the blossoming staff to Pope Urban IV, who became pope on 29 August 1261, when Wikerus was 63 years old and living comfortably with Brunhilde in her castle. It was Gregory whose staff blossomed and Gregory who spent the rest of his life searching for the Tannhäuser.

Großgebietiger [g ʁ o: s g ə b i: t ɪ g ɐ] – I high position in a Catholic order with dominion over all sects. There are five offices at the level. The Tannhäuser was promoted to the office of Marschall (Summus Marescalcus), the chief of military affairs.

Großkomtur [g ʁ o: s k ɔ m t u: ɐ̯] – A deputy to the Grand Master of the Teutonic Order.

Guérin de Montaigu, Grand Master of the Knights Hospitaller – 13th Grand Master of the Knights Hospitaller.

Gütel [g y: t ə l] – First Swan Knight spouse. She rescued Parsifal from the enchanted flowermaiden. She is the mother of Lohengrin.

Halb-Brüder [h a l p b ʁ y: d ɐ] – Half-brothers of the Teutonic Order. They were mostly foot-soldiers. They did not take the monastic vows of the knights, but were bound by every other rule of the order. They wore matching grey cloaks and either grey or black tunics.

Hamburg, Germany – Port city in northern Germany with access to the North Sea and Baltic Sea. Because of its strategic trade location on the Elbe River and the North Sea, it became a wealthy merchant port in the middle ages. In 1189, Holy Roman Emperor Friedrich Barbarossa granted it the status Free Imperial City, giving it tax-free status from the taxes of local nobility down the Elbe to the North Sea. The wealth that flowed into the city raised many working class families to the Bourgeoisie and lower nobility.

Heidelberg Castle/Schloß Heidelberg [ʃ l ɔ s h aɪ d ə l b ɛ g̊ k] – Home and political seat of the Counts Palatinate of the Rhine.

Heinrich V, Count Palatine of the Rhine – Count of the Rhenish Palatinate and Elector of the Holy Roman Empire. He married his daughter Otto von Wittelsbach, son of Duke Ludwig of Bavaria, the Swan Knight. The marriage secured Wittelsbach control of the Rhenish Palatinate for centuries to come.

Helleklinge [h ɛ l ɛ k l ɪ ŋ ə] – I mighty Unicorn warrior and companion of Duke Otto II of Bavaria. She was the head of her clan and was among the party who intercepted Wikerus on the Sweeter Realm side of the portal.

Helfen - Wehren – Heilen [h ɛ l f ə n - v e: ʁ ə n - h aɪ l ə n] – Literally Help-Defend-Heal, it is the primary precepts and the rallying cry of the Order of Teutonic Knights. During the height of the order, it could be found emblazoned on the walls and doorways of every fortress and stronghold of the order. The words were included in the vows that recruits took when joining the Teutonic Knighthood. It served as a reminder of the origins of the order, as keepers of hospitals and protectors of Christian pilgrims to the Holy Land.

Hermann von Salza [h ɛ g̊ m a n f ɔ n z a l ts a] – Fourth Grand Master of the Teutonic Order and one of the leaders of the Fifth Crusade. He came from a family of ministeriales. These were people raised from serfdom during medieval times for certain acts of loyalty and valor. These were poor people knighted for their own merits. The made up a bulk of the lower nobility and knighthood in the Holy Roman Empire. They were often indebted to one noble or another for their advancement.

Hildemar [h ɪ l d ə m a: r] – Daughter of Swan Knight Elsa and her husband Cunrad. She married Aldwin of Welf and moved to the castle on the Alpsee, near Füssen. She is the mother of Swan Knight Ermenrich. She is the first descendant of Parsifal to marry into nobility.

Holy Lance – Also called the Spear of Antioch or the Spear of Longinus, it is a sacred Christian relic. One of the few Christian relics to have touched the Blood of Christ, it is said to have Divine properties, like the True Cross and the Holy Grail. It is the metal spear head of the Roman Centurion Longinus, who used the spear to pierce the side of Jesus during the Crucifixion. It was taken by Christians during the first Jewish rebellion of Jerusalem and hidden in Antioch.

Holy Land – A region of the Middle East containing almost all of Israel and Palestine, and parts of Lebanon and Syria. The region is considered holy in Christianity, Judaism, and Islam, attracting pilgrims from all three religions.

Holy Grail – The Cup of Christ, it was the vessel used by Jesus Christ at the Last Supper to hold and serve the first consecration of ordinary wine into the Blood of Christ.

Holy Roman Empire – A political entity that loosely held a region that is now mostly Germany, Austria, and Northern Italy. It is often called the Holy Roman Empire of the German Nation. It developed in the Middle Ages and was dissolved by Napoleon Bonaparte in 1806. Some historians say that it began in the year 800 with the coronation of Charlemagne, when he claimed to be the new roman emperor and heir to the former lands of the Roman Empire. It was not called the Holy Roman Empire until four centuries later. The emperor was chosen by electors from the many kingdoms, principalities, duchies, counties, prince-bishoprics, and Free Imperial Cities that housed an elector. It is comically but truthful said that it was neither holy, Roman, nor an empire.

Honorius III, Pope – Successor to Pope Innocent III. The Papacy enjoyed tremendous political and military power during his Papacy. Pope Honorius III oversaw the Fifth Crusade, where Swan Knight Duke Ludwig I and the Teutonic Knight Tannhäuser were captured and met in a prison in Egypt. Pope Honorius III negotiated the release of the prisoners.

Hugh I, King of Cyprus – Hugh's father died while he was still a minor and unable to sit on the throne. His brother-in-law Walter served as regent until Hugh came of age. He was a shrewd politician and businessman. Hugh made trade deals with the Turkish Sultan of Rum, a relationship that would later help serve the Fifth Crusade. He joined Andrew of Hungary on the crusade and served as a voice of leadership early in the campaign.

Indulgences of the Church – An indulgence granted from the church is a relief of guilt from sins and a stay of any divine punishment for those sins. Indulgences were granted for some service to the Church, donations, or through prayers and penance. They were given to those who served the crusades, either by fighting, outfitting a knight, or committing to a regimen of prayer for the crusade. Abuse of indulgences was one of the primary factors that led to the Reformation.

Innocent III, Pope – Roman Catholic Pope who sided with Otto IV of Welf against Friedrich II of Hohenstaufen when the two families fought over the throne of the Holy Roman Empire. Otto sought land gains into Italy. This forced Pope Innocent III to switch his allegiance. Friedrich won the war. As repayment to the Pope for his support, Friedrich had to commit to the Pope's Fifth Crusade. Innocent III died before the crusade developed. The Fifth Crusade was continued by his successor, Pope Honorius III.

Innocent IV, Pope – Roman Catholic Pope born Sinibaldo Fieschi. As a cardinal, he was a close friend and confidant of Pope Gregory IX.

John Brienne, King of Jerusalem – King of Jerusalem from 1210 to 1225. John was a French noble who was solicited by the barons of Jerusalem to marry their queen, Maria of Montferrat. They were crowned co-sovereigns until Maria's death. John and his supporters believed that the crown should remain his despite the fact that he gained it only through marriage, until his daughter came of age. Others questioned his right to rule. The dispute caused tension between john and Hugh of Cyprus. John appealed to Pope Innocent III who supported his claim. Although the Pope brokered peace between John and his many rivals, tensions remained high while they served together in the Fifth Crusade. One by one, his opponents left the crusade effort. He solidified the support of most of the remaining crusaders when he joined in opposition to the will and leadership of Cardinal Pelagius.

Jonah and the Whale – A story from the Old Testament Book of Jonah, in which Jonah, a prophet of God, is told by God to go to the Assyrian city of Nineveh to warn them of God's wrath. Jonah decides instead to travel by ship toward a place called Tarshish. Storms rage and Jonah is thrown overboard and swallowed by a giant fish. It is only when he promises to go to Nineveh that the fish vomits and Jonah is free. He goes to Nineveh and gets the residents to change their ways and avoid God's wrath. The tale is used as a metaphor by the narrator of this story for the playful negotiations between the Meersburg blacksmith, Rikard, and the giant bellows cramp he uses.

Kandake [k a n d a k ə] – The Queen of the Land and Shallow Waters. She followed the Unicorn Achima as Queen. She is a creature of the Shallow Waters.

Kelheim, Bavaria [k e: l h aɪ m] – The ancestral seat of the Wittelsbach dynasty. It became a hub of political power in the duchy of Bavaria when the Wittelsbach assumed the dukedom. It was abandoned as a ducal residence after Duke Ludwig I was assassinated on a bridge in Kelheim.

Knights Hospitaller – The Order of Knights of the Hospital of Saint John of Jerusalem. The oldest of the three major military orders under the Pope, they began as a handful of individuals working to bring care to sick and injured Christian pilgrims in the Muristan district of Jerusalem before the conquest of Jerusalem in the First Crusade. After the crusade, they grew and became a monastic military order dedicated to Saint John the Baptist, taking vows of poverty chastity, and obedience.

Knights Templar – The Poor Fellow-Soldiers of Christ and of the Temple of Solomon. Founded in 1119, the Order was made its headquarters on the Temple Mount in Jerusalem, where it is believed the temple of Solomon sat. It is for that association that they received the name Templars. They began as a monastic military order for the protection of pilgrims in the Holy Land. But they received substantial charitable donations and grew to become one of the wealthiest and most powerful organizations in Europe.

Konradin von Buchhorn, Count [k ɔ n ʁ aː d iː n f ɔ n b uː x h ɔ ɐ̯ n] – The Counts of Buchhorn were rulers of the Meersburg area on the northern coast of lake Constance, residing in Meersburg Castle. Their influence stretched well beyond their own lands, as they were well-known for their generosity and loyalty, and for their strong allegiance to the Church. Konradin carried the title during most of the years covered in this story. He was childhood friends with the Tannhäuser's mother, Methildis and proved to be one of the most potent influences in his early life.

Lake Constance – A large lake in southern Swabia, around which many influential Swabian noble families grew and prospered.

Land and Shallow Waters – The known region of the Sweeter Realm, excluding the Deep Waters. It is the jurisdiction of the Queen. It includes in its citizenry all breeds except for the creatures of the Deep.

Lateran Palace in Rome – An ancient Roman palace, it was the primary residence of the Pope during the years covered in this story. It is adjacent to the Rome's Cathedral Church, the Archbasilica of Saint John Lateran.

Laws of Ermenrich [ɛ ɡ̊ m ə n ʁ ɪ ç] – A set of laws set down by Ermenrich, the first Swan Knight born into royalty. The laws mandate the structure of the introduction of spouses and children to the Swan Knighthood. They were formed in response to the spreading of Grail Blood and to the secular demands of royal Swan Knights. Ermenrich was the son of Hildemar and the Welf prince Aldwin. He was the grandson of Elsa.

Leopold VI, Duke of Austria – Known as Leopold the Glorious, he was a member of the House of Babenberg. A devout Christian, he founded several monasteries. He spent his life fighting for the Church, engaged in both the Albigensian Crusade and the Fifth Crusade, as well as the Reconquista of Spain. He was a member of the war council in Acre.

Lohengrin [l o: ə n ŋ r ɪ n] – Second Swan Knight and only child of Parsifal and Gütel. He married Nethe and was father to Elsa, the greatest Swan Knight.

Lords of Tannhausen [t a n h aʊ z ə n] – A family of Barons in northeast Swabia. Although they were not of notorious wealth or rank, they remained influential through shrewd political favors and some fortunate timing. Castle Tannhausen is a humble structure for German nobility of that rank, but the lands and villages of the estate were productive.

Löwschock [l œ v ʃ ɔ k]– King of the Deep Waters, a large, clawed, horned water creature with the face of a lion, muscular arms and shoulders, a scaled tail with short, knobby legs and webbed feet.

Ludmilla of Bohemia – Swan Knight's spouse, wife of Duke Ludwig I. They married for political alliance but developed an intense love over their years forced apart by war. Ludmilla oversaw the construction of Brunhilde's Castle.

Ludwig I von Wittelsbach, Duke of Bavaria, Swan Knight [l ʊ t v ɪ ç f ɔ n v ɪ t ə l s b a x] – Swan Knight and youngest child of Swan Knight Otto I, Duke of Bavaria and his wife Agnes of Loon. Ludwig became Duke at ten years old, when his father died. His mother served as regent until Ludwig came of age. His sister Agnes yielded the Swan Knighthood to Ludwig when he grew strong enough. Ludwig served in the Fifth Crusade as Commander of Imperial Forces.

Ludwig II, Duke of Bavaria, Swan Knight – The son of Duke Otto II and Agnes of the Palatinate on the Rhine, Ludwig's reign as Swan Knight caused him great personal grief. His first wife, Maria of Brabant, threatened the secrecy of the Portal Valley and the Grail. To maintain the sacred secrets, he accused her of adultery and had her executed. His guilt was severe and he opened a convent in her memory.

Luitpold von Tannhausen, Baron [l u: ɪ t p ɔ l t f ɔ n t a n h aʊ z ə n] – The father of Luitpold Wikerus von Tannhausen, this story's hero, he did much to lay the foundation of Wikerus' character, usually in our hero's

450

attempt to be less like his father. Luitpold was a good man, dedicated to the prosperity of his family, but his means were sometimes less than noble. He pushed his sons to war in search of family glory.

Luitpold Wikerus von Tannhausen [v ɪ k ə ʁ ʊ s] – This story's hero. He is commonly referred to as the Tannhäuser. His exploits laid out in the preceding pages led to the growth of a legend that found its way into paintings, songs, a Wagner opera, and even the pages of the Grimm Tales. Each captured some truths of his remarkable life. His poetry survives to this day in the Codex Manesse, where he left hints about the truly miraculous life he led.

Mainau Island [m aɪ n aʊ] – An island in Lake Constance. It was home to a stronghold of the Order of Teutonic Knights. It is where the Tannhäuser trained and took his monastic vows.

Marian Cross of Saint Mary – The most prestigious award granted to members of the Teutonic Order. The symbol of the Cross with a second crossbar at the bottom and a letter M hanging from it, also known as the Miraculous Medal, was placed upon an item significant to the recipient. In the case of the Tannhäuser, the Marian Cross was placed on the pommel of a ceremonial sword.

Martinstag/St. Martin's Day [m a g̊ t iː n s t a k] – The feast of Saint Martin (11 November). It is celebrated in Germany with the making of homemade lanterns and the giving of alms. The giving of alms, and particularly clothing, stems from a story from the life of St. Martin when he removed his own cloak and tore it in two so he could cloth a poor person.

Martinstag Lanterns – Homemade lanterns made in the celebration of the feast of Saint Martin (see also – Martinstag). The lanterns used to be made by poor children, so the tradition lives with the use of simple and inexpensive materials. The lanterns light the dining rooms of celebrants before the Martinstag meal.

Meersburg, Swabia [m e: ɐ̯ s b ʊ ɐ̯ k] – A town on the northern shore of Lake Constance. It is the home of Meersburg Castle, the family seat of the Counts who ruled the area. Many dynasties held the title and the land, but during the years covered in this story, the Counts of Buchhorn ruled Meersburg.

Meersburg Castle – Family home of the Counts of Buchhorn. It is today the oldest castle of constant residence in Germany. Its proximity to Mainau Island ensured a healthy relationship with the Teutonic Order. A wonderful old castle, its most notorious feature is a pit used by the counts to spiritual cleanse through the denial of carnal desires.

Meinrad [m aɪ n ʁ a: t] – recruit to the Teutonic Order for the fifth Crusade and son of a wealthy Hamburg merchant. During his training on Mainau Island he proved his unworthiness to join the order.

Mercedes – A Scherier who with her cousin Rei'mund was the first creature to step through the Portal to meet the Tannhäuser.

Methildis von Tannhausen, Baroness [m ɛ t ɪ l d ɪ s] –
Mother of the Tannhäuser, wife of Baron Luitpold von
Tannhausen, and daughter of Count Egon von Urach and
Elizabeth von Zähringen. She was a devoutly spiritual
woman and loyal advocate of the Church. Her sharp mind
was wasted in the staunchly patriarchal atmosphere of
Castle Tannhausen, so she dedicated herself to the pious
rearing of her children.

Ministeriales – Families that were elevated from serfdom
into the middle-class and lower nobility.

Minnesänger/Minnesinger [m ɪ n ə z ɛ ŋ ɐ] – A German
poet and singer of love songs during the twelfth,
thirteenth, and fourteenth centuries.

Muschelschale [m ʊ ʃ ç ə l ʃ a: l ə] – German term for a
conch shell. It was used by the noble-born members of the
Teutonic Order to denote lower-born members who reveal
their lineage through unseemly and crass behavior.

Nährenstadt [n ɛ: ʁ ə n ʃ t a t] – Capital of the Brunnen
homeland. It is where Wikerus and Caris were brought to
face the Brunnen council. It is from there that they were
banished into the wilderness.

Nethe [n ɛ t ə] – Second wife of Lohengrin and mother of
Elsa, the greatest Swan Knight. She died in the house fire
with Lohengrin and their grand-daughter, Birgit.

Neusiedl, Lake [n ɔʏ z i: d l] – A lake in Eastern Austria.
Its southern end extends into Hungary. It is where the
Tannhäuser awoke after the battle on the streets of
Vienna.

Nikephoros II, Emperor – Born Nikephoros Phokas, he was emperor of the Byzantine Empire form 963-969.

Nomadic Belt/Der Nomadengürtel [d e: r n o: m a: d ə ŋ ʏ r t ə l] – A strip of land in the Sweeter Realm, which wraps around the Queen's Lake. It is where the Nomadic Breeds roam. The Portal Point in the Sweeter Realm is in the southeast corner of the Nomadic Belt.

Old Digger – A Scherier of renown across the Land and Shallow Waters. He designed and single-handedly dug half of the Scherier capital of Eineklaue.

Old Mosque, Damietta – The city of Damietta Egypt had as its most remarkable feature an old mosque near the city center, with a marble mosaic of a crescent in the center of the floor. The dome above was an acoustic wonder, designed to magnify the voice of anyone standing upon the crescent. One humble, prayerful hum upon the crescent reverberated through the mosque like a full choir.

Oliver of Paderborn – Bishop of Paderborn and school master of the cathedral school in Paderborn, he was a practical but spiritual man. He was an influential voice among the leadership of the Fifth Crusade. His vivid chronicle of the Siege of Damietta, titled *Historia Damiatina,* has given historians the best images of Fifth Crusade.

Ordensmarschall [ɔ g̊ d ə n s m a ʃ a l] – A high-ranking officer of the Order of Teutonic Knights, answerable only to the Grand master and the Pope.

Ostrach, Swabia [ɔ s t ʁ a: x] – Swabian town and home to the Salem Monastery. The Tannhäuser stopped there on his way from Castle Tannhausen to Mainau Island.

Otto II, Duke of Bavaria, Swan Knight – Swan Knight and only child of Duke Ludwig I and Ludmilla of Bohemia. He married Agnes, daughter of Count Heinrich of the Palatinate on the Rhine. The marriage gave Otto's father, and later Otto, the electorship of the Count Palatine. During his late childhood/early adulthood, Otto was trained in the Portal Valley by the Tannhäuser.

Otto IV von Brunswick, Holy Roman Emperor – A member of the Welf dynasty of German nobility. Holy Roman Emperor who fell out of favor with Pope Innocent III. His reign as emperor was stained with constant conflict. His succession was no smoother. His fall marked the beginning of the decline of Welf prominence in Imperial politics.

Palatinate of the Rhine – An electorship of the Holy Roman Empire, governed by the Counts Palatine. Its seat of power is in Heidelberg. The Wittelsbach gained the Palatinate when Otto II married Agnes of the Palatinate of the Rhine.

Parsifal [p a r z i: f a l] – The First Swan Knight and a keeper of the Holy Grail. His spilled blood created the portal after he drank from the Grail. He and his wife Gütel founded the portal valley. He was father to Lohengrin. He was the first person to enter the portal and the only one to open the portal from the Sweeter Realm and return to the portal valley. He was the first to meet The Ancient One.

Parsifal's Valley – The name The Ancient One called the portal valley, later called Linderhof. It is where Parsifal was attacked by an enchanted flowermaiden and spilled his blood to open the portal. Parsifal and Gütel built their home there.

Peire de Montagut, Grand Master of the Templars – He assumed the position of Grand Master in 1218, after the start of the Fifth Crusade. His influence was felt immediately. He had a much more hardline approach to the crusade than his predecessor, Guillaume de Chartres. It was in great part due to pressure from Montagut that the many offers of peace that would have secured Jerusalem for the Crusaders were rejected.

Pelagius of Albano – Born Pelagio Galvani, he was a Catholic Cardinal and canon lawyer, granted the Italian diocese of Albano by Pope Innocent III. Innocent's successor, Pope Honorius III, wishing to keep the efforts of the Fifth Crusade out of secular control, appointed Pelagius as his papal legate, making him the ultimate authority over Christian forces. He was in every way ill-equipped for the position of military commander. His weak and faulty leadership directly resulted in the failure of the Fifth Crusade.

Peter Bartholomew – A monk of St. Peter's Church in Antioch during the First Crusade. When Antioch was under siege, and the entrenched crusaders faced annihilation, Peter Received a vision from St. Andrew the Apostle, telling him that the Holy Lance was buried under the church in Antioch. Peter dug through the church floor and found the relic. With the Holy Lance in hand, the crusaders rushed against their superior enemy and routed them with ease.

Pierre de Castelnau – The papal legate under Pope Innocent III, sent to southern France to excommunicate Count Raymond VI of Toulouse, a sympathizer of heretical Catharism.

Pit of Starvation – A pit inside of Meersburg Castle, with a waist-high circular banister surrounding it. It was used by the Counts of Buchhorn to purge their knights of dependence on physical pleasures. Each knight wishing to join the Buchhorn army had be lowered into the pit. They were raised when their spirits transcended physical needs.

Pontificate – The term of office of a pontiff. The term can refer to any high priest or holy person, but in the Catholic Church, it refers to the Pope, the Bishop of Rome.

The portal – A passage into the Sweeter Realm, opened for the first time when Parsifal's Holy Grail enchanted blood fell to the earth. It opens at the approach of all with Grail Blood —all descendants of Parsifal.

Queen/King of the Land and Shallow Waters – the ruler elected by the creatures of the Sweeter Realm to rule the known region on the other side of the portal, excluding the Deep Waters. The Queen from the Shallow Waters, who ruled during the life of the Tannhäuser was named Kandake.

Quia Maior – A papal decree by Pope Innocent III declaring among other things Innocent's intention to call the Fifth Crusade.

Rashidun – The Rashidun Caliphs were the first four Islamic successors of the prophet Mohamed. In 637, when the reference in this book is made, the Rashidun Caliph who took the Christian city of Antioch was Uthman ibn Affan.

Raymond VI of Toulouse, Count – A French count excommunicated by Pope Innocent III for his support of the heretical Cathar movement.

Rei'mund – A Scherier and the first creature of the Sweeter Realm, other than The Ancient One, to meet the Tannhäuser.

Rhine (river) – European river that forms borders for Germany, France, Switzerland, Austria, and Liechtenstein. It was a profitable trade route for German royalty whose lands it crossed.

Richard I of England, King – Known as "the Lion Heart", Richard was a leader of the Third Crusade. He drew his sword where fighting was most violent and perilous, not only proving himself an able warrior, but displaying such inspirational valor that his army won many battles that numbers and circumstances should have prevented.

Rikard the Blacksmith – A blacksmith in the employment of Count Konradin von Buchhorn, working in Meersburg Castle. He served as blacksmith for the Buchhorn contingent in the Fifth Crusade. Rikard designed the floating siege tower that won the harbor tower of Damietta and allowed the eventual crusader victory over that city. He and his friend Andreas, a knight in the Buchhorn army befriended the Tannhäuser and worked their way into a special place among the characters of this story. He was in possession of the Spear of Longinus, the spear tip that lanced the side of Jesus at the Crucifixion.

Rosary – A series of Catholic prayers honoring Mary, the mother of Jesus, or the prayer beads used to mark those prayers.

Rum Sultanate – Also known as the Anatolian Seljuk Sultanate, it was a Turkish Sunni Muslim political entity, led by Sultan of Rum. The name Rum comes from the Arabic name for the Roman Empire, as the territories held by the Rum Sultanate were previously Roman territories. Its proximity to Constantinople, the capital of the Byzantine Empire led to mutually beneficial trade relations. To maintain these lucrative relations, the Sultan of Rum struck deals with Christian crusading forces against the Ayyubid Sultanate in Egypt.

Sabatons – The foot coverings of a knight's armor.

Saint Michael the Archangel – Patron Saint of warriors, Saint Michael is the commander of the Army of God. The Book of Daniel in the Old Testament of the Holy Bible refers to Michael as "one of the chief princes" of Heaven. In European Christian tradition, he is often depicted wearing armor and carrying a spear or sword.

Saints – In the Catholic Church, a saint is any soul residing with God in Heaven. More commonly, the term refers to a selection of Catholics throughout history chosen by the Church for canonization. These are people whose services to God and the Church during their lives are honored and glorified, to be imitated. Catholics often pray to the Saints to intercede on their behalf to God. Saints are given feast days for the celebration of their merits.

Salem Monastery – A monastery of the Order of Cistercians, a branch of the Benedictines, in the town of Ostrach, Swabia, Germany. It was a wealthy monastery with beautiful structures. The monks lived strictly by the Rules of St. Benedict.

Saladin – Founder and first sultan of the Ayyubid Sultanate based in Egypt. A formidable military commander, he commanded the recapture of Jerusalem in 1187, after capturing almost all of the Crusader held fortresses and cities in the Holy Land.

Saul/Saint Paul – Born Saul of Tarsus, Saint Paul persecuted followers of Christ until his conversion. He was traveling from Jerusalem to Damascus to find Christians, arrest them and bring them back to Jerusalem when the Risen Christ appeared to him, striking him temporarily blind and knocking him from his horse. His sight was restored and he declared Jesus to be the Son of God.

Savelli, Cencio – Birth name of Pope Honorius III.

Scheriers [ʃ e: r i: r s] – Creatures of the Sweeter Realm, with white hair and short, flat bodies. They are social creatures who love to wrestle. After The Ancient One, they were the first breed to meet the Swan Knights. They came to love the Tannhäuser and he loved them.

Sharimshah, Egypt – Fortified city on the Damietta branch of the Nile River.

Siege of Acre – One of the most impactful victories in the mostly successful Third Crusade. Securing Acre gave the Crusaders a strategic fortress and military base that would be used to maintain and regain Christian holdings in the Holy Land until 1291.

Sign of the Cross – a self-blessing given by Catholics, in which the Trinity of God is acknowledged at the beginning and end of prayers by touching with the thumb, index finger, and middle finger of the right hand on the forehead, then the chest or abdomen, followed by the left shoulder then right, while speaking "In the Name of the Father, The Son, and The Holy Spirit." Blessing from the clergy that mark the symbol of the Cross with the right hand at head level, or with the right thumb on the body of the recipient is also referred to as the Sign of the Cross.

Simon III of Saarbrücken, Count –

Spear of Antioch – See **Holy Lance**

Spear of Longinus – See **Holy Lance**

Split, Croatia – A Adriatic coastal city in Croatia, from which crusading forces departed mainland Europe for the Mediterranean island kingdom of Cyprus.

Stefan, Father – A Catholic priest in the service of the Teutonic Order. A full member of the order, he served in a priestly, not knightly position. He was tasked with riding to Castle Tannhausen and bringing the young Tannhäuser to the Teutonic stronghold on Mainau Island. Highly influential in the Order, the Church, and the region around Lake Constance, his quiet but powerful influence manipulated many of the events that shape the nature of this story.

Swabia – A stem-duchy of the Holy Roman Empire, west of Bavaria.

Swan Knights – The line of the descendants of Parsifal, knighted by The Ancient One, whose Grail enchanted blood opens the portal. They are sworn to the protection of the portal and to the service of the Queen of the Land and Shallow Waters.

Sweeter Realm – The known world on the other side of the portal. It consists of two kingdoms, the Land and Shallow Waters, ruled by the Queen, and the Deep Waters, ruled by Löwschock.

Talkhah, Egypt – A city in the Nile delta. Its surrounding fields are subject to the annual flooding of the delta. Al-Kamil used the flooding to his advantage during the Christian march on Cairo during the Fifth Crusade. He entrenched his army there, using them as bait to lure the crusading army into the dangerous flood zane.

The Tanhuter – The name used by the soldiers of the Ayyubid Sultanate for the Tannhäuser after his performances in battle outside the walls of Damietta. They believed him to be a conjurer of unnatural abilities through evil means.

Tannhäuser [t a n h ɔʏ z ɐ] – A name referring to any descendant of the Lords of Tannhausen.

The Tannhäuser – While many of the Lords of Tannhausen have probably been called "The Tannhäuser", for the sake of this story, it is only referring to Luitpold Wikerus von Tannhausen, the title hero of this story.

Teutonic Knights [t ɔy t o: n ɪ k] – The Order of Brothers of the German House of Saint Mary in Jerusalem. They were a holy Catholic military order of German knights, founded in 1190. They had a particular hierarchy, including a Grand Master, but were ultimately under the authority of the Pope. They had fortresses and training grounds throughout Germany and beyond, including in the Holy Land.

The Ancient One – Creature of the Sweeter Realm, a giant swan, the first creature to meet Parsifal. He took the Grail from Parsifal and gave it to the Queen. He is the teacher of the Swan Knight children and the keeper of the Grail Blood history. He taught German to the Queen and the other creatures of the Land and Shallow Waters. He was heavily involved in raising Brunhilde, daughter of the Tannhäuser.

The Lord's Prayer – From the Gospel of Matthew 6: 9–13 in the New Testament of the Holy Bible, Jesus instructed his disciples, "This is how you are to pray: Our Father in heaven, hallowed be your name, your kingdom come, your will be done, on earth as in heaven. Give us today our daily bread; and forgive us our debts, as we forgive our debtors; and do not subject us to the final test, but deliver us from the evil one. Amen"

Third Crusade – Christian crusade to retake Jerusalem and other Crusader States lost to Saladin, the Ayyubid Sultan. Unlike the Fifth Crusade, there was no central leadership. Secular rulers established their own crusading forces and had differing objectives. The crusading forces of Holy Roman Emperor Friedrich Barbarossa were the best organized and promised to be successful. But on 10 June 1190, Barbarossa drowned leading his army toward Acre. With the death of their leader, thousands of German soldiers abandoned the campaign and returned home. Disease cost them many more. Only about a third of the departing force arrived in Acre. The campaign of English King Richard I gained greater success and notoriety, taking multiple cities back from Saladin. The crusade failed to take Jerusalem, but succeeded in regaining a strong Christian foothold in the region.

Tiefhorn – A Unicorn and close friend of Duke Ludwig I. She was light grey with a darker grey beard and mane. She was the first to express to the Swan Knight the Unicorn uneasiness with the darkness inside of the Tannhäuser.

Trazperch Castle/Schloß Trazperch [ʃ l ɔ s t ʁ a ts p ɛ ɐ̯ ç] – A Stronghold of the Teutonic Knights in Tyrol region of Austria.

True Cross – A Christian relic. A gilded cross containing a portion of the actual cross upon which Jesus was crucified. The wood fragments maintained the Blood of Christ and was rumored to hold great power. It sat in the Church of the Holy Sepulcher in Jerusalem and was taken into battle to lead the armies of the Christian King of Jerusalem. It was lost to Saladin in the Battle of Hattin, 4 July 1187.

Ulm, Swabia – A young and small Swabian town during the years covered in this story. It was founded in 1181. It sits on the north bank of the Danube River.

Unicorns/ Die Einhörner [d i: aɪ n h œ r n ɐ] – Creatures of the Sweeter Realm, single-horned goat-like creatures, with shaggy, bearded faces, the height of a horse, but with a slightly sloping back and narrow hips. They can communicate with each other and others through a touch of their horns. For many hundreds of years, they were the primary sentries of the portal valley.

Valkyrie [f a l k y: r i:] – A Norse myth that sprang from the actions of Brunhilde. She traveled north when she left her castle at Hohenschwangau. She descended upon battles, felt the character of the human hearts involved, and killed the soldiers with cruel and evil hearts, after which she disappeared high into the air. Her soft, pale skin reflected the sunlight like armor. Out of the direct sunlight, her bare skin appeared as soft and delicate as a Brunnen's. (See also Brunhilde).

Venetian Merchant Fleet – See **Venice, Italy**

Venice, Italy – The Republic of Venice was an independent sovereign state centered around the Italian city of Venice from 697 until 1797. The maritime state built a tremendous navy that was employed by the Pope during the crusades.

Vespers Hymn – An evening prayer in the Catholic Church and part of the required daily ritual of many of the Catholic monastic orders. It is performed at dusk. The Verpers begins, "Deus, in adiutorium meum intende. Domine, ad adiuvandum me festina. Gloria Patri, et Filio, et Spiritui Sancto. Sicut erat in principio, et nunc et semper, et in saecula saeculorum. Amen. Alleluia." (O God, come to my aid. O Lord, make haste to help me. Glory to the Father, and to the Son, and to the Holy Spirit. As it was in the beginning, is now, and ever shall be. Amen. Alleluia.)

Waffenbrüder [v a f ə n b ʁ y: d ɐ] – Literally "brothers-at-arms". It is a term that the German knights of the crusades used for other German knights, particularly those of their own orders or armies. When unity was strong, they used the term for crusaders of other orders and other armies.

Weichesholz [v aɪ ç ə s h ɔ l ts] – The Zweigwesen who met Wikerus in the Sweeter Realm when he crossed from the valley. He was particularly soft-hearted for a Zweigwesen. He took pity on Wikerus and spoke in his defense.

Werdenfels Castle [v e: ɐ̯ d ə n f ə l s] – A castle near the valley of the River Loisach, north of Garmisch-Partenkirchen. It was commissioned as a donation to the Teutonic Order by a collective of prominent familes of Swabian and Bavarian nobility. The land was donated by the Family von Vollrads. The construction was under the command of Count Gottfried von Löwenstein.

Wiener Neustadt [v i: n ɐ n ɔʏ ʃ t a t] – An Austrian city south of Vienna. It is the birthplace of Duke Friedrich II of Austria and the city to which he fled when banished from Vienna by the Holy Roman Emperor.

Wikerus, the farmer – Tennant farmer on the lands of Baron Luitpold von Tannhausen, he heroically rescued the Baron's wife, Methildis, from violent thugs and delivered her baby in the back of a cart outside of the Tannhausen home. He was frightened away by the rush of people from Castle Tannhausen who responded to the bustle. He fled into the woods and was never heard from again. Methildis insisted upon the name of Wikerus as the second name of the baby. The baby grew up to be Luitpold Wikerus von Tannhausen, also known as the Tannhäuser, the hero of this story.

Wolpertingers [v ɔ l p ɐ d ɪ n g ɐ s] – A creature of the Land and Shallow Waters, long thought to be extinct. They were hunted by the creatures of the Deep Waters for their flavor and because of their ability to fly over the waters. They appear as rabbits, with wings and the horns of a deer, and long, sharp fangs. The hid for many centuries in the Brunnen Wilderness, unknown by any, until discovered and befriended by the Tannhäuser and Caris.

Woodblock Printing – A form of printing used in China as early as the year 200. It appeared in Europe in the 13th century, when texts and images were printed on cloth. Sometimes, printed cloth was bound into books. Woodblock printing became widely popular in Europe and used paper instead of textiles around 1400.

Wrestling Tree – A large linden tree in the Portal Valley, just uphill of the Portal Point. The Scheriers called it the Wrestling Tree because of a game they play around it. Much like the game "tag", one player kisses the nose of the other, then runs around the base of the tree. The other chases. When the kisser is caught, they wrestle until they are too tired or laughing too hard to continue. They breathe for a moment before switching roles and starting again.

Zagreb, Croatia – Croatian city ravaged by Mongol invasions. The Tannhäuser settled briefly there, working as a stone carrier in the city's reconstruction effort, during his travels to find Rikard and Andreas after awaking healed on the shore of Lake Neusiedl.

Zanthie [ts a n t i:] – Childhood nickname of Brunhilde, daughter of Tannhäuser and Caris. It is short for Chryzanthoseude. See **Brunhilde.**

Zweigwesens [ts v aɪ g v e: z ə n s] – Creatures of the Sweeter Realm, branch-thin, chest-high, covered from head to toe in soft, almost glowing, coarse, brownish-orange hair. Their hair looks like tree bark on their thin bodies. They have the ability to seamlessly connect to one another and form balances in intricate geometric shapes. When many connect together, they can form into the shape of a tree that nobody could distinguish from a real tree.